CONFESSIONS OF A LYCANTHROPE

GENE L. EDWARDS

Copyright © 2013 by Gene L. Edwards.

Library of Congress Control Number: 2013902000
ISBN: Hardcover 978-1-4797-8893-4
Softcover 978-1-4797-8892-7
Ebook 978-1-4797-8894-1

All rights reserved. No part of this book may be reproduced or transmitted in any form or by any means, electronic or mechanical, including photocopying, recording, or by any information storage and retrieval system, without permission in writing from the copyright owner.

This is a work of fiction. Names, characters, places and incidents either are the product of the author's imagination or are used fictitiously, and any resemblance to any actual persons, living or dead, events, or locales is entirely coincidental.

This book was printed in the United States of America.

To order additional copies of this book, contact:
Xlibris Corporation
1-888-795-4274
www.Xlibris.com
Orders@Xlibris.com

I would like to suggest that the werewolf in many instances embodies a potent blending of masochistic and sadistic elements. On the one hand, man is degraded as he is forced to submit to the bestial metamorphosis; on the other hand, he emerges as a powerful sadistic predator who can, without regret, destroy other men. The werewolf as both the victim and victimizer, wrapped in magic, may arouse emotions in us that are hard to define.

—Anne Rice

PROLOGUE

I ENTITLED THIS WORK "Confessions" as I feel that I have much that I can no longer keep buried within myself. I do not believe that the disclosure of my sins, or even my very nature, will allow for absolution. It should be noted that I write these words not for the benefit of anyone save for myself. It is as though a great weight presses down upon my soul; I am tormented beyond any description I could offer. My hope is that by coming forward with the truth, I will lessen the burden that I carry with me. Not that I really feel any guilt per se. In truth, I haven't actually felt even the slightest tinge of guilt since late 1987, a story for another time perhaps. My lack of feeling does not diminish my recognition of the fact that I am a guilty party to countless atrocities. One does not require emotion to acknowledge right from wrong and to judge the actions through this acknowledgment.

If you are looking to read this for the sake of entertainment, then go fuck yourself! It is not at all my objective to offer fiction of any kind in this writing. Everything within these pages will be factual. I am not so foolish to believe that the majority of those who read what I am offering will view it as anything more then an invented story—at best. Many others will consider it the ramblings of a disturbed schizophrenic patient. So be it—you can go straight to hell; I have a very special spot reserved there myself!

I have invested far too much time concerned with what others will think of me—no more! If you choose to take my precautions lightly or to disregard the warnings I will offer, then you are absolutely stupid—and you deserve exactly what will come to you if you ever face the darker half of those I am required to speak of, myself included! Of course, if even a few lives are saved on account of what I offer here, then all the better. In truth, I honestly do not care if you die in droves—and that you very well may do.

Again, I write this for my sake; a method to lessen the pain of those few remaining human emotions, however threadbare and depleted they may be, that haunt me relentlessly.

So I write; there is much I need to say, but even more that I wish to bring out—much of it irrelevant. I very much wish to speak of a woman I fell in love with years ago; I want to put to paper the dreams I once had—those that were robbed from me; I want to talk about the desirable qualities—the goodness I once possessed. But you're not interested in this, are you? You want to know about me, or more accurately, you want to know about the monster that resides chained within me. I'm sure your morbid psyche's have many questions, and they will find both the answers they want and those they will wish to never have learned in due time.

Of course, your pathetic and feeble eyes follow these words that I have written, and yet you have almost certainly never experienced the gore and mutilation that I have witnessed, that I have caused. Consider this before you continue reading as my story will not make you a better person upon finishing it. If you were a reasonably intelligent person, you would probably not sleep well after what I offer in the coming pages. If you were quite intelligent, you would put this writing away somewhere and think no more of it. But you probably aren't the least bit intelligent—you are probably a stupid-shit that thinks you know everything! Actually, I cannot pretend to know who will read this or how it will be received. Take it as it is, I present everything in truth.

I could take a moment and tell you all that you would like to know regarding lycanthropes—or werewolves as popular culture has labeled them in this last century or so. I could do this, but I won't. Doing so demeans and devalues everything else I am here to "confess" to. I have my story—it is a tragic story; there is no happy ending, no light at the end of my tunnel, only pain and sorrow.

I will tell you this much for those who believe the werewolf is a myth—you are sadly and dangerously mistaken. There are things I intend to reveal in the coming pages that I will only touch lightly on now. I watched the Man of a Thousand Faces and his son portray what came to be known as the Wolf Man. Ah, yes, America's first taste of the disillusionment of the Hollywood cinema as it related to lycanthropes. Then of course, the next generation of werewolf—those much more frightening movies of the '80s and '90s when special effects could provide what would have been impossible in the decades before. And let us not forget the age of computer animation—which allows filmmakers to create anything the mind could conjure even if it does sacrifice a certain quality or realistic look.

Do you believe that the media has properly prepared you to understand the true monster it labels werewolf? Hell, even I've enjoyed watching these movies, but to be honest, they are quite far removed from the truth.

So do I offer my name? Do I even deserve a name? Yes, I was a person once, and I still like to think of myself as such. I walk among men and women, pass by them on the street, sit with them in restaurants, and although they pay me little mind, they see me. They see a man not unlike any other. I *am* the proverbial wolf in sheep's clothing. There have been those whom I have helped, and there have also been those whom I have killed.

Yes, for the sake of my confessions, I must have a name by which you will know me—whether you choose to admire me, love me, or loath me, I shall provide a name that you may offer and direct toward whatever emotion you choose.

My name is Caleb. I offer my story.

ONE

So I have your attention, do I? Good. So where should I begin, my childhood? I'm sure this would be a waste of time and paper. Still, I will offer some of my childhood for the sake of a small piece of information that would ultimately relate to the events that would later bring me to my current station in life.

My childhood was spent in southern Louisiana. My home was quaint—a bungalow. Essentially, it was nothing more then a double shotgun design under one roof with a porch facing away from the heart of the swamp toward the road that led into town. The town itself, M——, was a fifteen-mile trip that was infrequently taken unless it was necessary. The long and winding mostly dirt road leading into town was seemingly carved and elevated from the sea of sugar cane, tobacco, cotton, and rice that grew as far as the eyes could see.

My house was the last on this long and seldom used excuse for a road. Should anyone wish to have proceeded beyond its placement, they would require a boat in which to do so, for I lived at the edge of a bayou, a rather expansive one at that.

Ah, yes, the Louisiana bayou; it offers the most warm and inviting of my memories. Picture this. The moss hanging on gnarled cypress trees surrounding you in all directions as you travel by dinghy—a pram—into the beautiful and picturesque sunset. The striking orange hue of Louisiana's setting sun contrasted by the dark and eerie cypress trees and the shadows they cast. All around you, the sounds of life—fleeting birds of every conceivable shape and size, frogs singing and always happy, an occasional dragonfly darting to and fro, and of course, the alligator watching me, watching him. As for the flora, there are the beautiful yellow-flowered orchids that bloom in the spring and offer the sweetest fragrance with their massive bulbs and foot-long leaves. In addition to the cypress trees, there are others that I do not know the names of, and one other that I do know the name for—the impressive green buttonwood trees named for their unusual-looking fruit. These monsterlike trees possess giant arms that extend far overhead. And let us not forget the grassy foliage that finds its way to the surface of the water in the shallow areas.

What a beautiful image. Far from the often conjured idea of the loathsome smelling things and horrible creatures that make strange noises in the night. If you have never been to the swamp, it is a mistake to judge this environment solely by what you may have seen on television or in movies. This is where I lived, where I grew up, where I came from.

And the year, should I tell you what year? Why not? I was born in 1950 in Lafayette. My father worked in the gulf on various oil rigs, which meant that he was gone for thirty-day stretches at a time. My mother worked on and off, usually part-time, at a hotel in the nearby city of N——. Of course, none of this is important, so I will proceed to what was important.

So what can I say about the way of life in Louisiana, especially during the '50s and '60s? Louisiana, for all intents and purposes, possessed a culture unto itself. They did and probably still do things in ways completely unique to themselves, especially pertaining to ethnic matters. Yet to be honest, I actually felt more racial "tension" upon moving north some years later than I ever did while I lived in Louisiana. This isn't to say that life was without prejudice in the south, or at least where I lived, but there were no feelings of hatred or animosity between my white and black neighbors. Mind you, by "neighbors," I mean anyone within a twenty-mile radius from where I grew up.

My best friend was named Aaron, and he came from a very poor colored family who harvested much of the rice and sugar cane in the surrounding area. Aaron and I grew up neighbors, and although we went to separate schools, we nonetheless spent much of our free time together. I loved Aaron as he was like a brother to me, and I am sure that his feelings were mutual.

The summers were fun as we would often meet up and spend the day at play, exploring the bayou, building forts, "sword" fights—typical boy things. Once a week I was responsible for mowing the grass in my yard, and Aaron would always help. Of course, we used a reel mower with semidull blades, and if the grass had gotten too high, mowing was much more difficult. Sometimes, alligators would venture from the water into our yard to bask in the sunlight. Rarely cautious, Aaron and I, often foolishly, would chase them out of the yard and into the water.

One of the things I most enjoyed about my childhood was the way that several families would gather together and prepare some of the greatest meals I have ever eaten. Everything was prepared, from fish, cornbread, rice pudding, and let us not forget crayfish gumbo. Usually, once a week one of these get-togethers would take place, and everyone—my parents included—would attend and contribute.

Another event that usually attracted only the male members of our parish was cock and dog fighting. I remember going with my father only once to watch this gruesome and inhumane spectacle. He told me later that he didn't have the stomach to sit through another. Of course, when I could, I would still sneak out to watch the cockfights. For some reason that I can no longer comprehend, they seemed less cruel then the dogfights that would begin after them.

What kind of person would have anything to do with this kind of "sport"? Despite the type of savage image that comes to mind, most of the men involved were gentlemen and were well respected in the community. Again, this was simply a way of life in those parts and, although outdated and frowned upon by today's standards, considered acceptable during that time and place.

Although it seemed that everyone was especially kind to me, there was one man who frightened not only myself but also nearly everyone he came across. Everyone called him Old Man Pruitt although he didn't seem too old to me. He would usually arrive in time to watch the dogs fight—I was told that he used to breed dogs to fight as well. Although I usually left long before the dogfights, and the heavy drinking, began, I remember seeing Old Man Pruitt on occasion. He was as ugly and menacing looking as anyone I had ever seen. I used to jokingly think to myself that he was preparing to enter into a match and fight himself.

When we were about eleven or twelve, Aaron and I began exploring the bayou—deeper than was wise. For those who are not well acquainted with the bayou, the idea of a swamp monster may seem a bit strange; to believe in one—juvenile. Still, reports and sightings of these monsters over generations have led to the "unofficial" acceptance of their existence. To this day, witnesses claiming to have seen the Honey Island Swamp Monster surface. In fact, I am to understand there are even tours offered through the swamp, attracting visitors from quite a distance. Rewards are offered for photographs of this mysterious creature even though experts claim that the possibility of such a monster actually existing is quite slim.

While the validity of the majority of these sightings are in much doubt, the truth is that official reports of this monster date back to 1963 when it was spotted by a wildlife photographer. However, the monster was well known to anyone who lived anywhere near the area where I grew up. I remember hearing the old-timers talk about how, as young men, they avoided the bayou at night as this was when the monster lurked—they were considered "old fools" by my generation.

The monster was described as being approximately seven and a half to eight feet tall, with gray hair and yellow eyes. Of course, descriptions varied greatly from one sighting to the next. Some said that it held the resemblance to a giant ape while others stated that it possessed reptilian qualities. Clearly, no one had ever been close enough to it to get a reliable description.

While there were always accounts of individuals who knew someone who knew someone else that had come face to face with this monster, few, if any of them were taken seriously. Still, to two twelve-year-old boys with a talent for finding trouble, the idea of finding such a monster grew beyond daydreams or fantasies. The swamp was our backyard, and we weren't yet smart enough to know fear. Of course, we had rules that our parents expected us to abide by, and we were quite prepared to break every one of them. At the very least, we had no intention of informing our parents, who seemed to pay little mind to us anyway, our day-to-day activities.

It was the summer; and during the summer months, once chores had been completed, the remainder of the day was ours. We would even set our alarms to rise early just so that we could conclude our responsibilities and be done with them while having as much daylight to work with as possible. Armed with an old corn knife and a sickle, Aaron and I would hop into one of the available rowboats at our disposal and proceed into the swamp, each day exploring farther and farther.

The bayou was scattered with islands; some of them no larger then a couple of cars placed together—during heavy rains, these patches of land would disappear altogether. Of course other islands, the ones we were interested in, measured several miles across. It was in these areas that Aaron and I would spend our days exploring. What exactly we were looking for, I remain uncertain—footprints of this dreaded monster? A lair that it would use to hide away in? Maybe even the beast itself.

Although our adventures were fun, they seemed ultimately fruitless, and the summer of 1962 came and went without incident. Now you may be wondering why I'm taking the time to tell you this. Truthfully, I'm not entirely certain. I've spent the last three and a half decades since I first became a lycanthrope mentally revisiting the occurrences surrounding Aaron's disappearance. Yes, sadly, I lost my friend early that fall, and while at the time I had no way of knowing exactly what happened to him, a not too surprising set of factors led me to believe that Aaron may have met his demise in a way that would, years later, seem obviously apparent to me. I will share with you this part of the story now, at least what little I knew of it from my end at that time, and you may decide what you think. If I remember to, I will finish the tale at a later point in this writing.

It was during the month of October, and I had long since started back to school. I saw little of Aaron outside of the weekends—as I mentioned, Aaron attended a separate school and, even then, only with a semiregular attendance. It would seem that as Aaron was becoming older, his share of responsibilities within his family had increased. No longer a child, he was expected to take on the more adult roles of helping his father and brothers with work in the fields or whatever it is that the family did during that time of the year. Still, opportunity would present itself, and when it did, we did not hesitate to take advantage of it.

Anyway, as I had stated, it was October, on a Saturday afternoon. Aaron and I departed for the dock as we had a hundred times before. This time, we weren't alone. Holly, a cute brunette who also lived down the road, accompanied us on this outing. Holly was a year older than I, but I had the wildest crush on her. Each morning, when the bus would come, I would sit directly across from her, studying her lovely face, daydreaming about kissing her. Of course, that information I would never have shared with her and would have denied it if asked.

Holly's inclusion on our outing may have had little direct significance, but I believe she was an indirect factor in what would ultimately play out. To make an unnecessarily long story short, Aaron and I had plans to continue our search for the monster on that day, the day Holly came to visit me. To me, I had since lost interest in the search itself but enjoyed the idea of exploring just the same. You can imagine my surprise when out of the blue, Holly knocked on my door and wondered what I was doing. Had it been anyone else, I may have entertained them until Aaron was free, then I would have probably blown them off for the sake of "adventure and exploration." Holly, on the other hand, was an exception to that rule of thought.

When she arrived and wanted to hang out and talk, I began hoping that something would come up, and Aaron would be unable to come over. Time passed so quickly that I couldn't believe that an hour had elapsed since her arrival. Unfortunately, I saw Aaron quickly advancing toward my house. While I didn't want to send Holly, who I thought was the most beautiful girl in the world, home, Aaron was my best friend, and I couldn't abandon him without notice. Without considering the consequences or even discussing the idea with Aaron, I invited Holly to come with us. She hesitated at first but reluctantly agreed with coercion on my part. For a moment, I thought everything had been settled. I honestly didn't want to leave, preferring instead to spend more time alone with Holly. But this way, I could still be close to her without being a total jerk to Aaron.

Despite the good intentions of my plan, I could visibly see the disappointment that would eventually turn to anger in Aaron's expression. And yet, I assumed that Aaron would get over it once we embarked. Instead, a considerable amount of tension grew as our small rowboat proceeded into the darkest part of the bayou.

"I can't believe you guys come out here," she said. "My father would kill me if he knew I had come with you this far out."

"Then why did you come?" Aaron asked, his tone bitter and hostile. The question was rhetorical; any answer Holly could offer would do little to diffuse Aaron's temperament, a fact that she was apparently unaware of.

"I don't know," she began. "I just liked the way Caleb described everything. It sounded so creepy."

I looked at Holly who smiled as she spoke, seemingly unaware that her presence was causing conflict. My observations then turned to Aaron who returned my gaze. His eyes told me what his mouth would not. *Why the fuck did you bring this stupid bitch!*

It appeared that I was going to somehow play the role of mediator. Unfortunately, my own intelligence, limited as it was, was further hindered by the fact that my hormones were playing far too great a role in my decision making process. For the next two hours or so, the three of us passed a series of landmarks that Aaron and I knew well before proceeding into a part of the swamp there neither of us had yet ventured. During this time, conversation was kept to a minimum. When I would ask Aaron a question, he would merely nod or grunt "yeah," and when I directed conversation toward Holly, I could practically feel his hatred for her growing.

Now why Aaron felt the way he did, I am uncertain. Perhaps he felt that somehow our friendship was in jeopardy of being lost by work and family responsibility on his end, and by Holly's involvement in my life on my end. These thoughts, however, are purely speculative. The truth is I will never know exactly what he was thinking or feeling on that Saturday in October.

"You guys," Holly stated, "I'm not so sure that we should be here!" Her voice carried with it an uncomfortable trepidation.

"Don't worry. We'll be fine," I said, speaking before Aaron had the chance to reply. As I told her this, I gently placed my hand on hers, reassuringly at first but there was more to it than that as I'm sure she was becoming well aware.

Some time later, we banked the boat and proceeded on foot. Aaron was in the lead, taking an aggressive pace through the undergrowth, channeling his anger into hacking away any ivy, shrub, or fern that stood in his way. Holly remained very close to me, and although she said nothing, I had imagined that seeing Aaron swing the corn knife as wildly and seemingly rage-filled as he did, with an already foul temperament, may have caused her to fear him.

After zigzagging through almost a mile of foliage, Holly touched my shoulder; when I turned to face her, a worried look seemed painted across her beautiful features. "Caleb, I think maybe we should head back!"

Upon hearing this, Aaron turned and faced us in anger. "What?"

Before anything else was said, something nasty and grotesque caught my attention some forty or fifty feet away. I didn't speak, only pointed to it. Aaron immediately abandoned the argument he was about to engage in with Holly, focusing instead on what I had pointed out.

Closer investigation revealed that it was an incredibly large alligator that had been crudely and savagely torn apart. I estimated that this particular alligator would have been about eleven feet long or so, probably weighing as much as twelve hundred pounds. This was, of course, my best guess based on what little of this animal remained intact. All we knew for certain was that this was the largest alligator we had ever seen.

"What the sam hell could have done this?" Aaron asked.

The scene was absolutely gruesome; the largest part of the carcass consisted of its tail, one of its hind legs, and its abdomen. The remaining parts of this formidable animal, including its head, three of its legs, and the majority of its thorax, were strewn about. The intestines, as well as the majority of its organs—most of which I could not identify—appeared as though they had intentionally been thrown against a tree then simply flopped down into a pile beneath it. Although the smell was nauseating, we continued to circle around and study the bizarre spectacle. Holly stood very close to me as though ready to leap into my arms at the first sign of anything frightening. While I found the scene disturbing, I was enjoying the closeness that Holly offered. "What happened to it?" she asked.

"I don't know. I've never seen anything like this before," I replied.

"Was it another alligator?" Holly asked.

"No," Aaron answered. "An alligator would never do anything like this." His response to Holly's question was not hostile or mean spirited, and for that I was thankful. "What do you think, Caleb?" he asked me.

"It was probably killed some time yesterday or last night—more likely last night. There are a lot of flies, but I don't see any maggots yet, and it takes about twelve hours once an animal dies before the maggots start showing up. Also, if it had been dead longer, other animals would have scavenged it by now."

"What do you think might have done this?"

I shook my head. "I don't know of anything around here that would be capable of killing a fully grown alligator, certainly not one anywhere near this massive, let alone do this to it."

"A poacher?" he suggested.

"Maybe, but I honestly can't imagine. Look at the way its hide has been dismembered. I don't think it was done by a blade or saw." Indeed, it appeared as though the flesh had been ripped apart by brute force in much the way a chicken leg could be crudely ripped from its thigh with an aggressive twisting and forceful pulling apart of the tissues. But manually disarticulating a chicken leg from its thigh would be a relatively simple task. Performing something of this magnitude would seem virtually impossible, especially considering the impressive hide of an alligator.

"You guys, I'm starting to get scared, and I think we need to leave here," Holly pleaded to what would seem deaf ears.

"It must have been the monster," Aaron stated, totally ignoring Holly's request. As he spoke, a victorious grin crept across his lips.

In the weeks and months preceding this particular outing, Aaron and I had frequent and often heated debates over the existence of such a creature. While I had begun to doubt that such a thing could actually exist in the twentieth century without being long since discovered, it seemed that Aaron believed, almost religiously, in its existence and would not be convinced otherwise. Our find on that day suggested to

Aaron not only that the creature existed but that we were somehow closing in on it as well.

Still quite skeptical about the idea of a yet-discovered swamp monster, a skepticism that would haunt me in the years to come, I disagreed with Aaron. "This is hardly sufficient proof that the monster exists."

"Of course it does," Aaron argued. "Can you tell me what did this?"

"No."

"And you are the smartest person I know. What else could it possibly be?"

I answered in the only way I could, "I don't know."

"Caleb, I'm scared and I want to go home!" Holly said, now crying.

"Why are you scared, damn it?" Aaron asked his tone and expression stern. "If you were going to do nothing but complain, then why did you come in the first place?"

While I thought Holly was a good person and as beautiful as any I knew, I suppose that if I were to be honest, I would have agreed with Aaron; I should not have brought her. "Holly, it's all right. Nothing is going to happen. We're perfectly safe, and we won't allow anything to hurt you"—actually, Aaron probably would have abandoned her there if he had any say in it—"and we will head back home very shortly."

While I am sure that Holly, growing up where she did, had seen her share of snakes, crayfish, and all other creatures native to southern Louisiana, creatures that would probably freak out someone from New York or Chicago, she was nonetheless unaccustomed to being out this far in the bayou, an unsafe distance from help, if it were needed. From the look in her eyes, I could tell that while she wanted nothing more than to leave immediately, she found some comfort in my words. After a few more moments of examining the scene, with brief exchanges between Aaron and me, we departed. The plan was to invest a short amount of time searching the immediate area before heading back to the boat—that was the plan anyway.

Fortunately, Holly said not another word about wishing to leave, and Aaron made no further snide remarks. We began making our way slowly toward the boat, maneuvering through the dense undergrowth as we went. Aaron and I shared the lead, discussing what we had seen, while Holly followed several steps behind, seemingly lost in her own thoughts.

"Hey, you guys, look at this," she said. As we turned, we saw Holly's attention drawn to what appeared to be a well-established, well-groomed trail down the embankment from where we had been walking.

"Someone else had been out here," Aaron stated in an almost disappointed tone. The vegetation all around us was so thick that we walked within thirty yards of the trail, which was roughly five to six feet wide, without even noticing that it was there.

The three of us quickly descended the sharp embankment, crossed through a narrow patch of foliage, and found ourselves on this mysterious trail. Within moments, we found numerous tracks—human footprints, barefoot, in the muddy clay. "There are accounts of backwoods people who have reputedly lived their entire lives in the bayou," I said. "It is possible that they are responsible for this trail."

I waited for Aaron to comment on my newest hypothesis. When he offered none, I added, "With this in mind, it would seem plausible that they could be responsible for the alligator."

"You don't know that," Aaron argued. "Besides, you said that it couldn't have been done by a person!"

"No, I said that I didn't see how a person could have done that as it didn't actually look like the hide had been cut, but what do I know?"

We each began walking up the trail, ignorant of what we were doing or of what territory we were violating in doing so. I think we were like birds, eagerly rushing toward a cat's lair, too stupid to realize the potential danger of where we were. Our lack of concern for our safety as well as our utter obliviousness to the potential consequences of our actions continue to amaze me as I reflect back on that period in my life.

After almost a mile on the trail, we came to a small shanty-style hut with the smoking remains of a since-exhausted campfire. Hanging from the accessible lower branches of several surrounding trees were the skins of several dozen animals and a very large stack of bones next to the campfire itself.

"What the hell?" Aaron commented, not quite under his breath.

"I'm really serious, guys. We should get out of here!" came Holly's emotionally charged warning. For once, I was in total agreement with her. Something here definitely seemed wrong.

"Nonsense," came a voice from above and behind us, "why, you've just arrived."

Startled, the three of us turned to observe a man wearing shorts only perched some thirty or forty feet high in a cypress tree. With incredible agility nature usually reserves for monkeys and apes, this red-haired, red-bearded man dropped from his limb to one beneath it, to another beneath that one before landing like a cat in front of us.

We would have probably quickly retreated in the direction from which we had come had he not been blocking our path. As he raised his head to face us, I immediately recognized him—Old Man Pruitt.

"You know," he began while staring at Holly, "I don't know that there has ever been a woman in these parts. I'm certain there has never been a morsel so young as yourself."

"We're sorry to have bothered you, Mr. Pruitt," I said. "We'll be leaving now."

"Not so quickly, *mon ami idiot*. Why were you here in the first place?"

"No reason, we were only exploring," I answered, trying to be as brief as possible.

Taking no cue from me, Aaron said audaciously, "We were looking for the monster." When these words escaped his lips, I nearly cringed.

"Were you now, boy?"

"Yes, sir."

A malignant look crossed through the wild eyes of Mr. Pruitt as though his intention was to merely play with us before killing us. Most unsettling was the way his observations seemed to focus on Holly.

"There ain't no monster here, boy. Unless you count me," he said with a fake smile. Then quite suddenly, the smile melted from his face. "I should kill you right here and now, you *peu de merde*!" He spoke slowly, deliberately stressing every syllable. "I came out here to get away from the likes of pieces of shit like you, and I'll be damned if I let you come into my world!"

"Sir," I began as calmly as I could, "we will leave here immediately, and you will not see or hear from us again. On that you have my word."

12

"Yes, your word," he began condescendingly. "Is that supposed to mean anything to me, *mon ami idiot*? I'll tell you what, I'll give you my word if you ever step foot this far into my bayou again, I will gut your fucking asses like swine. I swear to God I will! And as for you, *mon cher*," he said, "I would look so forward to getting my hands on you." These words obviously carried with them a sexual connotation that was not missed by any of us. Somehow, this made Holly the biggest victim of the three of us. While angered by his statements, I more than anything wanted to return home safely.

"Now get the fuck away from me!" he said, stepping aside for us to depart down the very trail from which we had come.

Aaron wanted to speak more, to counterthreaten, but I pushed him forward while at the same time holding Holly close to me as we exited. We all seemed to hold our breath as we passed by him. It appeared that I was the one he paid the least attention to. His eyes regarded Holly as a piece of meat, and I had the very strong impression that he would have liked to have killed Aaron for no other reason than the fact that he was less respectful.

Once we were several paces beyond him, we quickened our stride and eventually put as much distance between him and us as we could by running as quickly as we could. Within twenty minutes, we had reached the boat, jumped in, and paddled away from that horrid island without hardly a glance back in its direction. It wasn't until an hour later, when we were a safe distance from Mr. Pruitt, that Holly broke down and began crying.

"I'm so sorry, Holly. This should have never happened," I said to her. "I understand if you hate me for bringing you."

"I don't hate you," she said as she breathed deeply through the tears. She then put her arms around me and held me tightly for several moments.

It was late in the day when we arrived at the dock just down the hill from my house. Holly appeared visibly shaken yet told me that she might try to come by the following day after church.

"What the hell were you thinking by bringing her?" Aaron asked as soon as Holly was out of earshot.

"I know, it was a mistake," I said. "But I really like her. And besides, how the hell was I supposed to know *that* was going to happen?"

"That guy was a damn asshole! If my brothers had been there, they would have kicked his ass! In another couple of years, I'll even be able to kick his ass."

"I don't know, Aaron. Did you see the size of his arms? I don't think I would want to mess with him."

"I think he's hiding something."

"What do you mean?"

"I think there might be something else on that island, something he didn't want us to find."

"I don't know, but I think it's best that we leave it alone."

"Spoken like a true pussy coward!" Aaron said hatefully in a tone he had never used with me.

"Aaron, Old Man Pruitt meant business with what he said. He wasn't screwing around."

"Well, I'm not afraid of him. I'm not afraid of anyone!" he stated, his temperament becoming less subdued. "And I'm going back there—tonight."

"Are you serious? Have you lost what little sense you had? First of all, we were damn lucky to get out of there today. I don't think we will catch another break if Pruitt sees us there again. And secondly, what's your father going to say about the idea? He would skin our hides if he ever knew where we went during daylight hours, let alone at night."

"You scared?"

"Aaron, how would we even be able to see where we're at or where we're going?"

"It's a full moon out tonight," Aaron said. "We won't have a problem seeing."

"This is an awful idea, Aaron. No, we're not going to do this."

"I don't need your damned permission!" he said with a deepening anger. "And my father and brothers can't tell me what to do either! If you're suddenly too chicken shit for this, then fine, go hang out with that dumb bitch you brought with us today! But I'm going tonight, and I'll go without you!"

"Aaron, I think you should leave now," I said politely though honestly

I wanted to hit him, to hurt him. "You can come back when you're thinking straight."

"I ain't never coming back here! I thought you were my friend, but you are nothing but yellow!"

And those were the last words Aaron said to me. We had had arguments in the past, even exchanged blows a few times, but never had Aaron offered such hateful words. I predicted, incorrectly it would seem, that after a day or two, Aaron would return; and although he would not likely apologize for his outburst, he would probably pretend that it never happened just as he had done in quarrels in the past.

Several days later, Aaron's father, visibly distraught, came to my house, hoping that I could point him in the right direction to find his son. I told him about Aaron's obsession with finding "the monster," and I also told him about the argument we had engaged in the last time I saw him. I did not, however, mention anything about Old Man Pruitt or just how far into the bayou we had ventured. I also did not make him or anyone else aware of the fact that I knew where he was planning on going or that he was planning on going out at night. I simply told him, as I told the sheriff's deputy who was investigating the disappearance later, that Aaron was angry when I last spoke with him and that I had no idea where he would have gone to.

two

IN REREADING THE pages I have written, it does occur to me that much of what I had put onto paper was unnecessary. Of course, the theme I wanted to spotlight was Old Man Pruitt. And while I was to never seen Aaron again, there is more to tell about Pruitt himself. But I do not wish to get ahead of myself.

As I stated earlier, I have no idea who you are or why you are reading this. If your intentions are to learn more about the monster that I would become, then I invite you to skip this chapter altogether. If, however, you have an interest in learning about me, this section will offer information that, while having nothing to do with lycanthropy, contains accounts that I cannot omit.

So as it has been a reoccurring pattern that I have witnessed time and time again, life goes on. Through tragedy and loss, through heartbreak and sorrow, life goes on. In the six decades of my existence, I have buried more friends than I can count, this personal record being a testament to many of them. Aaron, while never actually buried, was the first of many that I would lose. And yet, life goes on.

From time to time, I would see Aaron's brothers or father working and would wave to them. They seemed bitter toward me, however. For reasons that were never offered to me, they blamed me for Aaron's disappearance. They knew, of course, that I didn't directly do anything to Aaron, but I assumed that they felt that had I never existed, their son/brother would still be with them.

My relationship, if that is what you wish to call it, with Holly, lasted less then a year. She was the first girl that I ever kissed and the first I ever felt up. Our association ended when Holly's family moved to Arkansas. Apparently, her father, who was originally from Arkansas relocated due to a job offer. We corresponded through letters here and there until they eventually stopped coming. Eventually, she would become little more than a distant memory.

School was always difficult for me not because I lacked in academic skills but rather because I performed so well. Things may have changed by today's standards (from as best I can tell, they have not), but it wasn't a good thing to be too smart in my school. On more than one occasion, I was the target of cruelty by bullies with lower academic scores.

While high school had its upsides, the things that others seem to recall when reflecting back on their adolescent lives—new experiences, friends, parties—all these ideas were foreign to me. Yes, much of this was my own doing as I often chose to alienate myself, choosing self-isolation over inclusion. There were a number of acquaintances that I enjoyed the company of but never a true friend, never again anyone to fill in the gap that Aaron had left open. I was certain that if I were to disappear from the face of the earth, few would take notice, and none would truly care.

When high school came to a close, I was offered various scholarships to colleges across the country. Given that I seemed to have no attachments and no real friends to speak of other than my immediate family, there seemed little to keep me in Louisiana. Besides, I was looking forward to the idea of travel, something new where no one knew who I was, a totally fresh start. I had considered going into the military, the army perhaps. The war in Vietnam was becoming very intense, and although opposition for it was growing, for me, I viewed it as simply another opportunity, another way out, should I chose to take it.

But first, I was off to college. Why I chose the St. Louis area remains a mystery to even me. I suppose it was the representative from St. Louis University that somehow talked me into it. Besides, I did have family across the Mississippi River in Illinois—several aunts and uncles from my mother's side. College may have been a fun time for me if I had known then what I know now. After all, I was quite bright, had financial stability, at least for the moment, and I had my entire life ahead of me. Instead, I took things a little too seriously, including, I'm sorry to say, my love life.

I met Clarice at a party that one of my aunts insisted that I come to. Although it was her intention for me to meet some girl, she absolutely objected to me seeing Clarice. There was really nothing remarkable about her except that she was the exact opposite of everything I had become. She was the life of the party, the center of attention, seemingly wild and carefree. It seemed that she didn't know a stranger until she met me.

Clarice was considerably older than me, not quite a cougar by today's standards, though the term had not yet been coined (actually, I am not sure at what age a woman becomes a "cougar"). She was thirty-two and would, during the course of our relationship, often state that her experience in life more than made up for her limited education. Now technically, she did graduate from high school, and during that time, a high school diploma meant much more than it does today. Still, I believe that she often felt insecure about her level of education and, on more than one occasion, attempted to convince me to quit school. When we would argue, she would repeatedly say that because of my age, I lacked the experience to know or understand whatever the theme of our argument was. This from the semialcoholic, drug-induced, often-hormonal party woman.

Can you tell that I am still bitter? Even after almost thirty-five years, I still become angry when I think of how I was treated and taken advantage of by Clarice. I am uncertain but would imagine that she is still alive today. Clarice, if somehow your eyes ever find these pages, then I hope you rot in hell, you stupid bitch!

Wow! Somehow I have gotten way ahead of myself. Let me go back. As I stated, I was at a party, met Clarice, and for some strange reason, she asked me to go out with her the next evening. Again, we really had nothing in common, but I think that only served to make her more interested in me, and who knows, maybe I took an interest in her for the same reason.

The next evening, she and a group of her friends picked me up, and we went to several bars (I wasn't really old enough, but no one seemed to care as much in those days). Of course, not only was Clarice a heavy drinker, but she also took whatever drug was available—and there were so many available. Not that I really cared, but I found it interesting that someone who partied as hard as she did would have any interest in someone such as myself at all. And of course, late that night, Clarice took me back to her place where one of us seduced the other. If I had been half as intelligent as I believed I was, I could have had my way with her and left her the next morning. If I were to have run into someone like her today, that is exactly what I would do. But things were different for me then; the person I am now—the thing I have become—is far different from who I was; this idea will be a reoccurring theme throughout this writing. I don't think I had an unkind bone in my body. What was worse was that my upbringing, secluded and withdrawn, had made me ignorant of people like Clarice.

It seemed that I was so starved for affection that I disregarded the disaster that I was headed straight into the middle of. In so many ways, everything was my own fault. Yes, it's true that Clarice was an absolutely horrid person, bent on breaking my spirit, forcing me to surrender anything that brought happiness into my life, and taking away any personal freedoms, however slight they may have been. And yet, it was ultimately my decision alone that allowed everything to happen as it did. I was the weak person that just lay there and took whatever unjust and cruel punishment that Clarice's wicked tongue could offer.

I had no reason to disbelieve anything she said; after all, she told me that she loved me. And I, still too young to appreciate the complexities of such a theme, believed that I felt the same way. I remember being happy with the idea that someone cared about me, someone actually *wanted* to be with me. I was too stupid to realize that no one would ever want to be with me and that no one would ever care about me. Maybe I am less angry at Clarice than I am at my own passive role in the relationship. But again, I digress.

So to make a long story short, Clarice and I were married, and at the insane age of nineteen, I became the head of a ready-made family. I somehow knew that this was a poor idea, and yet I plunged headfirst into it. What can I say? I was lonesome, I needed someone to be close to, and in the absence of someone kind and generous, I found Clarice. Maybe she felt the same way, at least to some degree. Looking back, I realize that what I truly needed was someone to beat some sense into me, but that didn't happen.

Clarice's daughter, Erin, had just completed the first grade when I was introduced to her. She seemed to be the most generous and caring child, and we instantly bonded. Though technically, I was young enough to have been her older brother, I took on the role of her father. Erin's biological father, a man by the name of Sean, dealt drugs out of the back of his van until one day when one of his disgruntled clients put several bullets through his face.

My family, still residing in Louisiana, strongly, and wisely, discouraged the marriage for all the sensible reasons: she was thirty-two while I was only nineteen, she had a kid, she was too wild and irresponsible, she was a drug addict, and the list goes on and on. But I would not hear any of it. I don't even know why I did what I did, but I made my decisions and stood by them.

Clarice and I were married on April 8, 1970 in a small church just outside of St. Louis. At the time, it was the most awkward and uncomfortable social setting I had experienced. My decision was a disappointment to my family who sat on one side of the church while my age made me the butt of many jokes by Clarice's family who sat in pews on the opposite side of the church. In addition to this, Clarice and I had been in an argument a day or two before the wedding, and although we were still married, I remember each of us were bitter toward the other as we stood at the altar.

Somehow, I expected life to become more routine once we were married—fewer arguments, less partying, and of course, less drinking and drug use. I figured that once we settled down, Clarice would maybe become a bit more domestic, possibly even realize that she had a daughter. However, I was not yet experienced enough in life to understand that a leopard does not so easily change its spots. Clarice was who she was. It seems that we both made the mistake of believing that with enough time and effort, each of us could change the other.

For the first couple of years that we were together, we experienced more than our share of financial difficulties. While still in school, I held several jobs, including janitorial work and stocking shelves at a hardware store. Most of the work I did was part-time, which allowed me to focus on completing my schooling. My savings that had amounted to nearly three thousand dollars, a substantial amount for a post-high school graduate during the early seventies, had long since been withdrawn from the bank and spent by Clarice—again, my own fault for allowing her to do this.

Nineteen seventy-two was a remarkable year. Until then, everything seemed to move so slowly in my life. Weeks and months had dragged on, and although I would often daydream of what life after college would be like, a part of me seemed to doubt that it would ever happen. I was like a castaway, lost at sea and living day to day, just waiting to be rescued—losing a little faith each day that that rescue would happen. However, in May of that year, I graduated with honors—the first person in my family to have ever gone to college, let alone graduate.

Although I've never been one that felt bound by tradition, I nonetheless walked the stage and received my degree. My parents visited from Louisiana to congratulate me on my accomplishments and to see me graduate. Even my younger sister Terri, who was pregnant at the time, was there. There were photographs taken, cards offered, and someone had made a cake—it seemed that everyone was happy. No, not everyone—Clarice was visibly angry. Maybe because she wasn't on the best of terms with my family, who made every effort to maintain a pleasant relationship with her, maybe because, for this one occasion, she was not the center of attention. Of course, after a noticeable absence from the party, a party that I didn't really wish for or request, Clarice returned drunk and made an embarrassing scene.

By early July, I was offered and accepted a position with Conoco Pipeline. I started off as a pipeline operator, responsible for receiving various grades of gasoline, diesel, and liquid butane from one of two underground pipelines, then delivering these products to their respected thirty thousand barrel tanks through an elaborate maze of underground valves and pipes. I don't think it is necessary to elaborate on the specifics of my job, but I should at least offer some detail to the size and complicity of what I have already described.

In addition to receiving product on the main line from a refinery in Ponca City, Oklahoma, I would also move military-grade jet fuel—JP8—crude oil from Canada, and pump butane gasses to other refineries in the area. Suddenly, I had plans. Within a few years, I would become the facility manager, and there was no reason to believe that within a decade, I would have been promoted to a regional supervisor of the Midcontinental Division.

As if graduating college, my new job, and an impressive income weren't remarkable enough, I learned in October of that year that Clarice was pregnant. Although I was still married to and controlled by a vindictive bitch of a wife, the news of a coming child suddenly overshadowed anything negative within my mind and heart; my life at that moment seemed worthwhile and meaningful.

In January 1973, we purchased a nice home in B——, a St. Louis suburb, and began preparing for the baby's arrival. I worked long hours at Conoco only to return home and spend an additional two to three hours working on the house. During those months, I was exhausted, financially strapped because of the investment in the house, and as optimistic about the future as ever.

Jessica was born on June 30 at 5:00 PM. I was, for the first and only time in my life, happy. I remember holding her and feeling that her existence was a miracle, my personal miracle to think that I helped create another human being and that inside of her a piece of me existed. I was deeply sentimental, and while I have long-since lost the ability to feel that way, I do remember it. Not surprisingly, Clarice, while taking the time to hold our new child, did not seem to have demonstrated the profound and overwhelming emotional attachment to her that I had thought was instinctual. Over the course of the next several years, Clarice never became close to Jessica, at least not as close as I would have thought a mother should be to her child. To her, Erin and Jessica were both inconveniences.

Erin, on the other hand, was quite excited to have a baby sister. So many times, it seemed that it was just the three of us, and that Clarice existed but wasn't really a direct part of our family. Erin had long ago learned to accept her mother's disposition and had come to depend on me alone as a caring parent. It was sad to me that Jessica would have to spend her childhood in the way Erin had.

It was then that I began playing with the idea of separation, possibly divorce. I wasn't happy, at least not with Clarice. I had matured enough to know that she would never be able to offer me anything more than what she had so far. There were other women out there—I knew this by that point. How many of them would have made a better mother for Jessica? Then when I considered Erin, my heart sank. How could I leave and abandon her?

I went about my life, working long hours then coming home and playing the role of both parents while my wife went out to bars and parties every night. We argued about her nonsense spending and how it seemed that I was working for nothing. We argued about her absence on a daily basis. We even argued about how she would leave the house a cluttered mess. Time and time again, thoughts of leaving her entered my mind; I was uncertain of what to do or how to go about it. Someone told me once that our hardest decisions are often made for us. So was the case here in the most tragic possible way.

Jessica wasn't even four years old when the worst thing that could happen did. She was such a beautiful and smart little girl—I think all parents probably feel that way about their children though. During the day while I was at work, Jessica was in the care of her mother while Erin was in school. Generally, once Erin returned home, her mom would pass responsibility of her sister to her while she either slept or took off to do whatever she did. I remember returning home from work on several occasions and learning that Jessica was running a fever. I was assured that this was normal and that all children run frequent fevers and complain of aches and pains. "They are just having growing pains," Clarice would say.

Jessica had visited the doctor for all her regular checkups and vaccinations, and she always received a clean bill of health. I was worried, but what the hell did I know? I was a pipeline operator. Against the advice of Clarice, I took Jessica to the ER when I noticed her limping painfully. Interestingly, her nose began to bleed as we waited to be seen.

I could talk about the horrible things that I learned that evening—the bruises that had gone unnoticed, the loss of appetite that I was unaware of, and the anemia that accounted for her nosebleed in the waiting room. None of this alone meant anything to me—just symptoms. If there is a single word that is sufficient to put fear into any parent under any set of circumstances, it is cancer. That is what I learned was causing Jessica's problems.

For the next several days, Jessica was at the hospital with me by her side at every moment. Erin went to stay with her grandparents, who made frequent visits to the hospital as well, and Clarice even spent a considerable amount of time at her daughter's side as well. During those painful days, Jessica underwent a bone marrow biopsy, a lymph node biopsy, and spinal tap to see if the cancer cells had spread into the spinal fluid. It seemed cruel and terrible to subject such a weak little girl to such procedures, but I was told it was a must.

Things went from bad to worse, it seemed. Before we really had time to recover from the news that she had leukemia, we learned that Jessica's cancer was extremely aggressive and had quickly metastasized into her central nervous system. The doctors began administering cancer-killing drugs into her cerebrospinal fluid around her brain and spinal cord, attempting to halt or kill off the cancer cells that had already developed in those areas. We were informed that we shouldn't give up hope but that Jessica's situation was less then promising. It seems that they were right—Jessica died on September 14, 1976.

Looking back, Jessica's death seems almost like something I may have watched on television—a dramatic movie. Sad, yes, but somehow disconnected from me once I walk away from the screen. That's how I feel now and thought it sounds horrible to describe my feelings in such a detached fashion. They are feelings that I am currently unable to appreciate or even recognize in myself. But things were different for me then.

That grief was overwhelming, and I was seemingly unable to cope. I had heard the expression that it is unnatural for parents to outlive their children, but my loss extended far beyond that. Jessica was the center of my world and the key element that secured every other aspect. With her loss, everything else crumbled.

After all this time, I remain unable to truly understand the flood of pain and the reasons for the hatred that grew within me, nor can I look back and understand a reason for the decisions that followed. I will cover this quickly if I can.

The funeral seemed surreal, and I found myself without any real means of support. In truth, I probably had support, but I refused to accept it. Even my wife, especially my wife—I could hardly tolerate her presence before Jessica's death. Afterward, I loathed her. In fact, I didn't even sit with her at the funeral.

Now it's true, she was a mean-spirited woman concerned only with what she could acquire from others, but she suffered the same loss as I did. In the weeks after the funeral, the tension between Clarice and me seemed to steadily escalate. Whereas I would have previously ignored her cynicism or bitten my tongue, I was no longer willing to show or demonstrate my tolerance.

Clearly, we each had our coping mechanisms; I found that burying myself in work, often for sixteen plus hours each day, left little time for me to dwell on my domestic tragedy. It also kept me away from anything that reminded me of Jessica. Clarice, on the other hand, battled this demon just as she had all her others—with addiction. How much she drank and what drugs she did, I will never know.

I remember coming home from work and just wanting to sleep until I would wake and head off to work again. Each and every day, I would wonder if possibly Clarice had driven off a bridge in a drunken stupor, and I would find disappointment in learning that she was alive and well, passed out on the sofa.

My family did attempt to reach out to me, but I found no comfort in my dialogues with them. At first, I kept conversation with them brief, especially when Jessica's name was mentioned or when any question was raised about my feelings. I absolutely did not want to discuss my emotional status with my family. Eventually, I stopped taking their calls altogether. In truth, that was the beginning of the end for my association with my family.

Unfortunately, I was unable to work seven days a week—Conoco policy seemed to frown on it. So on my days off, I revisited the parks where Jessica played, strolled the paths where she bicycled, and when I was home, spent my time in her bedroom. I was so deeply depressed that I didn't even realize how my life was falling apart. Simple things like paying the bills were no longer a priority or even a passing consideration. And God knows that my wife did nothing to help manage our household.

It really should not have come as a surprise to me when I received divorce papers. It seemed that she had been seeing someone for quite some time—an antique dealer. I viewed it as good news, kind of like having a tumor removed. As it was, I was looking for an end to our marriage anyway and had no intention on contesting anything. The following week I moved into my own apartment, leaving the house and everything I had acquired over the course of my marriage, save for some of my clothing. It was an interesting time as I continued with my long hours of work only to return home to my apartment, which I had never bothered to furnish. I slept in a sleeping bag on my bedroom floor, which was more then sufficient for my needs. My refrigerator was sadly stocked—some milk, usually spoiled, maybe a couple of beers, and whatever fast food I hadn't bothered to eat during my evenings. Other than this, my apartment had the appearance of a recently vacated room.

Things progressed in this manner for several months—work, sleep, work some more, sleep some more—and all the while I kept to myself, avoiding even my family. How long had I planned on living this way, I cannot say. To say that I was in a depression would have been a gross understatement, and yet I was functioning, at least for a couple of months.

I had gotten so used to avoiding calls from my sister and mother that I would often erase messages they had left as soon as I recognized the voice, without knowing what they wanted to say. I assumed that they simply wanted to talk about the divorce or possibly even Jessica; neither subject I was willing to entertain a discussion of. However, I found myself more than a little annoyed when my sister showed up at my workplace, insisting on speaking with me.

"What the hell is wrong with you?" she began. "We've been trying to get a hold of you!"

"Terri, please! I'm not interested in talking. I have nothing to say. You know I love you, but I just need to be left alone right now!"

"Do you even know what has happened? Did you get the messages?" she asked. I only offered a blank though still slightly annoyed expression. "Dad passed away yesterday. He has been sick for a while. His funeral is on Wednesday!" Clearly and understandably, there was anger in her tone.

There would be a quote that I would reread and commit to memory many years later that would have been significant considering everything that had happened in such a short time. "Troubles come not as subtle spies, but in battalions." It was a quote from Shakespeare, and it was sadly fitting. I don't know, but it seems that there is only so much a man, any man, can bear on his shoulders before he breaks. I believe that the news I received that evening pushed me to that proverbial breaking point.

"It's two o'clock in Lafayette," Teri said. "You are coming?"

"Of course," I said with a lingering sternness. But while my answer indicated a clear decision on m part, this was a purely verbal response that my brain hadn't yet processed. It would take some time before my mind caught up with my tongue.

"Are you going to drive or fly?"

"What?" I asked with irritation.

"Do we need to pick you up at the airport?"

"No, I'll be fine," I answered. "Where is the funeral?"

"It is at Emery's Funeral Home in Layaffette. Do you know the place?"

"I've been there before. I can find it." My last statement was the only one in which I actually looked into they eyes of my sister. It was clear she had been crying as her eyes were swollen and red, but she maintained her composure quite well during our exchange despite my rudeness to her. I suddenly felt guilty. "I will see you Wednesday at two," I said as I gave her a hug. It was a feeble attempt to display a sense that I cared about what was happening, to convey that I was connected to my family. In truth, I was numb to everything and seemingly connected to no one. Funny really, in time I would truly learn what it meant to be disconnected. I remember thinking at the time that if God truly did exist, surely he had even forsaken me.

THREE

AS STATED earlier, there comes a point at which so much weight is pressing down on to one's shoulders that he simply cannot bear it. I wanted to go to the funeral out of respect, out of obligation, out of a need for closure. To the reader of these words, it would seem simple enough—go to the funeral! But I couldn't.

I felt as though I was faced with one of two choices—run away from my life, my problems, everything I knew, or lose myself in madness. The idea of taking my own life had crept into my mind, an idea that sits with me even now; self-destruction, it seemed, was a path I was becoming a little too familiar with. Yes, I wanted to lose everything, my life included. In so many ways, I had long since lost control of even the simplest aspects of my life and felt a crash was imminent.

And then, as if by providence, I remembered an offer my supervisor, Terry, had proposed several months earlier when he noticed the obvious—my depression. "Get away for a while," he said. "Go to Alaska and work on the pipeline. I can set it all up for you." Without a second thought, I called my facility manager and asked him to do whatever he needed to make it happen.

The next couple of weeks were nothing short of a blur. I had my utilities disconnected and moved all of my possessions into storage. I avoided the anger of my family by staying at a motel where no one would know where to find me or how to even get a hold of me. I missed my father's funeral, which I am sure made me a terrible son in the eyes of everyone that knew he had passed away. I felt bad about it but also felt that I had no choice in the matter. I just couldn't do it.

A short while later, I found myself on a flight to the Last Frontier state. I think I felt a little relief from the constant sorrow that had burdened me for so long. *Maybe this could be a new beginning for me,* I thought to myself as I deeply inhaled the brisk March Alaska air. They told me it was spring, but it certainly felt like a harsh midwinter. Alaska, it seemed, was a beautiful but less then gentle state.

Upon arriving, I was picked up by a Conoco pipe fitter named Rocky, and driven to H——, where I was shown the apartment that I would call home for the next several months. Now what would happen after my stint here was left undecided at the moment. Perhaps I would go back to St. Louis. Perhaps I would be allowed to stay in Alaska indefinitely. I didn't know, and at that moment, it was the furthest thing on my mind. In fact, all those horrible things I was attempting to escape from—Jessica's death, my father's passing, my horrid ex-wife, my depression in general—all these things were so far away from me while I was there in Alaska. I had found peace, at least a kind of peace.

I was also to learn that Rocky would be picking me up each morning, and I would be working primarily with him and another contractor named Jeff. Rocky was probably the most jolly and easy-going guy I had ever known—I immediately liked him. Jeff, I was to learn, while a little more reserved than Rocky, was equally enjoyable to work with. Finally, a fourth member or our team—Billy—was more of the comic relief/womanizing type. Billy had such a nonchalant attitude; few people really knew how brilliant he truly was.

For the next several months, we would work long days, doing a job that I wasn't especially good at under conditions that were anything but ideal. The pipeline itself was to span nearly eight hundred miles and would take about three years to complete. Of course, the group I was working with was responsible for only a small percentage of the entire line. Every day, large trucks delivered the forty-eight-inch-diameter pipeline, and slowly the group I worked with pieced it together in the trenches that were usually eight to twelve feet deep.

Jeff would often explain "telluric currents" and how these electrical currents would possibly corrode the pipeline. For this purpose, he would use zinc ribbons to ground these currents back into the earth. Personally, I often thought he was full of shit but went along with what he said.

After work, Rocky, Jeff, Billy, and I would all head to a small tavern called Eddies. Every night Billy would take home a different woman only to kick her out the moment he was finished with her. Rocky and Jeff, both married men, certainly entertained the thought of jumping into the sack with another woman, but as far as I know, they never actually did. As for myself, I was a wallflower. I watched people, interacted a little, but kept to myself. I did find enjoyment in spending my downtime with the coworkers that I came to know as friends. There are a number of stories I could offer about my time, both at work and at leisure, none of which really pertains to anything I truly wanted to write about, but all of which are fond memories to me.

At last, the unpredictable spring and the icy temperatures gave way to a more moderate season, which made work more productive and easier to tolerate. Suddenly, the mosquitoes came to life with a viciousness that even their Louisiana counterparts did not seem to possess. I settled into my day-to-day routine and found a certain serenity in the physical aspect of my job. Of course, I was nowhere near as experienced as was Jeff, nor had I the technical knowledge that Billy possessed. I always felt that I was just along for the ride but was happy with the group I was with. Finally, the day approached when, at least for me, the job was over, and I was scheduled to return home. I had considered staying, thought maybe I would meet some awesome woman who would sweep me off my feet, but that didn't happen clearly. Besides, I knew that I had obligations that I could not run from forever.

It was about two weeks before I was scheduled to leave that Rocky suggested that we go hunting. Now bear in mind, I was from the Midwest and had grown up in the Louisiana bayous; hunting was not an alien concept for me. The Alaskan mind-set, however, was one that I hadn't quite seen before. It was not uncommon for individuals to walk down the street with a pistol at their side and a shotgun across their shoulder. I often felt like I was in the old West!

"Have you ever seen a moose up close, a bull?" Rocky asked. "They are as big as a damn horse—sometimes eight feet or taller!"

Rocky was excited, and Billy and Jeff seemed all too willing to participate in the adventure as well. As for myself, I was again out of my element—this was their part of the country. But as always, I was willing to go along for the ride just the same. For two weeks, while I was dreading the end of my assignment and uncertain of what was going to happen to my job, my three coworkers went on and on about this hunting excursion.

My last day at work seemed a little anticlimactic. Mind you, I was the only one working temporarily on this job; everyone else would continue until some time in 1979 when everything was projected to finish. A couple of days before the conclusion of my assignment, Jeff needed to leave and go back home to Anchorage (I don't know the specifics, but there was something wrong with his wife).

So my last day at Conoco in Alaska was over; I was dropped off at my apartment, and I began to pack my belongings. I didn't really get too far though as I retired early to bed so that I would be ready for the big weekend. At 5:00 AM, I crawled out of bed and was met thirty minutes later by Rocky. "It's just you and I," he said. "Billy is sick and can't make it." I suspected that he was simply hung over, but regardless, what started out as a four-man hunting party had dwindled down to just Rocky and myself. Rocky didn't really care though; he, more than anyone else, had looked forward to this.

For almost four and a half hours, we drove deeper and deeper into what seemed an uncharted wilderness. I didn't really know where we were going or why the spot we were headed to was any better then the virtually uninhabited four hours we had passed to get there. Once we arrived to wherever Rocky had driven us, we got out and stretched our legs. Rocky handed me one of his shotguns—a double barrel, over or under twelve gauge—and a box of shells. Between the two of us, we had enough food to last a couple of days, sleeping bags, extra jackets in the event it rained, and of course, alcohol.

There wasn't really anything too remarkable about the rest of the day; we hiked then hiked some more, rested for a while, then followed that with a little more hiking. It seemed strange; there wasn't a single big-game animal. We spotted birds, rodents, even a wolverine running into its den, but not a trace of the moose, caribou, or elk that Rocky had been describing to me. It was as if these animals simply evacuated the area. The truth was that I didn't really care. While I wasn't altogether opposed to shooting a big-game animal, I really had no longing to do so either. My sentiments were not shared by Rocky, however, as I could tell that he was becoming increasingly discouraged as the day proceeded on.

I am guessing that it was some time around five or six that we found a semidecent open spot and decided to settle for the evening. We cleared the area and built a fire. Rocky opened his bag and removed a couple of warm beers and tossed one to me.

"Did you ever do much hunting?" he asked me as we ate.

"Years ago, I used to go out with a small .410 I had. Only rabbit and squirrel, never anything larger."

"I have been hunting throughout Alaska for the last several years. Let me tell you, there is no other place like it."

"Oh yeah?"

"Well, I know you are from the St. Louis area, and that there is a lot of hunting in that part of the country also. If you find yourself in trouble there, you are never more than a thirty- or forty-minute jog from some kind of civilization, a road, a house, a tractor shed, something. But you get yourself into trouble out here, you will find that you are in a world of hurt. This is the most beautiful place on earth, but it is also the most unforgiving."

Rocky also pulled out the bottle of Jack Daniel's he had been carrying with him. A short while later, I could tell that he was becoming more than tipsy. "Yeah, you will want to keep that shotgun close. Probably not much to worry about as far as wolves are concerned this time of year, but bears are a different story, especially if they have cubs. They become overly territorial."

I drank a little that night but nowhere near as much as Rocky. I remember thinking how funny it was that he fell asleep midsentence. I got up to throw a little more kindling on the fire but thought the hell with it and settled down for sleep myself; soon, my eyes grew too heavy to keep them open.

What happened next is hard to describe mostly because I was quite disorientated in the dark and having violently been awakened from a semialcohol-induced sleep but also because everything happened so quickly that I hardly had time to think.

I heard a scream, a horrible scream, followed immediately by a single gunshot. I then heard, very clearly, the growl of an extremely large animal—a bear. Startled, I quickly sprang to my feet and began searching for the shotgun that Rocky had advised me to keep close. The fire had died out, leaving only the embers that softly glowed but provided little illumination. "Rocky!" I called out but received no response. There was little that I could see, but I could hear the bear's heavy breathing every so often. From what direction though, I could not tell.

I pulled the butt of my shotgun to my shoulder, prepared to kill anything that might lunge at me from the blackness that engulfed the entire world around me. From behind me in the distance, I heard a twig snap, and I spun in that direction but obviously could not see anything. My heart raced; I really don't know how I knew it, but I realized that Rocky was dead. Still, I desperately called out his name, "Rocky!"

Another sound in the distance on the right, again I turned and aimed blindly in that direction, then a low growl 180 degrees in the opposite direction. *Fuck!* I thought to myself. At first, I assumed that there were several of them and that they were all around me, but within a few moments, I began to realize that there was only one. It seemed as though the animal was circling me, just playing with me.

I knew that Rocky had fired a shot moments earlier and that it obviously did not frighten off the bear. Despite that fact, the next sound I heard, I quickly aimed and fired in the direction from which it came. I thought perhaps this time the sound may frighten it off or possibly, if I were lucky enough, maybe I could have actually shot the damn thing. After firing the shot, I waited listening but hearing my own heartbeat and breathing over anything else. I continued waiting quietly and waiting longer still before calling out in vain again, "Rocky!"

I began to believe that I was alone, that my one and only shot had either killed the bear altogether or had frightened it away. I made my way to the sleeping bag that I had been comfortably resting in only a few moments earlier. After a quick search, I located the flashlight I had brought with me. With a hazy beam of light that only reluctantly pierced through the darkness, I made my way to the location where Rocky had been sleeping. Everything seemed so surreal, and while I was going through the motions, I couldn't truly accept what had happened, what was happening. I didn't see Rocky but located his sleeping bag, which was torn apart and blood soaked. My heart pounded as I knew that the worst thing that could possibly happen on this outing just did.

In that instant, as I attempted to rationalize and process all that had happened in the last 120 seconds or so, I was struck as if by a speeding vehicle, the shotgun and flashlight both knocked from my hands. I felt my body move through space almost in slow motion, it seemed, while in the clutches of this terrible animal. I'm sure the impact of the animal alone may have injured me or possibly the violent collision with which I hit the ground may have caused bones to break. All I know is that bones did break. It was interesting, though, even in that moment that I felt no pain—my adrenaline had numbed that sensation at least.

The bear was massive, and though I could barely see it in the darkness, I could easily make out its silhouette. For several seconds it growled, not a simple warning growl but a deep and deadly growl that sent a terror through me. Then as if it was the devil itself, it furiously ripped into my flesh.

There isn't really much I remember from that point. It was exceedingly vicious. I expected to be mauled as I had heard stories of bears mauling their victims, but it didn't really behave in that way. Either way, it really didn't matter; time seemed to stop, and what tiny light was available faded. The last thing I remember seeing were the dense clouds that rolled quietly above, exposing momentarily a nearly perfect full moon. Ironic really. I then lost sensation as well as consciousness.

All was black.

FOUR

I AWOKE... OR WAS I already awake? Did I ever even lose consciousness, or was I somehow awake throughout the ordeal and in the hours since? I do not know. I can say only that I realized in one moment that my surroundings were lighted and that I was in the most excruciating pain.

My breathing was deeply labored as I tried to raise my head and make a visual assessment of the extent and severity of my injuries. *Oh God*, I thought to myself and may have even said aloud. That strange and overwhelming trepidation passed over me in that instant—the fear that I could only imagine a soldier feels after stepping on and detonating a land mine. Knowing that my injuries were severe, the thoughts that raced almost instantaneously through my mind—am I going to survive? Am I going to be able to walk? How much blood have I lost? How many bones have I broken?

From a supine position, I lifted my head, feeling a jolt of pain radiate from my shoulders and neck on my left side and travel down my left arm. The sunlight broke through the tree branches and served to blind my view of anything toward my feet. My right hand crossed my body to first inspect the wounds I felt in my neck. What my fingers relayed to my brain served only to exacerbate the fear of the extent of my injuries. A giant gaping crevice that seemed nearly an inch wide and deeper than I cared to explore with my fingers ran from an area approximately one inch below and posterior to the mastoid process across my upper trapezium, ending at the anterior deltoid. Fluid slowly continued to spill and soak into the earth beneath where I lay.

I slid my left arm toward me, and together with the strength on my right side, I slowly sat up to continue my self-assessment. I suddenly bore witness to the most gruesome and gory scene I had beheld until then (in the years to come, I would see much worse). My abdomen had been spread open, and my intestines had fallen from the cavity that they belonged to, spilling onto my lap as I rose into a seated position. I wanted to scream in horror and disgust, to cry out for help that certainly would not be heard. Gazing down at the sausagelike viscera that had been soaking in blood and glistened as the sunlight showered down upon them, I realized that I would not make it out of these woods alive without immediate medical attention—and of that, there was no possibility.

After staring in disbelief for the longest time at the disgusting disembowelment of my midsection and debating whether to try to push my intestines back within the wound they had emerged from or it if was wise to even touch them at all, I noticed my right thigh had also been badly injured. While I could not visually ascertain precisely how large the trauma was due to my blood-soaked jeans, I did see the femur partially protruding from the medial portion of my thigh. I realized quickly enough that any attempted movement of my leg offered mind-numbing pain that proceeded through my body like waves in a great body of water.

All around me, the trees stood like quiet guardians, offering a false sense of shelter and security—much as the bayou did in my childhood. Slowly, I slid myself backward to rest my back against one of those gentle giants whose branches teamed with life—birds singing their songs with only a minimal awareness of me far beneath them. A fly darted before my eyes, and as I looked down at the intestines, I noticed I had attracted a number of small flying insects, like those tiny gnats that hover and swarm over fruit that has ripened beyond its perfection. In vain, I attempted to swat the tiny flying insects away before I realized the futility in it. *I am going to die,* I told myself. *My life has reached its end at the base of this tree.*

I wasn't really sure what dying would feel like—who is? I do remember expecting something more than this though. True, I had hoped to do more with my life and certainly could not ever have imagined leaving this world like this—mauled by a bear and left to die with only the trees, the birds, and the insects to keep me company and, of those, only the latter held any interest in me. Still, there was something strange I felt—a lack of finality that I expected would accompany death. I knew, barring some unforeseen miracle, there was no way for me to make it out of these woods; this was the end. It had to be. And yet, the strange feeling persisted as though I would see many more sunrises to come. Maybe I was simply in denial.

I looked up from the sad state of my oozing belly and scanned the trees to the east, and I saw her. Apparently, the streaming sunlight had provided her protection from my eyes while I lay on my back, but from my seated position beneath the tree, she was easily viewed. This feral-looking woman sitting on a low-lying branch not more than eighty feet from where I sat had been watching me this whole time. I am uncertain of what surprised me more—the fact that the woman had been there in the first place or the state of her condition.

She was beautiful and appeared to be in her mid to late thirties, with shoulder-length dark brown hair, unkempt as though she had just risen from sleep herself. A gray and black blanket covered her shoulders and back, but beyond this, she was entirely without clothing. Her breasts seemed to peer out, unprotected by the blanket that offered concealment to the shoulders, and as my eyes slowly traveled below her navel, I could see that her dark pubic hair was visible as well. Her bare feet hung unmoving from the branch, and I could see the well-toned muscularity of her calves. The image would have been extremely erotic had I not been in such pain and facing death. Looking back, it is easy for me to think of her in that moment in the most sexual, lustful way; at that time, however, lust was the furthest thought from my mind.

For the longest time, we each stared at one another, neither saying a word nor even moving. She had the physical and facial characteristics of a Native American Indian, possibly of Eskimo descent. Her face possessed high cheek bones and almond-shaped eyes. She was olive skinned, and her face, from what I could tell, was absolutely flawless.

"Can you help me?" I asked, my voice unusually strong considering my state.

The nude woman only stared back as though studying me. Strange how in that moment she suddenly reminded me of a cat studying a bird through a pain of glass—every subtle move and gesture I made analyzed as though she intended to pounce upon me. This strange behavior, or at least my perception of it, would have captivated my interest, enthralled me, had the setting and circumstances been different. Here, however, I became angered quickly.

"Did you hear me?" my voice no longer kind and gentle, my impatience becoming apparent. "I need your help!" When this second attempt to elicit her assistance failed, my anger intensified. "Are you fucking deaf?" I screamed aloud, regretting it as soon as the hateful words escaped my lips. How was I to know—maybe she was deaf, maybe she had a mental disorder. Why else would she be sitting thirty feet up in a tree, totally naked save for the blanket that offered no concealment from my eyes?

"I'm sorry," I said loudly enough that she could hear. "I'm in a lot of pain. I was attacked by a wild animal last night... I think my friend is nearby too. He may also be hurt." Actually, I did not believe that Rocky had survived the attack, but I felt that I owed him at least some degree of hope. "I think it was a bear... I don't know where he went to, but he may still be in the vicinity, so please be very careful whatever you do."

An instant later, I watched her drop from the branch where she had been perched, and land with the gracefulness of an Olympic athlete, much like the cat I mentally compared her to. During her drop, the blanket that provided her only cover had fallen from her shoulders, revealing the astonishing muscularity of her arms and shoulders. She slowly yet confidently approached me. I tried to look only at her face, to ignore or pretend not to notice her nude form—I at least tried to be the gentleman. I, of course, wanted to inquire why she wasn't wearing any clothing or even the blanket she had wrapped around herself a moment ago now discarded at the base of the tree she had been watching me from. I wanted to ask, "Do you live near here? Do you know were the nearest phone is? Or is there maybe a road somewhere nearby?" But I didn't.

Somehow I didn't expect an answer, and this woman did not surprise me by offering one. Instead, she studied my wounds. She glanced only momentarily at my neck, examined my abdomen briefly, then brought her attention to my obviously mangled broken leg.

"I need to find a doctor. I'm hurt very badly," I said to her, somehow convinced now that she did indeed suffer from a mental disorder of some sort. She knelt down before me, still gazing at my broken leg, seemingly oblivious to what I had just said to her. She then reached out to touch my leg. I caught her hand and pushed it away. "Please, I need a doctor." She turned her beautiful brown eyes to meet mine, and a strange chill ran down my spine and goose bumps arose on my arms and neck. Something I couldn't exactly put my finger on, something creepy in her gaze, put me on edge. Again, I felt like the small animal ready to be pounced upon by the cat.

She again reached for my leg, and again I pushed her away. This time, however, she struck me in the jaw. Strange, but this small woman delivered a blow that would rival that of any man, with seemingly no effort at all. For several moments, I was dazed, certain that she had broken my jaw. My face seemed to swell in the following seconds, my mouth filled with blood, and all sensation in my jaw was lost. In that moment of daze and confusion on my part, this unusual woman had pulled me away from the tree and, while I lay helpless on my back, straddled my broken right leg. With a quick and almost inhumanly powerful jerk, my femur was broken at another point. I screamed out in pain as I could actually hear the bones in my leg just distal to my hip crunch under this woman's pressure. My voice echoed off the trees, and my scream seemed to repeat itself for me to hear again seconds later. My eyes watered, and I began coughing on both the blood in my mouth as well as vomit that had erupted immediately following my leg being broken yet again. My head swam as though I had gotten off a circus ride, and as vertigo began to envelop my visual and proprioceptive awareness, I could see the woman hovering over me.

My hands went immediately to my right leg, and while the pain was excruciating and no longer bearable, I did notice that my femur was no longer protruding through my inner thigh. At that moment, my eyes rolled backward and up beyond my eyelids—I must have been looking toward the ceiling of my skull. I felt myself slipping backward though I was still lying on the ground; the vertigo had overtaken me. I fell. The world spun. I still searched for breath, then I was not conscious.

It seems that I remember waking, if for only an instant. I saw the small of the woman's back—the area I've always found so sexy in women. I remember gazing at her nude backside, the curvature of her muscular buttocks, the way her feet touched the ground so lightly that she seemed to almost float as she moved.

I did not see much of where we were or where we were going; clearly, we were deep in the mountains. I was being carried over her shoulder as though I was being rescued by a firefighter. I remember wondering how this was possible—not to sound sexist, but she was only a woman yet managed to carry my like I was a child or maybe even like a bag of dog food rather than a grown man who was much heavier than her. With remarkable ease, we ascended and descended the rugged landscape, hurdled large rocks and fallen trees, and even waded through an icy cold, waist-high creek—all without this woman even seeming to exert even minimal effort. This didn't make sense; nothing made sense at that point.

I remember opening my eyes and feeling bloody saliva fall from my lips, watching it slide down the back of this stunning woman. She either did not notice or did not care. So many questions raced though my barely coherent mind. How could she be carrying me? Who is this woman? Where were we going? I then lost consciousness again.

Then there were dreams. Of course, everyone has dreams; and it has been said that dreams can somehow reflect your personality, your drives, likes and dislikes, hidden fears. I don't know, maybe there is truth in that. My dreams, until then, had always been black and white—the kind of dreams that an accountant might have, very left-brained logical with little or no imaginative or creative component.

Yes, I had my share of nightmares—those dreams in which I was pursued by someone or something. Upon awakening from one of these, I could almost feel whatever entity had followed me from my dream, hiding in the darkness. Despite the lack of color in my dreams, they certainly seemed real enough in the middle of the night. I had never really had violent dreams, the exception to this being those during my adolescence. These were really nothing more than nightmares that involved me trying to defend myself against whatever was after me. These were not pleasant, and I believe they were probably brought on by the hormonal changes occurring at that time. All that changed here however.

I was at a party... Maybe it was a meeting. I'm unsure, but there was a gathering of several dozen people. They varied in age, ethnicity, even their attire as some wore business suits, some wore jeans and t-shirts while others were dressed only in house robes. There were both men and women in about equal proportions, some standing in groups. others seated at tables with papers in front of them.

I could smell the cheese and artichoke dip several of the guests were dipping their crackers into. I could smell the wine that was being poured, the colognes, hairspray, deodorants. I could even smell the sour breath of the overweight Asian man across the room as well as the rotten flatulence of the older red-haired woman in the corner.

Everything around me seemed presented in the most exquisite detail, enriched with a strange quality that I cannot truly describe. It was more real than my waking hours. The sights, sounds, and smells were of such high definition, it seemed strangely artificial yet alive. Most amazing of all, everything was in color, such amazing and brilliant color—the deepest blues and greens, every shade of red, purple, tan, and yellow. Even the contrasts in people's hair—the many different colors, shades, and tints of blond and brunette hair on any one individual, too subtle and invisible to the mortal eye and yet somehow made available for me to see. No details, not even the tiny specks of dandruff, were omitted. No detail could escape my eyes.

The building was a church of some sort. Most of the people gathered in a sort of large reception room. I slowly crossed the room, taking in the splendid sensations of my surroundings in all their rich detail. I ventured through a doorway and into the sanctuary of the church. Something about the large and open space seemed alive itself as though I had walked into and now stood within a living thing. The carpet was red with gold patterns that ran like subtle threadlike stripes crisscrossing across its length. The walls were off-white, mother-of-pearl color and were decorated with wall tapestries on either side, depicting the Christ on the cross. The tapestry above the pulpit was especially grand, and the words "Lamb of God" were presented over what was somehow a strange and almost morbid-looking crucifixion scene. Whether this was something I had seen before or my mind making this up as it went along, I could not say.

As I examined the pews, I quite suddenly heard a voice. It was something that I do not believe that anyone without unnatural hearing would have been aware of. Although I could hear it, I did not understand their meaning. "I can do no wrong, for I do not know what it is." The words were barely more than a whisper and yet I had no difficulty making them out.

I proceeded across the sanctuary and into a somewhat dark hallway, the temperature dropping considerably with every step taken. I estimated the hallway I had now entered into was nearly twenty degrees cooler than the reception room from which I had begun this journey. The whispers were coming from a place beyond this hallway. I considered turning back, revisiting the meeting room, or possibly lingering in the sanctuary longer. Somehow, I did not feel this hallway was safe, and I certainly did not feel that whatever lay beyond this hallway offered any protection or comfort. And yet the whispers were so familiar. "I can do no wrong, for I do not know what it is." What did this mean? I knew only that it was a message intended for me alone.

With reluctance and trepidation, I left the sanctuary and slowly advanced down the corridor. There were two small lamps on the wall—each with a bulb emitting no more than twenty-five watts of illumination. My shadow cast forth the entire length of this hallway—maybe forty feet. My senses were preternaturally acute, and I was using them to their fullest extent. Despite the extremely poor lighting, I saw every detail just as I had in the better-lit areas of the church—nothing could hide from my sight. I could hear my own footsteps practically crushing the carpet beneath my feet as though I were stepping across broken glass while wearing steel shoes—such impossibly acute hearing. My olfactory senses were no less impressive as I could smell the carpet I walked upon and could smell dust and mold ahead of me.

At the end of this hallway, a single open door; beyond it, steps leading down. I glanced back in the direction from which I had come and could see the light spilling out of the sanctuary into the far end of the hall. I could also still hear the people talking. Much of the conversation that was taking place, I could easily make out even from this distance. I then turned my attention to the dusty steps in front of me and descended them.

There was no carpet here—only the concrete in which despite my attempts to walk quietly, did little to lessen the sound of my footsteps with my sensitive hearing. There was also absolutely no light of any kind. Although my eyesight was functioning in an extraordinary way, it could not serve me in this total absence of light. Then again the whisper, this time louder, "I can do no wrong, for I do not know what it is." I hastened my descent and, upon reaching the bottom, discovered another hallway parallel to the one above it leading from the sanctuary.

Although I could see nothing, I could hear my footsteps, my breathing, even my heartbeat. These otherwise quiet sounds seemed to bounce off the concrete walls and echo back to me. Strange, it seemed that in addition to everything else, I possessed a type of sonar as well. Nice, though I found myself much less sure footed and crept along when I would have otherwise walked confidently though slowly, but I could clearly make out the walls, floor, ceiling, and would have been aware of any object should there have been one in my path—just as well that there wasn't. In other circumstances this "gift" would be fun to play with but could not serve in the place of my eyesight, even my greatly diminished nongifted eyesight. I continued through the pitch-black corridor for some distance, the lack of illumination made judging how far I had come an impossibility.

At the end of this lengthy hallway, which somehow had the feeling of a tomb, was a door from which a dim illumination seeped from beneath it. Opening the door, I observed a small room approximately twenty feet by thirty feet. Six red candles burned opposite the door on a small table, which provided more than sufficient light for this room, my eyesight being what it was now. Suddenly my eyes darted toward a man sitting in a chair, his back to me. It was from him the strange yet familiar whispers emanated. "I can do no wrong, for I do not know what it is," he said as he rose from his seated position. As he turned to face me, a severe chill ran down my neck, into my spine, and through my arms and legs. I stood, staring at myself across the room.

The face and body of the man I observed was the identical likeness of myself. He looked back at me but did not seem to share the deeply disturbing feeling that I was experiencing. In fact, he seemed absolutely void of any kind of emotion, more like a machine, no feeling whatsoever. He wasn't human. He looked like me. He stood like me. The sound of his voice was the sound of my own voice. He even smelled like me. Yet he was not me—he wasn't human.

For what seemed several moments, I looked into his eyes, at first expecting to see what I would if I were to gaze into a mirror. Instead, I saw something horrible and frightening—these eyes, they did not possess a soul. I cannot explain what I saw any differently. They were just windows into a dark and macabre abyss. Of course, he had pupils and irises, but I'm referring to something much more spiritual that he was lacking. I suppose it is something you simply had to see for yourself to truly grasp how creepy it truly was.

For what seemed the longest time, we exchanged stares, and though he seemed patient with me, he displayed little interest in studying me the way I was studying him. Finally, I worked up the nerve to speak to him, "Why are you here?" It seemed like a better question at this point than "who are you?"

"In here, you trespass. This is where I live. This is my realm." His voice was exactly as mine was except that it was monotone and dull. "Why are you here?" he repeated the question I had asked him, a question for which I had no answer. "In here, I live and you trespass." After a brief pause, he continued, "But know this, out there where you live, where you dwell, where you lie down and rest. There too shall I trespass."

Was this a threat of some sort? His facial expressions, like his voice, were without feeling—impossible to gauge. I examined his statement and tried to make sense of it, but it was like a riddle, one I could not see an immediate answer for.

He proceeded toward the table on which the six candles provided the only light anywhere downstairs. The table stood about four feet high and was made of oak; it also held a drawer. I said nothing more; I only observed as my twin, this doppelganger, slid open the drawer and withdrew a wicked-looking machete and unsheathed it. After studying this bladed tool or, more likely, this weapon in his hands, he lowered the machete to his side and took the six or seven steps required to reach the door through which I had entered moments earlier. In doing so, he passed me without further acknowledgment that I was even there.

At this point, I had to ask him the question with what seemed the most obvious answer. "Who are you?"

He stopped in the doorway and turned to face me, revealing once again those hollow and frighteningly empty eyes. "There is no line that divides you and I," he said before pausing, "not anymore." With those enigmatic words, he turned, exited the room, and closed the door behind him.

Strange, how even then I knew this was nothing more than a dream, and yet it was so real, and that realism seemed to have blurred my ability to rationalize what was happening and what was about to happen. Oh yes, people have said that about dreams as long as people have had dreams, but for me, I had somehow stepped onto a plane where fantasy became a conjured reality. Not only was this experience in color, which by itself was a deeply fantastic experience, but I possessed senses that exceeded anything human, allowing me to observe and become aware of my surroundings on a level unknown to me before. Despite all this, what made this dream most peculiar was the fact that I could still employ reason while having the dream, and yet somehow that reason, that basic logic, failed me.

I turned toward the door myself but, upon trying to open it, realized that it was now sealed tight. I panicked—again, indicative of my failed reasoning— began to beat wildly upon the door. After a moment of futility, I ceased trying the beat the door down with my fists. As I stood studying my circumstances, I began to hear screams coming from upstairs. My breathing and heart rate quickened in terror as the soulless version of myself had begun to massacre those upstairs. Yes, it was a dream. I was well aware of that, but that did not make any of this—the people upstairs included—any less real to me. As I experienced everything in a crystal-clear, precise quality that I never had during my waking hours, this dream took on a realism I would never have experienced in life.

"God, please help me!" I said as I again struggled with the door. Eventually, for whatever reason, the door opened, and I rushed into the darkened concrete hallway with as much haste as I could. Within only a matter of seconds though, I realized that the hallway had changed and *was not the same corridor I had traveled through earlier. Clearly, despite the realism this dream offered, it did not lack the unpredictable nature that all dreams possess.*

Again, in total blackness, guided only by the sounds of my footsteps bouncing off the walls, I proceeded right then fifty feet to another right, then eventually coming to a "T." Selecting left, I advanced quickly all the while listening to the screams of those in the church above me. Men, women, and even children screamed out in panic then in pain as the person resembling me came for them, killing them one by one as the others watched. Again, another left as I raced through the absolute darkness, desperate to escape this insane labyrinth. I advanced another forty feet in haste, then more steps leading further down... NO!

What did I plan to do once I had reached the church? How could I stop a madman with a machete? How many people had he already killed? I wondered all these things and more as I stumbled blindly though the darkness. Why hadn't I taken one of the candles? I could not even find the room I had been locked in—nothing but corridors. Right, then right, then left, then right again, then another "T." This was fucking insane! Surely this was my private and personal hell.

I stopped, exhausted, and began to cry, letting the tears roll down my cheeks in the darkness that drowned everything that I was. Was I even alive? Maybe I had been killed by the bear after all or that fucking nutcase of a woman. None of that really mattered here though. In fact, that experience seemed more like the dream while my existence here was the reality. I leaned against the wall and slid down to sit on the cold, hard, dusty floor.

For the longest time, I sat and wept as I listened to the screams become less and less frequent. I was helpless to stop any of it, not that I could have necessarily stopped it anyway. So many thoughts raced through my mind while I sat there in that underground prison. I thought about Jessica and wished I could hold her one last time, wished that I could feel her tiny hands cling to my neck one more time.

At first, I didn't know why the memories of my lost daughter had assaulted me at that most unlikely and seemingly unrelated moment. Then, of course, as those thoughts of her pressed deeper into my soul, I realized that the feelings of abysmal and unrelenting hopelessness I had experienced during her sickness were with me now in the tunnel. That old feeling of failure—that I could have or should have done... something to have stopped this.

The moments passed slowly, and I began trying to force myself awake without success. After an impossible measure of time, a very dim light quite suddenly appeared in the distance to my right—maybe eighty yards down the corridor. I slowly rose, sliding up the wall into a standing position. I feared that if I were to advance toward this light, it would either retreat from me with as much speed as I would use to approach it, or it would disappear altogether. Either way, I felt certain that this source of light was something to further torment or tease me.

Still, there was no reason for me to believe it wouldn't simply fade away should I remain where I was. With this in mind, I began moving toward the source of the light, which was almost a football field-length distant from where I had been seated. I proceeded slowly and cautiously at first, crawling along the hallway one step at a time, then suddenly sprinted the last half of the distance. I covered the final forty or so yards in mere seconds, the strength and power in my legs propelling me faster and more swiftly than I had ever moved in real life. To my surprise, the light, originating from a stairwell going up, did not fade, retreat, or disappear.

I quickly ascended the steps to find myself once again in the poorly lit hallway of the church. At first, everything seemed as I had left it when I went to investigate the voice from the basement. It only took a quick inhalation of air to recognize the all-too familiar smell of blood that permeated every breath I took, the copperlike aroma sending a chill down my spine. Although the hallway was dimly lit, it took several seconds for my eyes to become accustomed to the light as the blackness of the basement greatly enlarged my pupils. At the far end of the hallway, something lay on the floor. There was no need for me to approach the object to identify it— my newly acquired vision allowed me to clearly see what it was... a severed hand.

I gasped then again analyzed the breath I had taken. The air in my mouth, nose, and flowing into and out of my lungs was saturated with the fragrance that I was to become intimately used to. True, I could smell the thickness of the blood in the air, but I could have probably detected that much with even my pathetic and limited human olfactory strength. But I could sense so much more than that now. I could detect the blood, the urine, the excrement from multiple victims—dozens of people. But there was something more in the air, something faint and somehow preternaturally intangible and yet something I was familiar with, something from my past. It took my brain less than a second to recognize the blood and various bodily fluids that now soaked the already red carpet; but several moments had passed before I could truly identify this second and even more menacing odor. Yes, I suddenly knew what it was—the smell of death.

It's one of those strange and disturbing odors that has no physical basis or origin yet seems to cling to those who are sick and dying. Nursing home and hospital patients and, yes, even small children with cancer seem to carry this somewhat indistinguishable effluvium. No matter how hard one tries, it is a horrible scent that will not wash off.

I closed my eyes and allowed my hypersensitive hearing to work unobstructed by my vision. I half expected to hear the heavy footsteps of a madman, noisily patrolling the church, looking for anyone who had escaped his slaughter. I heard only faint breathing coming from one individual, somewhere in the reception room, where this nightmare had begun for me.

I moved in that direction in the same way a child would move toward a parent whose intention was to discipline. I had no idea of what to expect once I left the sanctuary and reentered the reception room. As best as I could tell, the sanctuary now housed the remains of at least six people, all of whom were badly mutilated and dismembered. But by far, the richest smell of death and blood came from the direction I was now heading, the direction of the breathing.

Approaching the reception room, the temperature increased substantially and with it my reluctance. Still, I pressed forward and opened the door that separated the sanctuary from this room. The floor was covered with bodies—some of them struck down without knowing they were under attack, others in defensive positions although they shared the same fate. Across the room, a pantry door was all that separated the breathing from within it to the ugly carnage outside.

Was one person spared during this massacre? A part of me wanted to run away as quickly as I could, and yet for whatever reason, I felt somehow... responsible for what had happened. There was no way I could possibly leave a victim behind; I had to reach out to whoever it was; I had to help. Then we would leave here together.

I walked as quietly as my feet would allow, making only the faintest of undetectable sounds, until I stood directly in front to the pantry door. I closed my eyes and listened one last time for the mass murderer responsible for this atrocity, but after several moments of hearing nothing else, I realized that we were alone here. I slowly opened the door and noticed a young woman curled into a ball in the corner, shaking and whimpering. "Miss," I called out quietly to get her attention. When she looked in my direction, she screamed with all her might. I could actually feel her voice on my chest as though I were standing in front of speakers.

I quite suddenly realized that the attacker looked identical to me—she thought I had killed everyone. I approached her quickly, attempting to calm her, trying to let her know that it wasn't me that was responsible, but my advance brought her hysteria to a head. Then as she screamed and kicked, the strangest and most horrible thing happened—I suddenly realized that I was holding in my hand the machete that had been pulled from the drawer of the table in the basement. Not only was I holding the murder weapon, but I was covered in blood as well—from head to toe. Even my hair had blood from several of the victims as though I had showered in it.

I dropped the weapon and heard it clang on the tile floor while stepping backward in disbelief. I couldn't have done this... It wasn't me... It was the guy who looked like me, the guy who had my face. I slowly exited the pantry and turned to see a mirror hanging above a small sink. As I looked at myself in the mirror, as I examined my bloody face, I was overwhelmed by the horror of my eyes—they were the eyes of my twin, empty and without a soul.

FIVE

MY EYES OPENED with the same horror that I had felt in my dream. As my eyelids lifted, I found myself peering upward toward the dark brown beams that formed the loft for the building I was now in. I remember it taking several moments before a sense of relief finally enveloped me. *Thank God it was only a dream.*

Around my body and face, I could feel the incredibly soft down pillows and comforters I had been wrapped in. I was quite warm and moved my upper extremities to push away the comforters that covered me when the pain in my neck and shoulder announced itself. However, the pain I now felt was significantly less intense than it should have been, considering the extent of my injuries.

Upon further inspection with my fingers, I was dumb stricken to learn that the wounds on my neck and shoulder were little more than scratches. Immediately I observed the same for the abdominal wound I had received. I ran my fingers across the length of the wound—yes, it was still ugly, and yes, it even oozed, but this was no more a mortal wound than was my neck.

What the fuck! I thought to myself. I tried to mentally envision the extent of my injuries while in the woods and compare them with what

I seemed to observe upon awaking; my conclusion—an impossibility. My mind attempted to rationalize the situation. Clearly, I concluded, I terribly misjudged the severity of my injuries. Perhaps… some kind of hallucination on my part?

I slowly sat up, feeling the much more reasonable pain in my midsection as my abdominal muscles contracted. Apparently, the wound had wept fluid onto the otherwise white comforters and one of the numerous pillows that had been placed around me. I pulled the rusty brown-stained comforter away from the wound it had become stuck to and, in doing so, mildly caused more bleeding as the fresh scab reopened.

My clothing had been removed, and upon scanning the immediate vicinity, I was unable to locate them. The bed in which I had been resting was essentially a pallet, a mattress on the floor with soft sheets, a dozen or more large down pillows, and two or three large down comforters. The room I was in was clearly the family room of a large cabin. I could smell the dusty, earthy, wooden walls and floors. Looking around me, thoughts of a retreat came to mind, the kind of place where Hemingway might have come to get away from the world. The ticktock of a large grandfather clock seemed to echo across the room while old pictures decorated tables and books lined shelves and were even stacked neatly on the floor.

Then my eyes met and locked gazes with the beautiful "wild woman" from the woods. Just as she appeared disconnected when I saw her the first time, so too did she now carry the same unemotional, robotlike expression on her otherwise angelic face.

"Hello again," I said to her, not sure whether to expect an answer or the continued silence she offered in the woods.

She sat reclining in an old rocking chair; her right leg slung over the arm of the chair, the left elevated on a stool. She wore a blue and black flannel shirt, sleeves rolled up to her elbows, exposing the impressive muscularity of her forearms. Also, several buttons were left unsecured as though she had little concern for modesty and simply wanted to secure the flannel with as little effort as possible. She wore loose-fitting black pants and left her feet exposed. Across her lap, a book she had been reading, now open and face up.

My eyes focused, and to my amazement, I could clearly read the text from across the room even with the book inverted. *This isn't happening*, I thought to myself. I focused again—the book was entitled *The Mysterious Stranger* by Mark Twain.

"You're feeling better I see," came the strangely accented voice from the woman holding the book. As incredible as my eyesight was, the sound of her voice was the one thing that could easily tear my attention from it. There was something about her voice, something strange and unidentifiable just as the voice of the man in my dream.

"You speak!" I said smiling. I was glad she was wearing clothing, but the fact that I was now nude, though under covers, still made our exchange awkward at least for me. Her face bore an expressionless and blank set of features that reminded me of a mannequin. "I was beginning to think that you didn't like me," I said, attempting to elicit a smile, maybe a frown, anything really.

"Why were you in these woods?" she asked coldly, her face remaining unchanged.

"My buddy and I were hiking, camping, and fishing," I responded. "I didn't think the bears would approach the fire we had made." As I spoke, thoughts of Rocky entered my mind, and I felt an intense sense of loss for my friend. So many emotions seemed to weigh down upon my shoulders. I felt anger, loss, sorrow, gratitude… and guilt. Guilt, because I had survived when Rocky had been not only been killed but also brutally and savagely torn apart. Beyond this, I felt guilt because I had spent only moments even considering Rocky's fate and had instead focused on my own condition.

"There aren't any bears in this area," the stranger said.

"I am sorry to disagree, but you are gravely mistaken. It was a bear that did this."

"There haven't been any bears in this area in many decades," she stated. Again, I began to question her mental/cognitive health. At this point, I could see no reason to argue the bear issue with her as it seemed her mind was made up and wouldn't be changed.

"So why the quiet treatment in the woods?" I asked, trying to sound mater-of-fact about the whole scene. In truth, everything that had happened in the woods and so far since seemed totally fucked up. It was as if Rod Serling had taken LSD then decided to write a *Twilight Zone* episode that I was to star in.

She looked directly into my eyes, and a cold chill ran down my spine. The hair rose on my neck and on my arms as she offered her answer. "I was trying to decide if the world truly needed another monster."

What the fuck does someone say to that? And why did this creep me out so much? "Am I a monster?" I asked, my voice lightly betraying the calm and collected presentation my demeanor offered.

"You are now," came her answer, followed by a long and uncomfortable silence. "You are hungry, I assume?" It wasn't really a question so much as it was a statement though. However, she was right; I was absolutely starving. In fact, I could not remember ever being quite so hungry in years… ever actually.

Without saying anything further, she rose from her chair, proceeded across the cabin, and exited through the doorway. Several seconds later, I realized quite suddenly that I could hear her footsteps, light as they were, as she walked to a nearby outbuilding, a garage or shed perhaps. I was both chilled and enthralled with this ability just as I had been in my dream. I began to wonder if this too was possibly only a dream.

Moments later, she returned carrying two rather large boxes. The instant she stepped though the doorway, my nasal passages were flooded with the beautiful smell of poultry and beef, still frozen. Yet their aroma seemed to scream to my olfactory senses.

"Holy shit," I whispered under my breath, again, both amazed and frightened by the abilities that seemed to have followed me from my dream.

"What's wrong?" she asked turning to me. It didn't seem possible that she could have heard the barely audible whisper I had made, but clearly she had.

"Nothing," I said. "I just had a really fucked-up nightmare before I woke."

Her lovely and frightening eyes looked directly into mine. "Get used to it. You are going to have many more in the months and years to come." Turning away from me, she placed the boxes on the countertop near the sink. "Everything is frozen and will take some time to thaw. However, if you need to eat immediately, we can make do with it."

"But it's frozen."

"I think you will find, at least in time, that in an emergency, food in any condition is still food."

"Well, maybe," I said, "but this isn't really an emergency." Although what I said made sense, in truth I was becoming so hungry that I could have eaten almost anything no matter what it was. My appetite was beginning to interfere with my ability to concentrate. The smell of the frozen meat was causing me to salivate, and it seemed that I had difficulty thinking about anything but my need to eat something. Still, I did what I could to force myself to focus on the beautiful, though questionably insane, woman who shared her time with me.

"As you wish," she said. "This should thaw in a few hours." She turned away from the kitchen area and returned to her chair facing me. "In the meanwhile, there is much we need to discuss."

Of course I agreed completely. There was the idea of getting medical attention for myself. And of course, alerting the authorities about Rocky's death. There would be many questions that would need to be answered— both by me and by crazy woman who apparently lived here.

"To start with, my name is Myra, and you should know that you are safe here, at least for the time being."

"Oh, I'm sorry," I said clumsily. "My name is Caleb. I guess my mind has been somewhere else with everything that has happened... I just totally forgot to introduce myself." I wasn't sure what she meant regarding my safety but did not say or ask anything about it.

Myra left the room, and I could hear her footsteps as she proceeded toward another part of the cabin, presumably her bedroom. She returned a moment later carrying jeans and a white t-shirt. "These probably won't fit perfectly, but they are the best I have." She tossed them at the foot of the pallet.

"Do you have a phone?"

"No."

"Well, how far is the nearest phone? I need to call the police. I need to let them know what happened."

"You are a long way from any kind of phone. You are a long way from civilization, period. Besides, we need to talk."

She gave me several moments to dress, and though in considerable pain, I managed to don the pants and shirt with minimal difficulty. The pants were a little large for me, but I could make them work. I was surprised that I could stand, let alone move and maneuver myself enough to get dressed. My right hip was terribly painful as I put weight through it, but not so much that I couldn't stand or even walk. Clearly, while my injuries were less significant than I had originally thought, I would still require medical attention, but at least I wasn't going to die from them.

I sat in one of the chairs, across from the recliner that Myra had been in earlier and took several deep breaths. "Your shoes were not torn up during your attack. They are fine," she said as she handed them to me upon entering the room.

"So you do believe I was attacked after all," I said as I struggled to put my shoes on.

"I never said that the attack didn't happen, only that it wasn't a bear."

"I can't imagine what it could have been then."

"It was me," she said as she sat in her chair opposite me.

"I don't think I understand."

"This isn't going to be easy to hear, but you need to know what it is that you are now a part of," she began. "You and your friend were attacked by a werewolf."

"So... you are a... werewolf?"

"We both are now," she answered.

For some time I listened to Myra speak about werewolves and the full of the moon and about how she had chosen to live here for its seclusion. I didn't really say too much, though clearly she was delusional. As she spoke, her tone suggested that she actually believed what she was saying—this wasn't going to be easy for me as I needed her to help me get back to the real world, and yet her fantasy was going to be an obstacle for me.

As strange as everything around me seemed, Myra included, it would have been easy for me to have become disillusioned by what she was saying. After all, here I was with what I originally thought were life-threatening wounds only to awaken and realize that they weren't nearly as bad as I thought they were. Additionally, while I could not easily explain my vivid dream or the frighteningly enhanced senses I seemed to experience since I had awakened, it might have been easy for me to attribute these to Myra's story.

After some time, Myra seemed to grow tired of hearing herself speak. Actually, I have no doubt that she was well aware of my opinion of what she was offering. While she showed no signs of changing her beliefs, she lost interest in trying to convince me that her story was valid.

Eventually, I wanted to stretch my legs, maybe go for a short walk. I hoped that maybe it would help lessen the stiffness in my right hip. I was relieved that Myra did not object. She stated only that our discussion would continue later then went into the kitchen to prepare what looked like a truckload of food. As far as I could tell, she had little experience with whatever she was trying to do there. I was becoming so hungry that it was good to put a little distance between the beautiful smell of the thawing meat and myself. So with that, I stepped out of the cabin and ventured into what seemed to be wonderland.

While the colors of everything surrounding me were so vivid and highly defined, it was the scent that I was now picking up that seemed so alien. I inhaled deeply through my nasal passages and was able to practically "taste" the mud, the grass, the trees, and water that was all around me.

I realize that much of what I have written here seems redundant. Yes, my olfactory senses were marvelous and new. As a human being, I would not have been able to understand or appreciate the role that my sense of smell now plays in my life. As such, I do not expect the reader of these accounts to feel any more enlightened than I would have been. So much time has passed since those early hours of my new life that I have forgotten what it was truly like to be and feel human. Maybe it is futile—attempting to define and describe a concept so fundamental yet totally invisible to all humanity. I'll try nonetheless.

It was as though I had been blind my whole life, and suddenly I had acquired perfect eyesight. Even the most simple things—sweat, blood, urine, things I had never been aware of and yet were all around me—were something beautiful and needed exploring.

I remember walking a short distance up the old dirt road leading away from the cabin when suddenly, something firmly grabbed my attention. I didn't know what it was, something in the breeze. I turned my head into the direction of the wind, facing the midafternoon sun. I could smell some kind of mushroom, a variety of blossoming flowers, even the earthy smell of the bark from different trees, but there was something else, something very faint in the wind. It was somehow "warm" and musky. I closed my eyes and allowed the gentle movement of the air caress my face while I took in a large dose of this somehow familiar yet mysterious scent. In that instant, an image came to my mind, revealing to me the mystery of this scent—it was a rabbit. How far away this animal was I could not say, but I could easily recognize its scent carried by the wind.

I began to consider Myra's crazy-ass story. I didn't believe it; I couldn't believe anything so stupid as "werewolf infection." At the same time, however, I had to consider—at least entertain the idea—of my abilities, my newly acquired sensations as well as how much I had healed in the previous day. The fact that I was up and walking around was, by itself, a miracle. And although I had not failed to register this "miracle," I was unable, at least at that moment, to offer credit to lycanthropy. But why then? Was I losing my fucking mind? Was I delusional? All I knew at that moment was that I was so fucking hungry that nothing else really seemed to matter too much.

The ability to detect the rabbit in the distance, awesome as it was, seemed only to fuel my somehow inhuman appetite. If I would have had the animal in my hands at that moment, I would have immediately twisted its head violently to break its neck and would have begun tearing at its flesh with my teeth. This powerful image ran through my mind and wouldn't leave my thoughts. It seemed to both welcome and revolt me at the same time. *Oh God, what is wrong with me?* I thought to myself.

"Caleb," came the strangely beautiful and enchanting though emotionless voice from a distance. "Food will be ready in a moment." The words were spoken in a conversational tone and volume. Yet as I turned, I observed Myra in her flannel and pants on her porch just under a quarter mile down the road. Despite the distance, I could see her in the clearest detail; even the buttons on her flannel shirt were easily visible. Beyond this, I could hear her words as clearly and plainly as if she had been standing ten feet from me.

After a moment of staring at each other, she turned and reentered the cabin. I knew that I needed to talk to her. I needed answers. I needed something. But again, this thought too seemed drowned out by my desperate need to eat. When stacked against this most basic of needs, nothing else seemed to matter.

Entering the cabin was enough to send me into a frenzy, but I did my best to suppress my urge to dash into the kitchen and tear the food from the plates and devour it like an animal. I was absolutely amazed at how much meat there was—occupying nearly every piece of table and counter space available. There was enough food here to easily feed twelve to fifteen people, maybe more.

I was uncertain at the time of what Myra was thinking as it seemed that some of the steaks were cooked very rare, some were seared only, while others hadn't been touched by fire and were still partially frozen. Several chickens had been crudely cut or torn apart, a couple in the sink with a couple more in the oven. The cabin was so permeated with the smell of prepared and semiprepared poultry and beef that I felt that I could almost swim through it.

"Please forgive me," Myra said. "I'm not much of a cook. I think you will find, however, that if you are hungry enough, food preparation hardly matters."

I didn't know what she meant with the last part of her statement, nor did I even care. I approached the near end of the table, sat in the chair allotted for the spot, and began devouring everything within my reach. I'm assuming that Myra was watching me though I honestly paid little mind to her in that moment.

So strange; it seemed that regardless of how much I ate, my appetite remained unsatisfied. I had never in my life ever even heard of someone eating so much in a single sitting. Between Myra and myself, we consumed every scrap of the meat she had brought in. No vegetables, no fruits, nothing that would have made this "meal" balanced, just the poultry and beef, and this was just as well with me. Even more interesting, while I began with the cooked steaks—in truth, they were burned on the outside and uncooked in the center—I soon moved to the unprepared steaks without any discrimination between the two. The fact of the matter was that I was so hungry that I no longer cared if it was cooked or raw so long as it was edible. What's more, there was something strangely enjoyable about the taste of the uncooked meat—the beef in particular. It would seem that whatever had affected and increased my olfactory awareness had also increased my gustatory perceptions as well.

Afterward, Myra and I returned to the cabin's main room, the one in which I had awoken, my pallet still on the floor in the corner. Myra sat in her chair, casually thumbing through her Mark Twain book while I sat across the room in another chair contemplating so many thoughts. I was actually still hungry as unbelievable as that would sound to a human being, but at least my appetite seemed under control. In the hour or so since we had finished eating, my body's miraculous ability to heal itself seemed to accelerate further. While I still had visible remnants of the wounds on my neck and abdomen, they had impossibly diminished from what they had been upon my waking earlier in the day. In addition, I felt little or no pain when standing or walking, an impressive improvement from just a couple of hours earlier when I was walking outside. Based on how rapidly I had healed thus far, I had no reason to think that by the following morning, I would have even a scar to remind me of the mutilation my body had suffered.

I wanted to speak with Myra, but I had no idea where to start, and although there were many things happening to me that I could wrap my mind around, I was in no mood to listen to her insane bullshit story about werewolves. But then again, it would seem that I may have little other choice. I watched her for a moment as she seemed completely absorbed in her reading. She sat in the chair at a funny angle, allowing her right leg to dangle over the arm of the chair while her left foot gently rocked her back and forth as it pushed off the ottoman.

I opened my mouth several times, attempting to initiate questions that I truly did not wish to ask but could not bring my thoughts to spoken words. I decided I would take the quiet time and explore this, the largest room of the cabin. Behind the chair I had been seated in, a large bay window with dark gray curtains pulled back to reveal the gravel road that I had walked up earlier in the day, now fading fast as darkness overtook what the sunlight abandoned. A very faint reminder of the setting sun remained on the horizon. It seemed that the only illumination provided in the cabin was by candlelight. On the window's ledge, one lit candle rested in a brass candleholder, which made the window reflect my image within it. In addition, several wood-carved figurines also rested on the ledge—a whale, a bear, and a deer, each amazingly intricate and detailed.

To the right of the window, the pile of pillows and down comforters I would presumably call my bed while I stayed here. To the window's left, a small table with a chess set upon it. It appeared that a game had already been started and abandoned before it had concluded as characters were set up at strategic points of the board on both sides. Further down the wall, a giant bookcase, stocked with many titles that I didn't recognize—nothing newer than thirty or so years old as best I could tell. Beyond the bookcase, steps leading upstairs to what I assumed to be a bedroom. Against the opposite wall of the bookcase, two small tables, each with a candle and with pictures. Between them, a large grandfather clock that indicated 7:55 or so. To the right of the clock, behind Myra's chair, the kitchen we had eaten in. I approached the pictures to look at them though I could see them well enough where I stood. Although her eyes never left the pages she was studying, I somehow knew that she was aware of my every move no matter how small.

Both pictures were black and white and looked as though they had been taken in the '20s or '30s, though I really had no way of knowing this other than that they were very vintage looking. Amazingly, the first picture was of an older-looking distinguished gentleman, maybe in his mid to late sixties, with a short white beard standing next to a person who appeared to be Myra. I picked up the frame, an ornate silver frame, to examine the photo closer. The man was dressed as a prospector may have been while the woman wore a long dress. Both smiled. The other picture appeared to have been taken during or about the same time as the first. In it, a native Alaskan Eskimo woman—also appearing to be in her late sixties. She was not smiling. "These are interesting photographs," I said.

Myra's eyes peered over the top of the book. So dimly was the room lit that I was surprised that she had continued reading. Her face was so beautiful in the candlelight as she stared in the direction of the photographs I had been examining. "They were my parents," she said.

"When were they taken?"

"It seems that it was around 1911 or so. My mother died in 1914, and that picture was taken a few years before that."

"That's not possible!" I said. "Is that you in the picture?"

"I'm afraid it is."

I was ready to object again when suddenly I was startled by the sound of the alarm clock. As the clock finished its chimes, Myra abruptly closed her book with a firm thump and sat upright in her chair, looking at me intently. "Sit down," she said in an almost frighteningly authoritative tone. I did as she asked, knowing that our "talk" was to begin now.

SIX

I'M AFRAID WE haven't much time," she said to me.

"Look," I responded as calmly as I could, "you don't honestly think I believe in werewolves, do you?

"The truth is not determined by whether you believe in something or not. And while I am well aware of the extent of your skepticism despite certain evidence to the contrary, the truth of the matter is that you are a part of something wicked and dangerous now."

It occurred to me in that instant that I had been attacked two nights earlier—before the moon was even full. "Is tonight even the full moon?"

"The full moon was last night," she responded.

"So apparently, the lunar cycle has nothing to do with werewolves?" I asked with an obvious tone of disbelief.

"The lunar cycle has everything to do with the becoming. Always when the moon is full—and on lucky months—you will change over on that day only. However, you are also susceptible to the becoming on the day immediately before and after the full moon as is the case for me this month."

"All right," I said, "when is this supposed to happen?"

"As I said earlier today, it varies from cycle to cycle and from day to day. The earliest I ever change over is at nine, and rarely, though not often, it can be as late as midnight."

"So what happens if you don't 'change' tonight?"

"I will."

"How do you know?"

"Because it has already begun," she answered. "You can feel it, often hours beforehand, when a very warm, almost burning sensation begins in your spine. Soon, the changeover will begin for me."

"And what happens when you change over?"

"That is what I want you to witness for yourself this evening."

"All right, let's see here," I began. "You have become a werewolf for the last two evenings, the first of which you attacked me, and you are going to become a werewolf again this evening."

"That is correct."

"And what about tomorrow night?"

"The cycle will conclude tonight."

"And you say that I am cursed now as well?"

"I have made no reference to a curse, but you are afflicted."

"Then why didn't I become a werewolf last night? Maybe I'll become one tonight?" My voice continued to carry with an obvious disbelief.

"You will not change over until the next cycle. However, you are already clearly exhibiting lycanthropic characteristics."

"What characteristics?" I asked.

"Come now! I think you know damn well what characteristics I'm referring to. In fact, if it weren't for the lycanthropic blood that now rushes through your veins, you would have died shortly after I came upon you early yesterday morning. Instead, you are all nice and healed now." The response she offered seemed to indicate an increasing irritability. I thought it unwise to push her further especially since I could not explain so many things that were happening to me.

For some time there was silence between us. During that time, I studied Myra—still calmly sitting there in her chair. She in turn merely stared out the window into the darkness. In the brief time that followed, something quite peculiar began to happen to me. At first, I dismissed it as part of my imagination, possibly a part of my subconscious that was open to the power of suggestion. It was a burning sensation that crept from my neck through my lower back, radiation from my spine. I tried to push it out of my mind, tried to focus on something else, anything else. It wasn't necessarily painful, though it was far from pleasant either. No, it wasn't an issue of pain or burning or discomfort of any kind, but instead I felt anxiety, anxiety and fear of what was happening to me. *What if she's right?* I began to think to myself. *What if this is all true?*

I did not want to say anything; I did not want to feed into what was certainly a delusion. But I could not escape the what ifs my mind created for me. "Myra, something is happening to me!" I said. My voice had now lost the sarcasm I had used in our earlier dialog, and in its place—fear and worry.

Myra looked at me, her lack of emotion made her even more frightening at that instant. "You need not worry. Nothing is going to happen with you this evening," she said. It was nice to hear her say this, but it offered little comfort as my spinal column continued to tingle. It was as though my body was telling me that something was changing within me. "I should offer you some words of caution," she said. "When I changed over last evening, I wasn't here. I was several miles north. Apparently the beast made no attempt to come for and kill you although it would have been well aware of your presence here. I have to assume that it intentionally allowed you to live last night and may also have purposefully let you live on the night you were attacked."

"What do you mean?"

Myra contemplated her thoughts silently then spoke, "There is and always has been the notion among those of our kind that the demon within us kills everything without thought or mercy. It simply kills. As we know, the bloodline is continued when the victim is bitten but not killed. There is some uncertainty within me that the monster accidentally leaves an occasional victim alive when it would seem well aware of anything alive or dead in its presence. I have proposed that the monster intentionally and purposefully selects those who will be the next generation of lycanthrope. My thoughts on this subject have been met with rejection by those older than myself. Still, logic and evidence at hand suggest a validity to my hypothesis."

"I don't understand what you are getting at."

For an instant, a look of frustration swallowed her otherwise emotionless face, then it disappeared just as quickly. "I'm simply stating that I believe in the possibility that the monster allowed you to live when it attacked you. In addition, although you were certainly infected, it made no attempt to end your life last night either. I am assuming, though not entirely convinced, that you will be safe tonight as well."

"That isn't reassuring," I said. At that point, I didn't know what to think. My rational mind couldn't conceive of such a preposterous idea. And yet, I wasn't about to dismiss what I was not feeling.

I then watched as Myra stood, unbuttoned, and removed the pants she was wearing. She gathered them from the floor and folded them neatly. She then unbuttoned her flannel shirt and let it slide off her shoulders before folding it also. She wore no bra or panties and was completely nude; she then returned to her chair. I was more than a little stunned and absolutely uncertain of what to say or how to go about it. "Why did you undress?"

"When it happens, the clothing you are wearing is generally destroyed. Knowing this, if you care at all for your clothing, you will remove them."

I saw her naked in the woods on the morning of the previous day but was in so much pain and in and out of consciousness that my glimpses were brief and even somewhat hazy. But now, I could observe her form as I couldn't before. I made no attempt to pretend that I wasn't studying her body—her beautiful and perfect breasts, the way the candlelight accented her toned and athletic thighs, legs, and upper extremities. Although she seemed well aware of the observations I was making, she did not seem to care. "You aren't very modest, are you?"

"Modesty is yet another trait that I have lost over time."

"You are absolutely beautiful," I said. "You could have been a model."

"Yes," she said quietly, "I could have been so many things."

We both remained quiet and waited for whatever was going to happen. I thought about talking to her as I wanted to ask more questions. But after several moments of silence, I felt that the time for questions had since come and gone. The clock soon struck nine—time was moving more rapidly than I wanted it to, and the tension I felt seemed to deepen with every passing minute.

"There is one more thing I need to tell you, Caleb, before it is too late."

"What is it?"

"When it happens, go into the corner. Stay out of its way and avoid direct eye contact with it."

"All right," I said.

"Remember, the thing you are going to see isn't me. I have no control of anything that it chooses to do or anything that happens, and as such, I cannot keep you safe."

"I understand." What would happen next? Was this all some sort of insanity on the part of Myra that had somehow infected me? Or was I to witness something impossible, something my mind would have objected to only hours earlier? What I was about to encounter I could not have possibly prepared for.

Myra did not speak any more to me, and I did not initiate anything myself. Instead, we both remained silent, listening to the clock—*tick... tick... tick*—as it seemed to thunder with every passing second. We listened as only preternatural things could. By this point, I knew Myra had been telling me the truth. Her nude body was far from relaxed as she had been earlier. Every muscle seemed tense, every part of her body contracted. Even the tiny hairs across her body stood at attention.

After a short time, Myra took a deep breath and clenched her hands tightly into fists. A look of excruciating pain came over her otherwise beautiful face. Her eyes tightly closed, and her jaw clenched tightly. One moment she was seated in the chair, the next she threw herself onto the floor. Without thinking, I quickly rushed to her assistance. "Myra!" I shouted, touching her shoulder, which felt as though she was running an extremely high fever. As I knelt beside her on the floor, she turned her head to face me, and what I saw was horrifying.

Somehow, the bones in her face were contorting, changing into something grotesque and large. Her cheekbones sunk in and appeared to pull toward her ears, tearing the skin that covered them. Her forehead and nasal bones were also contorting. Her nose began bleeding heavily. Suddenly and violently, her jaw broke on both sides of her face, releasing a bloody stream that mixed with her saliva and fell from her quickly dissolving lips.

I immediately pulled my hand away and returned in horror to the corner that Myra had instructed me to go to. From there, I continued to observe in disbelief at this bizarre and frightening metamorphosis. I could see the bones of her vertebrae as they appeared to pull out of her back then snap apart, elongate, then re-fuse again. She suddenly fell from her hands and knees to her side in a fetal position before twisting onto her back. She screamed out in pain as though being tortured. I wanted to help but had no idea how to.

I watched as her breasts, which were size Cs, seemingly deflate. I suddenly realized that the small dark patch of pubic hair now extended from her navel to her knees, creeping toward her rib cage to meet with hair that had started growing from her back and shoulders. Within no more than one minute, her body was nearly covered by thick dense hair. As I reexamined her face, there was no longer any sign of Myra—only this... thing.

I could hear the bones in her feet and ankles crunching, twisting, and breaking as they became something else. Her rib cage, no longer visible due to the growth of her hair, began to expand, snapping and reforming as it did. Her hands, which had been balled into fists, were now open, the bones of the fingers breaking and contorting, while the skin seemed to sprout rapidly growing hair as well. Her delicate fingernails suddenly popped off while a much more menacing and deadly clawlike nail grew from the beds of where her nails had been.

The painful screams coming from her were sounding less and less human until it lacked any of the qualities of a voice, becoming nothing more than a howling grunt. During the time of this transformation, all of which lasted only a couple of moments, her body mass had increased its size to three or four times what it was originally. The creature was absolutely massive, weighing every bit of five hundred pounds, possibly more.

Apparently, the last part of the changeover occurred with the head and face of the victim. At this point, its features became unmistakably canine although its body was much, much larger—a monster that would be easily mistaken for a bear.

For a moment after the changeover, the beast lay still then slowly rose to an upright position. It appeared that it could rise up on to its two hind legs or could just as easily move about on all four. Quickly, it turned its attention to me, and as it amazing teeth were revealed, my blood ran cold. I had retreated into the corner as far as my body and the room would allow, and I was terrified out of my mind. Clearly, the monster was angry and slowly approached with what appeared an intent to kill. The paws of the creature were horrific; the damage they could potentially inflict, lethal. They seemed designed for one purpose exclusively—to slash through and annihilate anything unfortunate enough to find itself in this monster's path.

The creature approached to within less than twelve inches from me; I dared not even breathe. Was there any part of Myra within this monster? With my heart beating almost out of my rib cage, I studied the monster at this most uncomfortable and dangerous distance. Its coat was quite thick and appeared rough and course. The color was gray and black, not brown as Hollywood movies would always depict. (Later, I would learn that the colors and patterns varied remarkably from one lycanthrope to the next.)

The seconds that elapsed during the time that the creature was practically on top of me were the longest seconds of my life. Was this "wolf" studying me as well? I realized that I could smell on its breath the poultry and beef that Myra and I had eaten earlier. I could smell the oil glands of its coat—producing a strange and distinctive scent that would have been impossible for a human to recognize.

Despite the sound advice Myra had offered, I turned my head and looked into the face of the wolf-monster, into the very eyes I had been told to avoid. For some reason, I expected to see something "human" in its eyes, some part of Myra in there somewhere. Instead, there was absolutely nothing recognizable in those eyes, no trace of Myra, only an overwhelming evil that chilled the blood in my veins. There was no doubt the devil himself stared back at me from the monster's gaze.

Unfortunately, by looking into its eyes, I may have unintentionally "challenged" the monster. I could hear it offer a blood-curdling growl only a split second before it swung its destructive claws at my face, slicing deeply into my jaw and cheek and tearing my left eye from its socket in the process. I felt the awesome power of the blow, but due to the volume of adrenaline in my bloodstream, I can't say that I felt any pain to speak of. I did not scream out, make any sudden moves, or even breathe. I stared, through my right eye only, at the floor and waited for what would happen next. For a long while, the monster simply stood there, waiting for me to do something stupid, like look at it. When finally it decided that I had assumed a submissive role, it began to turn and walk away. I could hear the sharp and distinctive *click click* sound of its claws on the hardwood floor.

When finally I looked up, I saw it exit through the doorway that Myra had left open. For some time, I remained as still as a statue, trying not to shake in fear, concerned that if I did begin to move about, the beast may come back again. After some time passed—I cannot say how much time—when the pain in my face became less masked by the adrenaline flowing through my veins, I began to inspect the damage done at first with my fingers then finally through a mirror that hung in the hall.

My inspections proved what I had feared—the gashes in my face were quite deep and would require extensive surgery, or at least they would have in my life before this experience. What was most frightening was the way my eye, removed from its socket, now hung just above my cheek, suspended by the optic nerve and bleeding heavily. *Would this heal too?* I wondered. Of course it would—I somehow knew this much. Any wound, regardless of its severity, would heal; my body would regenerate.

I returned to my bed on the floor and remained there as the hours proceeded into the dawn, fully expecting the monster to return at any time. Myra was right all along, and I was an idiot. I was even less certain of how I should feel than I was earlier in the day. A part of me felt as though I owed Myra an apology for my behavior, and yet another part of me wanted to hate her for everything she had done, everything she was.

It was a long night, and I'm not even sure that I remember blinking as I sat there listening to every sound that floated through the night air. Eventually, the sky began to brighten, the stars became less visible, and the songbirds began to sing. Yet I remained awake, wondering what I would do if the werewolf returned, wondering what I would say if Myra returned.

I remember the clock striking nine when I heard footsteps in the distance, slowly approaching—Myra. I felt fear initially, wondering how she would respond to seeing me after what had happened, but my concerns were relieved when she walked to the door and stood in its threshold. She even smiled as she looked at me, a gesture that meant nothing to her but was offered to comfort me. Of course, it didn't last long, and as it melted from her face, her expressionless features returned. Interestingly, I was much more calm in her emotionless presence than I would have been were she a typical emotional woman. Myra was a strong, reliable, dependable, no-nonsense person, the type you would want at your side in an emergency. She exhibited the traits that I both admired in others and found lacking in myself.

She studied my fucked-up eye for a moment. I expected her to say something though I honestly don't know what. Instead, she offered her silence only. Her body was, of course, nude, beautiful as ever, but she returned looking as though she had slept in the mud the previous night; she even had mud caked in her hair. After a moment of exchanged glances, she casually strolled in, lay on the pallet next to me, and closed her eyes. I watched her for several moments, and it appeared that she was fast asleep. Slowly, I laid my head back onto another pillow and turned my back to Myra. My eyes were heavy and I found myself quickly drifting off. The last thing I remembered was Myra's arm wrapping around me, pulling me close to her while she slept. I was uncertain what to think of this but enjoyed being close to someone after so long. We then slept.

SEVEN

THE FOLLOWING DAY marked the beginning of an entirely new life for me. "There are things that you are going to need to understand about yourself, some of which you will discover in time but much you must know immediately," Myra began. "As I told you, and as you have witnessed for yourself, the full moon is not the only day of the month that the becoming may occur. However, while the day before and after may or may not result in the changeover, the day of the full moon itself will always be one in which the wolf presents itself. So you see, it is possible that the becoming will occur only once during the lunar cycle. It is also possible that it may occur up to three times as was the case for me this month. There is no way of knowing from one month to the next how the becoming will play out during that lunar cycle."

"Is there anything that can be done that will decrease the chances of the becoming occurring on non-full moon days? Are there things that make the becoming more likely to happen on those days?"

"No," she said coldly. "It isn't like having a migraine where you simply avoid alcohol or chocolate or whatever triggers the headache. Nothing can be avoided in this case." Myra reclined back into her chair and brought her right leg over the arm of the recliner, briefly exposing her pubic area before concealing it with her left leg, which she tucked beneath her as she sat in what looked like a very comfortable position for her. I could not tell if she realized where my attention had been drawn, nor could I say if she even cared. "As far as our powers to heal and regenerate, it is the only reason that we could even survive the becoming. As you have learned, eating will accelerate that process, but so long as you are in the form of a man, the speed by which your tissues regenerate is still limited. If I stab you, you will heal, but you may need thirty minutes, an hour, or maybe even two hours to do so. And while it would be easily sufficient to kill anyone else, you will be left without even a scar to prove that it ever happened. As the wolf, however, your ability to recover from such a stabbing would be virtually instantaneous. As such, while you are very hard to kill as a man, you are damn near impossible to kill as the monster."

"So how do you kill one, the monster, that is?"

"Well, if you are expecting a silver bullet to do the trick, then you should know that there is nothing magic about that metal—it is just metal, no different than lead or iron or aluminum, nothing special, just a very expensive projectile. Fire works as does dismembering and decapitation. I suppose we can drown easily enough as well. If you did want to use a firearm, be sure to target its brain, and make sure you use a cannon for a gun. You will probably only get a single opportunity, make it count."

"So how do we typically die?"

"You won't live forever if that is what you are asking, but because of our cellular regeneration, we can expect to live a great many years while retaining a youthful appearance. Eventually though, even we succumb to age, albeit differently than you might expect from a human being. An individual who acquires lycanthropy at an early age, as have we both, could likely expect to live well beyond our sixteenth decade."

"More than 160 years old?" I asked with doubt in my tone.

"It's not really as old as it sounds," she answered. "Most lycanthropes, however, seldom reach such an age. It seems that after a century of so, many of our kind give up on the idea of a continued existence."

"So what do they do?"

"They kill themselves of course."

I was quiet for a moment, wondering if my next question was appropriate, and as Myra watched me, she must have known that I was debating on the propriety of what I wanted to know. With hesitation, I asked, "Have you considered doing anything like that?"

"Absolutely not," she responded. "I am at peace here and have little desire for much more. I can only hope that you find an equally contented life."

"So what more can I expect?"

"Literature always seems to romanticize the traits of the lycanthrope, and while you will experience all this and more, the price you will pay for these traits will far exceed anything positive offered by our condition. Be assured," she said sharply, "there is nothing romantic about what you can expect.

"With that said, I can tell you what you already know. Your senses, all of them, are so far beyond human comprehension that to offer a description would be futile—like discussing the laws of thermodynamics with a toddler still unable to speak. This is true of your physical abilities as well, and while I intend to introduce you to what you are capable of, it will be up to you to realize what your true potential is.

"You will never get sick, you will never know disease, and you will never suffer those conditions often associated with old age—arthritis, loss of hearing or eyesight. You cannot get cancer, you cannot be poisoned, and even radiation in its deadliest amount cannot touch you.

"As remarkable as your strength, speed, and reaction time have just become, they will grow stronger in you as time passes. Your new body will never again experience what you previously knew as cold. In even the most extreme Alaskan temperatures, I have never known discomfort with temperature, even when it drops well below minus thirty degrees. On the mornings preceded by the becoming, I will awaken buried in snow and ice, perfectly content with how I feel.

"As you have also become well aware and are no doubt experiencing even now, hunger will be a constant companion. You will never be able to consume enough food to satisfy that hunger, but you will try just the same. I certainly have. I usually take in somewhere around twenty to thirty thousand calories each day though I can get by on half that much.

While my intake may sound extreme, I could easily triple that amount and still fail to scratch even the surface of my appetite.

"While we are on the subject, allow me to offer you a suggestion—on the morning after the becoming, consume massive amounts of calories. It doesn't really matter where they come from—eat a tub of Crisco if you want. It's not like you are going to suffer a heart attack or anything. Do whatever it takes to get it into your system. You will find it a little easier to recover if you do."

"So basically, I'm fucked!" I stated.

"Yes, you're fucked," she answered. "Try to understand, this is as much a blessing as a curse. Humanity is a cage, and now you can experience a freedom that you could have never imagined. Yes, of course you enjoy your heightened senses—they allow you to observe, participate, and manipulate your environment in a way that no human being could. And our ability to rapidly regenerate tissues means that you will heal from even the most gruesome injuries. As I said, it is the only reason that we are able to survive the becoming. Your strength, your reflexes, even your mental faculties—inhuman. You will have absolutely no equal among men.

"On the flip side, like it or not, you are no longer human. In your interactions with people, you will find that they are none the wiser. But I have come to believe that on a subconscious level, they know that we are different. They will fear you, they will reject you, and if given the chance, they will turn on you and destroy you.

"Ours is a lonesome and burdened existence. I don't know if I believe in God, but if he does exist, he has forsaken us."

Quite suddenly, I was taken aback in my mind to the conversation I had with my sister when she came to inform me of my father's passing. I remember thinking that if God truly existed, then he had forsaken me. It was interesting to hear Myra repeat this very sentiment. I smiled. "You sound as though you have a lot of animosity toward everyone."

She did not return my smile. "Anger is all I have left. Try to enjoy your emotions as long as you can."

"I don't understand," I said.

"It is difficult to explain," she began. "You still possess your humanity—it is this concept that makes you human, more or less. In essence, you feel things."

I continued to smile while nodding my head. "I don't really get what you're saying."

Myra sighed. "No, of course not. If you see something that you find amusing, thoughtful, or even disturbing, it affects you. If I were to find an injured kitten, defenseless and weak, and I were to crush it in my hands, you would likely be appalled at the scene. Why is that? It is just your programming, a part of your humanity. And while it is possible for an individual to deprogram certain aspects of their psyche, as happens with war veterans, they still feel things—happiness, fear, sorrow, love. Even serial killers are capable of feeling emotions. They still have their humanity. Unfortunately, we lose ours."

"So I am going to lose my humanity?" I asked, still confused about the meaning of her lesson.

"When you talk to me, you offer less than subtle gestures. You smile or frown. You move your eyebrows to show a certain interest or pleasure in your communications. I used to do this too, you know. I can still smile, but it means nothing to me. I am no longer capable of happiness, nor am I capable of any other human emotion, save for anger. I'm not sure why, but it is the only emotion that I have left."

"So what does this mean for you? For us, I mean?"

"I used to enjoy music, but it is only noise for me now. I cannot experience fear. I will never know joy or sorrow ever again. Even the sentimental notions that I used to hold dear, are meaningless now. When I think of the friends that I once had, those friends who are dead now, I try to elicit feelings that no longer exist."

"I still feel things," I said.

"Yes, and you will for a while yet. You will find that as the years go by, you lose more and more of your humanity until the day comes when you can pick up that kitten in your own hands, crush it, and feel nothing, when you think of those closest to you that you have lost, and yet there is no feeling in that loss. We all essentially become machines, machines that are capable of anger. And that anger, it seems to grow and consume everything if it isn't controlled. You will, in the years to come, experience rage as no human could."

Some time later, Myra escorted me on a tour of her freezer, which she kept behind the cabin. "It runs off a generator during this time of the year. Through the cold months, however, a method of maintaining below-freezing temperatures is obviously not needed." The freezer was a somewhat large building, maybe fifteen feet wide by forty feet long, situated behind the cabin, the only thing on the premises that ran on electricity. Inside the freezer, there was seemingly enough food to last for a year or more—at least there would have been were Myra a human being. As it was, she could live off its contents for maybe four to six weeks. With me as an equal consumer, it would last only half as long. "I go into town every so often to pick up supplies and to restock the freezer. Also, about once a year in the spring, I have enough diesel delivered to run it for the season."

"It's impressive," I said.

"Are you ready for your first lesson?"

"My first lesson?"

"Yes. It's time for you to learn what abilities you have at your disposal."

"All right, so what do we do?"

"Catch me if you can," she said as she quickly darted into the woods, and within moments she was out of sight, all the while in bare feet.

I pursued as quickly as I could and immediately discovered that I could run faster than I could have ever dreamt possible. I navigated with the grace and ease of a gazelle—around trees, across ravines, over and under fallen branches. After just a few minutes, I had put an impressive distance between myself and Myra's cabin. Unfortunately, I had completely lost track of Myra. I turned 360 degrees to the left then to the right. My senses were seemingly overwhelmed, but at the last minute, Myra sprang out of nowhere and knocked me to the ground.

As she stood over me, she shook her head. "Okay, here's lesson one, and it is an important one—you aren't human anymore, so stop acting like one. You can easily track anyone wherever they might go simply by following their scent trail, especially when it's not raining. Your vision and hearing will allow you to detect the world around you in a way that few other creatures possibly could. This wasn't about running in a direction and hoping to get lucky. This was about utilizing the tools you have. Now again, find me and catch me."

Suddenly, like before, she was off. This time, I immediately bolted after her and kept her in my sight for a while longer. Finally though, she did disappear into the thick undergrowth. Just as she had advised, I stopped and focused on the world around me, and within a few seconds, I could smell her in the air from upwind. As I moved in that direction, I could even smell each step she had taken. As I moved, I listened with my newfound hearing. Sure enough, I could hear her running in the distance.

I tracked her for maybe three miles—funny how much smaller the world seems when you are a lycanthrope—until I came to a point where her scent trail stopped, or at least that is what I initially thought. After a second of study, I could tell that she had climbed a tree. It was amazing; there was no move she could possibly make that I couldn't follow. I ascended the tree with as much ease as a squirrel, more or less. I started to believe that this was a fun game until she again came out of nowhere, this time striking me and knocking me out of the tree at sixty feet up. This was only the beginning of my training.

EIGHT

The following weeks passed quickly, and in that time I had developed every part of my physical abilities. Myra was a brutal sparring partner and expected the same from me. With human beings, men have an absolute physical advantage over women on any day of the week, but with lycanthropes this isn't necessarily the case. Myra easily possessed the strength of three men, and she struck like a fucking Mack truck.

I was never a fighter; I was the kid who either ran away or got the shit beat out of him. No, I was a person of intelligence, not brawn. And here I was, having never thrown a punch at anyone, being expected to defend myself against, of all people, a woman. My hesitancy to strike a woman did nothing to make Myra go easy on me; instead, I believe that it only served to fuel her anger.

During the course of the next month, I lost count of how many times she broke my arms, legs, my jaw, knocked teeth out, even ruptured a testicle—yes, she did. It's interesting, really, how unafraid one becomes of the idea of injury, even serious injury, when within a few hours everything is healed as if nothing had ever happened.

As I stated, Myra was angry, and what she seemed to loath more than anything else was weakness. She believed that if one was to survive, especially as a lycanthrope, that that individual had to be faster, that person had to be stronger, that person had to be tougher, more so than anyone or anything they might encounter.

As far as I know, after all the years since I was there with her, Myra was the only one of our kind who lived with this mentality. Make no doubt, she was a vicious animal, and she fully expected me to be the same. Looking back, I have her to thank for the very fact that I am alive now. I took her lessons, I listened to what she offered, and I strived to become what she wanted, and I seemed to fail constantly, at least during my time with her.

Now bear in mind, as a lycanthrope, I was already physically superior to any human being under any set of circumstances. In Myra's mind, however, to be anything less than the best of the best was absolutely unacceptable. She strived not only for powerful and deadly excellence, but perfection as well. She pushed me to my limits until I broke. It was finally in one of those breaking moments during a sparring session that I swung with all my strength and swiftness and barely struck her. Even though she had moved with unbelievable quickness to avoid my strike, I still made contact and, in the process, fractured every bone in her face. Immediately, I felt an overwhelming sense of guilt; it didn't matter really that she had, by then, injured me countless times. For the first time, I had injured her. I quickly lowered myself and looked at her bloody and disfigured face.

"I am so sorry!" I said in a panicked tone. She looked as though she had been pulled from a gruesome auto accident. I didn't know what to do except cradle her face with my hands and try to wipe the blood from her eyes. In that moment I had altogether forgotten what she was. It was almost instinct for me to try to help, for me to offer comfort. Of course, she and I were creatures that required neither medical attention nor comfort when injured.

Suddenly, her lifeless body reawakened in an explosive manner. Like a wolverine, she sprang upon me and struck me repeatedly; I could feel my ribs cracking violently with each blow. She rose to her feet and began kicking me with the same ferocity as she had used with her fists. I begged for her to stop as blood began to spill from my mouth—she did not stop, at least not until I lost consciousness.

I awoke a short while later, fully aware of everything around me and of what had happened, aware but confused. The taste of blood was in my mouth, and as I spit it out, a tooth followed, another tooth. With my tongue, I could feel the gap where a new tooth was quickly growing to replace the one I had lost. My side was sore and bruised, but the broken ribs had already mended, and within an hour, I would be as good as new. I was aware of Myra's presence, but I did not initially look at her until she finally spoke.

"How do you feel?" came her cold question.

This may sound funny, and as I think about it now even, I find a bit of amusement in it, but I was terribly afraid of her, afraid and angry. I didn't answer her question.

"So you aren't talking to me now?"

I turned to look at her, momentarily surprised by the still-apparent injuries I had inflicted to her face—like my wounds, hers too had healed at a miraculous rate. Still, her ordinarily perfect and beautiful features were replaced with two black eyes and a less-than-perfect broken nose. I paused for a moment as I studied her then spoke. "What the fuck was that all about?" I demanded of her!

She shook her head slowly, seemingly disappointed in me. "It's amazing really," she said, "how you continue to cling to your human rules of behavior." Her expression seemed even more frighteningly stern with her gaze accented with blackened and swollen eyes. "What injury have you given to me that I will not heal from? If I break your neck, you will heal. If I sever your arm, it too will eventually heal. There is nothing short of killing you that will prevent you from recovering from whatever happens to you. So what is the problem? Are you afraid of a little pain?" Her tone was calm but with a hint of hostility.

"Why do you have to be such a hateful bitch about this?" Those words I wanted to ask my ex-wife for so long and on countless occasions, and yet I never did. Instead, I asked this woman who had made me into a monster—almost as though I had been waiting my whole life to make such a statement.

"Why do you have to be such a pussy?" she returned bitterly. "Have you forgotten that the whole point of me working with you was to prepare you for what you have become?"

"And to do that, you beat up on me like some kind of schoolyard bully!"

"In case you haven't yet figured this out, you and I aren't human anymore! The next time you have the upper hand in a fight and you back down with me, I promise I will tear you apart in a more painful way than you could ever imagine. As it was, you deserved exactly what happened to you and more. If I had been a real opponent, do you honestly think we would be having a heated debate while you sit there and heal from your wounds? No, because you would be dead right now, so don't tell me about how unfair I am with you when you not only get to live another day but are also healed and healthy within two hours." She rose from the spot where she had been sitting at the base of a tree and approached me. "And I was actually impressed with you for several seconds there. You did very well for just a moment when you struck me!"

"I don't like fighting, especially with you!"

"Why?" she demanded.

"Because you are a woman, for starters!"

"Yes, I am a woman. So what does it tell you that you get your ass handed to you on a regular basis by a woman?"

"It tells me that I don't want to hit a woman!"

"You have already hit one several times. This last time, you hit me hard, which was something I wanted to see you do. No, your problem is that you are severely ill-equipped to handle what it is that you and I are. If you are unable to fight me, knowing that you will not hurt me, then how exactly do you expect to survive once you come across someone whose intention is to kill you especially if that person just happens to be female? I suppose in that case, you should just lie down and let her kill you. Is that what you think?" She did not give me time to respond to her statements. "It's true, you will have an awesome advantage over any human being that ever crosses your path, a virtual guarantee that you will emerge as a victor in any encounter under nearly any set of circumstances. But I promise you that you will encounter things out there that aren't human. Other lycanthropes may not show you the mercy that you so graciously offer. And there are other enemies that exist for us also. It's not good enough that you are stronger than you were. It's not good enough that you are incredibly and impossibly strong now. None of this is good enough."

"So what do you want me to do?"

"You are alive right now because, first, the beast didn't kill you and, second, because I didn't kill you. Don't let that miracle and my reprieve be in vain by getting yourself torn to shreds within six months of leaving here."

Myra and I continued with our sparring session until long after the sun had set. I would love to say that she went a little easier on me, but that wasn't the case. She continued kicking my ass over and over again. I did begin to show a little more aggressiveness, however, and I believe that she was pleased with at least that much.

"How many lycanthropes exist?" I asked as we made our way back to her cabin. The blackness of night had long overtaken the wooded area that we walked through, and yet my eyesight could easily make out every detail of her expression as if it were midday.

She looked at me for a moment, pondering, I'm sure, on whether to or how to answer my question. "There aren't many, but I should offer you a word of caution. When you encounter them, and you *will* encounter them, take care. Some are like me, preferring isolation rather than risk the lives of others. Although we may not have the friendliest nature, we do the best we can with the hand we are dealt. And then there are the packs."

"Tell me about them."

"It is unfortunate that they exist, but I suppose if the wolf has a nature, it is at least in part, an animal that runs in packs. These are groups that work to either recruit new members or savagely tear apart anyone who would oppose them. When I think of them, I am reminded of a simple street gang, a gang with godlike strength and abilities. They relish in their savagery and should be avoided at all costs."

"I guess so," I said. "So what do I do if I come across a pack?"

"They will probably kill you."

"I was hoping for a word of advice," I said with a smile.

Myra did not return my smile, though if she had, it would have been insincere. "They travel, often great distances. If they learn about you, they will hunt you, they *will* find you, and they will absolutely kill you. My advice is to avoid them," she repeated.

Later that night, all was quiet and all was peaceful. I remember it strange to think that earlier in the day we were seemingly killing each other. Well, actually she was seemingly killing me. And now, here in the cabin, we enjoyed the quiet that each of us offered the other. Still, I had questions. A part of me hated to ask such things as I felt that they annoyed her, but I was ignorant, and she was the only means by which to pull information.

"So where do we come from?" I asked.

As was often the case when she had downtime, Myra busied her mind in whatever books she had picked up while in town. It always seemed peculiar to me—and it still does—how she seemed so content in her isolation so long as she had her reading materials. Myra glanced at me for a moment then quickly returned her attention to her reading. "I don't know," she answered. "I doubt that anyone knows the answer to that question."

"Well, what can you tell me about our history?"

After a deep sigh, Myra folded her book and offered me her somewhat sleepy gaze. "I wish I had something more to offer, but all I have are stories, myths, superstitions, but nothing credible, nothing worth telling." She paused for several moments, and as the room grew silent, Myra shifted from her relaxed position in her chair, bringing both of her feet onto the floor and facing me directly. "I can tell you a story if you like."

"Yes," I answered eagerly. "Please do."

"There is an old Eskimo tale about a young man who was hunting. During this outing, he was attacked by a wolf that fatally injured him. The story says that the man used a knife given to him by his great-grandfather and killed the wolf by plunging the blade into the animal's heart. Some versions of this story suggest that the knife was a gift from the gods. A moot point, really.

"It was in that instant, the instant that the wolf died, that its spirit, upon leaving its body, entered into the young hunter, and they became one. Because of this, the man did not die from the wounds that he had sustained, but healed.

"He lived for many, many years with the spirit of the wolf silent within him, yet he still benefited from the wolf's presence. He became a great hunter, better than any of the other men in his village. He was unnaturally strong and resistant to the harsh winter cold. Sickness and disease could not touch him, and old age was starved off in him for longer than was possible.

"Then men came from a great distance away, a far place that the hunter had never heard of—some say that they were Russians. These men were savage and unnecessarily cruel, attacking many villages, including the village of the hunter. Their armies killed the male members of his family and friends and would have killed the hunter too if the spirit of the wolf had not been with him.

"Crawling from the icy waters that he and the bodies of his kinsmen were thrown, he watched as his village was burned to the ground and the women raped. Even with his great strength and enhanced attributes, the hunter was powerless to protect what he held most dear. It was then that the spirit that had dwelled peacefully within him was quickened and brought to life with a fury.

"As vengeance flowed through his veins, the wolf awakened and tore through what was the quiet hunter's character. He was no longer a man with the spirit of a wolf, but became a wolf with the spirit of an avenging angel." Myra paused for a moment then added, "And that's the story."

"That's it?"

"That is all I know. It is vague as are most of the old stories, but it seems to describe lycanthropy and offers a mythical tale to explain its origins."

"Do you believe it?"

"Absolutely not. It's horseshit—surely you know that much. It's just a story, likely concocted by one of our kind then offered to others. If humanity cannot definitely determine its origins—evolution, creation by God, aliens—then why would you believe that something as obscure as lycanthropy would have an easy and simple to understand beginning. Maybe we have existed as long as people—maybe longer. Like I said, I doubt that anyone would know."

There was a part of me that was saddened to hear this story though I am not sure as to why; I suppose it was like a tragic movie that suddenly ended without a proper conclusion. Myra returned her focus yet again to her book, and I remained silent, listening to all the sounds of the world around me, sounds that no human could ever possibly hear. For quite some time I continued in this fashion, losing myself in this extreme sensory awareness with a lingering melancholy that would never in the years to come leave my side. I was so drawn into my own thoughts that I did not at first notice Myra's eyes on me. We locked gazes, and for several seconds, we simply seemed to peer into each other's souls. What a strange look, and then I noticed something.

"I finished with the last of my books," she said in a dull tone.

I did not really know what to say, so I only nodded.

"We should go into town tomorrow," she said.

We retired for the evening, and as Myra proceeded toward her room and disrobed, seemingly without the slightest degree of modesty, I took to my pallet on the floor. I considered many things as I lay there. I reviewed the events of the day, including striking and injuring her. I invested some thought on the story she offered and even considered what the following day might bring. However, this wasn't really the main theme running through my mind at that moment.

The truth is I wanted her. I wanted to ravage her. I wanted to kiss her neck, her breasts, the inside of her thighs. I wanted to be inside of her. As a lycanthrope, I could smell the excitement from between her legs and could see it in her eyes when she stared at me—surely she knew this. How audacious would it be if I were to proceed directly into her room and touch her? Would she welcome my touch or be insulted by my actions? For some time, I simply remained there frustrated.

I think most men are fairly sexually aggressive. They will do anything, including getting themselves killed, for sex. As a lycanthrope, I realized that my libido was several times stronger than it was as a man. At no point was I out of control of my actions, but I wanted her really, really, really bad. Enough so that I was willing to take whatever risk necessary. If she told me to leave, I would, but I was going to walk into her room one way or another.

Her senses were every bit as keen as mine. She heard my footsteps as I crossed the living room. She heard and could even smell my presence as I entered her room. She heard my breathing and heart beating just as I heard hers. Yet she lay motionless on her bed with her back turned to me, her nude form revealed through the dark by my preternatural vision. I carefully climbed into the bed, expecting her to quickly strike me, but she didn't. I kissed her neck and could feel the beating of her heart quicken with my lips. I gently bit down on her neck, and she offered only an invitation for me to proceed further. For hours, we explored each other until we had no energy left for anything further. Never before had intimacy been so strong. Climaxing was, it seemed, the closest to death I had ever come without actually dying. We were powerful creatures—I suppose it only made sense that sex would be powerful as well.

Horrible nightmares plagued me as I slept. Apparently, the throes of passion did nothing to offer me comfort from those terrors. I awoke when Myra slid out of bed and proceeded toward the door.

"How do you feel this morning?" I asked.

She stopped and returned the look I offered. After an almost awkwardly silent moment she spoke, "I am not angry with what you did or with what happened, but please don't do that again unless I ask it."

There was nothing in her tone that suggested even irritation, yet I felt as though I had somehow trespassed. "I am sorry. I didn't mean—"

"Not a word of it," she interrupted me. "An apology isn't necessary. We both wanted the same thing. In the future, let me come to you, all right?"

"Of course," I answered.

An hour later, we were on our way into town. "How often do you go into town?" I asked during our lengthy drive.

"Usually once a month, just for supplies—food, whatever I need, books, whatever."

Myra owned an old Ford pickup truck. I remember thinking it was old even then. I never asked, but I got the impression that she was her own mechanic. For nearly sixty miles, we found ourselves bouncing down what could barely be called a road. Despite the sorry condition of the route on which we were traveling, Myra drove at speeds that made me clutch my seat nervously. Soon, we reached a better maintained road that took us to the town of P——.

"I hate being around people," she said.

"Why is that?"

"They annoy me. They ask questions, want to know about me, then expect me to engage with them."

I smiled at her, thinking that maybe she was joking, but the look on her face indicated that she was clearly disturbed. "Why do you feel that way?"

"I wouldn't expect you to understand, not yet anyway. Right now you haven't *even* begun to lose your humanity. Trust me, in ten years, you will be disgusted with them too. I have a rather large bank account that will likely last far beyond my death. Because of that, I need not deal with the foolishness of a job or the day-to-day interaction of others."

The remainder of our trip, which lasted almost an hour, was quiet. I considered Myra a wise "old" soul but could not imagine living in her shoes. She had chosen to isolate herself then added a self-punishment mindset to her isolation. I have always wondered what had happened in Myra's life that led to such a way of existence. I had asked her on several occasions to tell me her story, but she refused.

In the years that would follow, I would learn, all too well, just how accurate Myra was with her prediction of how low my thoughts of the human race would sink. And yes, at that moment, while no longer human, I didn't really understand how disconnected I truly was from the world; at that moment I still felt human.

The town of P—— seemed quiet and serene, the kind of place where you would want to raise a family. With a population of only three thousand, I quickly learned that it was a community where one person's business would immediately become the talk of the town. As the old pickup rolled past the grocer, the filling station, and the city diner, all eyes were upon us. It seemed like we had driven into the twilight zone, a very creepy feeling to be assured.

"It seems like everyone is watching you," I said to Myra.

"Well, you would be wrong to believe that. The people of this town are well acquainted with me. At least they are acquainted with who I am. I have been coming here for nearly fifty years, and many of the town's older residents have come to fear and dislike me. Still, they know my truck and ordinarily pay me little mind. No, they are not watching me. They are watching the newcomer that I have in my company. You will probably not find much of a welcome here."

We first visited the meat marked where we were met by a tall and jolly butcher; at least he seemed jolly until he saw me sitting in the truck with Myra—his smile quickly dissolved from his face. "It takes a long time for people here to warm up to outsiders," Myra stated as we observed the butcher's reaction to seeing me.

"He looks like he wants to butcher me," I said.

"He does," she said in a matter-of-fact tone. "He has been hitting on me for a decade and desperately wants to take me home with him. You are the first man he has ever seen me with. I suspect that he will be jealous."

We exited the truck and approached the back entranceway to the meat market. "Hello, Dan," she said while offering the same false smile that she had used with me. At that moment, Dan's smile returned to meet hers. While he and Myra exchanged warm greetings, he absolutely ignored my very presence. As far as I could tell, it seemed as though Myra and this butcher were flirting with one another.

It was at this point I noticed something about myself. I recognized a part of me that had never before existed—jealousy. Even when I was married and other men would openly flirt with my wife, I always found myself cool and unbothered; but that was when I was human. Apparently, as a lycanthrope, I was now subject to feeling things that would have been absolutely out of character for me beforehand. My first instinct—and I use the word *instinct* only for lack of a better word—was to attack and beat the butcher to a pulp, a task that would now have been easy enough for me to accomplish despite his size. I was immediately startled by my irrational and violent reaction to his behavior and maybe even Myra's. I didn't like the way he looked at Myra, I didn't like the way she spoke with him, and I didn't like the way he disregarded me.

So frustrated and angry I became that even my hands began to tremble. I wanted to tighten my preternatural grip around his neck until I had crushed even his vertebrae. So strange how this intense and absolutely uncalled-for rage flooded my mind. At the same time, I felt an intense confusion and even guilt for hating this man so much, and yet, I continued to hate him. I continued wanting to not just hurt him but also to torture him cruelly.

Dan was actually the first human being that I had been close to since becoming a lycanthrope. I was amazed at how detailed my ability to detect even the most subtle odors emanation from him was. I not only could smell the alcohol on his breath, but even the beef and broccoli he had eaten an hour or so before. I could smell the deodorant he was wearing, but from me, it could not hide the odor drifting off of him from his axially area and even his groin. I could smell the perspiration in his hair, his low back, and how it saturated parts of his underwear. I could even smell the fungus that was growing in his socks and between his toes.

I found it interesting that while he looked well put together as far as his appearance goes, he was disgusting to me, and I found myself loathing him even more. What was worse, I was becoming increasingly upset by the way Myra was acting with him—the way she smiled at him, the way she looked at him, the way her voice seemed sweeter than it normally was, all a deliberate act.

I think that maybe she was offering me a lesson. Of course, I was so upset that the lesson certainly had gone unnoticed altogether. The lesson—how to easily manipulate the human race—was a lesson that I would become all too versed with in the years to come.

As far as my jealousy goes, I had no excuse for it. As I stated, I was never a jealous person in my life, and I certainly didn't hold any claims to Myra, or maybe I thought I did somehow. After all, I was attracted to her, we had been intimate, and at this point in my life, she was my only true friend, the one person I could trust with whatever I was to become. Although I did not know why I was feeling what I was and I could not rationalize it, that feeling would be one that would revisit me again and again.

Twenty minutes later, three high school boys loaded up the back of Myra's pickup with her enormous purchase—more poultry, pork, and beef.

"You should take some time and explore the town," Myra said to me. "Observe the world and everything around you with your new gifts."

Apparently, Myra had more supplies to purchase, and she informed me that we would meet up at the park in the center of town. So I set off on foot and listened with my enhanced hearing to the tremendous activity that everyone was engaged in all around me. I could listen to conversations people were having at great distances and even inside of buildings. I could also hear automobiles bustling about all over town, music playing on radios in the distance, even machinery at the sheet-metal facility across town.

As I have already described, and will likely continue to describe, my olfactory system was also operating in the most incredible manner. The world of human interaction was a totally different experience to me now. Nothing could be hidden from me, and I would forever walk through life observing the world through the eyes of a demigod.

"Is there anything I can help you find, sir?" asked a dark-haired woman of about eighteen or nineteen as I strolled through the poorly stocked library.

I brought the full power of my sensory awareness into play as I turned to face her. What could I learn? What information could I acquire simply by being in her presence? As I focused on her eyes, I seemed to almost become a part of her. There is really no way I could properly describe what it was like for me in that instant—I can say that I listened to her heartbeat and could practically feel the blood rushing through her vessels. Her pupils were dilated slightly. Her breathing was heavy. I could smell her hairspray, her cheap makeup, even the blood between her legs.

"I was just browsing," I said to her as I smiled.

Another woman walked past me, and I could smell the disease that was in her body, the sickness that coursed through her veins—cancer. No human being could smell it, but it couldn't be more apparent to me. No one walking by her would have ever known her compromised state of health.

"Heather," a woman in her early thirties called out to the young woman who had offered to assist me. "Did you check in the Fairbanks shipment?"

I didn't really care about the question itself or even the words; it was her tone that I found fascinating. It was absolutely beautiful on a level that no one but myself could have possibly noticed. As I proceeded past her, my nose alerted me to what I already suspected. She was pregnant. She smiled at me and I wondered how far along she was. I wondered if she even knew herself.

I left the library and proceeded toward the town square, a small grassy area with several picnic tables spaced throughout and a central flagpole with a wide sidewalk leading to it. I watched for several seconds as Old Glory waved proudly in the wind. There were a number of buildings that circled the square—a hardware store, grocer, Laundromat, and the one I chose to enter, the town diner.

My appetite was inhuman, and although I was able to suppress it while at the butchers, I think my anger with the fool Dan served to distract me. Here, however, I was overwhelmed with the scents of greasy foods, breads, pastas, pastries, and rich desserts. I seemed unable to help myself and entered the café with the same aggressiveness that a heroin addict might approach his dealer after a lengthy and painful withdrawal period. I had almost two hundred dollars in my wallet and was willing to spend all of it if need be on anything that would help satisfy my demanding appetite even if only slightly. At the time, I still hadn't learned enough to know that what I wanted would forever be impossible for me. I thought that if only I had enough to eat, I could walk away satisfied. What a thought!

The waitress was cold and impersonal to me. I could tell that she had recently had sex—I could smell it on her, on her clothes even. The semen was still wet, staining her underwear. She was attempting to cover any kind of odor with a cheap perfume and baby powder.

I ordered three of their large omelets, and when I finished with them, I had the waitress bring me a large stack of pancakes, two hamburgers—each with fries—and two country-fried steaks along with three large milkshakes. Although my bill was impressive, I hardly made a dent in my appetite. My waitress and others that had bothered to take notice of the orders delivered to my table were in awe of how much I had eaten. I had easily consumed enough for eight people and yet remained unsatisfied and wanting more.

I left the diner and met up with Myra who was already waiting for me. "Did you have fun?"

"It's an interesting town," I said.

"You made quite an impression on Dan," she said. "I have never seen him act so strangely. I'm pretty sure he wants to kick your ass."

"Why? Did you ever have something going with him?"

"Oh, please, I find him annoying!" she returned. "That is just the way he is."

It was later that afternoon before the sun had completely set that Myra and I were sitting in her candlelit family room discussing matters of no real importance that she had finally opened one of her newly acquired books. Quite suddenly, I noticed as Myra's expression had changed—she was alert, listening. I studied her strong yet delicate face for a moment as we both sat in silence. "I don't think that we are alone," Myra said calmly.

I listened carefully, then I too became aware of what sounded like creeping footsteps, deliberately quiet, some distance away. Despite that distance, the wind, and the fact that we were indoors, I could hear the crunch of leaves underfoot as if the individual was in the room with us.

"Who is it?"

"I don't know," she answered without stirring. "I have not had a visitor here in a very long time, certainly no one to ever approach the cabin on foot or at this hour." She reached for one of the new books that she had purchased earlier in the day and made herself comfortable in her chair. "You should go check it out," she said calmly.

"What should I do?"

She closed her eyes and cocked her head to the side, again listening. "There is only one person," she said. "Unless it is some sorry bastard who got himself lost, then he is trespassing intentionally in which case you should feel free to take whatever measures you feel are necessary."

"What does that mean?"

"You figure it out," she answered nonchalantly, turning her attention to the book. "I would hurry though. He is getting closer."

An instant later, I bolted through the kitchen and out the rear exit. With what seemed the speed and agility of the Roman god Mercury, I maneuvered effortlessly through the timber in a large semicircle, leading me to approach the individual from behind as he slowly and stealthily proceeded toward the cabin. The instant the wind shifted in regard to my position, I caught the scent of blood, blood and flesh along with other human odors. It took me only a second before I realized who this individual was; and with that realization, my blood began to boil.

I caught sight of Dan as he slowly and cautiously moved forward. He was only about one hundred yards from the cabin and had since left the road and was now tracking through the wooded area, attempting to use the trees as cover. Clearly, his obsession with Myra—or his need to investigate who I was—had gone too far, and he had now degraded to stalking.

Dan was a worthless excuse for a man, but I had come across many people worse than him, much worse. So why did I loath him so much? I wanted that piece of shit to feel pain as he had never before felt it; I wanted so badly to get my hands on him. With every swift and powerful step that brought me closer to him, I could feel the rage within me, consuming every other emotion, every other thought even. It seemed that there was such a strong hatred running through my veins that it would eventually spill out of my pores.

I am going to describe exactly what happened next in detail. I realize this will do nothing but further villainize me, but I also don't care. You may, if you wish, skip the next section or so, especially if you find distaste in violence or are a bit squeamish. What I did wasn't pretty.

Dan turned to see me as I was practically on top of him. The expression on his face—a startled look—quickly became one of anger. Before he could respond with anything more than a fearful jump, I shoved him with preternatural strength and watched as his body left the ground and moved though thirty feet of space before violently colliding with a large and unforgiving tree.

Never before in my life had I been so angry. Never before would I have felt so driven to such violent actions and thoughts. I was becoming so enraged that I began to feel that I was losing control of myself. I immediately slowed down, closed my eyes, and focused on the simplicity of breathing. In, out, in, deep and relaxing breaths. I could not allow myself to sink into the state of being out of control. I was frightened of myself, frightened of what was happening to me.

I looked at Dan lying on the ground but still conscious with blood running from a gash on the back of his head. His arm had also been broken and the humerus was protruding wickedly through his skin. He did not make any verbal noises, but he followed me with his eyes as I approached him, his face grimacing all along. In that moment, I found a calmness that could not have existed a moment earlier. In fact, as I looked at him, I could not help but to feel sorry for him. I still hated him for reasons that I did not entirely understand, except to say that I was quite territorial over Myra, but I felt that he was reduced to nothing more than an organic blob; I was prepared to let Myra determine his fate. Even as I squatted down to examine this loathsome man and could smell the liquor on his breath, I thought of Myra and realized that she surely had heard the brief encounter that had taken place.

"You were stupid to come here!" I said to him.

In that instant, he swung at me with his left unbroken arm. My reflexes were inhuman though, and I grabbed his wrist with no more difficulty than had he been a small child. Unfortunately, I had not buried the hatred and rage I felt for him as deeply as I should have, and I retaliated against his act by degrading into the animal that I virtually was. Without thinking, I bit into and removed his left thumb, before spitting it onto his chest. I could taste the alcohol in his blood as I listened to him scream once he realized what I had done. Almost instinctively, I struck him in the mouth with my forearm, sending what was a nice set of teeth onto the ground and tearing apart his bottom lip in the process. I then grabbed his right cheek and, with a violent jerk, tore it from his face, exposing his jaw and tongue as he continued screaming. "Shut up!" I yelled at him as I punched his sternum, breaking his fragile rib cage and sending him into shock.

How easy this was, how incredibly easy. I had grown accustomed to my fights with Myra, with her savage and fierce power that exceeded my own. By comparison, a human being seemed so weak and slow and easily broken. But how easily broken?

I grabbed his leg, and with power that I was not used to possessing, I tossed him like a rag doll, an impressive distance, his arms and legs flailing as he landed and rolled. I approached and stood over him as he attempted to speak. Unfortunately, with a huge portion of his face removed moments earlier, I could not make out anything he was saying—it was just babble as blood and saliva spilled from the ugly hole in his face.

I put my hand across his face with my fingertips at his temples. Slowly and with enhanced human power, I squeezed and crushed his skull until his eyes burst from their sockets like broken hard-boiled eggs. He did not yell out. Maybe he was no longer able to. After a moment or two, he stopped squirming, and then his heart stopped.

The world went quiet for an instant, an instant that swept all the anger from my system like a toilet flushing. When that instant passed and anger and rage were removed, I felt guilt—I had killed a man. I was a murderer, a cold-blooded murderer. I looked at the mangled and mutilated body—it was so disfigured that one could not identify him. His blood and brains were on my hands. What had I done? How could this have happened? What kind of horrible thing had I become? I felt as though I were in yet another dream, one that I could wake from and all would be right again… if only.

I could smell Dan's blood everywhere along with the excrement and urine that soiled his pants the minute he died, maybe even before he died. And then I smelled Myra's scent as the gentle breeze carried it to me. Looking up, I expected to see a scowl, an evil and angry look that would immediately indicate to me that I had committed an unforgivable act. Instead, her look seemed rather matter-of-fact, almost as though I had done something like tip over a vase or spill water on the floor.

"Well, this is interesting," she said.

"Myra… I don't even know how to begin… I can't even begin to express what I am feeling. I… I am a terrible thing and I beg you not to hate me. I… I—"

"I cannot imagine why you would think I care," she said interrupting me. "You eliminated a pest to me and a potential threat to the safety of my home."

"I've killed a man… I've never killed anyone before! I deserve to die myself!"

"Don't be foolish," she said calmly. "You did what you needed to do. That is all."

"I didn't need to kill him!"

"I would have if you didn't!" she quickly responded. She then sighed quietly. "Don't feel bad. I've done worse things to better people."

"So what do we do now?"

"He didn't walk all this way from town," she responded. "Find what he drove and bring it back here. Then take him and his vehicle and bury them on the far end of that open area." As she spoke, she pointed to an open and grassy clearing behind the cabin. "It's a task as you'll be using a shovel. Whatever you do though, don't dig on this side of the open area."

After offering an odd look, I asked, "Why?"

She offered that fake smile that she usually offered to human listeners. "I've buried a few people out there myself."

Still feeling horrible and wicked in my conscience, I did exactly what Myra had instructed. I found Dan's pickup parked about two miles down the road and drove it into the field. I then used only a shovel and, with remarkable ease, dug the largest and deepest hole I had ever made. As with anything that would have presented a challenge to me previously, the task of tearing an enormous crater into the earth proved to be an easy accomplishment.

The sun had set hours earlier, and as I walked back to the cabin after finishing the job I had been instructed to perform, I noticed an almost full moon rising above the tree line. As I thought back on what I had witnessed with Myra the month before, I grew frightened of what would happen to me in the nights to follow. I was still holding on to the hope that maybe I could somehow escape the becoming altogether, that maybe I could exist with all my newly acquired lycanthropic qualities without becoming the monster. Somehow, as I stared at the moon though, I knew better then to truly believe this.

NINE

THE DAYS FOLLOWING the incident with Dan were the hardest for me since Jessica's death in part due to the fact that I was riddled with guilt over killing a person, not just killing a person but the savage and malicious way in which I did it. And yet, this wasn't even the main issue confronting me; I knew that time was ticking down, and the becoming was something inescapable for me. I had wished many times that Myra had killed me on that morning following the attack in the woods. After all, there was little that I truly had to live for; and now, not only had I killed a man before even the beginning of my first lunar cycle, but I also had the most painful experience of my life to look forward to.

Myra had mercifully discontinued our sparring sessions for which I was quite grateful. In addition, she had become exceedingly attentive to me. Her constant reassurances that everything would be all right and for me to try not to worry, however, seemed only to create more tension within me.

I remember that night as if it had happened only last week. Myra and I had gone for a long run earlier in the day, trekking through the dense timber as only two lycanthropic beings could. Just as had happened the month before, I could feel the subtle and peculiar tingle running through my spine.

"It has begun in you," she said to me after our run. My body had been quite warm since I awakened after first being attacked, but it was unusually warm on that day, and the heat radiated off of me like a furnace.

"What about you?" I asked. "Are you going to change over also?"

"I'm afraid not," she answered. "But I am here for you, right up until the end."

"What happens then? Will you be safe if I become the wolf and you do not?"

"Probably, I guess we'll see."

It was around eight when Myra approached me yet again as I stared off into the direction that the sun had set like a convict awaiting execution. She gently placed her hands on my neck and shoulders and caressed me as though to comfort me, terribly out of character for the often vicious sparring partner I had come to know. In truth, I did need someone to provide the sentiment she offered; my nerves were more on edge than I cared to admit.

I kept remembering the scene four weeks earlier as I watched Myra change over. That image seemed seared into my mind, and it terrified me. While I welcomed Myra's more tender gestures, they did not ease my trepidation. "You should disrobe," she said to me. "You won't really have time once it begins."

"Myra, I'm scared!" I admitted with emotion in my tone. "I am frightened of what is going to happen to me... I don't want this!" Surely she must have been able to see the level of fear and anxiety that was manifesting within me without me telling her. Though she continued to provide physical attention to me by holding and caressing me, it was as though a machine was attempting to ease my concerns—no real emotion whatsoever.

As though reading my mind she stated, "I don't even remember what it is like to feel fear."

"Why are you being so warm to me?"

"I may not remember what fear feels like, but I remember that I was once afraid, very afraid. I can recall what it was like for me," she said. "I was left ignorant of what I was and alone to face this demon on my own. I think you deserve better than that. I'm trying to offer you something that I was never given—support."

"I appreciate that!" I said quietly and emotionally.

The next few hours passed quickly as I sat in the chair in the corner. Myra brought me a blanket to wrap around myself as I was a bit more modest than she was. Our conversation during that time was light and brief as we both awaited the inevitable. Nine o'clock came and went, then ten. All the while, I could feel the mildly uncomfortable heat emanating from my spine. It seemed as though a red-hot steel rod was running from the base of my skull all the way to my tailbone, just beneath the skin. I remember as the clock chimed at eleven thinking that maybe, possibly, nothing was going to happen. I didn't dare say anything to the ever-vigilant and watchful Myra out of fear that I would jinx the peace that preceded that moment.

I did begin to feel very odd, as if nausea had set in. And like a child doing his best to avoid vomiting, I was trying, determined to hold back this unpleasant sensation that had descended upon me. I was uncertain if this was the start of the becoming or possibly just my terrible nerves making me feel ill. Myra released her hold on me and rose to her feet, intimately aware of everything that was happening to me.

"Don't fight it," she said as she slowly backed away from me. "It will only make it worse and more painful."

Suddenly and without warning, the heat that had been resonating from my spine intensified tenfold. I could not even tell heat from pain at that moment. The muscles running along each side of my vertebral column tightened and began to twist. The bones of my back began popping, cracking like ice cubes in lukewarm water. I tried to scream out in pain, but I was unable to even breathe. Just as Myra had done the month before, I threw myself to the floor, abandoning the blanket I had been wrapped in. In what was the most sentimental gesture she could possibly offer, Myra lowered herself and touched my naked back and hand.

"It will be all right," she said with as much compassion as she could offer.

Seconds later, the bones in my hands and wrists began twisting and breaking. The pain I was experiencing was indescribable as I could feel my skin pulling and tearing open, my bones snapping like twigs, and my organs were as if on fire and would at any point burst through my abdominal wall. Even my eyes felt as though they too would burst from their sockets.

I was focusing on Myra who still held my quickly deforming then reforming hand. She was still speaking to me, but I could no longer hear what she was saying. The last thing I remembered was my shoulders involuntarily being torn from their sockets, followed by my hips. Still unable to scream, I blacked out from the indescribable pain. Although I lost consciousness, I knew that my body was still active. Such a strange sensation—to feel your consciousness disconnect while something else takes control of your body. It was like being carjacked then tossed into the trunk while the thief drives where he wants—you know the car is moving because you can feel it, but you have no idea of where to.

I don't really know that I dreamt, which was a relief from the terrible nightmares that I had become used to experiencing. My mind existed in a void—a blackness, nothingness. It seemed that I was aware of myself; at least I think I was, but even time was immeasurable—minutes, hours, days, and weeks; concepts such as these had no meaning for me. All I knew was that my consciousness swam through an endless vacuum until it was finally released, allowed to return to the body that it had involuntarily abandoned the night before.

I was something else for several hours before dawn; and yet during that brief time, a part of my awareness had been sent away for what seemed an impossibly long period of time.

I opened my eyes and pulled my face from the mud. My naked body rested half in, half out of a creek bed. The always icy cold water that flowed through this shallow creek washed over my lower extremities up to my waist. The sun had just risen, the birds were singing, and all seemed right with the world, except for the fact that I was somehow a part of it. I pulled myself up and, with the running water, brought several handfuls to my face. I was absolutely exhausted despite the fact that it seemed—at least to me—that I had been unconscious and had just awakened. My body felt as though I had not slept in days. After a brief assessment of where exactly I was, I began the three-mile walk through the timber and back to the cabin.

As I suspected, Myra was waiting for me, and as I entered the cabin, she handed me the clothes I had removed the evening before. "You are very dangerous when you change over," she said to me. It was only then that I noticed the deep and horrible gashes that had been carved into her neck and chest by the teeth and claws of the monster.

The month earlier, when Myra's inner demon cornered me in the cabin, it had swung at me and in the process removed my eye from its socket—punishment, I'm assuming, for gazing into its eyes and thusly challenging it. While this may sound like a horrible injury from a somewhat human standard, I healed up nice and quickly. In addition, the wolf that Myra had become left me otherwise unharmed and very much alive. Not exactly a kind and gentle monster, but clearly she was not interested in tearing my body apart. The same could not be said for what had happened with Myra.

Wearing only a long flannel shirt and nothing else, Myra appeared as though she had been a victim in a terrible sexual assault / murder attempt. I pulled her shirt open and noticed that the deep crevices that began in her neck, traveled to her navel. I found myself without words as tears began to well in my eyes. Myra, though emotionless and seemingly robotic in her lack of humanity, nonetheless stepped forward and placed her arms around me as I broke down.

"I am so sorry!" I said as I wept.

"There is no need for that," she responded calmly. "The beast behaves differently in each of us. For me, it is exceedingly territorial. It would hunt and kill anyone who trespasses within its territory, which was the fate of you and your friend. In addition, I'm sure it views you as belonging to it. As for the wolf in you, it is extremely aggressive. I don't need to caution *you* about how dangerous the wolf is during the lunar cycle, but in your case, it seems considerably worse."

There was something more Myra began to say but immediately stopped. Her eyes looked away from me, deliberating what to say to me next.

"What is it?" I asked, still crying somewhat. "Tell me... Whatever it is, don't keep anything from me!"

Her somewhat sleepy gaze returned to me. "I think that there is a darkness inside of you, something that eclipses anything I've seen before."

I asked Myra to elaborate further, but she would not. She pulled me inside, and after we disrobed, we lay together on my pallet. She wrapped her strong arms around me and pulled me close to her. As she did this, I could smell the rich blood still flowing from the wounds that would have killed any human being. I knew that Myra did not love me. I knew that she was not capable of such a thing—or was she? Still, she and I had a bond that could not be felt by men and women under any set of circumstances. In a sense, she was my creator, and while I realized that emotion was absent from her association with me, I felt relieved and safe to be in her arms. I could not even imagine dealing with this condition without her at my side. And so we slept, and the nightmares that had eluded me the evening before revisited me here.

TEN

"YOU ARE GOING to need to leave here soon," Myra said to me.

Every once in a while, there are discussions, phrases actually that seem to sting so deeply that I carry them with me always in the back of my mind, always a reminder of something painful that once happened like an ugly scar. Those words, the tone, even the expressionless look she offered, haunt me still to this day. It was the third morning following the full moon. It was a warm morning when she offered those words, but I can remember feeling something in the air, something to let me know that autumn would eventually kill off summer.

"Have I done something wrong?"

"Of course not," she answered. "But your stay here was always a temporary one. We knew that from the very beginning."

"I know," I said, "but I'd like to stay if that is possible."

"I'm sorry. It isn't possible." After spilling those words from her lips, she must have noticed what was an obvious look of hurt on my face. After a heavy sigh, she continued, "You are very unsafe during the becoming. It isn't your fault, but that is the way it is. Besides that, while I have enjoyed your time here with me, I miss the solitude that I have been accustomed to. Again, I am sorry, but that was the plan all along."

Her words, while not cold or calloused, cut through me just the same. My life had changed so drastically that I could not even consider myself "Caleb" anymore, at least not the same Caleb that had stepped into this wilderness a month or so earlier. I would be leaving a different man than the one I was when I came, reentering the world as a preternatural being. I suppose in a lot of ways, I considered my stint with Myra not unlike a departure from the world. I wasn't even sure that the world outside of the one Myra had carved for herself still existed. So what would I do? Where would I go? I was like an unprepared adolescent, being thrown out of his parent's home and suddenly needing to survive in a very frightening world.

Two days later, I walked away from the cabin with a backpack filled with clothing that Myra had offered me. My plan was to revisit Myra within a year, possibly within six months. As I slowly distanced myself from the home I had lived in for those weeks that I had been there, I began to form a plan by which I would reintegrate myself into the world.

As those thoughts flowed through my consciousness, I became aware of what had slowly become an accepted part of my nature—the extreme extent of my sensory awareness. I tried considering who or what I truly was, what it meant to be a lycanthrope. I listened to the birds singing in the nearby trees as well as those miles away. I inhaled and savored the ten thousand vivid scents that were carried on the wind. I was even aware of something so subtle as the way the ground felt through my shoes. I was not a man. I was a demigod.

"Caleb," came a voice from behind me.

I turned to see Myra in the distance approaching with a quick stride. As I waited for her, I took in, for what would be the last time, her stunningly beautiful body, the way her unkempt yet unnaturally healthy hair hung to her shoulders, those delicate features in her face that suggested that she might break if handled too roughly. Oh, how misleading. I was hoping that she had maybe changed her mind and was prepared to offer me a reprieve. I wanted so badly for her to tell me that I was welcomed to stay with her, that I could remain with her for as long as I wanted. Unfortunately, that invitation would not come from her.

"Caleb, there is one thing more I need to share with you."

"All right."

She paused for a moment, selecting her words carefully and making me nervous about what she had to say. Finally she began, "I want you to know that I deeply regret what has happened in your life. I apologize for bringing you into this existence. If there was anyway for me to reverse what has happened, I promise you that I would.

"If there is a final lesson that you will take away from me, then allow me to offer it now. We lose our humanity—that much I have told you already—and while you still have your full spectrum of emotion and feeling, that won't always be the case. In time, all that will remain is anger. It's like eating the same food over and over again—it's fine at first, then you grow tired of it, you lose your taste for it altogether, and eventually, you hate it and gag at the idea of swallowing even one more bite. But this, too, I've explained.

"Once we lose all else, we invest our energies in attempting to maintain and control that one last terrible emotion we are left with. How difficult it will become for you to even converse with others when anger, a dark anger, is all you feel. But even on our worst days, we never truly give into the gravity-like pull that anger presents to us. We never want to lose control of ourselves. Kind of like falling backward, you go down a little, but you instinctively want to catch yourself. Even when you try to relinquish self-control, a huge part of you will fight desperately to regain it. And rightly so. We are nothing but animals without it.

"But in certain circumstances and under the most extreme conditions, you may find yourself in a situation where utilizing the rage you carry in check is necessary. I won't lie—it is unsettling, like falling, but if you give into the anger, stop resisting and pull it forward into you. You will discover a destructive force that you were not aware that you possessed. Self-control will be sacrificed, of course, but it will allow you impressive power."

Once again, I was felt uncertain what to say as I didn't really know what she was trying to tell me. "I don't understand."

She smiled, a fake smile, but it felt like a gift—something she wanted to give me before I left, just a smile. "I know," she said. "Just please remember what I have told you. Someday, when you are further along, you will understand."

We invested the next several moments gazing into each other's eyes. I wondered what she might have been thinking at that moment. I hoped it was an intimate and endearing thought, and not something awkward. "You should leave now," she said, still smiling. She gave me a final hug and embraced me as a friend, lover, instructor, and a one-time temporary companion though life. I think I knew instinctively that this would be our last moment together though my mind would not allow me to accept this as truth. I wondered if she knew this also.

Once I made it to the highway, I hitched a ride to C—— and from there rode with a trucker who dropped me off back in H——. My apartment was just the way I left it, except the flowers that were alive and vibrant when I had last seen them were now brown and dead. Ah, my stoic and priestly Alaska home away from home. I remember the landlord being upset at what he thought was the abandonment of my apartment. Ironically, I gathered what possessions I needed and did just that—walked away.

With plans on revisiting Myra in the not-too-distant future, a part of me wanted to stay in Alaska just to be close to her. And yet, I found myself longing to return home. Though to be honest, I can't really say as to why. I really had nothing to return to.

Alaska will still be here when I am ready to come back, I said to myself as I flew from Anchorage to Seattle. A long bus ride later, I was back in St. Louis. It was amazing to me really. I had been gone just over a year, and yet it seemed and felt as though a new generation had come of age and everything was different now. At the time, it seemed as though the entire world had changed in my absence. Looking back, I was the one who had changed. Nothing would ever be for me as it once was.

Although I have alluded to them several times, I realize that there are concepts that, unless one becomes a lycanthrope, one would find difficulty wrapping their mind around. I can talk about my life before I went to Alaska, about the person that I once was. But from that time forward, I was a different person. I doubt that I could truly offer that difference in my writing, but the old me would not recognize the new me. I had all the memories of my former life, but none of the personality. I was a lost soul, searching for my new place in the world. As impossibly harsh and deep as my depression was before leaving St. Louis, it seemed to return to me sixfold upon stepping foot into the city once again. Previously, I suffered from loss and the consequences for the decisions I had made. But now, I was overwhelmed by a sense of isolation I could never have imagined as a human being.

Every day, my thoughts seemed to linger on Myra. I wondered what she was doing, wondered if she ever thought about me; mostly though, I spent my time wishing that I was still there with her. I never truly loved Myra, at least not in any romantic sense. Yes, she and I had been intimate, but those acts did not extend beyond anything purely physical. Our moments of intimacy were void of feelings on both our parts, I'm sure.

I missed Myra not only because she was the only other lycanthrope I knew, and knowing that she was in the world made me feel a little less alone, but I also shared a very special bond with her that all lycanthropes share with those who "sired" them. Just as I indicated earlier, when Myra and I were close, we shared a very personal link. It wasn't exactly psychological. It was almost spiritual. Either way, we had a bond, and I missed feeling the safety of that bond. It was as though every other being in the world had disappeared, and Myra and I were the only ones left. At the time, she was all I had, and when she made me leave, I was without anyone. True, there were people everywhere, some of who I truly cared for, and yet it didn't matter, I was utterly alone.

Although money wasn't really a pressing issue, at least not yet, because of how much I had earned while working in Alaska, I felt a need to do something constructive with my time, a need that would come up again much later in my life. Looking back now, it seems a total waste of my time, but at that moment, I felt it necessary to behave and live life as normal as possible. It was necessary for my sanity.

I picked up a few menial jobs—custodial work for a while, stocking shelves at a shoe store, sales associate at a home improvement store. All of these jobs were part-time and allowed me the flexibility I needed to manage my "condition."

As far as that goes, during the full of the moon, I would retreat from the city and endure the becoming as far from people as I could. Usually I would head to the Ozarks or out in the middle of farm country—the area around Kampsville, Illinois, seemed to be a frequent destination for me. Generally, I would drive to a remote area then hike out on foot until I felt that I was at a reasonably safe distance from anyone—whatever a reasonably safe distance meant. I would take with me a generous amount of food and sometimes even a tent. As time went by, I learned that shelter was unnecessary—sleeping on the ground in the snow or rain was no less comfortable to me than were I to rest my body in a five-star hotel. Anyway, I would basically camp out until the lunar cycle had yet again passed. Just as Myra had instructed, I would remove my clothing an hour or two before the becoming and place the garments in a protective bag in the event it would rain—not that it really mattered.

I would always hope each time that it would become easier, less painful as time went on—it did not. Oftentimes it seemed quite the contrary as though it were even more excruciatingly painful each month. The transformation played out the same way each time, however, with the pain of my bones and muscles contorting, twisting, and breaking until I lost consciousness. The following morning, I would find myself in some unusual place—lying face down in the mud, sleeping in a tree, or even at the edge of a lake as though the beast had been swimming. It was and still is such a strange and disorienting feeling to awaken and have no idea where you are or how you may have gotten there. Interestingly, I would often retrace the path that the creature had taken the preceding night, and I learned that rarely would it venture outside of a one- or two-mile radius from where I was camped. There was a tiny sense of relief in knowing this; at least I thought so at the time.

For the better part of a year, I operated in this manner, growing less and less cautious, becoming at times almost reckless with where I chose to camp. And yet during that time, I never experienced any problem with people. This relaxed mind-set would eventually prove to be a deadly mistake. But for the moment, life was calm and uneventful.

There were a number of things I began now that I had never before even contemplated. I tried new restaurants, visited the Arch, took an excursion on a riverboat; I even dated someone for a short while, a woman named Alice, nothing serious. I remember one of the really interesting things that I wanted to do after returning to St. Louis was to go to the gym. I could feel that the strength I possessed had increased in an impossible way over what it had been just a few months earlier.

I hadn't really gone to the gym much before this; I did have a membership at one for several months some years earlier but had never used it. While it was one thing to run and pick up and throw heavy branches or whatever I could find while staying with Myra, I wanted a more objective measure of how strong I had become. I joined a medium-sized gym and immediately proceeded to the free weight room. When I was in high school, I had bench-pressed 135 pounds—nothing to brag about. I remember looking at the bench in front of me, a little nervous about what it would feel like to press the two forty-five pound plates and the bar off my chest. I had done it only once years earlier. I positioned myself beneath the bar and spaced my hands wider than my shoulders, lining up my pinkies with grooves set into the bar. I straightened my elbows, lifting the weighted bar from the safety of the pegs, and held the bar far above my chest as I stared at the ceiling. Slowly, I lowered the bar to my chest, then pressed it away as easily as if it had been a broomstick. I repeated movement again, then again and again until I had completed twenty repetitions.

Now I realize that for anyone who has never lifted weights, much of what I am saying here might seem a bit unimportant or even difficult to envision. If someone would have offered me information about lifting weights before I started, even I would have not really known how significant what they were telling me was. The reason I am including this is to show just what a miraculous transformation had occurred in me.

After doing the 135 pounds for twenty repetitions, I sat up and could feel the blood surging though the muscles of my chest and shoulders. I definitely wanted more; I wanted to test the limits of what I could do. I added a twenty-five pound plate on each side of the bar and pressed it fifteen times just as easily and just as controlled. I took the weight up to 225 pounds, 275 pounds, then 315 pounds. At this point, others in the gym began to take notice.

"Hey, man, do you need a spot?" someone asked.

"Please," I answered.

With 375 pounds on the bar and a spotter on each side, I pressed the weight for twelve reps, struggling with the last one. I was speechless. I knew that I had become strong, but I did not know just how strong, and this was just the beginning for me as I would become even stronger as time went on. I also learned that moving that much weight around in a small gym would cause it to come to a standstill as people would tend to stop whatever they were doing and watch. Clearly, I needed to find a larger gym. I went on about my workout, a bit clumsily, as I really didn't know much about lifting weights. In every instance, however, I moved poundages that would have been nothing short of a dream for most individuals and, until then, impossible for me.

Another discovery about myself—just as my body would miraculously heal from injuries, so too would it recover from my workouts. In the weeks to come, I would work out in the morning then repeat that same workout in the afternoon and show impressive gains in that short of time. My already impressive body became what someone told me "fucking intimidating." Within six months, my bench press was up to 750 pounds, I squatted well over 1,000 pounds, and my shoulder press topped out at over quarter of a ton. And yet despite the massive increase in strength, I was still able to sprint the mile in under four minutes—inhuman. Myra would have been proud.

There came a point when I really didn't need to go the gym anymore. The strength and gains I had made, though impressive, would eventually be outdone by a preternatural power that was owed to me through time. Essentially, as I stated earlier, I would simply become stronger as the lycanthropy progressed in me.

Anyway, while my initial workouts were intended to discover what I was physically capable of, my reason for continuing in this weight training regimen was really nothing more than an attempt to occupy myself; after all, what do werewolves do in their spare time? Yes, I was lonesome in life, and yes, I was afflicted with a terrible condition. However, as I look back on that era of my life, it really doesn't seem too bad. No, things were going to get much worse for me in due time. For that brief period, I would work a few hours each week, eat constantly, and live leisurely. And then everything changed.

It was in the late spring, April or May 1979, and I had gone into Calhoun County as I had done for several months before. I had hiked out and camped at a new location, knowing fully well that a residence was located less than three miles from where I was. Still, after almost a full year, the beast had never really done anything too aggressive, preferring instead to remain in proximity to wherever the becoming took place. I should have known that I was becoming foolishly careless with an incredibly dangerous "thing." Unfortunately, as I would learn, there is no way to control the beast; neither can its motives nor behavior be forecasted. It works almost as if to deceive. I would learn that lesson that Myra had so desperately worked to teach—the monster is a *killing machine*.

There was nothing peculiar or unusual about that particular lunar cycle. Everything seemed to go as it had for many months earlier, with me simply playing the waiting game until the change would occur. I remember that it was raining particularly hard that night, and I had removed my clothing and placed it into the tent that I had pitched so that everything would remain dry. The next thing I remember after the becoming was waking up in a demolished house—demolished by the monster, no doubt. I rose to my feet with an overwhelming sense of confusion at first, replaced quickly by absolute horror. *What had I done?* I thought to myself.

I was standing in the kitchen, the cabinets ripped from the walls and their contents smashed and spread across the linoleum floor. Interestingly, a chest freezer that had been positioned in the corner had been torn open like a wet shoebox, the contents removed and presumably eaten by the monster. In fact, I could even taste the raw chicken still on my breath. Quite suddenly, I realized the smell of blood also permeated the air. My already terrified heart sank, and a tremendous panic overtook me. Again, those same thoughts ran through my mind, *Oh dear God!! What have I done?*

Slowly, cautiously, I proceeded through the kitchen and into the dining room, the direction from which the coppery scent was originating. This room looked just as destroyed as the kitchen. Pictures were knocked from the walls, the large oak table was overturned and two of its legs were broken, and a smashed television on the far side of the room. Strangely, a large curio cabinet rested untouched; its contents, fine china, still proudly displayed and now strangely out of place in this house. With the exception of the curio cabinet, the entire house so far looked as though several men had violently thrown each other back and forth in a long struggle.

I exited the dining room and entered the living room where I noticed that the front door had been smashed in and blood was splattered across the crème-colored carpet and along the walls. It seemed as though the bleeding body had been dragged across the entire length of the wall. I don't think my heart even beat in those moments. I stepped around the blue sectional sofa and exhaled as tears practically overtook me. Before me, three dead bodies—German Shepherds. As gruesome as the scene truly was, I found myself in an incredible state of relief. I doubt many people could imaging the instant and incurable guilt associated with killing someone unintentionally—ask someone who has done so in an automobile accident. There is nothing more haunting. While under ordinary circumstances, I would feel terrible about even killing these dogs. At that moment I would have been fine with the idea of slaughtering a hundred more animals if it meant that I hadn't killed any people.

I quickly proceeded through each room of the house and learned that no one was home, only the dogs who had apparently been killed defending their home. Although the fact that I had not killed anyone brought a sense of relief to me, I was more than a little upset and disturbed at what had transpired. Unfortunately, I didn't have time to dwell on the situation—I heard a car approaching the house on the long driveway, an old Oldsmobile. There was nothing more I could do. I bolted out an exit in the rear of the house and ran as quickly as I could across a quarter of a mile open field. I am uncertain if anyone saw me or not—a naked man running from a gruesome scene and demolished house. I returned to my camp, immediately dressed, and left without delay.

The only semi-silver lining was that the cycle was a brief one that month, with the becoming happening only once. The next several days, I pondered the situation I had found myself in. Everything I thought I could somewhat trust and rely on was false. I was a danger to anyone and everyone, and during the becoming, I could not be trusted under any set of circumstances. I kept thinking, *What if that family had been home? What if I had killed the family? What would have I done?*

As it seemed would almost always be the case, my dreams did not allow me the comfort that even my conscious mind denied me. In them, I found myself in the house just as I was, expecting to walk around the rear of the sectional and see the mutilated dogs. Instead, there were two small girls—one about ten years old and the other fourteen or so, each with dark brown hair. The youngest one was missing her throat while the oldest sister had been eviscerated, with her intestines pulled from her and twisting around her feel presumably while she kicked.

For most people, in the worst of dreams, there is a point where the individual becomes so horrified that they awaken, but there is no such mercy for me. On and on the dream went, and no amount of horror could force me to wake before my subconscious was ready to release me.

After several days of calling off of work and doing nothing but sitting in a chair staring at the wall reflecting on every element of the situation, there was one certainly that became crystal clear—I could not allow this to happen again.

ELEVEN

OH, HOW I hated myself. What had I done to deserve this existence? Why me? I left my home in St. Louis in an extreme state of depression. Little did I know at the time, but even my deepest sorrows would be robbed from me by this "disease." Ah, but that would come later.

It wasn't enough that my daughter had died. I had lost a wife, as awful as she was, and I had alienated pretty much everyone I had ever known, my family included, but I was now a horrible thing. I wished Myra had killed me when she had considered it. The world would have been a better place without me. As it was, I had *nothing* to live for.

With a heavy heart, I headed west, knowing that I had to distance myself far away from anyone during the next cycle and all further cycles. I had considered going into the Arizona desert, but for whatever reason, I felt that the Rockies would be safe, somewhere in the mountains. They would offer the isolation I needed. After all, if Bigfoot could remain hidden, surely I could too.

The drive was unremarkable; I had an old Suburban at the time, not the most beautiful automobile but one that would allow me to carry all that I needed and, if necessary, one I could even sleep in. I took my time getting there, stopping off at countless greasy diners along the way, always feeling in a constant state of starvation, unable to ever eat enough to satisfy that hunger. This would forever be how it I would live.

I did find a mild sense of peace once I had reached the mountains, an interesting parallel to how I felt when I first landed in Alaska. I arrived in a small town called Pinedale and stayed at a motel for a few days before hiking many miles up to the summit of several nearby mountains. It was there, above the snowline, that I began to feel my soul quiet a bit for the first time in many, many years in fact.

I was alone here, far, far from anyone. Still, my self-loathing seemed to haunt me. I wasn't really sure what I had planned to do with myself; after all, I couldn't just be a mountain man from this point forward. The isolation did offer a sense of safety during the becoming, but then what? I examined Pinedale and several other surrounding communities and had considered possibly relocating here maybe.

On that particular month, I was spared from the becoming on the night before the full moon and had successfully managed well on the night of the full moon. Essentially, no people equated to no real problems, and the wolf behaved as he had during the many other uneventful cycles—staying within a reasonable distance from wherever I had camped out. But on the evening after the full moon—the last night of the cycle—things went horribly wrong.

I awoke just as I had every other morning following the becoming—confused, uncertain of where I was, and lying naked and dirty on the ground. I sat up and scanned my surroundings while my mind raced to establish where I was, how I got there, and the date and time, much as I imagine most everyone does for the first four or five seconds upon awakening. I instantly knew that something wasn't entirely right but did not panic; after all, what damage could I possibly have caused? I was in the middle of nowhere. I rose to my feet and ran my fingers through my hair, removing the snow and ice that my body temperature had not melted. But I then detected something peculiar and unsettling as I brought my hands from my hair. I could smell something very... human on me. My first thought was that maybe the wolf had gotten into garbage—that had happened before. However, as I inspected my fingernails, a painful and sobering realization violently shook me to my core. Tiny traces of blood remained in my cuticles. That, along with the human smell that clung to me, caused me to fear the worst. Now I was panicked.

It was easy for me to track the direction from which the monster had come. As I had stated earlier, the creature did not ordinarily travel long distances, preferring to remain within a mile or two radius from wherever I decided to let the becoming happen. Evidently though, this was an instance where the creature behaved unpredictably. I tracked the wolf's path nearly ten miles down the mountain. From that point, I could smell smoke, food, and unfortunately, human beings. I proceeded slowly until I found the source of the fire—a nearly exhausted campfire outside of a lone RV. I hung my head as I knew what had happened—the monster was here, and it had killed. My worst fear realized.

If I would have had a gun at that exact moment, I would have placed the barrel into my mouth and would have pulled the trigger. I remember thinking that I should have done that very thing long ago. Many thoughts ran though my mind in those following moments, and among them, *Why did Myra not kill me when she had the chance?*

I approached the campsite, still unclothed, as the monster had taken me far from the Suburban. I did my best to remain composed as I examined the scene. Even now, it is hard for me to write what I saw. It isn't that I feel a particular emotion one way or the other, but rather a sense of respect for those involved in the atrocity that I committed. I will relate the facts however.

There were two boys, one of about thirteen or fourteen and another whose age I guessed to be about ten or eleven—the younger one was without a head. I then came across the body of a young woman in her late teens or early twenties with blonde hair—she was lying face down with her back broken in several places as well as deep claw marks extending from her neck to her sacrum. I ventured around the opposite side of the RV to discover the body of man in his late forties who had been literally ripped in half, with his legs and pelvis nearer the RV while his torso and upper body lied nearer the smoldering campfire; between the two halves, his intestines strung about like confetti. There are no words to describe how I felt at that exact moment.

Suddenly, I heard something. My attention was drawn to a grassy area roughly forty yards from the RV. After all this time, I cannot say with certainty what was more horrific, the savagely mutilated remains I had come across around the RV itself or the woman I discovered as she attempted to crawl toward her family, bitten and now infected. This woman appeared to be in her forties and was clearly the mother this family. Her right arm was torn to shreds, along with her throat all the way to her sternum. As best as I could tell, her lower back had been broken along with both legs. Despite her injuries, she was attempting and succeeding to pull herself from the wooded area where she had either been attacked or dragged and toward the dirt road that had brought her family here in the first place. I began to suspect that her body was already beginning to heal itself. She was badly shaking, and when she saw me she cried out, "Please help me!"

I knelt down beside her and, for a moment, wondered what she must have thought of a naked man coming to assist her after being attacked by what she would have thought was a wild animal. Then suddenly, I realized the irony of my situation—I was in an identical place when Myra approached me the following morning after I had been attacked. The irony continued when I considered the thought that ran though my mind not ten minutes earlier. *Why did Myra not kill me when she had the chance?*

"Please help me!" she repeated as she rolled onto her back and reached out to me with her left arm. "There was an animal that attacked us!"

I took her hand and held it tightly as I came close to her. "It's okay," I said to her. "You are going to be okay."

"What about my family... my husband?" she asked as she cried hysterically.

I didn't know what to say; I certainly didn't know what to do. I just held her hand and let the words come without considering what decision I was now forced to make. "Your family is fine, and help will be here shortly."

She clutched my hand even more firmly, "Oh thank God for you!"

In all the time since becoming what I am, I frequently asked myself why Myra had spared me, a question I have presented in this writing several times. Had Myra done what she told me she had considered and killed me upon discovering me, the monster would never have existed, and this family would be alive and enjoying this remote camping excursion. And here I was, presented with an identical quandary to the one that Myra was facing. There were repercussions for allowing me to live—this incident was but one.

"What's your name?" she asked, unaware that I was trying to decide her fate.

I smiled at her. "My name is Caleb."

"Are you sure my family is okay? Please go check on them!"

"Just relax," I said as calmly as my voice would allow. "Your family has already been taken care of, but you've been injured, and I am here for you."

"God bless you, Caleb," she said. "Jesus must have sent you here to us!"

"I doubt that very much. Everyone here, including myself, was just at the wrong place at the wrong time. Where are you from?"

"We're from Texas," she answered. "This was supposed to be our last family outing before Nancy went off to college. Nancy is our oldest daughter. Coming here was my husband's idea. He wanted to take us as far from the city life as he could. He would have preferred Alaska, but we couldn't afford that, so here we are."

"Trust me when I tell you that bad things can happen in Alaska too."

"What are you doing so far up this way?"

"I wanted to get away from people for a little bit. I thought this would be a good spot."

"Looks like we ruined that for you," she said trying to smile. Her smile seemed to fade quickly as she looked at me directly. "Why aren't you wearing any clothes?"

It seemed that in her state of shock, she hadn't acknowledged that I wasn't wearing anything. I ignored her question. I was torn between not speaking with her further and simply doing what I knew I must and offering her some kind of respect through conversation. After all, I killed her entire family and turned her into a monster. Surely, I could spare a few moments for kind words.

"Why aren't you wearing any clothes?" she asked again, this time with a hint of distress in her tone.

I surveyed the immediate surroundings—tall and wet grass that ran up the hillside to the road, a few small limbs scattered about, and rocks, large rocks, like the ones used to surround the campfire.

"Sir, please tell me what you are doing here," she asked, her relief now replaced with panic.

"As for the state of my condition, I lost my clothing some distance from here. Unfortunately, my lost clothing is the least of your concerns. I am very sorry for what has happened to you and your family. None of this was your fault." As I spoke, I approached several of the bowling ball-sized boulders and selected one. "If there was anything I could do to fix what I have done here, I promise I would. But what's done is done."

"Sir… Caleb, what are you doing?" she asked, trembling in fear as I approached carrying the fifteen-or-so-pound rock.

Surely she could see the tears in my eyes and knew that the person she initially thought was sent by God to help was in fact the devil incarnate. "I know this won't come as any consolation to you because it doesn't come as a consolation to me, but I have to stop the cycle here, and by doing so, maybe I can save the next family from being killed like yours has been."

"Please don't do this! Please don't do this!" she pleaded with me as she cried in mercy.

For a long moment, perhaps the longest single breath in my life, I listened to her soft heartbeat and considered the unforgivable act that I was about to commit. I told myself that it wasn't too late to reconsider; I could take her away from this massacre and teach her how to live with this condition just as Myra had done to me, couldn't I?

Suddenly, the left-brained analytical side of my thinking came to bring reason to my flawed mind-set. I could smell the blood and excrement and death from her family that I had caused the night before. Maybe it was too easy for me to forgive Myra for what had happened not only to me but for Rocky's fate as well. Obviously, it wasn't her fault any more than this tragedy was mine, but that would be a minor detail to a grieving mother and wife. She would never forgive me were she to learn the truth about her attack. Beyond that certainty, the idea that I could teach her to respect and maintain her newly acquired lycanthropy would have been laughable if not so tragic—like taking a gun safety training course by a man who accidentally shot and killed your loved ones.

"I'm sorry, but this must be done," I said to her as I brought the heavy boulder over her head. The last image her face revealed was a terrified one; she screamed initially but then fell silent as I proceeded with what I did. I brought the stone down upon her head with all my force and then repeated that action again and again and again, even after her heart stopped.

When I was finished, I slowly backed away from her body. She was no longer identifiable. I don't know what to say about myself regarding this act. I told myself that it was necessary. Myra was wrong to let me live—the world certainly did not need any more monsters. I could of course offer reason for my actions, but they did little to comfort me. I knew that it should have been me on the receiving end of that boulder and not this unfortunate woman whose life I took, not out of anger as I had done with Dan the pervert stalker/butcher, but out of what I felt was a sense of responsibility for actions that I could not control.

It seemed that after a few moments with the remains of the woman whose name I never even learned, I could no longer bear it. I fled the site and ran as quickly as I could away from the scene that I would never truly escape in my mind. Eventually, I did find the Suburban, another seven or eight miles to the east of their campsite.

TWELVE

AFTER THE INCIDENT outside of Pinedale, I immediately distanced myself from the area and spent four or five days at a motel in Cheyenne. I was in a strange depressed state, still trying to digest what had happened. What was I to do with myself? I had committed my first atrocity and couldn't even stand to look at myself in the mirror. When I closed my eyes, I could see the face of the woman as clearly as I had when I saw her in person. I could see the pain and despair in her eyes, having helplessly watched her family torn apart by something she could not even begin to understand. Over and over, I replayed the scene that would haunt me for many years to come. I tried to rationalize my decision, telling myself that I had no other choice. Easy enough for someone reading this to understand—but you weren't there. You can't imagine what it was like for me to hear her desperate cries for help and to see the horror on her face when she realized that I had come not to help but to finish what the demon had left undone the night before.

In my room in Cheyenne, I sat at the edge of my bed and sobbed quietly for so long that I had no tears left. I'll say it again—I wished that Myra had chosen to kill me instead of letting me live; if she had, that family would have still have been alive. I was in need of help in the absolute worst way. Myra had suggested that I search out and speak with Arthur Denham from Madison, Wisconsin. Unfortunately, her last contact with this individual was nearly half a century earlier, and I had no way of knowing if he was even still alive, especially considering that he was supposedly well over a hundred years old when she knew him.

I left Cheyenne on a Thursday and headed to St. Louis to pick up clothing and a few things and withdraw money from the bank before heading north. I remember feeling as I have countless times since—that time wasn't on my side. Always mindful of the calendar and the cycles of the moon, I had only about three weeks before I became the monster again.

I was in northern Illinois, just south of the Wisconsin border, and decided to stop for gas and to get something to eat. I remember that I had not left St. Louis as early as I had hoped, and because it was getting late in the afternoon, I was considering getting a room for the night. After filling the tank, the attendant offered me directions to a local butcher about three miles down State Street. I was told that I couldn't miss it.

One of the problems that lycanthropes experience is the need to consume so many calories, that eating in front of people will only serve to draw unwanted attention. No, we don't eat like animals, but an individual who takes in as much as ten thousand calories in a single sitting is bound to draw notoriety. With this in mind, I generally do not eat out, preferring instead to order half a dozen pizzas or something else in an equivalent portion as carryout. In this case, however, I simply ordered my usual—twelve New York Strip steaks, cut one and one-fourth inch thick, and five pounds of ground beef.

After thanking the butcher, I exited and proceeded toward my car. As I stepped outside, the hair on the back of my neck rose and goose bumps became visible on my arms. I quickly placed my purchase in the passenger floorboard of my car before scanning my surroundings. I was unsure why, but my body had never responded like this before. My heart rate quickened, my muscles became tense, and a huge amount of adrenaline was released into my bloodstream. It seemed as though my body knew something that my mind did not.

My eyes searched the street frantically, but saw no one of interest, just people going about their lives. I smelled the air, filtering through all the odors that the busy street carried: automobile exhaust, perfumes worn by people walking around and upwind of me, trash both on the street and disposed of in receptacles, the smell of fried food that drifted for as much as two miles in the wind, the strong copperlike odor of blood coming from the butchery that I had only exited moments ago, even the sewer that existed like a living thing beneath the street. Suddenly, I detected a very faint inhuman scent coming from upwind. Apparently, my subconscious mind had detected this scent before my conscious mind was even aware of it. I realized that whoever or whatever I had picked up on was not on this street with me but possibly some distance away. It also occurred to me that it was possible that my presence there had not yet been detected by whatever supernatural being that I shared the proximity with (this was assuming that this being possessed sensory levels equal to my own). This, of course, left me wondering what I should do—investigate what I had discovered, and possibly stumble on to something I would later wish I had left alone or I could simply get into my car and depart the city of Rockford as quickly as I had entered it.

Again, I allowed my nostrils to take in and examine this strange scent. What can I say about it? How could I possibly describe something so intangible? It is an issue I have had some difficulty with since beginning this written work. It is simply not possible to offer a description about something so complex, so multidimensional, and such a fundamental part of life as I experience it now. Ah, take my word for it. It was a beautiful scent, and I wanted to know what it was. And so, foolish as it may have been, I decided to follow it and see where it led me.

I locked my car and proceeded on foot several blocks down the street. By the way, it is not as easy to track a scent as one might believe. Dogs make it look much less difficult than it actually is. This is true at least as far as my humanlike form is concerned. Sure, anything is easy enough to detect, but with a breeze blowing and other odors getting in the way, tracking the origin of a particular scent is quite difficult and requires some patience. I turned left on to one of the northbound streets, and slowly walked toward what appeared to be several empty buildings. I was alert and on edge the whole time, expecting something to jump out at me at any moment. I was still too much a pup to understand that technically, I was trespassing onto a claimed territory.

As I turned and examined the area, it occurred to me that this was not likely the nice part of town. I stood before a three-story brick building; the weathered sign that hung over the center of the building read Martin Tool and Dye. Beneath the sign, a long row of windows, many of which had been broken, and in the corner, steps leading to a locked steel door. Clearly, whoever or whatever I had been tracking was in this building.

Again, I began questioning what I should do. The locked door would have presented little challenge for me if I wanted to tear through it, and yet, even I knew that such an act would have demonstrated a rude audacity on my part. For an instant, I considered walking away, only to disregard that notion as I had already seemingly committed myself by coming this far. I circled around to a narrow alleyway between this building and the next seemingly abandoned building. Several small windows in the same condition as those in the front of the building also lined this side. Without proper thought or hesitation, I lifted one window open and quickly slid inside.

The inside of the structure was even less remarkable than the outside—a couple of chairs and tables, some colorful graffiti on the walls, and an impressive amount of settled dust covering everything. It was difficult to determine, but I estimated that this building had sat empty for as long as twenty years.

"Hello!" I called out, hoping to hear a friendly response in return. However, I heard nothing except the sound of my own voice bouncing off the walls of this all but empty building. Still, I was well aware of the fact that I was not alone in this building, and I knew also that whoever was here with me was quite aware of my presence as well.

I cautiously advanced toward a stairwell leading to the second floor. Allowing my senses to scan every sound, scent, and sight as my preternatural abilities were capable, I slowly took one step after another. "My name is Caleb, and I have only come to talk!"

Reaching the second floor, I gazed into the thick darkness at the building's far end. Then suddenly, I detected the slightest hint of movement in my periphery. I turned quickly toward the movement while also retreating several steps away from it. Not twenty feet from where I had been standing, a workbench spanned the last third of the length of the otherwise wide-open room, the side of the room I was presently on. Sitting on the workbench, looking back at me, was a beautiful blonde woman wearing a long pink coat.

Clearly a lycanthrope, she appeared to be in her late thirties though, with our kind, it is virtually impossible to determine age based on physical appearance. She may well have been in her seventies or eighties for all I knew. I examined her lovely and delicate facial features and could not see any anger or animosity in her eyes, only a benign sadness that she attempted to conceal with the slightest hint of a smile.

I wanted to say something, but when I opened my mouth, I could not find the words. I must have appeared like a clumsy child to this woman who seemed to study me with her gaze with as much interest as I had with her. While I fully expected to find someone when I entered this building, I was ill-prepared for seeing someone so stunning and, at the same time, so strangely out of place in these surroundings.

"You know," she began, clearly sensing the struggle I was having to initiate a dialogue. "You must be quite bold coming here. Our kind doesn't necessarily always get along with one another."

"I don't know about bold. I'd say ignorant of protocol as it relates to our kind. Still, please accept my apologies. I meant no disrespect by my trespassing. I only wanted to learn who you were… possibly talk."

"You don't owe me an apology," she said. "In fact, I am very happy that you have come to find me." As she spoke, her smile broadened, revealing what appeared to be a kind and gentle disposition. Her emotions, though obviously blunted, seemed genuine, which led me to believe that she had been a lycanthrope for less then twenty years. But of course, what did I know?

"Do you live here?"

"Oh God no!" she said, amused at the idea. "I was aware of you when you were at the gas station. After that, I just watched you from a safe distance, but not safe enough, it seems," she said cheerfully. "After that, you simply followed me wherever I walked. This seemed as good a place as any if a confrontation was going to happen."

"I see."

She then slid off the workbench and approached me. She was like a

Barbie doll: tall, shoulder-length blonde hair, perfect features, and quite well dressed. She was very image of what I would consider a lady.

"My name is Trish," she said as she extended her hand to me.

There are people you come across from time to time who somehow click with everything you are. These relationships are unique as there is an instant chemistry that is felt. Trish and I immediately became friends, and in the years to follow, there would be times when she was the only friend I would have. In fact, I owe my very life to her. Ah, but again, I am getting ahead of myself.

Trish and I left the abandoned tool and dye building and returned to my car. As we walked, she spoke about this building and that building, what was once on this street, and how that street used to look, Rockford's history in general. She appeared to have a very intimate and personal understanding of how the city had changed in recent decades. I got the feeling while we walked, and in the days to come, that more than anything, Trish wanted someone to talk to, someone to share her story with. She seemed lonesome, desperate to offer a piece of herself to someone. Maybe, like me, there was only so much for her to offer to anyone not afflicted with our circumstance.

Unlike Myra, there was something so calming about her company. While I had the utmost respect for Myra, I never felt any sense of comfort while I was with her. In fact, I was quite afraid of her at times; and although I viewed Myra as a teacher, I was never certain that we would ever develop a true friendship. I am uncertain as to why I felt such a natural sense of peace with Trish, and not with Myra. When I made eye contact with Trish, she would smile at me, and seeing her smile brought a welcomed happiness. The only time I ever saw Myra smile was the morning after she had returned from her becoming, and even then, there was no sincerity in her gesture, only a mild attempt to comfort me.

Of course, until I met Trish, Myra was the only lycanthrope I had known. Every idea that I had about what others of our kind were like was based on Myra's coldness and detached nature. Now it's true that Myra was much older and therefore much less human, but Trish showed me that we didn't necessarily have to approach life with a "gloom and doom" mind-set.

To my surprise, Trish offered to let me stay with her while I was passing through. While I was quite pleased with her offer, she seemed equally happy for my company. I cannot pretend to know what was going through her mind or why she was as welcoming as she was other than simply suggest again that she was lonesome and wanting to talk to someone that she had something in common with. Although she had driven into town herself, she told me that she would retrieve her truck later, possibly the next day.

By the time we had reached my car and left Rockford, it was already six o'clock., and the sun would be setting soon. Trish lived on a large farm only about ten minutes outside of town; but despite this fact, she enjoyed a seclusion that seemed equivalent to that of Myra. It was as though we had driven into another part of the country with only a brief trip.

"Would you like the twenty-five cent tour?" she asked, still as cheerful as ever.

"Certainly," I replied.

The two of us strolled around and behind her impressive ranch-style home and proceeded to a large outbuilding, located some forty or so yards behind her home. There was also an impressive-sized red barn set off to the side. My nose and ears alerted me as to what was in the building we were walking toward before we arrived to look inside it. As Trish opened the door, I observed chickens, more chickens than I had ever seen before, settling in to roost for the night.

"My gosh!" I said. "How many are there?"

"About two hundred give or take. They're an ideal animal really: low maintenance, excellent producers, and relatively inexpensive." As she spoke, I could tell that she was proud of them. It almost seemed as though she was attempting to sell me on the idea of raising chickens.

"I guess I never really thought of them like that."

"Consider this," she said enthusiastically. "I get somewhere between 170 to 190 eggs every single day. Every three or four months, except during the winter, I butcher around a hundred roosters and maybe another twenty or thirty hens.

"The best part is that other than gathering the eggs, all I usually do is open the gate in the morning so that they can roam, then at dusk when they have all returned for the night, I close the gate to keep them safe from animals. Of course I make sure they have water and cracked corn too, but nothing that takes more than five or ten minutes at most."

"Well, I'm impressed!"

After closing the door on the side of the building and sliding the gate closed in the back, we walked over to the barn and went inside. Once in the barn, we were greeted by five more than friendly goats.

"You have your own milk goats," I commented.

"I do, and I usually get around three or four gallons of milk each day; and on occasion, I'll butcher them too. So as you can probably guess, I am at least not going to go hungry."

I watched as Trish knelt down and offered affection to her goats. I was quite speechless as I myself could think of nothing more than wanting to kill and eat them right there. Not only was she as tender with them as would a mother be to her child, but strangely, the goats had no fear of her. I wanted to ask how she as able to control herself but did not. I certainly would not have trusted myself to put my arms around and pet the goats or even the chickens for that matter.

After Trish secured the barn for the goat's safety, I retrieved the meat I had purchased from the butcher, and we went inside the house. Trish's kitchen consisted of a small table in the center, surrounded by large freezers and refrigerators—each well-stocked with poultry, eggs, milk, and one with beef and pork presumably not raised or butchered here.

There was really no need to bother with cooking the meat as far as I was concerned. I had actually long since gotten over the notion that meat should be cooked. As Myra had once told me, "It really doesn't even matter." Apparently, Trish had no reservations about how to prepare food either, or at least she didn't act like she cared. Either way, there was no stove or oven in the kitchen anyway. Of course, we are civilized—we do eat with knives and forks, and we do use plates. I am hoping to convey an understanding that just because we often choose to eat our meals uncooked, that we no not eat off the floor. And unless we are starving or are simply barbaric, we are perfectly capable of using utensils, despite what Hollywood may have demonstrated in cinema.

"So you live here alone?"

"I do now. My husband and son used to live here as well."

For a moment, the room became strangely quiet. I wanted to ask about her husband and son but was afraid of what I would learn. I quietly wondered if their fate was the same as the family I had killed less than a week earlier. Suddenly, an overwhelming sense of guilt seemed to tear into me.

Trish looked at me and must have guessed what I was thinking. "My son and his father live in Chicago now, and they are both doing very well."

I found some relief in the idea that her family was alive and well; as for my sudden guilt, I tried to suppress it, to bury it as deeply as I could. I was hoping that Trish was unaware of the change in my demeanor. However, it was as though the temperature in the room had dropped by several degrees, and when she looked into my eyes, I felt as though she could see right through me.

"If you don't mind me asking," I said, attempting to reestablish a more positive atmosphere. "What happened? I mean… why did they leave for Chicago?"

"Oh, that's a story for another day," she answered, still smiling. "Tell me, where are you from? Where are you headed?"

"I live outside St. Louis, but I don't really spend too much time there these days. Right now, I'm headed to Madison. There is an old man there named Arthur Denham that I am looking for. You don't, by chance, know this person?"

Trish nodded her head slightly while still smiling. "I'm assuming he's one of us?"

"Yes, I'm hoping that maybe, if he's still alive, he can answer some questions for me."

"I guess we all have unanswered questions," she said softly with a hint of sadness in her voice. I wondered about what she meant by that as it seemed that she had thoughts racing through her mind just as I did. Perhaps, she too, had demons that haunted her.

"So this is what you do? I mean, the farm thing?"

She smiled broadly. "I also dance."

"You're a dancer?"

"Yes, and I teach. I have a dance studio in Rockford." There was something that lit up in her eyes as she spoke. It seemed to me that I must have asked the perfect question because suddenly whatever ill thought had occupied her mind was now replaced with something that brought her much joy. "I began dancing when I was a small child, and I never stopped. It is the only thing I have ever felt good at. It is the only thing that has ever truly made me feel... alive."

It was so interesting. I was sitting across from this woman whom I had only met a few hours earlier, and yet I felt this intense closeness to her. I seemed to hang on her every word, and I observed and analyzed her every gesture. It was amazing really; she was the easiest person in the world to for me to develop feelings for.

I know it seems unrealistic, doesn't it? As I sat there, enthralled with her company, I wondered what she thought or felt. Something? Nothing? I may never know. Propriety, it seemed, was the one notion that prevented me from acting or addressing what I felt, and as such, it in turn prevented me substantiating one way or the other if those feelings were mutual.

"I don't suppose you dance?" she asked.

I smiled back at her. "I may have a long time ago, but I certainly wasn't graceful."

"Well, I don't know if you are in a hurry to leave or make it to where you are going, but if you would like to stick around, I would love to show you my studio tomorrow. And of course, you are welcome here as long as you would like to stay."

"I would like that very much," I replied.

"Excellent," she said, rising from her seat at the table. At this point, despite the volley of dialogue back and forth, we had both managed to consume every bit of the purchase I had made.

"It has been a long day. Would you like a glass of wine before retiring?"

"Yes, I would indeed," I answered.

She entered the pantry and brought back a bottle of 1973 Chateau Larose Trintaudon, a rather expensive bottle I would imagine. After pouring each of us a generous glass, she recorked the bottle and left it on the table. Before we drank, she held up her glass for a toast. "Here's to a lovely evening, and for many more to come." There was something in her expression that made me believe that she wished that she had toasted something differently or perhaps had said more. Either way, that expression quickly passed. "I have developed a rather peculiar habit each evening before going to bed. Do you like saunas?"

"A sauna? I've never actually been in one."

"Well, that's a shame. They're addictive actually, at least they are for me. I couldn't live without mine. I would love for you to join me—if you wish, of course."

Working together, we cleaned the kitchen in minutes. I then followed Trish into her basement, which actually had a very warm ski lodge feel to it. On one end was a bar with various liquors stocked on the shelves. Off to the side of the bar, a billiards table. It looked as though a game had already begun but had been temporarily paused.

"Are you any good at pool?"

"Not really," I said. "I was once beaten by a twelve-year-old girl."

"Wow!" Trish said laughing.

In the center of the basement, against one wall, an enormous fireplace rested, waiting for use. It is difficult to say, but I guessed that it hadn't been used in many years. On the opposite wall, a large whirlpool that, unlike the fireplace, appeared to have been used quite frequently. In the wall between the sauna and fireplace was a solid oak door. "What's behind there?" I asked.

"I'll show you later," was all she said.

As Trish removed the whirlpool cover, the smell of chlorine filled the basement. The sauna itself was in the corner, on the same side as the whirlpool. She set a timer on the wall, and within seconds, steam flooded the sauna and was contained only by the glass doorway. Then the most interesting thing happened, something I certainly did not see coming nor did I know how to take. Without giving it a second thought, Trish disrobed completely, gathered her clothes, and tossed them into a laundry basket in the opposite corner from the sauna.

You know, I was human once; and since I'm being honest, I can say that I generally didn't fare too well with the opposite gender. I could easily fill the pages of this book with the failures I have had in my dating life; I remain uncertain as to whether it would be considered a comedy or a tragedy. The truth of the matter was simple—I had absolutely no idea what women truly wanted. Of course they say they want someone who will treat them well and always be there for them, but they demonstrate this by choosing guys who will ultimately beat the piss out of them, take their hard-earned money, and essentially, use them until someone better comes along. Am I supposed to have sympathy for them? I used to, a long time ago. But now, I believe that they deserve everything they have coming.

Again, it seems that I have gone off on a tangent. Accept my apologies. I will add this one final note however; in the years following the ones I am currently writing about, I came to a point in life where I didn't *even* give a shit about how women felt, and suddenly, they seemed to flock to me. Ironic, isn't it? I was a nice guy: sincere and caring, and during that time, I was either very much alone or being taken advantage of. Then when there is a darkness that surrounds me, when I really don't care, when outside of sex, women are absolutely worthless to me—disposable, wouldn't you know it—I suddenly have my choice of women to take home every night of the week. What's more, even though they were fully aware that I was going to get rid of them the following morning, they continued to treat me like I was fucking royalty. No, I really cannot imagine why anyone would have sympathy for them.

But I'm writing about things that have yet to come in my story. The point I wanted to make before I distracted myself was that one would think that as a supernatural being possessing such heightened senses that I am capable of experiencing life and everything in the world in an almost godlike fashion, that I would have a fair understanding of what a woman in my presence wanted or intended. One would be sadly mistaken.

I watched Myra as she while completely nude moved throughout her house and even outdoors, never giving my presence a second thought. While nothing would have pleased me more than a romantic partnership with Trish, I was less than certain that this was what she had on her mind. Based on her nonchalant manner in which she removed her clothing, I believed that, much like Myra, there was simply no modesty within her. I wondered if all female lycanthropes shared this trait.

I watched as she entered the sauna and disappeared into the steam before closing the door. Her body was less muscular than Myra; Trish was quite lean, exceptionally toned, absolutely beautiful—everything you would expect an unclothed dancer to look like. After a moment,

I too undressed and joined her in the sauna. We spoke very little once inside. After about thirty minutes of perspiring, I was quite ready to exit. While I was somewhat tired before entering the sauna as I had driven a considerable distance that day, I was absolutely exhausted as I stepped out. She was right though. I could see how this sort of thing could become rather addictive.

The cool basement air felt so wonderful and inviting as I stepped into it. Trish then took my hand and led me into the whirlpool where we relaxed for another fifteen minutes.

"I cannot ever remember feeling so relaxed," I said.

When we got out of the whirlpool, she handed me a pink towel to dry off with. I then followed her upstairs and into her bedroom, which was, yes, pink.

"You must really like this color," I commented.

"Pink and sparkly," she said smiling.

We lay next to one another, and despite the very intimate setting we shared, there was nothing sexual that happened—much to my disappointment. Within seconds of closing my eyes, I was unconscious. The last thing I remembered was Trish's hand caressing my face.

THIRTEEN

I AWOKE IN THE most peculiar fashion. The midmorning sunlight blazed through the window and seemed to kiss the side of my face. Strangely, something seemingly annoying began scratching the other side of my face. My initial reaction to something like this would usually be to quickly smash whatever dared touch me. Fortunately for the small kitten that had climbed into bed with me and was currently sniffing my face, my reaction time was a little slow that morning. I slowly sat up in bed and examined the animal further. It appeared to be a couple months old, and like most kittens its age, its head was disproportionately large compared to the rest of its body. I picked up the small grey tabby and almost instinctively brought this miniature cat to my chest. I was reminded of a talk I had once with Myra in which she had commented on crushing a small kitten in one's hand and feeling nothing. As I held this future predator, I remember hoping that I would never sink that low, never lose that much of my humanity.

After a moment, the kitten began to squirm, and I gently placed it on the floor and watched as it scurried out of the room. Although I could smell Trish all around me, she had risen much earlier. I lifted her pink pillow and brought it to my face. Inhaling deeply, I attempted to capture her beautiful presence in my nostrils. As I sat in bed, I realized quite suddenly that the preceding night was the first since I had become a lycanthrope in which I wasn't tormented in my sleep by horrid and merciless nightmares. Mind you, that while all my sleeping hours are filled with horrifying images, they had been especially gruesome since the incident in Wyoming.

The fact that I could go a single night without a nightmare was absolutely nothing short of a miracle as far as I was concerned. As I questioned the cause of my miracle, I first considered the sauna and whirlpool experience from the evening before. While it's true, my body was as relaxed as it had ever been, I did not believe that this was the reason for my pleasant night of sleep. This, of course, left only one other possible explanation that I could think of—Trish. Was it possible? Could it be that Trish's presence ensured my first horror-free slumber in over three years? If I hadn't fallen in love with her already, I certainly did at that moment. I was quite anxious to see Trish and speak with her.

I crawled out of bed and walked toward the living room and kitchen. Listening carefully, I determined that there were two kittens and myself in house—Trish had evidently stepped out. Outside, the occasional crow of the roosters reminded me that Trish had let them out and that they were freely roaming. They were, quite possibly, the happiest chickens on earth.

As I entered the kitchen, I immediately detected the scent of fresh blood—not human of course but of poultry. I approached the table, and on it a large bowl with maybe thirty eggs and a plastic bag, its contents a freshly killed and prepared chicken. Maybe the rooster crowing outside was happy only because he was spared the fate of this particular rooster. There was also a note:

> Hey Caleb,
> I ran into town to take care of a few things. I will be back soon. I hope you enjoy breakfast.
> —Trish

I removed the bird from its bag, impressed by how well it was butchered and cleaned. I ran it under cold water at the sink and then consumed everything except the bones. Fortunately, werewolves don't have to worry about salmonella poisoning as we don't get sick. I then retrieved a large plastic mug from the pantry and, cracking the eggs seven at a time, swallowed them *Rocky* style from the mug. Doesn't sound appealing to you? Lycanthropes live in an almost constant state of starvation. There are very few food items that we would find unappealing. If you've ever gone for an extended time without eating—maybe a couple of weeks—then you might have a somewhat vague idea of what we endure each and every day of our lives. If you haven't, then don't fucking judge me, especially when you are probably too ignorant of anything outside of your pathetic and worthless life.

I left the kitchen and, while still undressed, walked to my car to retrieve another set of clothes from my trunk. From what I could tell, Trish's nearest neighbor lived nearly a mile up the road, so at least the sight of a naked man roaming around outside did not send some little old lady into cardiac arrest.

After shaving and showering, I got dressed and went for a walk. My mind seemed overwhelmed as thoughts raced through it. I tried to force all my concerns and issues into a box and simply enjoy the beautiful pre-Thanksgiving scenery offered in this part of the country. Unfortunately, it seems that there is no box that can contain such thoughts as my own. I thought about the family in Wyoming that I had killed and how I had avoided watching the news in fear that I hear of the story. It seemed unlikely, but the news media may air a story such as this even as far as northern Illinois. I then wondered about Arthur Denham. How difficult would it be to find this man? Was he even still alive, and if so, could he possibly help me? If there was a chance that he had something to offer, then why didn't Myra seek him out decades ago? It seemed that a cloud of futility was constantly hanging over my head. Finally, there was Trish, a woman that I hardly knew and yet felt an immediate and deep-rooted connection to. Who was this beautiful peculiar woman? I would learn, at least that much, soon enough.

As I was walking back down the dirt road toward the house, I noticed a white pickup pulling into Trish's driveway and parking next to my car. I hastened my stride though I attempted to appear as casual as I could. All these years later, I no longer seem to recognize what I was feeling then, but I was quite excited and at the same time nervous to speak with Trish.

"Hey there," she said to me as she pulled eight large pizzas from the passenger side of her truck. "Did you sleep well?"

"As a matter of fact," I began as she handed the pizzas to me and I followed her inside her house, "I slept better last night than I had in years."

"Well, I'm glad to hear that," she said smiling.

"No, you don't understand!" I said enthusiastically. "I didn't have nightmares last night. It was the most incredible thing!"

"Really?" she asked though clearly less excited than I.

Of course, I was assuming all along that Myra and I weren't the only lycanthropes that were haunted by malevolent dreams while we slept. But it did occur to me that Trish and I had a very limited exchange the day before, and while I had learned a great deal in a rather short period of time, most everything I believed about her was really nothing more than an assumption at this point. "You do have... dark dreams, don't you?"

Suddenly, the smile seemed to dissolve from her face, her features instantly reminding me of Myra—lifeless, cold, robotic. "Let's eat, shall we." Her tone was still pleasant, but I felt as though I had dropped and broken something of value. This was nothing compared to what would happen shortly however.

"Trish, did I say something wrong? Are you upset with me?"

"Oh, please don't think that. I have my demons that I deal with, just as you seem to have yours. I will tell you about them some time if you like. But for now, I'm very hungry." With that, a lesser degree of happiness than what I had been seeing came into her face. At that moment, just as with Myra, I felt that her smile was insincere, an attempt to put me at ease.

We immediately sat down at the table and began to eat. "Thank you for breakfast," I said. "It was very thoughtful of you. It was also the best chicken I can ever remember eating."

"Farm raised and free range is always better."

"I also met one of your kittens this morning."

"Ah yes, I probably should have warned you. I have two of them—Simon and Garfunkel. You probably met Simon. He is the brave one."

"So what have you been up to today?"

"Well, I volunteer a few days each week at the Rockford Pediatric Oncology Center."

"Really?"

"It's an inpatient center for children undergoing intensive radiation and chemotherapy. I help out there with whatever they need. Usually though, I just spend time playing with the children. Lately, I've been reading to them."

Deep inside me, there was a great swell of sorrow upon hearing this. Of course you know why. Do I really need to mention her name again? Actually, it is quite easy for me now, given that I have lost nearly all of my old emotional abilities. At that time however, I had been trying desperately to push Jessica out of my mind—at least during my waking hours. I guess in a lot of ways, I never really coped with Jessica's loss. In fact, the whole Alaska trip was really nothing more than an attempt on my part to run away from my feelings, from my pain. Interestingly really how my "disease" has taken all my pain away.

"Are you all right?" Trish asked.

"Yeah, I'm fine. I just... I just thought of my daughter is all. She actually died of cancer. It's been about five years now."

Trish stopped eating and offered all her attention to me. "I am very sorry for your loss. Children have always held a special place in my heart. It is the worst kind of tragedy when the world loses one so young."

"Well, it's odd really, but everything that has happened in my life, everything—becoming what I am, everything that I've done, even being here with you—all this is an indirect consequence of her death."

Trish listened closely as our talk took us from the uneaten pizza in her kitchen to the slightly more comfortable living room. I offered her the same story that I have provided the reader of these pages with maybe more detail to some issues and less to others. It was good to be able to speak to someone, to get these issues off my chest.

"There is one more thing I really need to tell you, something horrible that I have done." I considered omitting the events that happened in Wyoming but realized that there weren't many people who would understand what I was feeling, what I was going though. I could think of no human being that would understand my contingencies. I had hoped that Trish, because of the fate we shared, would understand. "Last week the monster killed an entire family—two young boys, their older sister, and their father in northwestern Wyoming." I did my best to fight the tears back, a task that, because of my lycanthropic condition, was easier for me than should have been.

It seemed that no amount of stoicism, however, could mask the disgust that became apparent on Trish's face. Considering what she had told me earlier about her fondness for children, there is little doubt that this particular confession had deeply impacted her. She tore her angry eyes from mine and rose to her feet before stepping toward and gazing outside her large living room window. Somehow, I had, in the moment before, shattered the conception of who I was in her mind. I knew that she was upset, but I had no way of knowing exactly what she was feeling in those minutes, those seconds that she had turned her back to me, facing the window instead.

"Trish, I understand if you loath me now. If you want, I will leave right now, and you will never have to look at me again. Please understand though, I never meant to hurt anyone... I thought I was far enough away!" I said, the emotion in my voice impossible to hide.

Trish offered no response, only her silence. After several moments of this awkward and uncomfortable stillness, I rose to my feet. "I will show myself out. Thank you for your kindness and your hospitality. And I am sorry for any problems I have caused while I was here." I turned and proceeded toward the kitchen door. My feelings at that moment were impossible to describe. Almost like winning the lottery but knowing that you accidentally destroyed the ticket. How does one describe how he feels after doing that?

"I read the story in the newspaper," she said, her attention still focused on some distant point in the far distance. "I somehow suspected that one of us was responsible for that atrocity. You cannot imagine how upsetting it is for me to learn that it was you." Her voice, without emotion, seemed to hurt me more than if she had yelled at me in anger. After a lengthy pause, she continued, "The article cited that an animal—a bear likely—was responsible for the killings. However, they also mentioned the murder of the children's mother."

I hated to offer anything further as I had already caused enough damage here, but at this point, I was committed. "I am sorry to say that there is some truth to that. She had survived the attack, and I came upon her the next morning. It was quite difficult for me, but I had no other choice. I only wish that I had had been offered the same mercy after my attack."

I watched the back of her head as she dropped it slightly and slowly nodded. Knowing that I had disappointed Trish and was most likely beyond forgiveness, I hung my head in sorrow and opened the kitchen door to step out into the garage.

"Please don't leave," she said.

I turned again to see her still facing away from me. "Trish, I understand that you must hate me for what has happened. I don't want to cause any further problems for you."

"I'm not angry. At least I'm not angry with you. I think you are a kind and gentle man, and that you don't deserve what you are going through." She then turned to face me, and with tears in her eyes, she quickly approached me and put her arms around me. We held each other for the longest time. Maybe there was something therapeutic about this. Maybe this was what my soul needed. Either way, I felt a large burden lifted from my shoulders.

"So you don't hate me?"

"Of course not. You are a good person, a much better person than I am. Let me show you something."

I followed her into the basement just as I had the night before. This time, she led me past the whirlpool and sauna and directly to the door that I had inquired about. When she opened the door, I noticed steps leading into a sub-basement. The stairwell was quite narrow but still easy enough to descend. There was nothing but absolute darkness when we reached the bottom of the steps.

Trish pulled a cord attached to a lightbulb that brought a very dim illumination to the dungeonlike room. The room was both dark and damp. I could smell the mold growing on the concrete floor and walls as well as a bleach cleaner that had been used some time ago to kill it. I could also smell Trish's scent in this room, quite strongly in fact. The room itself wasn't particularly large, maybe forty feet by thirty feet. The larger part of the room, maybe two-thirds, was separated from the rest by an immensely thick set of steel bars—like a prison for a gorilla on steroids.

"This is where I come when I changeover," Trish said. "It isn't too fancy, but it works."

"This is… impressive!"

"My husband built it for me. It was kind of a live-and-learn lesson for us. He built the first set using bars from a shark tank. You would have thought that if it was strong enough to hold off a great white shark, it would have sufficed against me, but that wasn't the case, and the wolf tore out of it rather easily. These bars are stronger than prison bars, and to date, I have had no further escapes."

"This looks like it would stop a truck."

"It would," Trish said.

As I turned to leave, Trish quickly grabbed me and put her arms around me again. "I am sorry that I was angry. I do appreciate your honesty with me."

"You don't need to apologize," I told her.

"Would you like to see the studio? I have a class in a short while."

Forty-five minutes later, Trish drove us into Rockford. "As a child, I did mostly ballet, but as I got older, I kind of grew into ballroom dancing. You say you're not much of a dancer, huh?"

"I'm afraid not."

"Well, you're in for a treat tonight. On Mondays and Thursdays, I teach my favorite American dance—the Viennese waltz. I would invite you to join, but the members of the class are fairly advanced."

"I appreciate that," I said laughing. "So what is a Viennese waltz, and what makes it different than a regular waltz?"

"Do you really want to know?"

"Not really," I said.

"Well, the Viennese waltz actually originated in Austria. It is similar to the English waltz in that it is danced to a three-quarter rhythm, but it is a little faster, a kind of gliding and flowing dance.

"You know, while most take my classes simply to learn to dance, several of my former students have gone on to work in Hollywood either in front of the camera or as choreographers for dance scenes in movies.

And others have gone on to work as dancers in touring shows, Broadway, Vegas, backup dancers for musicians, among other things."

Trish pointed out the building as we drove by it and into its parking area. Rockford Academy of Dance, the sign read. "I don't suppose there is any kind of Kung-Fu class available?"

"Not yet. Are you interested in teaching?" she said sarcastically.

The studio was quite beautiful inside, with three large dance classrooms, each with impressive polished hardwood floors. Each classroom had a full view mirrored wall, portable barriers, presumably to make one large classroom into two smaller classrooms, and a small waiting room with a window into the classroom. There were two classes already in progress—one with children, all girls, in pink leotards. Their instructor, a harsh-looking woman in her mid to late forties, wore black and reminded me of an evil movie villain. The waiting room for this class was filled with gossiping mothers and one absolutely uninterested father.

The other classroom had students that appeared to be rehearsing a high school musical play. There were about fifteen individuals inside, each dressed in gangster-style clothing. A play set in the Prohibition era perhaps.

Each classroom was acoustically solid—for lack of a better word. It was, of course, intentionally designed that way to provide quiet classrooms despite what was happening in another class, but I was amazed that even with my hearing, sounds from the other rooms were quite muffled.

I watched Trish teach her class while I sat alone as the only observer in her waiting room. To be completely honest, I really don't get into dancing and ordinarily couldn't care less about the Viennese waltz or any other ballroom dance for that matter (I would never tell Trish this, of course). Still, it was important to her, so I did my best to act enthusiastic and impressed about her class; it was an act she surely saw through.

Her class lasted an hour plus another thirty minutes of socializing with her students and other instructors. She introduced me to several of them, and from a distance, I overheard some of the ladies making somewhat flattering though still obscene comments about Trish's plans for me. I assume that Trish heard these statements as well as her preternatural hearing was no doubt comparable to my own, but she said nothing about it. I remembered smiling at them, and as we left, I winked in their direction.

"You really shouldn't encourage them," Trish said, apparently amused.

It was a beautiful studio and an interesting experience, but I'm sure I don't have to tell you that I was glad to get the hell out of there. On the drive back, Trish's mood seemed to be disappointed. At first, I figured that it was because I was less than interested in her dance class. As I contemplated how to approach the subject, Trish spoke. "Is there anything I could say that would make you want to stay here in Rockford?"

I was totally surprised by her question. "You want me to stay?"

"Not if you don't want to, but yes, I wish you would stay."

I wasn't sure what to say nor did I understand what and if there were implications behind her statements.

"I understand that you have things in your life that you need to do, but it isn't often that I feel so... comfortable with someone. just think that we somehow click."

"Well, I like Rockford, at least what I've seen of it, and I absolutely love your company. Actually, you're a person that I could see myself with—you would be the perfect partner."

Trish smiled. "Thank you for saying that."

"But I do need to take care of some things, to deal with those demons. After that, I don't know what I will do. Maybe I will take you up on your offer."

"Well, I'm going to keep trying to talk you into staying."

We arrived back at Trish's home, and I noticed as she removed her bright pink jacket and hung it up, her mood was still rather somber. Not knowing what to do, I approached her and put my arms around her. It felt wonderful to hold her.

"Would you like to learn about me?" she asked hesitantly.

"Yes, of course."

She proceeded to pour each of us a glass of wine, finishing the bottle we had began the night before. "My circumstances are quite unique. You see, unlike you and probably most others, I was never attacked by the wolf. I was given the opportunity and made the decision to become what I am."

"I don't understand."

"Well, I told you that I was a dancer from the time I was a child. But there is so much more to my story than that." Trish took a deep breath and paused as though looking for the words, looking for the perfect place to begin. "I married my high school sweetheart soon after graduating. My parents actually encouraged this marriage. They were quite old-fashioned and expected me to take on a traditional housewife role. I am sure that they were ultimately disappointed in my desires to do more with myself than to simply have dinner on the table when my husband returned home. But I figure, at least after I got married, they assumed that I would automatically conform to meet their expectations.

"To support us, John went to work for his father in construction, a job that his family somewhat expected him to go into anyway. I chose to go to college, however, and eventually earned my bachelor's degree in kinesiology.

"For a while I did odd part-time jobs while also teaching several classes at the Y. Eventually, I had saved up enough money to open my own studio." Finishing the glass of wine she had initially poured, she rose and reentered the pantry, bringing back another bottle. "Those were the happiest years of my life—at least that's what everyone believed," she said as she uncorked the newest bottle. "I was married to John, and he was a truly wonderful man, I had finished school, and I was doing the one thing in life that made me happy.

"It seemed that there was really only one thing missing in my life, but it wasn't missing for long. When I learned that I was pregnant, John and I moved out here. At the time, 'out here' was a little farther out then what it is now. Rockford has grown in the last twenty years. Anyway, the house wasn't much to look at when we first moved in, but that's where being married to a carpenter has its advantages.

"Todd was born on April 8, 1961, and it seemed that my life was perfectly complete. You would have thought I would have been happy. I put on a great act for everyone. I was like June Cleaver in the eyes of my family and friends. Even my parents were mildly pleased with me. Looking back, I cannot understand why I was so ungrateful, but

I'm a different person these days—so much so that I barely recognize the memories I carry with me. I know what's wrong with me now. As complex as that is, I am able to wrap my mind around it. But I honestly don't know what was wrong with me then. Hell, most women would have killed to have been in my place.

"While everything seemed perfect and picturesque on the outside, there was a kind of empty void within me. Of course it had always been there, but I figured that as soon as my life was arranged the way I wanted it, the void would be filled. My marriage, college, opening the dance studio, even the birth of my son—all this, an attempt to cover or bandage the canyon that existed in my heart.

"Don't get me wrong, I loved John very much and still do. And Todd, he was my whole world really. Of course, you already know how I felt about my dancing. And yet despite all this, I couldn't help but wonder if there was more to life—there had to be more. I began doubting all the things I had done, all the decisions I had made.

"I began going to church as I was told that what I truly lacked in my life was a relationship with God. Now bear in mind, John was absolutely oblivious to everything I was feeling. I would never have wanted him to know how depressed I truly was. He would have believed that it was somehow his fault—maybe it was.

"Needless to say, I really did not find that magical happiness that I had been promised, at least not at first. I had met and gotten to know many friends from church. There were times when John and I would even entertain guests from church in this very home.

"While John certainly supported whatever whim I decided to pursue—he assumed my interest in going to church was a whim—he really did not get into it that much, and eventually he stopped going altogether.

"I didn't really remember too much about the first pastor who was at the church when I began attending. I remember that he was dull and monotonous. Although he seemed friendly enough, he never really made any attempt to get to know his congregation. I cannot even remember his name.

"Then, for whatever reason, he left, and we received a new pastor—Michael Cass. He was a rather attractive man with a distinctive Southern accent. And like flies to honey, the women did certainly swoon for him. The fact that he as a man of God did absolutely noting to dissuade his female parishioners—young and old alike—from practically throwing themselves at him.

"There was something remarkably charismatic about him, something that I couldn't really identify or put my finger on. Susan, another housewife who attended church without her husband and usually sat next to me, would often say that he must have been an angel. I remember thinking that she would have probably left her husband and never given it a second thought if Michael were to ask her to. Interestingly, I used to think less of her for that. It's funny—we see in others what we most dislike in ourselves.

"Unlike his predecessor, Michael went out of his way to get to know everyone who sat in his pews. Not just a simple handshake, but he took a genuine interest in me—well, everyone actually.

"I'm not sure when it really began or why, but I began thinking about him. For a long time, it was just a minor Sunday infatuation. But soon enough, Michael began entering my thoughts every day of the week. You realize surely that these thoughts I was having were hardly the proper thoughts of a happily married woman toward her church leader. I'll be honest. I even fantasized about him when I was with John.

"But despite how awful that does sound, they were nothing more than thoughts. I never intended to act upon anything of that nature even if I did enjoy going to church more than I should have. While I was never really a deeply religious person, I had my morals." Trish laughed lightly. "Do you believe that?"

"Of course," I said.

"Well, I certainly believed I did. When my female church friends and I would talk, Pastor Cass was frequently mentioned. We certainly weren't Catholic, so it was strange that considering he was in his mid to late thirties, he wasn't married. It seems that all Protestant ministers are married—usually with rebellious kids. One of my friends even suspected that perhaps he was gay, but no one really believed that.

"Todd was about five years old when I began taking him to church with me. Although he was rather young to sit through a Sunday sermon, he did enjoy the day care that the church offered. One day, as I was picking Todd up from the play area after church, Michael approached me and softly put his hand on my shoulder. It was almost as though electricity flowed through me when he touched me, not in a bad way, but in a very excited way. He just wanted to talk for a minute and ask how I was doing. Although I had spoken with him briefly on a number of occasions, this was the first time that I really looked into his deep blue eyes. I remember thinking, that while he seemed a very happy man, his eyes seemed so sad—like a lonesome abandoned dog. It's funny, but that is what I was reminded of.

"Our exchange was brief, but I felt like I had learned so much about him in those few minutes. Watching him engage with Todd seemed to reveal his tender and gentle side. Michael lowered himself to one knee and spoke with him, shaking his hand before standing. Before I left, Michael told me that if there was anything I needed, even if I just needed to talk, not to hesitate to get a hold of him. I am certain that he said the same thing to every member of the church, offering the same gestures of concern, even touched others on their shoulders as he spoke with them. But as much as it may sound like the simple ravings of a stalker, we somehow... connected on that day.

"I don't know why, but I think I began to obsess about him. I would often chose my eyes and think about him. I relived the talk we had a hundred times in my head. On one occasion, I even called John by Michael's name."

While she spoke, Trish seemed to stare into the wall, almost as though she was watching a stage drama being played out, as if in a trancelike state. Occasionally, she would bring the wine glass to her lips and take the slightest sip. It was clear to me that her recount of things that had happened was more for her own sake than for mine.

She then looked directly at me. "Doesn't this sound crazy to you?"

"I don't know. It definitely sounds... human."

"I was out of control. Unhappy with my wonderful marriage, dissatisfied with my life in general, I wanted something more. And yet, I did not act on it, not until one day in early November when somehow my car managed to drive right by the church. A part of me hoped that I wouldn't see him and that I would just keep driving. Then there was the more audacious part of my mind-set, the part of me that seemed determined to destroy everything I had cherished in my life, all on an unlikely gamble. And of course, there he was, working outside—raking leaves.

"I made the argument that it was only polite to stop and speak with him, and so I did. He seemed very eager for the company though I don't think he had any idea of what I truly wanted or why I just 'happened' to show up.

"We went inside where he poured us each a cup of coffee, and then we just sat and talked for hours. It's funny—I honestly don't even remember anything that we talked about, but nothing was important except that we shared each other's company. You kind of remind me of him really—your mannerisms, you're both well spoken, and of course, the way you carry yourself with a degree of class.

"I've never really been a fan of period pieces. They often annoy me more than they entertain. However, it would be easy for me to imagine him in the midnineteenth-century London, a gentleman, and the same for you, considering the seemingly comparable similarities you share.

"I'm probably boring you with all this, aren't I?" she asked as she looked at me. It seemed that she may have also been blushing.

"Not at all," I answered, uncertain if maybe the wine was contributing to her story. "Please proceed."

"Anyway, I don't wish to go into the details of what transpired, not that I really need to, I suppose. Michael and I began an affair that afternoon that lasted for almost two years.

"How nice it would have been if that were the end of my story. I would love to tell you that because of this or that, we both decided to go our own separate ways, and we were both the better for it. But that isn't even close to the truth.

"I always knew that there was something different about him, something that set him apart from everyone else I had ever known. Then one day, he felt compelled to offer me insight as to what he was. I'm sure there is no need to describe to you what he told me about himself, but for the sake of clarity, he informed me that he had been cursed by God with lycanthropy.

"My reaction to his declarations was also quite predictable. I felt that this was a very juvenile and stupid way to end our affair. It seemed to me that if he wanted to break up, which he did say was in our best interest, then he shouldn't have offered something so outrageous as this. He insisted, however, that what he had told me was true, which served only to make me even angrier with him. Reluctantly, I drove with him to a place he owned about sixty miles north of here—out in the middle of nowhere in Wisconsin. There was something there he wanted me to see.

"The house looked like something a serial killer would live in—unattended and practically falling apart. There was farmland all around—empty fields during the winter months. One could see someone coming for miles before they arrived. If he had been anyone else, I don't believe that I would have followed him into his basement, considering the crazy talk he had given me. In the basement he showed me a less than perfectly designed giant cage. He told me that it was for him when he became the wolf. Apparently, it was no longer sufficient to hold him as he had evidently broken out during the previous cycle.

"Still unable to believe his story, I began to give more credence to the notion that maybe he was a very disturbed, very sick man. I began to wonder just what I had gotten myself into. I should note that I had fallen in love with him almost immediately after our coffee date I had mentioned a moment ago. Michael wasn't just some lunatic that I had just met and didn't yet know fully. He was a man that I known and loved for a considerable time and would have gladly married myself if under different circumstances.

"While still in the basement, we sat down and talked for a long time about his condition. He told me everything about what he was and how he was and had been a vessel of evil. He told me about how he wasn't able to feel things the way he once did. He spoke of his ability to restore and regenerate damaged tissues. To my horror, he withdrew a knife, and before I could stop him, he plunged the blade deeply into the inside of his elbow then dragged the blade to his wrist, creating the most gruesome and bloody wound I had ever seen.

"The whole scene was surreal and completely terrifying to witness. Here was a man I loved who had just lost his mind and was now mutilating himself. I didn't know whether to run from him or to stay and try to help him.

"When he had finished with the knife, he tossed it to the floor and brought his badly injured arm to face me so that I could see the extent of what he had done. I didn't know. It looked pretty human to me, and he was clearly losing a lot of blood. He never moved from the chair he had been sitting in while we were talking. He just sat there, telling me that everything was going to be fine. 'Just be patient, watch and see,' he told me.

"I begged and pleaded with him to come with me to the hospital. He had severed an artery, and blood spilled from his arm to the floor almost as quickly as you could pour it from a glass. I remember that I backed myself into a corner, sat down on the floor, and began crying. Michael did his best to comfort me with his words, and eventually, his arm did stop bleeding. Although it still definitely needed medical attention, it didn't seem that he was going to bleed to death anyway. Still visibly upset about what he had done to himself, we left his isolated home and drove back to Rockford. Before we left, he had wrapped a dirty old rag around the wound, telling me that it wouldn't be possible for him to get an infection. He told me that he had done this because it was the only way to prove to me that what he was saying was true.

"When we finally got back to his Rockford home in the late afternoon, all I really wanted to do was to go home myself, to get away from him for a while. I needed time to absorb the insanity that I had been listening to and watching. He promised to let me go if I could just have one more look at his arm. I protested as I absolutely did not wish to look at his mangled arm again, but he insisted. Pulling away the nasty rag tore some of the scabbing, which actually caused it to begin bleeding lightly again. But after watching him run the arm underwater, I was astonished by what I saw.

"While I wasn't quite ready to accept the werewolf story he offered, the wound on his arm was not the same wound he had inflicted upon himself ninety minutes earlier. In fact, it was little more than a scratch really. Well, at least he finally had my undivided attention.

"I decided to stay with him for dinner. I always thought it was strange that he so rarely ate anything despite the church barbeques that he attended. Well, the fact of the matter was, as you and I both well know, he ate a lot. He must have consumed fifty or more hot dogs and at least a dozen cans of soup. He was still eating when I left and went home.

"Before I left that evening, I could see no trace of the awful wound from earlier that day. To me, this was the closest thing to a miracle I had ever seen. My mind automatically began to envision ways of utilizing this miracle, making it practical. If even a fraction of what he told me was accurate, he may have held the cure to cancer, disease, birth defects, you name it.

"To Michael, this was not a miracle, but rather an abomination of God. He tried to serve God the best way he could, but ultimately, he saw himself as an evil thing, not worthy of mercy. I refused to believe that this man—the most patient and kind man I had ever known—had anything evil within him. But that was that. His self-conception was well established and wouldn't be changed. He told me that he loved me and wanted to share this terrible secret with me, hoping that I would not forsake him for it. I think what he really wanted was someone to confide in, the same thing that we all want.

At that point, the intimate part of our relationship had ended. He offered his apologies, apologies that I never accepted because I never felt that he had done anything wrong. He was his own absolute worst enemy—constantly beating himself up and always expecting more of himself than what he gave.

"Despite the change in the nature of our relationship, I deeply cared for him. I still deeply loved him. We remained close friends for the next eighteen months. During that time, I watched as the man I had so admired and respected seemed to become someone I didn't recognize.

"Years earlier, when he had first come to Rockford, he was deeply caring and compassionate. Yes, he was always quite reserved, which I had always thought was one of his interesting and more appealing traits, but by now, he was nothing short of apathetic. He told me that this was a part of his disease, that he wanted to care, but simply could not. He wanted to 'feel' things, but he told me that there wasn't much left within him that could feel.

He had begun to describe the world as a painting—once colorful and beautiful, but now dull and unremarkable. Isn't it interesting?" Trish said, turning to me for a moment before resuming her stare into whatever void had her attention. "Almost cruelly ironic, that we experience everything in the world—all the otherwise inaudible sounds, the extreme spectrum of colors, aromas and scents that no one else can, even flavors that seem to explode on our tongues—all this, and yet we cannot appreciate the beauty of the world. Being able to experience life in this way but losing the ability to feel emotion, it is nothing short of tragic."

While she expressed her sentiments in a way that I had never thought of, I was in total agreement. The older we become, the more we appreciate what we have lost, the more alien those emotions we once felt seem as well.

"Finally, one day he was gone. It was quite the story around town really. He just seemed to pack up and leave in the middle of the night. There were rumors that he had done something illegal and was on the run from authorities, that he had run off with some woman, and that he had been killed and his body was buried in the woods somewhere. These are the kinds of rumors that you would expect about a well-loved pastor by his congregation, right?

"I didn't really know what happened to him, but I certainly didn't believe the outrageous things that were being said. It wasn't until almost a month after he had gone that I received a letter from him, still apologetic, though this time I felt I deserved one.

"In his letter he stated that he had drifted too far from humanity, too fast. He felt that it was in everyone's best interest that he be alone from this point on. He believed that he could no longer perform God's work in his present detached state. He wished me the best of luck with everything in life, promised to pray for me, but asked that I not contact him.

"I was relived to learn that he was not buried somewhere in the woods but upset that he felt that he needed to run away from what was plaguing him. He had tried to talk to me about what he was experiencing, but I'm sure that I was little help as I wasn't really able to understand. I guess it wasn't like he could just go to a shrink and spill his problems with them either. There was an overwhelming sense of helplessness that I felt when listening to him explain his loss of humanity. It was almost like watching someone die from and incurable disease over weeks and months, knowing that there is nothing you can do to help."

"Well, I understand that this is the expected thing to happen," I said, referring to his loss of emotion. "But it seems to have overtaken him prematurely or at least much less gradually than it should have."

"I don't know. Maybe it affects each of us a little differently."

Strange really, how until that moment, I had never really considered that notion—that our lycanthropy had affected us each in different ways. I did consider Arthur Denham's unique circumstances, the fact that he had never lost his humanity. If this was the case, as reason implied, then there would be nothing to be gained by seeking Mr. Denham's help.

"Anyway," Trish said, "I assumed that he was simply a wonderful part of my life that inevitably was to be lost, kind of like a grandparent that passes away. I went on with my life, just as would be expected—with family and work being what I devoted my energies to.

"Until then, the dance studio was certainly underutilized, almost a hobby for me really. I hired other dancers that taught everything from swing to tap and offered more classes to a much broader clientele, including the most lucrative group—children.

"Todd was in the second or third grade, and I became a soccer mom and a PTA member, all exciting stuff," she said sarcastically. "John, who by the way had absolutely no idea of my relationship with Michael, wanted another child. Unfortunately, after several visits to my doctor, I learned that I would not be able to have any more children. As sad as that news was for me to accept at the time, it was for the best.

"All was going well though, more or less, until December 23, 1969. That is when my life forever changed. I was at a party, had too much to drink, and decided to drive home. John, who was also at the party, left early as he really wasn't much of a party person anyway. As I was driving home, I lost control of my car and drove head-on into an unforgiving tree.

"You would never guess it by looking at me now, but this face was put directly through my windshield at around sixty miles per hour. Even John was unable to recognize me due to the severity of the injuries to my face. But believe it or not, my face was really the least of my problems. My spinal cord had been severed in three places, the highest being at C6 level.

"I certainly wasn't an expert in spinal cord injuries, but I knew enough—I was fucked! When I woke up in the hospital, I remember them telling me that I wouldn't be able to walk again. I was either on one too many medications or had a more extensive brain injury than I had suspected because this news didn't really seem to bother me initially. 'I'll be able to dance though, right?' I asked them.

"After months in the hospital, I came home mostly because John refused to accept the idea of me being in a nursing home. He was such a good man and certainly didn't deserve someone like me. Not only was I incapable of being a good wife in any sense of the word, but I had been unfaithful to him as well. I had always felt a sense of guilt for that, but now it was consuming me.

"I was in such a deep depression that I wanted to kill myself. I just lay there all day and night, being turned every couple of hours so as to prevent bed sores, which I got anyway. The nurses that would take care of me during the day would try to get me up and have me sit in the chair, but I refused them usually.

"Even my son was afraid of his mother now and didn't want to come into the room to see me. Do you have any idea what that felt like for me? Can you even imagine how awful life is when you rely on others for even the most basic needs? Do you know how dehumanizing it is when you don't even have control of your bodily functions? No, I begged to die. I begged John to have mercy and end my suffering—he wouldn't. He told me that he would do *anything* I asked him, just not that.

"I'm not sure at what point my mind came up with this... insane idea. I'm sure by now you've already guessed what it was. Since there seemed no practical way of making use of Michael's gift—at the time, I ignorantly considered it a gift—I was fully prepared for impractical measures.

"I didn't know how this worked, but I knew that it would require John's help, and for that I would have to tell him the truth about Michael. As you can imagine, this was not an easy talk for me to have with him. It's probably a good thing that I was already paralyzed as there was really nothing more that he could have done to me.

"He was angry, and he said some very hard things to me that I absolutely had coming. I knew that I hurt him terribly. I wanted to throw my arms around him, hold him as tightly as I could, and tell him how sorry I was. But I couldn't do any of those things, so I just lay there like a slug, crying.

"Eventually, John had calmed down slightly and asked why I wanted to see Michael now. I told him the crazy reason why, and he looked at me like I was the stupidest human being on earth. No one could really blame him, considering the nonsense about werewolves and their ability to heal up all nicely. I played the only card that I had—I reminded him that he promised to do anything for me.

"After much conflict, John reluctantly agreed to comply with my wish. A week later, when the moon was full, we made the ninety-minute drive to the desolate-looking building that Michael had been calling home.

"As you might imagine, Michael was not at all pleased to see John and I showing up unannounced on his doorstep. 'You don't *even* know what you're asking from me!' Michael shouted when I told him my plan.

"'Look at me!' I pleaded with him. 'You have the power to fix this! You have the power to heal me!'

"'I don't have any such power! Whatever it is that I have, it is not of God, but of Satan. You do not want this cloud hanging over you!'

"'Michael, you're my only hope!'

"Michael took a deep breath and closed his eyes for a moment. When he opened them again, I saw the gentle and kind-hearted man that I knew was still somewhere in there. 'Trish, it breaks my heart to see you like this, and I would do almost anything to give you back what you have lost, but even if it would work, and I don't know that it will, there is such an enormous price to pay for this.'

"'Please, Michael, I beg you! I beg you! I beg you! Please help me!'

"I honestly do not know why he changed his mind, but there were no words that could have expressed my appreciation. That night, he locked himself within his reinforced steel cage while John and I waited for him to become the werewolf.

"When it happened, it was the most frightening thing we had ever witnessed. The massive beast seemed almost in a frenzy trying to get to us. John immediately abandoned our agreement and lifted me from my chair and tried to carry me up the steps and out of the basement.

"'No!' I screamed at him. 'Take me back now!' But John wasn't about to listen to me. Since there was no other way to physically resist John, I did the only thing I could to stop him from carrying me away—I bit him as hard as I could, sinking my teeth into his chest until blood ran down my chin.

"After another heated exchange between him and me, he returned me to my chair and cautiously rolled me toward the hideous thing in the cage, desperately trying to tear its way out and get to us.

"At that point, everything happened very quickly. The monster clawed at my face and hair, and once it got a hold of me, it savagely yanked me from you chair and pulled me toward him. I slammed abruptly into the steel bars, breaking a couple of ribs in the process before he bit into my arm, viciously tearing away my left triceps. It would have certainly killed me if John hadn't jabbed a broken broomstick deeply into its neck.

"This distracted the wolf monster only long enough for John to pull me from its grip, tearing a huge portion of my hair out in the process. I watched as within seconds, the monster had removed the broom handle from its neck and healed up almost instantly. Evidently, we heal even faster when we become the wolf than we do otherwise.

"The last thing I asked my husband for was to not take me to the hospital but to let me lie on the floor. I don't know what happened after that as everything went black. The next memory I had was with me in bed, kind of half in, half out of consciousness. John and Michael were both there, though hardly friends with one another. I can't remember much, but I do remember moving my hand. As I dozed off again, I knew that it had worked. That was the last time I saw Michael.

"In the weeks to come, the miracle I had hoped and prayed for had not only come true but had also given me a lease on life that I could never have dreamed possible. I not only walked but could also outrun an Olympic sprinter. I was strong, even stronger than my husband. I could see and smell and hear things that were always around me but I never knew existed.

"To the astonishment of everyone I knew, I returned to work and began right where I left off. In fact, I was even better then I was before. When anyone would ask how I managed this, I would simply tell them that it was a miracle and best left accepted for what it was and unquestioned.

"Todd was still scared of me but was slowly warming up to his new and improved mother. As for John, well, what can I say? We enjoyed the best sex of our lives, and more of it than he or I had ever had.

"So my life was perfect, right? Well, actually, it was pretty damn close at least for a few weeks. But then, the inevitable occurred. During the time after my recovery, John had constructed a prison similar to the one Michael had in his basement. I locked myself up just as Michael had, and John and Todd left for the evening.

"I thought I was prepared for what was going to happen to me. I had had long talks with Michael about what it was like. I had even witnessed it for myself when Michael changed right before my eyes. But I had no idea what pain truly was until that first time I changed over. Human beings were never meant to experience that much pain, but then again, we're not human beings.

"Apparently John had underestimated the power that the wolf monster could generate as I ripped the bars from the concrete then destroyed much of the house as I went though it. During the next month, John prepared the basement room to its present condition, and I've never broken out since."

"So what happened with you and your husband? It sounded like things were maybe going well."

"I do believe that he had come to a point where he had accepted what I had done and forgave me for it. Still, I think that in his mind he questioned whether I could be trusted again. If I came home a little late from teaching a class or if I was talking to someone on the phone he didn't know, he never said anything, but the subtle expression on his face was always there—suspicion. He truly did want to make the marriage work, but everything unfolding as it had injured him in such a way that it would always bother him. But the reason he ultimately left had little to do with Michael. He was unable to accept the wicked and horrible thing that I had become."

"Do you believe that you are a wicked and horrible thing?"

"I certainly do."

"I can't believe that. You're practically the salt of the earth. You read stories to children with cancer for God's sake!"

"It's all about compensation," she said. "Michael was right about a lot of things. I did gain the ability to walk and dance again, and who could put a price on that? But I sold my soul in the process. How much did I love when I was human? How much did I love my son? How much less did I love him when I woke up a lycanthrope? How much do I really love him now? Sure, I can say the words. I can say them all day long, but how much meaning is still there?"

I couldn't argue with that. I considered Jessica and how I felt about her. If the pain of her loss was an expression of the depth of my love for her, and I felt less pain than I once did, especially since becoming what I am, does that mean that I have lost a certain amount of love for her? Would it be possible that at some point in the distant future, I cease loving her altogether? At that time, I couldn't imagine a more unacceptable notion. But less than three months ago, I found myself at her grave site, and yet I felt nothing. But we'll come to that in time.

"John left with Todd about eight years ago. I guess he figured that it wasn't necessarily healthy to raise a child with something like me in his life or at least in his home. I miss them and wish they were here, but I know it's for the best. Every once in a while, I will make the trip to Chicago and see them. Todd graduated from high school last year, and I was so proud of him. He wants to become a fireman. I think he'll be great at it.

"But that's my story. Now, I live my life with as much simplicity as I can, trying to hold on to as much of who I was as I can, for as long as I can. I can say that I am not unhappy, just very much alone in the world."

"Trish," I said, "promise me that we will always be friends."

"That is an odd thing to ask," she replied.

"I don't really have so many friends these days. It seems that I have buried or abandoned the majority of them. I too feel alone in the world."

"Then we have that in common, but at least we're alive," she said. "Caleb, I promise I'll always be here or there for you if you ever need me. Just please don't bury or abandon me."

I smiled at her and she returned the smile. I poured myself a glass of wine from the mostly consumed bottle on the table. "Friends forever," she said as we toasted.

We were both quiet then as I leaned back in my chair and began to stare off into the same void that had held Trish's attention all this time.

FOURTEEN

TRISH WAS ESPECIALLY affectionate with me the morning that I left. She tended to her animals, but beyond this, she did not leave my side. As I gazed out the window, reflecting on the events and conversation of these past days, Trish approached me from behind and put her arms around me while resting her head on the back of my shoulders. I certainly did not discourage these little moments of tenderness. It may be difficult to believe, but I had never been touched like that before. I cannot ever remember a time before or since that I can honestly, truly say that I was wanted. In *every* other experience I have ever had with the opposite gender, I felt that they were either using me or that I was simply using them.

I packed what few items I had brought in back into the car. "You don't have to go," Trish said, pleading with me right up to the last minute. She did not cry or tear up (I don't know that she was even able to by this point), but her blue eyes revealed waves of emotion that she maintained behind a seemingly impenetrable dam. I wanted to ask her why she wanted me to stay, but I did not—perhaps I was afraid of what she would say. I only returned her sad gaze, considered offering comfort of some sort but decided against this too.

I drove away, watching her slowly disappear in the mirror. I told myself that I would be back soon while feeling all along that I was quite possibly doing the one thing that she asked me not to do—abandoning her. Yes, I do hate myself for that.

The drive to Madison was faster than I had imagined. Ordinarily, I would listen to the radio on such a drive, but on this trip I relived in my mind the events from the previous night.

After finishing the bottle of wine, we retired to the den where we continued discussions of lesser significance. We sat together on her sofa with a fair amount of alcohol streaming through our veins and the music of Pachelbel, Chopin, and Rachmaninov filling our ears from her record player. I remember she was speaking about her childhood memories with her grandparents. There was something very human in her voice as she spoke. She then slowly and deliberately put her hand on my shoulder and turned to gaze directly into my eyes, into the depths of the abyss that is my soul.

I needed no further invitation; I moved forward to kiss her. I think she attempted to pull away at the last second, but I pulled her toward me forcefully, and she—we both surrendered completely to each other. It was a moment of intense passion that we somehow stretched to cover the entire evening.

We made love three times before the sun offered even a suggestion that it would rise. Afterward, she slept soundly, resting her head on my right arm with her back to me. My body was exhausted and wanted to sleep, but my mind forbade it. Instead, I listened to her breathe deeply, wondering if maybe her dreams took her to happier places than mine take me. Occasionally, I offered sweet kisses to her neck and back, tender sentiments that she would never know about because she slept. But it was for my sake that I offered this affection, for I was absolutely enthralled with this woman.

I needed her; I needed her as surely as I needed food, water, and air. My mind tends to build walls, compartmentalizing anything foreign and irrational. While I loved the company Trish offered, the feelings that I was experiencing were certainly foreign to me. As for love, it is absolutely irrational; it is, however, a beautiful irrationality that I may have found as frightening as I did inviting. As I look back on that situation, I know for a fact that I was afraid of what I was feeling. Yes, I needed her; I didn't know that I needed her, however, until I was gone. It seemed that the ninety-minute drive to Madison was the beginning of an extremely low point in my life.

So why did I leave? I honestly don't know. I could offer something lame and inexcusable, but why waste my time? I think that I assumed that I had time on my side, that I could go, do what I needed to do to satisfy the questions I had then could return and pick up where I left off. If it were possible for me to go back in time and change decisions that I had made, I would absolutely have chosen to remain with her. Here was a beautiful blonde woman who wanted me to stay with her, someone who would understand the complexities of the life I was now cursed to live, someone who I could tell my deepest fears, offer my most lofty hopes and aspirations, the most perfect companion I could imagine. And yet, I was on a mission, like a deranged man on some fool-hearted quest into the great unknown.

Is it possible to fall completely in love with someone after knowing them only a couple of days? I've argued with myself over this notion for many years now. I had known my ex-wife for what would be considered a traditional amount of time before proposing—a little less than a year. And yet, I never loved her, and I was well aware of this when we walked down the aisle. Maybe being in love with someone has less to do with how long you've known them and more to do with simple chemistry and raw compatibility. I don't know. I'll leave that debate to the philosophers and the poets. As far as I was concerned, when I left her house that day, I was deeply in love with her.

I arrived in Madison, and for the next several weeks, I searched for and eventually found evidence of the man I had been looking for, the man that had, decades before, called Madison his home. I even hired private investigators to continue the search in a more professional manner. It seemed that Arthur Denham was an educator, the dean of a small but prestigious prep school during the late forties after the war.

I learned that he had purchased and sold a number of properties during that time, that he had amassed a sizable fortune though it was unclear how he came into those funds, and that he married a woman named Juliet Casper in 1937. According to documents, he also reputedly had three children, which would have been impossible as lycanthropes cannot have children.

At first, I thought perhaps I had located the wrong person. Maybe there was more than one Arthur Denham in Madison at that time. However, I knew that I was at least on the right track when peculiar irregularities concerning the life of this individual were becoming apparent upon deeper inquiry and research. For starters, though there were three children, two of them seemed to be nothing more then ghosts—other than birth certificates and the fact that they were named in a will by Mr. Denham, there is no other proof that there were such people. It seemed that they existed on paper only.

Upon the supposed death of Arthur Denham in 1964, his assets were divided among his three children in his will. Within two years, two of the siblings had also died, leaving their property and assets to the third whose name was Jacob Denham. Unlike his possible fictitious brothers, Jacob Denham left a paper trail every bit as unusual as his father before him and a signature that was just a little too familiar. The investigators that I had hired were deeply puzzled by what they had learned but eventually dismissed everything due to poor recordkeeping. I believed, however, that Arthur and his son Jacob were one and the same individual, and that he had devised a clever way of operating over a much longer period of time while maintaining his acquisitions.

Unfortunately, everything that had been uncovered had led to dead ends. It was like working a maze that had no exit. Even the information that we did find was old and questionable in validity. It seemed that I had reached the end of my search; and while I knew the odds of finding this Arthur Denham were poor, I felt that I was so close. I had walked down the same streets that he had walked, visited the same parks, even explored the lavish homes that he had once lived in.

Then finally, after almost three months of fruitless leads and unproductive searches that amounted to little more than educated guesswork, I caught a break. One of the higher-priced investigators came across information leading to a paper trail, an old one but something solid nonetheless. From what I could ascertain, Arthur had made a habit of dying every so many years and leaving his considerable wealth to whoever he would become. It appeared that he found a perfect way to legitimately operate within the public eye for a long, long time without raising an eyebrow as to why an impossibly old man would still be paying taxes.

It took some work and a fair amount of financing, but I eventually followed Arthur's ghost from Wisconsin to New York and finally to Vermont, where it seemed that he operated under the name of Arthur Matsko. The address I had, along with a truckload of information about Arthur, indicated that he was now operating a boarding school of some sort. So that is where I decided to head.

I flew into Montpelier and stayed there for the night. I would hop onto a bus the following day and finally meet this man named Arthur. I was strangely excited and nervous at the same time. As for that night in the state's capital, I rested my mind fully aware of the nightmare that would come for me, but I wasn't quite prepared for its theme.

I found myself standing in a familiar driveway, looking at a familiar house, with no real idea of how I got there or what my intentions were. All I knew at that instant was that I did not immediately recognize where I was, but I knew that I should have. Then suddenly, I was made aware of the most beautiful scent in the world; this welcoming fragrance could only belong to the most beautiful woman in the world. Only then did I know that this was Trish's home and that I had returned to visit her.

My mind was not working as quickly as it should have been. Was this a dream? I looked around at my surroundings, the soft moonlight, the shadows cast by everything in that moonlight, the summer breeze gently whipping the leaves on the trees. The stars were as clear and visible as I had ever seen them. The frogs in the distance sang as though they owned the night. Closing my eyes, I felt as the warm air seemed to kiss my face; with it, a kaleidoscope of scents—flowering goldenrod and columbine from a nearby field, smoke from a distant fire possibly many miles away, and of course, the scent of goats and chickens.

I slowly proceeded toward the door, noticing that my heart seemed to be skipping beats in my excitement. What would I tell her? Of course, I would let her know that I had missed her and thought of her every minute of every day. Aren't these the kind of things one says to a woman he is so taken with? I would also tell her that I never wanted to be without her in my life, that I would never again leave her. Yes, I would tell her how much I loved her and how much I needed her.

But while I could not wait to look into her lovely blue eyes again, I could not help but fear the possibility—maybe the probability for all I knew—that her feelings were not mutual. I had, at times, wondered how this impossible-to-read woman felt about me. 'I am what I am,' she would tell me. She seemed totally unaware that she was so much more at least to me. I felt that I could handle nearly anything in my life, regardless of how painful it would be just so long as Trish was by my side. The only thing I felt that I could not bare was her rejection.

I approached the door and attempted to open it, but to my surprise, it was locked. I knocked several times but received no answer. She was here though—I could smell her, and surely by now she would have been aware of my presence even if I had not knocked. I circled around to the rear entranceway where I found that door locked as well. As far as I knew, Trish never locked her doors—most lycanthropes don't—and yet everything was securely locked.

Quite suddenly I detected a scent that had become all too familiar to me. In only a second, I was aware of its origins and hastily made my way to the barn. Slowly opening the door, I was struck by the sweet and frightening scent of blood. I knew immediately that it wasn't human, and yet this did little to comfort me once I had witnessed the scene that was left.

Trish's goats had been savagely torn apart; their blood and organs spanned the length of the barn's floor. It seemed as though they had intentionally been scattered evenly—like toppings on a pizza. A drop of blood struck my forehead, and as I looked up, I saw the intestines and blood vessels strung across the rafters just as one would string decorations at Christmas. I slowly backed away from the scene, trying to make sense of what I was seeing. I then noticed the heads of three goats hanging from the inside of the barn door—their eyes had been plucked from their sockets.

Had Trish gone mad? There was no sense to any of this, especially knowing how she cared for her animals. I turned my attention to the other outbuilding, the one housing the chickens. I quickly found that the *senseless slaughter had continued there. There was not a single chicken spared, and while the scene was less gruesome than the barn, it was no less disturbing—feathers, blood, and violently dismembered chickens.*

Everything I had seen had been done within a relatively short time, possibly within the last fifteen or twenty minutes. Where was Trish? I was afraid to see her now not because I feared her rejection at this point but rather because I was terrified at what I would find.

I suddenly considered the fact that I was terrified. How long had it been since I felt such an intense emotion? Could this be real? My mind attempted to slip out of whatever trance I was in, but my mind wasn't really working as it should. But why? Was it because I was so afraid? Why was I so afraid. How could I be? I was a lycanthrope, and generally we don't really feel much in the way of fear (it tends to be the first emotion we lose).

Just then I heard something—the distinctive sound of a door opening and closing, the house! As quickly as my legs would allow me, which was much slower than they should have been able to, I sprinted to the rear entranceway, which was now unlocked.

"Trish," I called out as I stepped across the threshold and into her foyer. I could smell that she has just come through here. Still standing just inside the entranceway, I heard something… something faint. I closed my eyes and listened with as much preternatural power as I had. I could hear breathing, maybe even the faintest heartbeat. I continued listening, cocking my head slightly. Yes, it was a heartbeat, but it was beating much too quickly. It wasn't human nor was it Trish.

Suddenly, a small black animal bolted from beneath a curio cabinet in the kitchen, ran between my legs, and exited through the still open doorway. Startled, I watched as the deeply frightened cat circled around the corner of the house and disappeared from sight.

Turing my attention again to the task of finding Trish, I proceeded slowly into the kitchen. "Trish, it's me! I need to talk to you!" I called out louder than what would have been necessary for her to hear me. As far as I could tell, the kitchen and dining room were as immaculate as ever. Then I noticed a single white feather resting gently on the floor in front of the basement door. A strange feeling seemed to cross my mind as I studied this feather. It seemed ironic, something so peaceful as this feather coming to rest on the floor, like a gentile snowflake, with no awareness of the violent act responsible for its current setting.

I disregarded the feather and opened the door to the basement. "Trish," I called out, "I'm coming down to talk to you!" I tried to carry a calm tone in my voice, something that surely she would be able to see though.

When I arrived at the house, I had no reason to believe that anything was wrong with Trish, but as I proceeded into the basement, I took each step with extreme caution. It is not uncommon for those who suffer from lycanthropy to, at some point, find themselves in a state of madness. I would imagine that under such circumstances, they are a danger to everyone around them, even other lycanthropes.

I was hoping to hear her say, "Hey, come on down," or maybe even, "Give me a minute and I'll be right there." Instead, I heard only the soft creak of each step as I proceeded with my descent. While I was hoping to hear a pleasant response, a part of me feared she would quickly leap from the shadows and bury a knife into my throat. As I neared the bottom of the steps, I realized that no lights had been turned on in the basement itself. I directed my attention to the kitchen entranceway, looking for a switch—there was none. I reached the bottom of the steps unscathed... so far. The only illumination seemed to come from the open door to the kitchen; unfortunately, as I stood at the base of the steps, the light from the kitchen was like a spotlight shining down on me—not an entirely comfortable feeling when sharing a dark basement with the unknown.

Slowly, I stepped into the darkness and felt no less vulnerable than I had when I was in the light. As lycanthropes, we have terrific nocturnal vision, enabling us to locate and see what no human could. Even on the darkest nights, we move about with ease, hunting or avoiding humanity. Still, illumination to at least some tiny degree is necessary for us—or any animal for that matter—to see. Even we are blind in the absolute absence of light.

While the basement was quite dark, I should have had more than enough illumination to see everything in precise detail. Instead, the darkness seemed to dissolve any and all illumination almost as though it was a living conscious thing with an intention of reducing or eliminating altogether my ability to see. It was a strange and frightening darkness *unlike anything I had ever seen, and yet, it was somehow familiar to me.*

But I wasn't alone in the basement; Trish was here with me—quite possibly an angry and disturbed Trish that no longer cared who I was. Should I call out to her? Would it matter? And what would I do if I found her in a state of madness? I could never harm her. I loved her.

"Please, Trish, I need to talk to you!"

I waited patiently, hoping to hear a friendly response. Suddenly, I heard something from the far end of the basement—a chair being dragged on the floor. "Trish, I'm here to help you. Please let me help you!" I pleaded.

The entire basement then lit up so bright that I was no less blinded than I was in the pitch blackness that preceded it. Within a few seconds, my eyes grew accustomed to the extreme brightness now offered. Looking around, I saw everything just as it had been when I visited her last, but how long ago had that been? No, my mind still was not performing right. Then suddenly, I saw her at the distant end of the basement, near the sauna. She was unclothed and seated in a ladder-back chair, facing away from me. My first thought was to rush to her at once, wrap my arms around her, and tell her that I would take care of everything. Still, something—my intuition—told me that something was horribly wrong with this scene. Yes, even my most basic logic backed up this cautionary thought.

I studied the scene as though I was attempting to solve a puzzle, but after several moments of silence on both our parts and no further understanding of the situation based on my observations where I stood, I began to slowly advance in her direction. She did not move. In fact, I could not tell that she even breathed. Cautiously, I took one step then another followed by another until I reached out and touched the back of her left shoulder with my fingers. "Trish, whatever is wrong, I'm here, and we will get through this," I said to her. Her skin was unusually cold (lycanthropes never have cold skin), and I became increasingly alarmed.

With my fingers remaining on her shoulder, I circled around the chair to face her. I immediately withdrew my fingers and took several steps backward in horror! I drew in a gasp but seemed unable to exhale without great effort. Trish's face had been removed as though a child with scissors cut out her face from a magazine. All that remained was a deep and blood-filled crater extending from her lower jaw to her forehead. Even the bones of her face were cut away. In her right hand, she clung tightly to a large kitchen knife.

I didn't say anything; I didn't really know what to say. I watched in helpless silence as she brought the knife to her own throat and pulled the blade across, deeply severing arteries and even her trachea wide open. As her head cocked backward, a crimson river fell from her neck, and her body dropped from the chair and onto the floor.

I awoke, relieved not only to learn that it was a dream but to also have once again escaped the emotions that I now viewed as unnecessary and counterproductive to my life. It was only two in the morning, but I decided to get up and prepare myself for the following day.

FIFTEEN

I APPROACHED AN IMPOSSIBLY large palace, which was built to impress and intimidate. Wealth beyond imagination—this was the only thought that could possibly describe the grand monument that I was viewing. As best as I could tell, the estate spanned ten to twelve acres and was surrounded by a twelve-foot-high limestone and iron fence that bordered the property on all sides. The entranceway into the estate was marked by large sculpted iron gates, which fortunately for me were open.

I proceeded inside the property and walked on the manicured gravel driveway, lined with maturing pin oaks and red maples that were presently covered in ice and snow. I was met by a boy of about thirteen or fourteen who was walking toward the gate by which I had entered and was obviously paying me little mind. "Excuse me," I said. "I am looking for a man named Arthur Denham. Is he here?"

"Mr. Matsko?" he asked a little hesitantly. "He is inside. Just let yourself in, and he will probably find you. He's funny like that."

I wanted to ask him about Arthur as I did not really know about this Mr. Matsko he had directed me to, but the student had begun walking away already. So I continued to the front entranceway and ascended the steps leading to the doors. As I walked past its massive Corinthian columns that rose like giant oak trees, I opened the door and stepped into a landmark of high Victorian architecture.

"It's you!" a feminine voice called out in surprise. I turned to see a woman, a *very* young woman with a long black dress, wearing a ruby necklace, bracelet, and ring on her right hand. She was maybe fifteen or sixteen years of age, tall and slender with dark hair that nearly touched her shoulders. She was clearly happy to see me almost as though I was a long-lost relative returning from a war. I could tell by the subtle pheromones that seemed to flow from her skin, however, that she viewed me as anything but a family member.

"I'm sorry," I said. "Do I know you?"

"No, but I know who you are. My name is Anne, and I have been waiting to speak with you for so long!"

"I think you must have me confused with someone else."

"Not at all," she replied. "You are Caleb V——, born in January 1950 in Lafayette Parish near the Vermilion River." She smiled. "You are a lycanthrope, but you are not alone. You have come in search of Arthur, but you are also destined to meet me."

I found her statements more than a little disturbing; in fact, she was genuinely creepy, creepy with a pleasant and seductive smile. "You have my attention," I said. "And I am afraid you have me at a disadvantage."

"I'm sorry," she said, approaching me. Her eyes were dark, very dark; her scent, peculiar and sweet. Clearly, she was human, but she was far from typical. "I see things before they happen," she said. "Sometimes, long before they happen. I have been seeing you, seeing you come into my life for a long time."

"Is Arthur available?" I asked, intentionally ignoring her ambiguous statements.

"He is," she answered, "and he is going to want to see you. I'll take you to him, but I am going to want to talk to you also. Maybe when you are finished with Arthur?"

"Sure," I said hesitantly though I really was not willing to commit to anything with her.

"We really *need* to talk," she said, attempting to drive home the significance of what she had to say.

I followed her through what seemed a maze of corridors, each with historic print wallpaper and rich red carpet with gold trim. I could smell dozens of people in various rooms, classrooms, and could hear voices muffled but easily clear enough for me.

"What is this place?" I asked.

"A school, of course!" she answered with a deep smile.

"It isn't like any school I've ever seen."

She continued smiling and walked uncomfortable close to me. "You're right. It isn't like anything you've seen before."

"So, Anne, how long have you been here?"

"Almost two years, but I have been waiting for you for a lot longer than that."

"When you say that you've been waiting for me, what does that mean?"

She stopped momentarily at the bottom of a stairwell and turned to face me, stepping almost dangerously close to me. She brought her right hand to my chest and touched me gently. "There is so much I want to tell you, so many things I want you to know. Please talk to me when you are finished with Arthur."

I stepped back, pulling myself away from her awkwardly intimate touch. "I promise that we will talk," I told her. Seemingly satisfied with my statement, she turned and proceeded up the steps. As I followed her, I could hear a distant piano playing, playing very well in fact.

Again, my attention was drawn to the pleasant scent emanating from Anne. No human being could ever understand, but certain people, women in particular, smell so intoxicating, so inviting, so warm, that they are hard to resist. Anne was certainly one of them. Add to this her uninvited and seductive advances, and I felt more than a little uncomfortable. She intentionally walked a certain way—you know the way. She was a cute girl, and I do want to emphasize the word *girl*, but I wanted nothing more than to get away from her. I felt that she was even more dangerous than I was.

She led me to an office, where behind a large mahogany desk sat a man who appeared in his late fifties or early sixties—Arthur Denham no doubt. Anne proceeded around the back of the desk while I remained at the doorway out of respect. Arthur, while fully aware of my presence, seemed captivated by a book he was reading. In that way, he reminded me of Myra, somehow able to devote an enhanced human attention to anything that was happening in the room while concurrently focusing on reading.

"It's him!" she whispered into his ear, seemingly unaware that I could hear just as plainly as if she has said it aloud. "He's the one I've told you about!"

"Is he now?" Arthur replied in a conversational tone. As he stood, he brought his gaze to meet mine. Though it appeared that he offered me just a friendly glance, I knew that he had assessed everything about my presence in less than a second. "Arthur Matsko," he said as he extended his hand.

I proceeded forward and took his hand. "Matsko? You aren't Arthur Denham?"

He smiled. "Ah yes, that is a name I haven't used in some time. And you are?"

"Caleb," I answered. "Caleb V——."

"Anne, could you please excuse Mr. V—— and I. We have some things to discuss." His tone with which he spoke to Anne seemed to convey a gentle and caring feeling, suggesting that he was maybe a father figure to her.

"Of course," she responded, and as she walked past, she offered one last seductive look with a smile. As the door closed behind me, I wasn't sure if I felt relieved that Anne had stepped out or more nervous that she was now gone.

"So," he began, "you've had the pleasure of meeting Anne. You probably don't realize this, but you have made her day."

"I really don't know what to think at the moment. What was that all about?"

"Well, Anne is a remarkably special individual with a truly unique gift."

"What gift is that?"

"She is precognitive," he said. "She sees the world a lot differently than you or I. Whereas we live in the moment and blindly make plans for the future, she seems to wait for the inevitable."

"And she knew that I was coming to see you?"

"I don't know about that, but she claims that you are to play a significant role in her life. I suspect, at least at her age, that she was a little overcome by seeing you and may have lost her composure. Forgive her if her words or actions made you uncomfortable. She has been in love with you since before she came here."

"Doesn't this seem a little inappropriate," I asked, "considering her age?"

"Mr. V——, I am not suggesting that you engage in anything inappropriate. I am advising that you try to understand her for the sake of her circumstances. As far as I know, Anne has never once been wrong about anything she has ever predicted—not once. You are one of her most significant predictions. If she says that you will play an important role in her life, I wouldn't even question it. Even if you do find it unbelievable, she knows a hell of a lot more about what is going to happen tomorrow than either of us do. See what she has to say."

"Is she a student of yours?"

"One of many, but certainly a jewel among jewels. I would be happy to offer you a tour of the school if you like. I think you would find it quite interesting."

There was a certain aura around him. I don't really see auras, mind you, but in his presence, one could feel power emanating from him. He sat across from me. His eyes were a void that stretched the boundaries of my imagination. He looked like a man in his late fifties perhaps, but if one were to gaze into his eyes, if one dared, he would find something old and frightening. He had the look of a gentleman, an almost royal elegance to him. When he moved, even his most simple of gestures, it was as if done so magically. There was no question, he possessed something... chilling. I felt a strange mixture of both safety and fear in his presence.

"So let us talk. You have gone to a lot of trouble to find me. What can I do for you?"

"I learned of you from a woman named Myra F——. She told me that if there was anyone who could answer my questions, it would be you."

For a long moment, Arthur pondered the name I offered in silence. "Myra," he began with a warm smile. "How is she?" As he asked this simple question, I found myself intrigued not by the question itself, but rather at his smile—it seemed genuine as though he was a human being.

"She is well," I answered. "So you've known her for... fifty years?"

"Not exactly. I knew her fifty years ago," he said laughing. Laughing? "You may find that people change so dramatically over extended periods of time, that they aren't really the same people anymore. It is disheartening really, and particularly true with those like us."

"What about you?" I asked. "Have you not changed?"

"Only a fool would truly believe something as such. No, I have certainly changed, just in different ways. You are exchanging words with *very old wolf*, my new friend. I have had over two hundred years worth of change in my life," he said with a smile. "In any case, a friend of Myra's is always welcome here, and if need be, I can accommodate you during the cycle."

"I do appreciate your hospitality. You are kind."

"Ah, I could do no less," he stated. "So tell me, what questions do you have for me?"

"Well," I said before taking a deep breath, "there is really no delicate way of saying this, so here goes. Several months ago, I killed an entire family while they were on a camping trip. I'm not really dealing well with the blunted emotions that should naturally come with such an atrocity, but more importantly at this point, I don't want to hurt anyone else."

Arthur sat across from me and listened carefully while I spilled out every detail of my experiences, just as I have done in the preceding pages. I gave him every opportunity to interrupt, and yet he did not. Upon concluding my story, he simply stated, "I see."

"So what can I do?" I finally asked after a moment of silence. "Is there any way to stop this?"

"I am a bit surprised that Myra did not tell you more about your circumstance."

"She did," I said. "Trust me, she made sure I was well aware."

"In that case, I am not sure that I can dispense any further wisdom."

"She told me that lycanthropy had affected you differently, and as I've sat here and interacted with you, I can see that she was right. I guess that I came to you hoping for a miracle."

"Well, I am sorry, my young friend, I haven't any miracle to offer. As for my somewhat unique disposition, all I can honestly say is I don't know. Whereas others of our kind have slipped further and further into inner blackness or nothingness, it seems that I alone have been spared that fate. But as for a reason why, I simply haven't an answer."

In an instant, my only hope seemed extinguished.

"I am curious about one part of your story," he said. "And of course, I cannot help but wonder why it isn't more significant to you."

"What is it?"

"This woman you met—Trish? You claimed that you had no nightmares while you shared a bed with her?"

"That's right."

"Well, I'd say that if you are indeed looking for a miracle, that is where I would start. Evidently, you've come here in pursuit of the counsel of a wiser wolf when it seems, at least to me, that she has much more to offer to you than I ever could."

And like a slap in the face, everything suddenly became clear to me. As I sat there and listened to him speak, I knew he was right. I had to have been the stupidest thing to have ever walked the earth to not have already known what he realized after a thirty-minute exchange. I needed to find Trish. I needed her!

A short while later, Arthur escorted me through some of the more interesting areas of the school. "The mansion was once called the Vanderman mansion. It actually set the precedent for extravagant estates build during the gilded age," he told me as we revisited the great hall where I had first met Anne. Actually, it was amazing just how much I failed to realize initially that I suddenly noticed on this particular tour.

Descending the towering red-carpeted grand staircase, I paid particular attention to an enormous stained glass window above the main entranceway. As the quickly fading sunlight still streamed through it, it caused the marble floor in the enormous room to take on blue and red shades. Against each wall perpendicular to the mouth of the staircase, were massive tapestries depicting scenes that I did not recognize. "Those are older than I am," Arthur stated. "They are from the seventeenth-century France and attempt to illustrate the generosity and leadership of Louis XIV's long reign.

"Constructed in the style of a French Renaissance chateau, the Vanderman has 170 rooms and boasts 120,000 square feet. Most of the rooms, decorated in French and Italian styles, were designed and assembled in Europe, shipped to the U.S. and reassembled in the house."

Throughout my time there, I had been listening to a piano playing in the distance; Arthur continued our tour in that direction, taking me down a long hallway to the left of the main entranceway and through an impressive set of double doors where the music originated. It was a giant solarium that looked more like a greenhouse than a sunroom. The domed ceiling rose, at its highest, nearly thirty feet. All around, lush plants grew as small fountains filled the air with the tranquil sound of running water. The air was very moist and earthy but in a pleasant way. As for the glass itself, it was difficult to see through as ice and snow covered everything outside, allowing only a small amount of light to penetrate through. Seated at the piano was a young man of about nineteen or twenty; his shoes were untied, his hair uncombed, and his clothing disheveled and badly wrinkled.

"Do you recognize the piece?" Arthur asked.

"I am sorry, I do not, but it is beautiful."

"This is Andrew, another of my very unique students. From the time he was five years old, he was a virtuoso pianist. To say that he is a musical genius would be a gross understatement. However, he is a savant of sorts and, if left to his own devices, would do nothing but play and in the process neglect even toileting tasks and eating."

Arthur and I approached the man as he seemed to disregard us altogether. "Andrew, this is Caleb. He is here visiting us." Andrew continued playing as though he hadn't heard what Arthur had said. "Perhaps you would like to share with Caleb the title of this composition?"

"Hello, Caleb. This is Fredrick Chopin," he said in a strange and monotone voice. While he spoke, he continued playing almost as though one part of him was disconnected and willing to say a few words so long as it didn't interfere with the part of him that was playing. "Chopin himself never named an instrumental work beyond a number for whichever genre it belonged. This piece was entitled 'Revolutionary Etude' and was composed around 1831. If you listen carefully to the end of this piece, you may be reminded of Beethoven's last piano sonata, Opus 111 No. 32."

Arthur and I remained quiet and listened as Andrew completed this particular piece before immediately beginning another. "Andrew can hear a song only once and repeat it perfectly. He has never read music but has composed a large number of pieces himself."

"Impressive," I said. Though I enjoyed listening to this young man play, it seemed to me that I was not educated enough in classical music to truly appreciate the talent with which he played. Arthur, who, on the other hand, was a bit more refined than I and had actually been born long before Chopin, seemed enthralled with the music.

"Andrew, Caleb and I are heading out, but Stephanie will be in to work with you in a while."

Andrew appeared to disregard Arthur's statement; he seemed almost oblivious to our even being there, but as Arthur and I were walking away, he spoke as his fingers continued dancing across the keys, "Nice to meet you, Caleb."

After we exited the solarium, we proceeded through a set of double doors that led to an outdoor garden. The cold winter breeze brought wind chills well into the single digits, not that Arthur or I were affected in the least.

"So tell me about the school," I asked as we strolled.

"Well, you could say that the school is really nothing more than an extension of myself. Even when I was just a man, I was a professor. It seemed only natural, at least for me, to continue with this as it has always been something by which I have identified myself with. For some time postlycanthropy, I continued as I had done so beforehand. Eventually, as I knew I would have to, I stepped out of the public light and thought that those days were simply behind me.

"Then just this century really, I encountered a man by the name of Sebastian who, like myself, existed outside of conventional standards. As a child, he was ostracized by his family who believed that he had the devil in him. In truth, he had a very remarkable gift, one that even he didn't fully understand. You see, Sebastian was empathic, meaning that he could see into the true intentions and feelings of others.

"An empath?"

"It is something difficult to understand, and for those who possess it, they hardly view it as a gift as it creates more hardships that cannot really be ignored. Most people have a certain degree of intuition, but with empaths, it goes far beyond that simple two-dimensional realm. Sebastian would actually absorb the feelings of those around him and would experience them himself. He was so sensitive, no one in his presence could ever deceive him as he would feel even the most subtle emotion. In fact, his ability would often manifest physically—he could even feel pain and sickness that those around him felt."

"And he had a problem with this?"

"Empaths, especially powerful ones like Sebastian, absorb so many feelings during the course of a day that they often need time to process what they are feeling. They prefer surrounding themselves with positive energy because they absorb that. However, it is always the negative energy that seems to seek them out, and they absorb that too.

"Sebastian had to learn to shield himself from the darkness that would accompany those who were in his presence—simply stated, there were things people felt that he didn't want to feel. As a man, he had gained the ability to utilize his talents to his advantage—useful when playing cards." Arthur laughed. "Sebastian and I worked together to begin this school to help gifted students that conventional schools are ill-equipped to understand—those like him."

"And those like Anne?"

"Yes indeed," Arthur smiled.

"So are all your students here exceptional?"

"Everyone here is here for a reason. For some, like Andrew, they would either fall through the cracks in the system and find themselves in a low-quality special education school, or so heavily medicated that they would be useless and unable to function. Either way, Andrew's true gifts would have never been recognized had he not come here.

"As for Anne, there isn't really anywhere equipped to work with someone like her, at least not in a productive and benign way. She, as was Sebastian, is a special case, and she isn't the only special case here."

"More psychics?"

"I wouldn't advise using that term around Anne. She hates it. In fact, she isn't entirely keen on *precognitive* either. But to answer your question, no, Anne is the only one here with her specific talent."

The garden itself, though snow-covered and dormant, had been well maintained in warmer months. In the garden's center was a fountain covered and tightly secured with a tarp. Rosebushes and various flowers were arranged in semicircular rows that increased in size as one traveled away from the garden's center. To the west, the sun had only just peeked behind the horizon line, and though the sky was still brilliantly lit up, the last tiny, direct ray of sunlight seemed to touch me gently before disappearing altogether.

"I will introduce you to Markus if he is around," Arthur said as he led me out of the garden through a snow-covered path. "He is an instructor here and helps me with the day-to-day operations. I should warn you though. He isn't likely to offer a warm greeting to you."

"Why is that?"

"I can't really say too much, except that he isn't really a fan of those like us."

"Then why is he here?"

"This school is an academic institution. Of that, make no doubt. But it is also something of a sanctuary for those like your new friend Anne. Markus is one of those individuals as well, and he now calls the Vanderman his home."

"So what's his story?"

"I'll let him tell you if he wishes to. All I can say is that there is an entire world of the unknown that exists—you and I are a part of that, but it hardly ends with us."

We rounded the school and approached the front entranceway. At the base of the steps was a man who appeared in his late forties and was smoking a cigarette. He wore a thick black wool coat, but was obviously still cold and trembled ever so slightly. He offered only an ugly scowl as he noticed Arthur and I approach—untouched by the cold that discomforted him so.

"Good evening, Markus," Arthur said pleasantly.

"Arthur," Markus said respectfully as he nodded his head.

"This is Caleb. He is here visiting us. Please extend to him the same courtesy that you would for any of our guests." Arthur's tone was soft and gentile, but it carried with it an obvious message, a message that wasn't intended for me to understand.

I stepped forward and extended my hand. After a moment of thought on his part, Markus reluctantly took my hand. In that instant, I felt an intense pressure surge through the bones of my wrist and arm. The pressure didn't really seem to come from the grip he offered, which was loose really, but instead seemed to originate from inside of my arm, a force pushing outward. It was quite painful.

"That's enough, Markus," Arthur said with a hint of authority in his voice, and in that instant, the pressure was gone, and Markus withdrew his grasp on my hand.

I wasn't really sure what to say or how to act but respectfully nodded and stepped back as though nothing had happened because as far as I could tell, nothing did happen. And yet I knew that this wasn't really the case. I was just not sure what.

"We have a new student coming on Monday," Markus said in a very matter-of-fact tone. "It's the boy from Michigan. I am setting him up with Lucas and Henry."

"Excellent. I have been looking forward to having him join us here."

A moment later, the three of us entered the school, and while Arthur and I continued with our tour, Markus left to perform whatever business he tended. I wanted to ask Arthur about him but decided not to, thinking it unwise should my questions be viewed as an attempt to sow seeds of discontent, especially considering that my stay here would be brief.

"This is the dining hall," my guide stated as he opened one of the many thick oak doors off of the main lobby. The dining room continued the elegance with its own set of twelve marble columns, glittering chandeliers, wall designs in gilded bronze, and three enormous tables that could each seat at least thirty. I could smell the rich cheeses and meats that the students and their instructors were eating. The smell of food caused my mouth to water; and as Arthur looked at me, I could tell that he felt guilty for not offering me anything to eat before now. "I know that you are hungry. So am I—that is a fate I have not been spared. You are, of course, welcome to as much food as you wish. I ask only that you exercise a mild reserve when eating disproportionate quantities in the presence of others."

"Yes, of course," I said.

The dining room itself was nearly the size of a basketball court. I estimated approximately sixty or more students. As were the other rooms of the school, this one too had a very vintage feel—like walking into the nineteenth century.

I heard footsteps quietly approaching from behind me and immediately recognized the scent over everything that the dining room had to offer. "Hello, Anne," I said as I turned to see her smiling face.

"Ah, Anne," Arthur said warmly. "Have you eaten?"

"I ate early, thank you."

"Well, perhaps you would be so kind as to show our new friend here around a bit more while I take care of a few things for one of our new students coming in next week?"

"Certainly," she answered with an obvious enthusiasm. Arthur himself even seemed amused at her excited state as he smiled at her. I, on the other hand, found no humor in it. I didn't really know what I felt about Anne. A part of me was intrigued, a less-than-sensible part of me. The more sensible part of my psyche seemed to feel that it was in my best interest that I keep a safe distance from Anne, but it didn't look like that was going to happen.

"Do you like what you've seen so far?" she asked.

"It's impressive."

As Arthur stepped through the entranceway from which we entered the dining hall, I noticed a dark-haired gothic-looking boy offering me an evil look. As if she read my mind (hell, maybe she did) Anne spoke. "His name is Ron, but everyone calls him Blade. He has been chasing after me since the first day I arrived here."

"Blade?" I asked laughing slightly.

"That's what he does—knives, swords, razors. You name it, he's mastered it. Not really a person to have angry with you, but that is what's great about being you—you don't have to be afraid of anyone."

"Is that what you think?"

"You intimidate everyone in this room just by standing here. You intimidate everyone you come into contact with, and they don't even know what you *are*. Imagine how they would feel if they had any idea. No, I don't think you have anyone to *ever* be afraid of, not *even* someone as deadly as Blade."

"I don't know. He looks kind of young to me. I don't think I would worry too much about him anyway."

"That is a mistake most people would make about him."

"So he's interested in you. That's good. Why don't you pursue him? He's about your age or a little older, right?"

"I'm not interested in him," she answered. "I have my heart set on someone else," she added softly as she stared into my eyes.

"Well, that's insane," I said as I walked through the door that Arthur had exited through a moment earlier.

"We will be together!" she said with a convincing tone. "And you will love me, and you will hold me, and you will take care of and protect me! I've seen it! You are the person I am going to be with!" As she spoke, she followed me into the hallway leading to the lobby.

"Are you listening to yourself? Do you even know how that sounds?"

"I know, and I am sorry, but there isn't really any other way to tell you. This *will* happen. And I know that maybe you don't love me now, but in time, you will."

"I don't even know you. Besides, you are just a kid!"

"Well, I'm old enough to realize when someone is too ignorant to listen to what I have to say—even when I know what I know. But fortunately for you, I am patient enough to wait until you can rationalize what I have to offer."

I wanted to laugh again at the ridiculousness of the dialogue but thought that it would be an insulting gesture. So instead, I smiled lightly and redirected the conversation. "Tell me about you. Tell me what you believe about me."

"I wish it worked that way, but it doesn't," she said. "All I can tell you is that we are going to be together. You will travel with me and I will be kind of... an apprentice."

"An apprentice?"

"Well, that isn't really what I mean. It's just for lack of a better word. And while I know that you don't want to hear this and I know that you don't really know me yet, I promise you that I have seen us together, and despite everything you think, it *will* happen just as I said it would."

I chose not to disagree with anything even though I was as convinced that she was wrong as she was about being right. I also got the impression that she knew much more than she stated. However, if whatever she was withholding proved as absurd as what she offered, I figured that I wasn't missing much. I simply listened patiently as she told me about her childhood—much of it in hospitals while she was examined for a psychiatric condition that could not be diagnosed.

She was actually fascinating to listen to, and I found myself actually wanting to believe her. She told me about a number of other predictions that had come to fruition, some of which were insignificant or pertaining to people on a very personal level. Others, like the Ted Bundy killings were more headline making. Then she spoke briefly about things going gray.

"And what does that mean? Gray?"

"I don't know. It is something that will happen in the not-too-distant future, but things stop. It is almost as if the world will stop—there is nothing more to see when it does. But that won't happen for a while yet, and there is a lot I see before that."

While we spoke, she did offer me the remainder of the tour that Arthur had started. I wanted to ask her questions like "So what are your plans upon leaving here? Or where are you going to college?" However, I decided not to ask as I figured this would ultimately lead to something like "I am going to be with you, of course."

My mind was on one woman and one woman only—Trish. Even as I walked through the corridors and viewed different classrooms, my mind was actually lingering on Trish. What was she doing now? Has she thought about me? Will she be happy to see me? My intention was to spend the night then depart the next morning as soon as I rose.

"Let me show you my favorite room," Anne stated as she led me past a number of guest rooms—one of which, would be mine for the night—and into what appeared to be a sitting room. The richness of everything I had seen so far continued here as this room too was filled with fine furnishings and decorations. On one wall of this impressive room was a massive marble fireplace, and on the opposite side, a beautiful grand piano. Its main feature, however, was an immense window that provided a gorgeous and panoramic view out to the Atlantic. "When this was built," Anne stated, "they certainly enjoyed entertaining. This was originally a room for the men to smoke in but was eventually made into a music room. We have a student who sometimes likes to play in here."

"Andrew?"

"Yes," she said with a smile. "This is where I come when I want quiet time. I sometimes just sit and watch the ocean. I am a romantic, you know!" she said impishly.

"I suspected that," I replied with a smile. Of course I had no interest in this young girl, but even I had to acknowledge her charm. I did like her.

Anne showed me to my room, and though she wanted to continue talking, I bid her good evening and rested for some time while my thoughts lingered on Trish. The ceiling of my bedroom had a mural painted on it, and as I lay on my bed, I gazed at it and was amazed at its rich detail. I recognized the painting from an art class I had taken in college—Botticelli's *Primavera*.

For the next several hours, I listened with hearing that only Arthur could appreciate as the business of school-aged children and teenagers wound down for the night. I heard conversations, I heard toilets flushing, showers running, and even a couple of arguments. When it seemed that the mansion was still and that even the most restless sleepers were quiet, I ventured from my room and proceeded into the now calm palace of a school. I maneuvered the dark hallways and easily found the dining room. From there, I simply followed my nose that led me to the kitchen. From the refrigerator, I pulled a very large tub of spaghetti that had been made several days earlier. Though it did not satisfy my appetite—nothing ever does—I devoured enough to stuff six people.

As I cleaned up after myself, I felt that I wasn't alone. "Good evening, my new friend," Arthur said as he advanced across the kitchen with the grace of a cat. "Can't sleep?"

"Just a lot on my mind," I said. "I have been thinking about Trish and wondering why I am spared the dark dreams when I am with her."

"Our circumstance affects us in varying degrees and in different ways. All I can say is that she is remarkably special if she can offer you that. It also makes me wonder if perhaps you provide some benefit for her as well."

Oh, how foolish I felt, chasing after a fleeting dream. "So what's your excuse?" I asked. "Why are you up so late?"

Arthur smiled. "We all have our demons. Come, let me show you something."

I followed Arthur out of the kitchen and down a hallway that I had not been shown. At the end of this hallway was an elevator that Arthur entered a code to open. "I had this built many years ago as a bit of a retreat for me."

A few moments later, the elevator opened and we both stepped in. It was a strange and almost eerie feeling of silence that we shared as the elevator took us to its destination. Basically, we had descended into the basement of the Vanderman, but when the elevator opened, Arthur led me into what could only be described as a museum. I was never really one that got too hung-up on the idea of antiques, but even I could immediately appreciate the items he had collected over many lifetimes—swords, books, paintings. There was more than I could possibly describe and certainly more than I could remember as I write these words.

"You are the first individual, outside of myself, to have seen these walls in almost three decades. These are my private quarters, but this is also where I confine myself during the full of the moon," as he spoke he pointed to a large prisonlike cage on the far opposite wall.

"Trish uses something like this during the becoming as well. It seems to work for her."

Arthur and I sat in recliners as the fireplace warmed and illuminated our faces. For many hours, I listened as he told me stories of the days of long ago. He also spoke of myths that described lycanthropic origins, including that of Lycaon, who, according to Ovid's *Metamorphoses*, was turned into a ravenous wolf by Zeus. He also spoke of myths originating from Old Norse countries, Russia, and even those of Far East. Unlike Myra, Arthur had no desire to hold back information and offered it freely.

"Are we evil?" I finally asked, hoping for a philosophical answer from an individual who could easily be the wisest and most intelligent on the planet.

"Do you think you are evil?"

"I don't know," I answered. "I sometimes feel evil. I must be—I killed a family."

"Well, unfortunately for those of us who are less than evil, there is no exemption from the guilt and depression that accompanies a conscience. I am reminded of something I heard once—'hoping, dreaming, believing, and finally, listening to evil itself hammering on the door.' I think that there is something inside of us that we cannot identify. There is something less than tangible but forceful and overwhelming. I am not really a dichotomous thinker, but if you allow this force that calls your soul its home to overtake who you are, then yes, you are very much evil. However, just because you will eventually lose your ability to feel, don't think that you've lost your ability to reason—you know right from wrong. You are a lycanthrope—that is a fact, one that you cannot argue. It is what it is. But I don't think *lycanthrope* and *evil* are synonymous terms."

"That was a very Myralike answer," I said.

Arthur smiled. "Let me show you something." Rising from his recliner, Arthur walked across the room, and from a large display case, he pulled an enormous mace. "This was used by a seventeenth-century German foot soldier."

He handed me the mace, and its weight was surprising—probably twenty-five or thirty pounds total. While I never pretended to understand the use of such weapons, I knew enough to understand that this object that Arthur had handed me was impractical, at least in the hands of a human being.

"Can you imagine the individual who yielded such a weapon? While other maces would have easily maimed or killed if used correctly, in the right hands this weapon would have smashed any armor and removed heads from their shoulders."

"That is something I couldn't imagine."

"As far as I know, this is the largest and heaviest mace ever made and ever used in battle. So tell me as you hold it in your hands now, what do you think of it? Do you think it is a horrible thing just because of its weight?"

"No."

"Well, I think of us in the same terms. This is an extraordinary mace, and it can certainly be more destructive than others but only in the hands of someone who means to destroy. In my hands, it is a piece of history and art. The question is what is it when I place it into your hands?"

I had no answer to offer.

"Are you evil? I don't know, maybe, but if so, I don't believe it has anything to do with lycanthropy. Furthermore, if an individual is evil, I don't believe that he is necessarily a lycanthrope. It only means that regardless of what kind of mace he holds in his hands, he means to cause destruction."

"I understand what you are saying, but it doesn't really answer my question."

"You like dealing in absolutes. Great if you are talking about math, but in life, there is really no such concept. Why don't you keep that?" he said to me as he nodded to the mace. "Consider it a gift."

"Absolutely not," I said. "I couldn't accept such a gift."

"Nonsense, it's yours."

We talked for a bit longer, but both of us soon grew tired and decided to call it a night. I thanked Arthur for both his hospitality by allowing me a place to sleep and food to eat and for the time he graciously offered to me. I intentionally left the mace next to the chair where I had been sitting before getting onto the elevator and returning to the main floor.

The next morning upon awaking, the mace was inside my room, leaning against a small table.

SIXTEEN

I AWOKE EARLY WITH the intention of slipping away before anyone had realized I had left—one sixteen-year-old girl in particular. More importantly though, I seemed to discover, or maybe rediscover, a new focus, a new direction for myself—I was headed back to the Land of Lincoln with an almost obsessed mind-set. My newly recognized soulmate served not only to preoccupy my thoughts but also distracted me from everything that was happening around me.

I turned and made one final observation of the Vanderman mansion before exiting through the gate and returning to the real world. After leaving the property, I proceeded on foot toward a downtown coffee shop I had visited in the early hours on the morning before. From there, I would catch a cab and make my way to the airport.

As I made my way, I was distracted by my thoughts, so much so that I not only failed to notice that someone had been watching me but had also managed to follow me for some distance. Just so you know, most lycanthropes are more than keenly aware of what is happening in their immediate surroundings and are virtually impossible to sneak up on. On that day, however, I was not myself. Only when I heard the bittersweet voice call out, "Caleb, wait!" was I snapped back into reality.

Anne advanced toward me with an obvious enthusiasm. She wore a thick black coat that covered her to her knees, black gloves, and a checkered wool scarf that had been quickly thrown around her neck. As she scurried along, she pulled behind her a large suitcase on wheels; her hair was a bit wild and blew in the wind.

"Sorry about my hair," she said, seemingly aware that I had made a mental note of it. "I was in such a hurry to catch you, I didn't really have time to work on it."

"What are you doing here?"

"I want to come with you," she said. Her tone suggested to me that she actually believed I would probably go along with this idea.

"Are you out of your damn mind?"

"Please, please take me with you!"

"Anne, I don't even know how to say this delicately, but you belong here. This is your home."

"My home will be wherever you are! Please take me with you. I promise I will do whatever you tell me to do. I won't cause any problems and you—."

"Stop!" I shouted. "What the hell is wrong with you? Don't you see? I don't want you to come with me! I don't want you anywhere around me!"

The momentary silence that followed was one that I will never forget. My words must have struck her harder than I intended as her eyes began to well and tears quickly fell from them. "But—" she began then I cut her off.

"Go home, Anne!" I shouted. "Get away from me and go home!"

She paused for a moment and looked as though she was going to offer something more; but she didn't, only her hurt expression and her tears. She turned without saying another word and walked away. I almost called out to her, almost ran to her and told her I was sorry, almost. As I watched her walk away, I could not help but feel bad for her... but not that bad.

Despite the drama with Anne, I returned to Rockford with high spirits. I had imagined and reimagined how my reunion with Trish would be. Of course, I couldn't help but wonder if she would invite me back with arms wide open or if she would be bitter at me for my extended absence.

As I pulled into the driveway, I was immediately reminded of the nightmare from a couple of nights earlier. However, as I exited the car, those initial concerns fled; my relief was momentary only though. I quickly realized not only that Trish was not at home but that the house had been vacated as well. Confusion set in, and I tried to look for impossible-to-find clues that would offer some reason to what had happened. I examined the outbuildings, and while they were blissfully free of mutilated animals and bloody carcasses, they were empty nonetheless.

The house was unlocked, and I let myself in. I could still smell Trish in the air, in the carpet, and even in the walls, but she was long gone as was her furniture. The house had been totally cleared out. Not one item remained. As I walked from empty room to empty room, my heart sank. I entered the basement only to find it as abandoned as the upstairs had been. The sauna was cleaned, the whirlpool had been drained, and there was no sign of life. I even opened her kitchen cabinets and drawers, hoping that maybe she had left some kind of note, some way for me to contact her. I immediately left her house and, with a mild effort, located the dance school that she operated—perhaps if she wasn't there, there might be someone who could possibly direct me to her.

Everything was as I had remembered it here, which actually served as a bit of a relief. As I entered, about a dozen small girls wearing leotards seemed to scurry past me and into one of the classrooms for their lesson.

"Can I help you?" a friendly voice asked. I looked to see one of the women Trish had introduced me to during my last visit here.

"I hope so," I answered. "I was looking for Trish. Do you know where I might find her?"

Her expression changed ever so slightly with a smile as she remembered me. "Ah, yes of course! You are her friend from out of town!"

"Yes," I said as she shook my hand. "I actually just returned to Rockford, and I was hoping to meet up with her."

"Oh... well, I'm not sure where she's at now," the woman stated clumsily. "She actually left here a couple of months ago. In fact, she sold the school here to me. I'm sorry, I wish I could tell you more."

"Is there anything you can tell me that would help me locate her? She doesn't live in her old house anymore."

"Nothing I can think of," she answered. "Trish was a very private person and didn't really share a lot about herself. It's kind of sad to say really, but even after working with her for as long as I did, I didn't really know too much about her—you were the only person she ever introduced us to really."

I thanked her for her time and prepared to leave when she offered one final observation. "Everything seemed to be going pretty well until the last week she was here. By then, she didn't really seem herself though. She asked if I was interested in buying the school, and when I said yes, she sold it to me for much less than she could have made if she offered it to someone else. I don't know if any of that helped, but I hope you find her. I thought you two made a lovely couple."

I spent that night at Trish's abandoned home. *Why me? Why me? Why me!* Was I such a fun target for fate and misery that they couldn't bear the thought of leaving me be? Did God hate me so much, he wanted nothing but constant agony from me? I was lost. I was in despair. I was an empty vessel.

The following day, I drove into Chicago. I had no idea of where I was going. I just drove. My car ran out of gas, and I pushed it into a motel parking lot—I would deal with it later. So I walked. I had nowhere to go, no destination, just one foot in front of another. I didn't give a fuck about anything at that moment. All I could focus on was walking, and so I walked.

The world went on all around me, but it wasn't really something I was tuned into. It was more of a blur actually. And then, someone with a loud voice spoke to me. "Hey, man, do you have any money I can borrow?" I remember hearing the words but disregarding their meaning. I continued on my way, more or less ignoring the question. "Hey motherfucker, I'm talking to you!" Ah, a threatening tone, now this was enough to pull my attention from the abyss it had been residing in.

I turned to see a young white man maybe in his late teens or early twenties, staring intensely at me as though he intended to melt me with his eyes. He wore an old denim jacket, and from its pocket he pulled a knife. Behind him were two other men of about his age—one black and the other white Neither of them spoke, but clearly they served as lieutenants of the one who did. Unlike him, their expressions seemed more amused with each of them sporting impish smiles. They must have figured this was an amusing situation—some poor bastard in the wrong neighborhood.

Of course for most, this would have surely been a frightening position to have been in, maybe even a life-and-death scenario, depending on the extent of their intentions. Mind you, while they couldn't have possibly known about my preternatural nature, I was nonetheless a somewhat intimidating presence—a fact that would likely dissuade many from attempting anything aggressive toward me. But for three arrogant and territorial gangbangers with something to prove to each other and their neighborhood, I am sure that they had little doubt that they would easily emerge victorious from any kind of altercation.

I could tell that for just an instant upon my facing him, the man who had spoken withdrew his cocky expression; it returned just as quickly, however. "My friends and I need your money, your watch, whatever you got!" His tone was stern but insidiously playful—like a bully simply tormenting a weak classmate. I had seen more than my share of his kind.

"Well," I began with an obviously condescending tone of my own. "I have about six hundred dollars on my person. It's yours... if you can take it from me."

Clearly, that was the one statement that he wasn't expecting as he offered only a dumbfounded expression for several seconds as his mind tried to reevaluate how he would proceed. Of course, my choice of words were nothing but a challenge, and under the circumstances—with his posse backing him up—it was a challenge he had no choice but to accept.

It is easy for me to sit here now and comment on how virtually impossible it would have been for them to take anything from me, let alone hurt me. A challenge from them would have been comparable to a delusional four-year-old on a tricycle challenging a NASCAR driver to a race. In that moment though, there were doubts running through my mind as to how this might turn out. Foolish, foolish me.

I was more than willing to engage in a confrontation even if I needed to provoke it a little. There was no real sense of confidence in what I was or what I could do; instead, it was my sudden compulsion for self-destruction that not only led me into this part of town but also had me ready to throw down then and there. Myra was right about me—I had absolutely no understanding of my potential. The events that followed would ultimately redirect the course of my life and would serve to shape the individual I would very soon become.

"Are you fucking serious, man!" the man asked? "We're gonna fucking gut you!" He held up the knife as he spoke in case I had been too stupid to notice he had been holding it.

I didn't even bother to acknowledge his threat; instead, I simply stepped toward the three of them, daring them to do something, anything, and they didn't let me down. As I stepped dangerously close to him, the knife-carrying man withdrew quickly and, in doing so, backed into the two men standing behind him. As he raised his knife and clumsily pointed it at me in that same instant that he nearly tripped over his companions, I quickly grabbed the knife with my left hand while forcefully shoving him with my right. He and those behind him toppled like bowling pins.

He quickly began to spring to his feet only to be met with a powerful kick to his face, easily sufficient enough to hospitalize him. I didn't even kick him as hard as I could have; had I, I may in all likelihood, have killed him. The denim jacket he was wearing became red with the blood that spilled from his nose and mouth as he flew backward into the arms of the black man who hadn't yet recovered from falling initially.

Continuing my role as the aggressor, I stepped toward his left and grabbed his white friend—a blond-haired slender man with most of his teeth already missing. As I grabbed his collar with my left hand, I easily lifted him from the ground. I was going to strike him with my right but instead intercepted a quick punch he threw at me. With his left fist in my right hand, I squeezed until I could feel his bones breaking in my grip while his feet dangled helplessly off the ground. In that instant, I quickly tossed him to the side and evaded what looked like a powerful strike from the much larger black man who had finally joined in the fight. I remember taking a mostly defensive role initially against him not so much because I had to but mostly because I was interested in testing myself and my reactions to his attempts to injure or kill me. Every swing he made seemed to move so slowly and was forecasted in advance by subtle indicators that, while seemingly unnoticed by most, seemed to scream out at me. I almost seemed to know what he was going to do before even he did. For several moments, he swung at me with all his power and charged at me with everything he had while I simply stepped left or right or gave him a quick shove into the wall of the building next to us.

I could tell that he was becoming increasingly frustrated while at the same time exhausting himself—all within thirty seconds or less. I ended our exchange with a single blow to his floating ribs on his left side, instantly breaking them and sending him helplessly to the ground.

My exchange with these three was overly anticlimatic. They may as well have been small children. There were three of them, but it wouldn't have mattered if there had been six. There was nothing they could have done to me; suddenly, this much became very clear.

For the moment, they distracted me from Trish, which was a welcomed blessing. Still, there were ramifications stemming from this conflict that I hadn't even begun to consider. My life was about to take a 180-degree turn, leading me into a world that I would never have seen myself in.

I left the three injured idiots bleeding on the street and walked on; I really didn't want to attract any more attention than I already had. There were a number of people who witnessed the scene. Most of them stopped what they were doing long enough to marvel or laugh at the brief entertainment I had created for them. Afterward, they went on about their business and would have certainly denied seeing anything if asked.

But there was one man who had watched what happened and had taken enough of an interest to follow me as I proceeded away from the scene. He kept a safe distance but did not let me get too far ahead of him to lose me. I had no idea who he was, but whatever his intentions were, I needed to crush them. I turned right into an alleyway and waited for him to approach by listening to his footsteps—left, right, left, right, as swiftly as his legs could bring him. He slowed down to cautiously peer around the corner of the alleyway when I grabbed him, pulled him into the alley, and violently pinned him against the wall.

"Have you been following me?" I asked firmly.

"No... I mean, yes... kind of. Actually, I wanted to introduce myself—I'm Charlie... Charlie L——."

Ordinarily, I am an easygoing person, pretty laid back and willing to engage with whoever wished to speak with me. On this particular day, however, I was absolutely not in the mood to provide this lowlife the time of day, let alone engage with him in conversation. As I looked at him, all I truly wanted to do was to knock him across the street in a fashion similar to what I had done twenty minutes earlier. Still, even I realized that my temper was beginning to control me—a state that I'm sure Arthur would have advised me to subdue.

This Charlie character was a little too well-dressed considering the neighborhood. He was a decent-looking guy, tall, blond hair, brown eyes, slender build, maybe in his mid to late twenties, and wore a quart of cologne.

"What do you want?" I asked.

"Hey, I just wanted to talk to you for a minute. I saw what you did back there, and I have to tell you—that was fucking awesome That big black guy, his name is Rodney, and in addition to being a local thug, he is also an underground fighter and a pretty damn good one too."

"Look," I began, "I'm sorry if he was some kind of friend of yours, but—"

"No, he wasn't a friend," he said, interrupting me. "More like a client I used to represent. You see, I'm kind of in that business."

"You're a fighter?" I asked in disbelief.

"No. In fact, I've never actually been in a fight before. I work more behind the curtains. Like I said, I represent people. Those other two guys were just clowns, but the way you went through Rodney, you could make a lot of money."

"Sorry, friend, I'm not interested," I said as I released my grip on his collar and began to walk away.

"What kind of work do you do?" he said loudly. "If you don't mind me asking."

"I'm between jobs at the moment," I answered as I continued walking away from him.

"Then what else do you have going for you? You could make five grand tonight!" he shouted.

I stopped in my tracks. He was right—what else did I have going for me? What was my ultimate plan here once I stopped walking aimlessly around Chicago's shady areas, that is? There was no reason for me not to at least investigate what this goofy ass was talking about. I was a werewolf in Chicago, and I had two weeks before the moon was full.

Later that night, Charlie and I met up with an assembly in an old parking lot behind an out–of–business office building not too far from the docks. There were about two dozen cars, some of them BMWs and Mercedeses and a lot of money being bet. To be totally honest, I have no idea what Charlie did or who he talked to, but despite my size, the odds were set against me as far as the betters were concerned as I was an unknown and their champion was nicknamed the Beast.

Apparently, the Beast was Swedish born and the winner of virtually every fight he had been set up with. He stood six foot four and was every bit of a solid 280 pounds. He had a large scar that ran down the left side of his face; I heard someone say that he acquired it during his childhood.

"Are you sure this is smart?" Charlie asked. "We could have started with someone besides this guy. Why did you want to fight him first? You're gonna get your ass kicked before you even get started in this!"

"Isn't there more money in it if I fight him?"

"Yes, but only if you win. The loser walks away with nothing. That's assuming he can ever walk again. This dude means business, and he will rip your fucking head off. I've seen him do it to people!"

"He's still human, right?"

"Yeah, but you're gonna have to be a fucking animal if you want to last more than a few seconds with this guy."

"I've think I've got that covered," I said to him.

The group was cheering for my opponent and booing me as everyone prepared to watch me get the holy shit beat out of me. "Hey there," a red-haired woman called out to me. She wore a black miniskirt and a white sleeveless top that left little to the imagination. "If you win, you can take me home tonight," she said with a seductive smile.

"Oh great," Charlie said. "Now you're distracted by a fucking prostitute!"

"I'll be right back," I said as I stepped into the ring of cars and faced the Beast.

As much as the crowd had been cheering and whistling when the fight started, everyone fell deathly silent when, after fourteen seconds, I walked away from the former champion as he lay with a broken leg, dislocated shoulder, and ruptured kidney. I won nearly eight thousand dollars that night. Twelve hundred of which went to Charlie.

Of course, as my secondary prize, I took the prostitute for the evening. We stayed at a rather nice hotel that night. As for the sex, it served the same purpose as did the fight—to momentarily distract me from the all-consuming darkness that loomed over my soul like a horrible storm cloud.

I suppose that if I'm going to offer my story, I should offer it without omitting the ugliness. As far as my life is concerned, this is the ugly part. So as for the prostitute, I used her, and when I was finished, I tossed her ass into the hallway. As far as I was concerned, she could go jump off a building at that point—I couldn't care less. After all, she served a purpose, and once her purpose was completed, I really had no other use for her. She would be the first of many.

The next morning, several men in business suits met me in the hotel lobby. Apparently, they provided the same service as did Charlie—only with a little more class. They each promised me money, cars, drugs, women, everything; all I had to do was let them arrange my fights, and of course, take a percentage of the profits from my wins. I wasn't really that interested though; after all, what use did I have for drugs or cars or even money for that matter? True, money is nice; it's what makes the world go around, but I'm a fucking werewolf. What did I care? Of course, women were great, but I would soon learn that women were a virtually inexhaustible resource.

Maybe I was just going with my instincts, but I chose to stay with Charlie. Besides, I kind of felt that he would be less apt to sell out on me or set me up for something horrible. When I finally did meet up with him, he was still in shock over what had happened the night before. Not just the fact that I walked away from the fight a winner, but that I had also beaten the total shit out of this guy of all guys in a matter of seconds.

For the next week or so, we stayed in Chicago and during that time, I had two more fights, both ending in the same manner as the first. While everyone was amazed, this was certainly no challenge for me.

Every night, Charlie would set me up with different women—a redhead, blonde, brunette, black, Asian. I didn't care. It was as though I had opened some kind of sexual floodgate. My carnal appetite was almost as insatiable as my hunger—no sooner would I finish with one than I would discard her for the next. There were times when I could go through three women a night then sleep half the day away.

Maybe on some subconscious level, I was angry with the fairer sex, and I was going to punish them by treating them like shit. Like I mentioned earlier, the worse I treated them, the more they seemed to adore me. As a nice guy with good ethics, women totally ignored me, but as an abusive alcoholic who beat people up for a living, they flocked to me. It's no wonder the world is as fucked up as it is—assholes are rewarded and revered while good men are laughed at and taken advantage of by women. That is what I've come to understand anyway. Fortunately for me, I was now an official asshole.

We couldn't stay in Chicago forever though; we had to go where the fights were. All in all, Charlie was a pretty good manager—if that is what you'd want to call him. He basically took care of arranging everything, never once trying to screw me over. All I had to do was wake up and fight. In fact, there was only one minor problem that Charlie had.

"Listen," he said. "I don't know how the fuck you do it, but you step in there and make killing those motherfuckers look effortless, and that's awesome, but it's also a problem."

"Really?"

"Yes, really," he answered. "No one wants to put their fighter against someone who is not only going to kick their fucking asses but also humiliate them by doing it in fifteen fucking seconds! If you're fucking invincible, then that's awesome as shit, but it doesn't do us any good if everyone knows that. We want people to think that their fighters don't just have a chance at beating you, but that they have a pretty fucking good chance at beating you. To do this, we have to make every fight look good, and I'm sorry, but fifteen seconds isn't a good fight. In fact, doing that is just going to piss everyone there the fuck off."

"So what do I do?"

"Give them a fucking show. That's what they want. That's why they're there in the first place. Don't get me wrong, you definitely want to win. You just want to make it look like you barely did it."

It was actually sound advice, and from that point forward, I did just as Charlie suggested. We traveled from New York to Philadelphia to Miami, new cities, new fights, win after win, but just barely. Then we traveled west through Dallas, Los Angeles, Portland, living out of hotels and doing my best to preoccupy my often-dismal mood.

Each month during the full of the moon, I would slip away for a few days to find a quite and safe location for the becoming. I took every precaution I could to prevent anyone else from getting hurt, and as far as I know, nothing like Pinedale ever happened again.

This went on for several years, one fight after another followed by one meaningless sexual encounter after another—it was monotonous but a welcomed pattern that I could easily lose myself in. Charlie was cool about most things and did not cross any boundaries with me, nor did he attempt to become something more than he was—a business partner. We had a good rapport, but in the end, I did my job and he did his. Over the course of our travels, we had each made a fortune.

It seemed that everyone wanted an opportunity to fight me. Often, these so-called managers would videotape the fights and have their fighters watch them, trying to find my weak points, trying to develop some strategy for ending my winning streak. It was highly amusing. Eventually though, we had to increase the quality of our show. We started by allowing my opponent to step into the circle against me with a weapon of some sort, usually a knife or something like that. Eventually, two then three opponents at the same time would challenge me.

I've said it before; my life was hollow and meaningless. Most of the time, I felt as though everything that had happened to me before I started this part of my life was so distant, so far away. I sometimes wondered if Trish was real at all or if maybe I only dreamt her up. On those rare occasions when my mind seemed less clouded, I would wonder how much longer I planned on living this way, wonder when I was finally going to put some kind of order back into my existence. These were unwelcome thoughts, however, and easily remedied with Jack Daniel's and another lay.

Still, I knew that the winds of change would blow my way sooner rather than later.

SEVENTEEN

THEN THE DAY came that would forever change the course of my life. I was in Vegas; and though I had fought there many times before, this particular bout consisted of three groups of three men, each with bladed weapons trying to kill me—nothing too spectacular. Funny, everyone seems so confident in their abilities when they are hopped up on enough speed. The fight took place in the underground parking garage of a large hotel casino.

It didn't really matter if it was one or three or five opponents or, in this case, nine; in the end, they are still human—slow and clumsy. Despite the overwhelming odds, I won the fight in less than six minutes. It was, as were most fights, anticlimatic—like spending an hour setting up dominos only to knock them down in thirty or forty seconds. But I won, which was really no surprise to me or Charlie, another quarter million dollars that we earned.

Generally, there was always a certain amount of chaos and pandemonium following such an event. People would crowd together to congratulate me and shake my hand or threaten me with one of their fighters. The mood of the crowd usually depended on how impressed they were with me or how much money they won or lost while betting.

There was nothing too remarkable about this fight versus the many I had won in the past—Charlie set everything up, and I beat the holy fuck out of anyone and everyone that was in the ring with me. On this particular day, however, there was a certain scent, ever so faint but absolutely and definitely there. It was something I knew once—someone, that is, but different. Who was it? Who? People were speaking with me, and while I could see their lips moving and could hear the words that they were saying, I was totally ignoring them all. My mind was desperately trying to recall that sweet fragrance and who it belonged to.

"Nicely done," Charlie said to me, doing his best to suppress his true excitement. "By the way, there are a couple of blondes that wanted to meet you. They are in the corner."

"Thanks, Charlie, but I need to check on something first."

"All right," he said puzzled. "What is it?"

"I don't know," I answered as I walked away. I glanced at the two women who were planning on sharing a bed with me. They were nice—one with short blonde hair, the other with longer blonde hair and each in their early twenties, maybe. I turned away from them, and in that instant, a most horrible and painful thought entered my mind—Trish. Maybe it was because of the blonde hair combined with this mysterious scent from my past, but for a moment, and a moment only, my heart was saddened some. A thought ran through my mind, *Where is my friend when I need you?* I quickly banished this from my mind and went in pursuit of whoever was here.

I disregarded the two women, assuming that they were be available to me upon my return and walked out of the garage, following my olfactory senses and trying to remember where I knew that peculiar scent. I climbed a flight of stairs that led me to the sparsely filled lobby. For a moment, I lost the fragrance that had totally captured my attention; but then suddenly I found it again, stronger than ever—the individual I was looking for was very close.

I proceeded across the lobby and exited through the sliding doors that led outside. The brisk air seemed to slap at me with violent gusts and tore away the fragrance that I had been pursuing My nose is good, damn good, but tracking the scent seemed next to impossible in these circumstances. I turned to the left then the right, scanning all the faces and hoping to see someone familiar. I was going to cross the street but caught a slight trace of the person I was looking for before I did and instead continued to the right and moved away from the hotel entranceway.

My mind seemed a blur as I attempted to recall who this individual was—someone familiar and yet not so familiar. Again, as if she were meant to haunt me forever, Trish came to mind. Though I knew that I was seeking out a woman, I knew it wasn't Trish. I could also rule out Myra—it certainly wasn't her. I began to consider the possibility that that someone who was watching me I had known as a man. Was it possible that I recognized an odor from a time before I became a lycanthrope?

For two blocks, I walked, putting the relative safety of the hotel far behind me. The street was busy, the wind was blowing, and ten thousand scents swirled in every direction. I had lost her, and I didn't even know who she was. The street was busy, and as I watched pedestrians pass back and forth for several moments, I began to turn and walk back to the hotel.

Before I took even a single step, however, my attention was brought to an alley across the street. I don't really think I possess a sixth sense, and I don't really believe that animals do either. Despite this, I am very highly aware of considerably subtle hints. I use *hints* for lack of a better word, little things that catch my attention; and while, at first glance, seem to have no real significance, they draw and hold my interest for reasons that I can't really describe. Maybe I will write more about this later, but in this instance, the alley seemed to attract me. It was offering me a hint.

I crossed the street, ignoring the oncoming traffic while staring down the alley While the street and sidewalk was bustling and active, brightly lit and almost polished to make it attractive, the alley was dark, dirty-looking, and seemingly empty. Sandwiched between another casino and a restaurant, the alleyway provided a back entranceway for deliveries to be brought in and trash to be taken out. It was exactly what one would expect—sinister and dank looking.

I began to walk away from the street and into the unknown. I could smell rodents. I could smell urine on a wall where someone had relieved himself. I could smell the garbage dumpster and all the foul odor associated with it. I could smell a dead and decomposing cat beneath wet cardboard boxes. I could even smell the maggots that consumed it. Is it necessary for me to add that there was little pleasant about the area I walked?

Then suddenly, there was that scent again—soft, beautiful and sweet, and strong now. Yes, she was here with me in this alleyway, and she was hiding. I knew that I recognized something about how she smelled, but until then, I really wasn't sure if she was human or not; I just didn't have enough for my nose to go on—only traces. But now, I was fully aware that the individual I had sought out was not human at all, but another lycanthrope.

As I cautiously advanced deeper into the alley, I remembered the last time I came in search of an individual with a beautiful scent who also wasn't human that happened in Rockford when I met Trish. Again, her memories tried to overwhelm me, and again, I brushed them aside to focus on the here and now.

The real difference between what happened in Rockford all those years earlier and what was happening at that moment was interesting to note. When I followed Trish, I was relatively new with my condition and seeking out someone much more advanced in their condition. As it was here, lycanthropy had run in my veins for some time—it made me an old soul somehow, just as Trish was when I met her. I had the impression that whoever I shared this alley with was very new with her condition.

I proceeded past two side doorways and stood in the darkest part of the alley. I considered calling out, and maybe I should have. Instead, I remained quiet, listening; and while I could hear a great many things that were happening all around me, the woman I was looking for was quiet, especially quiet... and afraid. Yes, she was afraid of me though I wasn't really sure how I knew that. I just did.

In an instant, with preternatural speed and strength, this person lunged from around one of the many corners that allowed her to hide in its dark shadows. In less than half a second, she moved an impressive distance and attempted to strike me. If I had been human, she would have killed me there in that alleyway, and there would have been no way that I would have had the reflexes or strength to have stopped it. Instead, however, I quickly evaded and countered by striking her—very hard.

Without even a moment to examine who this individual was, I shoved her, throwing her body into the brick wall of the restaurant.

She had dark hair but wore a hood that provided a mild barrier, preventing me from seeing her face as she attempted to recover. I had broken her ribs and probably created internal damage when I hit her. I suspected that I injured her back, maybe broke it even, when I threw her into the wall in the way I did.

It was an odd moment for a flashback, but I thought about Myra's warnings and remembered how hateful she was with me when I offered even a reluctance to defend myself by striking a woman. Well, it seemed I had gotten over that reluctance easily enough.

The side door opened, and two large men exited. They looked like they worked in the kitchen. "What the fuck is happening out here!?" one of them shouted as he saw me standing over the severely injured woman. They were, no doubt, investigating the crash that they heard as I sent this woman's body into the wall of the building. I was ready to answer them though I really didn't know what I was going to say when I noticed something that silenced me immediately—the face of the woman who attacked me.

She had changed from when I last saw her; she was a little older now. At that moment, I couldn't even remember her name, but I knew exactly who she was. It was the girl from Arthur's school, the one who had tried so hard to have me take her with me when I left—Anne. I suddenly felt ill for what I had done.

"Get the fuck away from her!" one of the men said aggressively as he approached me. I wanted to warn him away, not that it would have done any good, but I had no time. He advanced quickly and swung at me. He missed. I didn't.

With a broken jaw and severe concussion, his body rested at the feet at the other man who had come out with him and now watched me. "This has nothing to do with you," I said, trying to offer him a warning that I didn't have time to provide to his friend. I gently picked up this former student of Arthur's, and as cautiously as I could, I carried her in my arms, and we left the alley as the other kitchen worker looked on.

I am sure I attracted many gazes on the street with this bloody and battered woman in my arms; no one stopped or questioned me. Maybe they were afraid, or maybe they didn't care, or maybe they were too busy to interfere; I didn't really want anyone to bother us, but it seemed to bother me some that no one did.

It wasn't until I made it back to the hotel lobby that the men and women working behind the desk rushed to see what they could do. "Oh my god! Is she okay?"

"She is fine," I answered, fully aware that considering how she looked at that moment, my response was hardly appropriate.

"We'll call an ambulance," another man said.

"There is really no need for that. She will be fine."

My room was on the twelfth floor, but I had no intention on taking the elevator—it was just as fast for me to use the stairwell. I was suddenly a little surprised when I found that my room had been unlocked. As I opened the door, I realized that the two women who had been watching the fight downstairs were here now.

I had been gone for about thirty minutes though it seemed like no time at all. Charlie had apparently brought these two up and let them in, assuming that I would be up to join them soon. On any other night before this one, I would have used them just as I had used countless women for quite a number of years. I wouldn't have cared about how they felt. I wouldn't have cared if they liked me, wanted me, needed me. The only thing I seemed to care about was that they put out—that was all I wanted.

I must have had an epiphany that night, however. I had thought about Trish every day of my life over and over again. I felt guilt for leaving her, and in some strange way, I felt guilt for how I had been living my life. It was her I truly loved, and there wasn't a single other woman in the world that could possibly be a substitute for that. Still, I tried to fill whatever dark void that had been growing inside of me by sleeping with thousands of women (maybe thousands, hell, I don't know). Something about seeing Anne though, changed all that inside of me (I did eventually remember her name).

I rested her on the bed, and even though I knew that she was going to be fine and that she really needed no comfort in order to heal, it was important to me that she be made as comfortable as possible. As I positioned her head, I could tell that her neck had been broken when she hit the wall. I took a corner of the blanket from the bed and began to clean the blood that was coming from her mouth.

"Hello," came a sexy voice from behind me. "I'm Chelsey. I hope you don't mind, but your friend let us in."

I turned to look at her as she exited the bathroom. It was the short-haired blonde woman, wearing only a white towel. It wasn't until then that she noticed the lifeless body on the bed. Her expression told me that she was wondering what I had done to her.

"She will be fine," I said. "She just had an accident outside, and she just needs a little time to recover. But I need you to get dressed and leave."

A moment later, the long-haired woman emerged from the bathroom. Apparently she and Chelsey had been in the Jacuzzi. She, unlike Chelsey, wore nothing and stood in the nude. I was quickly losing my patience with the both of them. The epiphany I mentioned all but totally took away any need to have these women in my vicinity. Even as I could smell the lust coming from between their legs, I found myself revolted.

"I want to make you feel sooo good!" this woman stated seductively.

"Listen to me as I am going to say this just once more! Get your damn clothes, and get the fuck out of my room! I don't even want to look at you. Just go!" I didn't yell or raise my voice, but my tone was vicious.

Of course, I had absolutely pissed them off, and they were saying horrible things about me as I firmly closed the door in their faces, but my attention was on Anne at this point. Why was she here? Why now?

I suddenly noticed that her eyes were open and that she was looking at me. "Can you speak?" I asked her.

The tiniest smile emerged from her face, and her eyes welled up in tears. "I am so happy to see you," she said in a whisper.

"What are you doing here? Why did you attack me in the alley?"

"I can't move my arms or legs!" she said in a horrified tone.

"That is because your neck is broken," I said in a less-than-sensitive tone. I had assumed, incorrectly it seemed, that she was somehow versed with what she had become. Upon hearing my statement, her eyes opened wide and were filled with terror.

"Am I going to be okay?!" she asked.

"Anne, do you not realize what you are?"

"Please tell me that I'm going to be okay!" she said in an almost hysterical tone as tears streamed down her face.

"You are going to be fine," I said reassuringly, but my words seemed to do little to calm her. "Listen to me. You have been hurt. In fact, you've been hurt really bad, but it is okay—you are healing up even as we are speaking now. By tomorrow morning, it will be as though you were never injured at all. In the meantime, I want you to focus on moving your fingers. Make them move."

"I can't!" she said desperately.

"Keep working. Keep trying. They will move soon."

It was another thirty minutes before the first signs of life reentered her upper extremities and another thirty after that before she had a minimal usage of her arms and shoulders. She had, by this point, calmed down and was at least a bit more rational. I retrieved the large cooler that I normally brought with me in my travels. Generally, I kept if filled with ground beef, sausage, sometimes even just butter—anything with calories. I pulled out several pounds of the ground beef, placed it on a plate, and offered it to Anne.

She offered me a most queer look. "It isn't cooked?" she said as though I had lost my mind. "It also doesn't smell right."

"How does it smell?" I asked.

"It smells tainted. It has been out for too long."

"How does it smell?" I repeated the question.

"It smells good, but it still isn't cooked."

"Oh God, have you gone through even one lunar cycle?"

"I don't know what that means," she answered.

"Well, the answer is no because it is definitely something you would have remembered. I will tell you this much though. It doesn't matter how badly the meat is tainted or even if it is totally rotten altogether. It can't make you sick—you will never become sick again. There is nothing wrong with this beef, however. It is your olfactory system noting subtle peculiarities that your nose would have never been able to detect before. In time, you will get used to it and utilize it just as much as you would your eyesight and your hearing."

"So we don't cook it?"

I was surprised by her lack of knowledge about lycanthropy, having lived with Arthur for as long as she did. Still, I recalled how private he was, especially concerning the less-than-pleasant aspects of our condition, such as eating unfathomable portion sizes or even how old he truly was. "Anne, I would never have hurt you if I had known who you were, if I had known it was you, but why did you attack me?"

"I thought you were someone else," she answered. "I have to tell you some very bad things."

"So talk to me," I began. "What happened? Why are you here?"

For several moments, Anne was silent, collecting her thoughts and trying to mentally establish a point at which to start with an answer to my question. Clearly, she had a lot to tell me. "Several years ago, I started going out to recruit new students. The school had grown considerably since you left, and we actually began another school in South Carolina. I was in Florida, interviewing a potential student and his family—it was someone that Arthur was very excited to have come and join us.

"As I was in the middle of a conversation with them, I saw the most horrific vision. I left the interview, probably making the family believe I was out of my mind, and tried calling Arthur or anyone at the Vermont school over and over again. After an hour still unable to get a hold of anyone, I decided to head back.

"Sometimes I see things years before they happen, and sometimes I only know an instant before it occurs. I immediately caught a flight north and returned to the school, trying to call at every chance I got. But it was too late. By the time I arrived, the school was in flames. I couldn't bring myself to even move. The Vanderman had been my home for many years—it was all I knew. I was in a state of shock.

"I didn't even think of the full moon, not until Arthur—it wasn't really Arthur, but it was the monster. It leapt at me from the darkness, knocking me down, then it bit into my neck. I don't think it even meant to hurt me because it could have easily done so. It was savage and frightening, but at the same time, it was gentle somehow.

"Just at that moment, guns were being fired from all directions. There were maybe ten men shooting at the monster at the same time. As I watched what was happening, it occurred to me that maybe he had jumped out of the shadows not to kill me but to protect me from these men. They were hunting him but had intended on killing me when they saw me.

"As I lay on my back, I watched as the gunshots seemed to heal and close up almost as soon as he was hit. It wasn't until one of the men ran directly up to him and shot him several times in the head that he finally collapsed on top of me.

"In a few moments, he wasn't the monster anymore, but Arthur again, only he was missing most of his head. The men who had killed him were responsible for setting fire to the school, and in the process they set Arthur, the monster, free from whatever he was in. As far as I could tell, they selectively killed whatever students that they thought might have been lycanthropes as well.

"I just lay there, completely covered in blood—some of it mine, but most belonged to Arthur. I was so afraid that I didn't even move. Everyone had assumed Arthur had killed me even though he hadn't really injured me much at all.

"When the coast was clear, I got up and ran as quickly as I could. I didn't go to my car. I just ran into the night for as long as I could until I got to the bus terminal. I later learned that our sister school had been razed as well—a massacre. It was all over the news. I'm surprised that you didn't hear about it."

"I don't really watch much television these days," I said coldly.

"Then the next day, I started on the road, and I have been running ever since, looking for you."

Her story, while abbreviated and brief, was a little much to take in. Arthur dead? The school gone? "Who were these men?"

"They are some kind of fanatical religious group. Their goal is to find and exterminate lycanthropes in the name of God. When they learned that I wasn't dead, they began hunting me also. In these last few weeks, I have barely escaped with my life on a couple of occasions. They are relentless, and they know that I am here—here in Las Vegas. I'm sorry, I didn't know where else to go or who else I could turn to."

All the while, I had expected my potential enemies to be other lycanthropes or maybe even something I hadn't yet encountered—after all, this is what Myra had warned me about—but human beings?

"So what do we do?"

"Anne, tomorrow night is the beginning of the lunar cycle. We're going to need to get out of town for the becoming. I have gone out to the Valley of Fire State Park before and have found it pretty isolated and very large—it is about as far from civilization as one can get. That was my plan for tomorrow. That is what you and I are going to have to do."

Over the next several hours, Anne filled me in on all the stories she had, and while I listened quietly, I began to feel a slight jealousy creep into me. It wasn't really a bad envy or anything, more of a guilty one on my part. I felt that my life over the last decade had been poorly utilized; the world had been spinning, and I wasn't really a part of it. Part of my epiphany seemed to dance around this concept—the live-one-day-at-a-time mind-set that I had slipped into. It was an absolute and senseless existence with the pursuit of immediate gratification only.

Eventually, Anne regained her ability to wiggle her toes, and before we had fallen asleep, she was able to move her legs with ease. I told her that by the time we woke, she would be as she was before the incident Anne fell asleep before I did; I watched as she tossed and turned while violent and terrifying images swept through her unconsciousness. Eventually, I could fight the inevitable no longer. While Anne slumbered restlessly in bloodstained bed, I closed my eyes as I lay on the floor.

It was midday by the time we awoke. Anne crawled from the bed and examined her legs that had healed completely at that point. "This is miraculous!" she said. She then ran to me and wrapped her arms around me.

It seems that I keep saying this throughout this writing, but there was no way that I could really describe the conflict that I was experiencing at that moment. While it wasn't necessarily easy to resist her when I met her in Vermont, I could at least use the excuse that she was only a kid to walk away from her. But now... I didn't really know what to think or how to feel. The women I kicked out of the room the night before were a bit younger than Anne was now.

Until that point, the energy that she had offered was fear and surprise; but suddenly she was as seductive as she was ten years earlier. "You should probably go get in the shower," I said to her as I noted the dried blood caked to her hair.

"Get in with me?"

"Maybe," I said, not knowing what I was going to do or even how I was supposed to feel. Without giving a second thought, Anne removed her blood-spattered hooded sweater and slipped her black bra off as though she had been rehearsing for this moment for a long time. Like Myra and Trish, Anne demonstrated no modesty around me. Unlike Anne though, Myra and Trish, who also undressed in front of me, seemed to pay little mind to what I felt about it as though I was the family pet; there wasn't really a sexual element to the act. But this display from Anne, on the other hand, was a purely sexual gesture, and Anne's eyes paid very careful attention to my reaction to her exposing her breasts.

And what she saw was me looking away and finally turning and walking toward the suitcase. After retrieving clothing that I intended to wear for that day as well as an outfit that Anne could wear until I found something more suitable, I turned to see that Anne had completely disrobed and was walking into the bathroom to shower.

Did I find her nude body attractive? Yes. Did I want her? Yes. So why didn't I take advantage of that? I have an answer, kind of, but I don't expect anyone to understand. It would be easy for me to say I had an epiphany, a lame excuse that fails to have any real meaning once I have an erection. No, my initial reason for denying myself this newly created lycanthrope in the midst of physical and sexual perfection was that I was afraid of how I would feel about her afterward. For the countless women I had slept with over the years, I had developed a strange aversion, a disgust with them as soon as I had "soiled" them. In those cases, as I have described, I *never* wanted to look at them again. They were whores to me and nothing more. I discarded them just as one would a used condom.

I wanted to help Anne. I wanted to protect her, to keep her safe if not for my sake or hers, then for Arthur who was the best of us all. Sleeping with her, I feared, would change that respect I had for her as well as the newly found respect I had for myself. To me, she would become nothing better than the pathetic women I had thrown from the warmth of my bed.

There was one other issue running through my mind, but it was one that I didn't entirely understand myself. Obviously, after all this time, I still held a dear and almost sacred place in my heart for Trish. It occurred to me, much earlier in fact, that I would never escape her memory. I hated and so often regretted ever even meeting her. And yet I loved her. I loved the idea of loving her. Suddenly, since my supposed epiphany, I felt a harsh guilt rush over me as though I had betrayed her by giving into my carnal urges and impulses. In truth, I had felt guilt for giving up on finding her and settling for the life that I now had. In my mind and in my heart, I had become worse than even the monster—I was a horrible man, a horrible thing.

Somehow, seeing Anne cut away the ugly façade that had grown like an outer skin and had consumed the Caleb that I had once been. There was little emotion left in me, but I still and would forever possess a strong sense of right and wrong. It was my love for Trish that would ultimately rescue me from my own despair, but it was Anne's presence at that exact moment that allowed me to reestablish that part of me that I had lost—by finding her, I found myself again.

I considered showering myself. I certainly needed to, but didn't trust myself to take my clothes off, and I certainly didn't trust Anne. I assumed that the minute I got into the shower, Anne would immediately hop in with me. I laid a shirt I selected for her on the shelf just inside the bathroom. It was a very poor selection as it was much too large for her, but it would suffice until we could purchase something else. I figured she could wear the same pants that she had—they weren't bloodstained like her sweater.

After showering, Anne dressed and we prepared to leave. I made a quick phone call to Charlie while I was in the lobby, informing him that I was going to need a little time to take care of some personal issues that had arisen and would be in touch. I had expected him to become upset, but surprisingly, he took my news well; apparently, he was still counting the money from the previous night's earnings.

Then as I hung up the pay phone, I noticed something disturbing that required my intervention. I turned to see Anne across the lobby and an individual who was paying particularly close attention to her as she stared off into the distance through the lobby windows, oblivious to the man who had her in his sight. It would have been easy to assume that he paid her the attention that he did because of what she was wearing—my extra-large shirt—or possibly because she was such a beautiful woman. But again, there was that feeling deep inside of me, that subtle hint that something was wrong with this picture. Meanwhile, the psychic just waited patiently for me to finish with my phone call.

I continued to watch as he pulled a walkie-talkie from his coat pocket. "I have the target in sight," he said as I listened with preternatural hearing. Clearly, he had no idea that Anne had contacted me. He had no idea who I even was or that I was even here. I casually strolled up behind him and quickly placed my left hand around him and secured his forehead while I punched the back of his head with my right fist. His skull collapsed, killing him before he could even call out. I lowered his body to the floor as his legs jerked and quivered. I looked around and was surprised that no one had noticed my violent act, but I knew that within seconds, someone would turn to see the man whom I had killed.

I quickly grabbed Anne. "We're leaving now!" I said to her.

An hour later, we sat in my car at a gas station in Coyote Springs with Anne still wearing my oversized shirt.

EIGHTEEN

THERE IS REALLY no need for me to offer detail into the transformation of what Anne was and what she was to become. The only silver lining—if you wanted to call it that—was that Anne's metamorphosis preceded mine. I cannot imagine what she might have felt had I changed over before her, nor could I say that her safety would have been guaranteed, considering the aggressiveness of the monster I was.

Just as Myra had done with me years earlier, I did my best to comfort Anne, to explain with as much detail as I could what she was to experience. Of course, there is really no way one could ever prepare for such a traumatic event. Still, at least she wasn't ignorant of what was about to happen to her. Anne cried, and as I looked into her eyes, I knew all too well what she truly wanted to ask, "Please, is there anything I can do to keep this from happening?"

As I stood at the edge of an uninhabited desert, Anne's change was complete. Although I had become the monster hundreds of times by this point, watching someone go through it was nothing short of chilling and deeply unsettling. It is really not much different than watching someone you know and care for tortured to death and unable to do anything but watch.

As for the transformation itself, as well as the monster, I had only seen it once before—with Myra. It was during that episode that she attacked me and tore my eye from its socket. While I wasn't really sure of what to expect with Anne, or more precisely, I wasn't really sure of what to expect from the monster that she would become, I did not expect anything violent from her. Although I knew that the beast was unpredictable and certainly capable of killing me once the changeover was complete, I was not the same person that I had been during my encounter with Myra's dark side. I was older, much further along in my condition, and had lost nearly all fear that I had carried as a man.

Not surprising though, while the beast stared at me, snarled, and paced back and forth, it kept a reasonably comfortable distance. It could have attacked me, or it could have run off, but it chose to do nothing, nothing but wait. I wondered what was going through her/its mind as it watched me; surely it knew what I was. It waited for the inevitable, and the inevitable happened.

While I cannot say what happened when my inner demon came out, I can discuss the events that happened the following morning. I opened my eyes to a most peculiar scene. The midmorning sun blazed across the horizon and made the ground seem even more orange and Martianlike then usual. An insect buzzed annoyingly at my face, and in my arms, the beautiful woman whom I knew only as a girl until thirty-six hours earlier. We were in a spoon position, with Anne curled into a semifetal position while I wrapped my arms around her.

I moved my body away from Anne and felt the sweat that had accumulated between the two of us. As I moved, Anne woke and looked at me with a degree of terror in her eyes. "What happened?"

"Just what I told you would happen," I answered in a tone more calloused than I had intended. I was upset, less at Anne, and more at the situation. It was a scenario that most men would welcome—to wake up in the middle of nowhere with a beautiful naked woman who worshipped the ground you walked on But to me, it was upsetting. I was upset that I woke up with her in such an intimate embrace. I was upset that it wasn't Trish.

"What happened last night?" Anne asked timidly.

"I wish I knew. I wish there was a way of knowing."

Both of us naked, we walked nearly three miles back to the car where we donned the clothes we had taken off the night before. After dressing, we drove into Overton and purchased enough food to satisfy our needs. I rented a motel room, and Anne and I slept most of the day.

At first, it was my intention to keep a safe and healthy distance from Anne who, despite her change in sexual aggressiveness following the becoming from the preceding night, certainly still retained her feelings for me. However, I finally gave in—not to anything sexual but rather to a very tender intimacy, an intimacy I offered to no one before her.

Although Anne had demonstrated a demanding persona the day before—and when I knew her years ago—she was now very quiet and seemingly withdrawn. As she lay on the bed, I wrapped my arms around her. Although we were now wearing clothes, we were positioned much as we were upon waking that morning. We rested, and eventually she turned and seemed to bury her small and petite frame into my chest, with her head tucked under my chin. I didn't sleep, but I held her closely as she did and as the nightmares tormented her.

By five o'clock, we left the motel and returned to our secluded location in the middle of nowhere. As we drove, Anne held my hand and looked out the window. Clearly, she did not wish to go through with this again—neither did I.

"I am sorry this is happening," I said to her. "You don't deserve this."

She looked at me and brought a smile to her face that I hadn't seen since the day before. "It's okay as long as I am with you!"

The events of that night unfolded much as they had the night before. We parked for a while, ate some, then disrobed. Anne's changeover preceded my own, then, within thirty minutes or so, mine followed.

There was nothing terribly unusual about my sleep. I dreamt restlessly, and I had my usual night terrors that, despite how long I had suffered them, I would forever be unable to get used to them. But something strange happened that morning that had never happened since becoming a lycanthrope. Generally, when I slumber, especially during the lunar cycle, I am imprisoned within my dreams, my nightmares. Despite how desperately I attempt to awaken, I seem unable to; to us, dreams are like a sickness that must run its course.

On that morning, however, I awoke early as though I had been released early from prison. At first, I wasn't certain as to why; I was just grateful that I was given even a tiny reprieve from my nightly torture. As I sat up and looked at Anne's nude body that had come to rest next to mine, I suddenly heard several engines approaching quickly. With haste, I swung around and violently shook Anne, trying in vain to wake her. "Anne!" I yelled out as I shook her forcefully. Her deep sleep, it seemed, rivaled my own, and she was slow and reluctant to respond. I quickly scanned the horizon line, trying to assess where the hell we were when I saw the four SUVs fast approaching.

I am not really sure what was going through my mind at that exact moment, nor can I say for certain why I felt as alarmed as I did—after all, what could they or anyone possibly do to me? Still, something about how my inner demon released me from my dreams prematurely seemed desperately unsettling to me. If I have instincts, they told me at that moment to be alarmed.

Anne had only barely opened her eyes when her body tensed up with fear. "They've found us!" she said in a panicked tone.

We rose to our feet as the four enormous black trucks pulled to a stop about one hundred feet from us. I felt like a character from one of the *Planet of the Apes* movies as the doors opened and men spilled out with rifles. There was no time to talk or negotiate; in fact, not a word was spoken. They simply opened fire. I hadn't really been shot before, and I had no way of knowing how this would play out. I was in a situation that, despite what I was, I was at an absolute disadvantage and had no control over, a situation that I never wanted to be in.

To my surprise, we were struck with darts—tranquilizers. I learned that morning that lycanthropes, at least when we are not the wolf, have no immunity to tranquilizing drugs, and based on how quickly they took affect, I think it is safe to say that they used more than was necessary to subdue us. I remember standing helplessly as the shots were fired, and I remember looking at the odd-looking projectiles as they projected from my body by the dozen, and while I don't remember hitting the ground,

I do, just for a moment, remember the taste of the sand and dust as my face came to rest on the earth.

I awoke, but it seemed to be a gradual release from unconsciousness, not just asleep one moment, awake the next. It took me a while to pull out of it. When I was awake enough to realize what my surroundings were, I found myself suspended from the ceiling by a cable that was wrapped around my wrists. I was wearing pants—someone must have put them on me—but no shirt or shoes I was strung up so that my toes could not quite touch the floor.

I was surrounded by six or seven men, who seemed to be waiting impatiently for me to awaken. As soon as I did, two of them held my back so that I wouldn't swing while the others struck me like a punching bag. It didn't take long before my ribs began breaking. This went on for some time. Across the room, a blond-haired man in his midforties observed.

I could hear Anne screaming in another room; I could also hear the captors that were with her laughing in amusement. I could not bring myself to imagine what they were doing to her.

"Wow, that's quite a beating you've endured!" the blond-haired man said with amusement in his voice. He approached me from behind and circled around in front of me, coming face to face with me. "If you were human, this would probably be the time where you would begin to offer up whatever information necessary to make us stop inflicting pain upon you," he said as he stared directly into my eyes. Then quickly, a smirk crossed his face. "And then suddenly, I remember, you're not human, and so, your punishment continues."

He quickly pulled a small blade from his pocket and punctured my right eye, instantly eliminating my vision on that side. As I tried to pull away, he dug the small blade into my orbital socket as deeply as he could while twisting it to and fro. Unsatisfied with this, he withdrew the blade and made several deep slashes across my face—my nose and cheeks taking the brunt of this action.

After another extended period of beating from the man standing behind me, the blond man—who clearly was in authority here—slowly dragged a chair across the concrete floor and positioned himself in front of me. "Do you have any idea who I am?" he asked.

I looked at him with my remaining eye but said nothing. "I am the hammer of God," he said, answering himself. "And he has given me the authority to trample on serpents and scorpions."

"What's your name?" I finally asked.

He did not immediately answer; instead, he pondered the wisdom in offering me his name as though I might gain some kind of control over him if I knew it. Finally he spoke, "I am Brother John."

"Well, fuck you, Brother John!"

He smiled. "This is exactly what I would have expected from your kind. But when we are finished with you, we are going to send you straight back into hell."

"Well, finish this because I am tired of listening to you."

Brother John glared hatefully at me. "Do you have any idea of what pain is in store for you?"

"Do you have any idea of what pain I go through each and every month? This is child's play by comparison. You're a fucking amateur who doesn't even know what true pain is!"

With as much power as he could direct at me, he struck my face repeatedly, screaming throughout the process. After twenty seconds of the most violent blows he could offer with his fists, he stopped. "I demand that you tell me where the others of your kind are!"

"Even if there were others of my kind, there isn't anything you could do about them. You are under some fucked-up impression that you are doing something constructive by keeping us here, by interrogating us. But you're wrong. The world will not be any safer for you after we are dead. The truth is we're not what you think we are."

"You have killed how many people? You are an abomination, an agent of Satan in our presence. You are the very manifestation of evil!"

"And you, a God-fearing man who takes pleasure in torturing those he doesn't know, those who exist under the cruelest circumstances that you don't even care to understand. And your men, God-fearing as well I would assume. What carnal punishments have they inflicted upon the woman in the next room I wonder? Do you pretend not to hear her screams?"

In a moment of uncontained rage, Brother John quickly rose to his feet and drove the blade of his knife into my chest and neck several times, its blade penetrating deeply into my flesh. I did my best to remain as stoic as possible, denying my torturer the pleasure of knowing the pain he had caused. "Neither I nor my associates are accountable or answerable to you!"

"Before this is over," I replied, "you're going to be accountable to her."

His face, angry and hateful until that moment, quickly took on an impish and jovial expression before he began laughing. His amusement seemed contagious as the others in the room began laughing as well. "Now that's funny!" he said. "Hell, I'll even give you a small break for that one!"

There have been moments in my life—in particular, those times before I lost too much of my humanity—when I would question not only my own nature but that of those around me as well. Did I deserve to die? Would the world be a better place without me? Do I have anything truly worthwhile to offer—beyond these written words? Am I evil? If I am to be honest, then the answers to these questions become self-evident. But it's never quite so simple, is it? I can make the argument that opposes everything that, at first, seems so evident. Am I a truly evil thing? Haven't I *tried* to do the right things? Beyond the man in the Vegas hotel lobby, had I ever intentionally killed anyone? (Eventually, I would intentionally and purposefully kill many people, but at that moment, this wasn't the case.)

And what of these men? What of the whole damn human race? Do you really want my honest opinion? I hate nearly every one of you, fuckers! There are hardly a handful of you that I've come across in the last three decades that deserve even a peaceful death! If and when the time comes that an outrageous epidemic consumes the human race, leaving myself and other preternatural entities untouched in its wake, you'll get no fucking sympathy from me!

"You see," Brother John began, still seemingly entertained by my previous statement, "the full moon was last night, so I'd say that you are both out of luck there. And you'll both be long dead by the next full moon. Besides that, she's just as drugged and bound as you are. Wolf or not, I don't think either of you are going to do anything to anyone."

Brother John then proceeded confidently toward the fire pit and withdrew a red-hot stoker. As best as I could tell, this stoker was a welded piece of rebar that had been sitting in the fire for some time. Slowly, intentionally dragging each step, he approached me. It was as though he was savoring these acts by delaying every aspect of them, dragging them out for hours... or maybe days.

Unfortunately for him, he didn't have days, and his hours were limited. From what he had indicated, Brother John was quite ignorant of lycanthropes. It wouldn't matter how drugged we were, it would have absolutely no effect on the beast. As far as the chains go, they may just as well have been made of paper because when one of us would change over, we would have little difficulty tearing through them.

This fool, John, was correct about the full moon having occurred the previous night, and while I knew that there would be no further changeover for me this cycle, I also knew that the process had already begun with Anne—I could sense it. If they didn't kill her very soon, it would be too late for Brother John or his followers to stop her. I felt no obligation to warn them.

"All right, I'd say that your time was about up," John stated authoritatively. As he spoke, he slid the very tip of the stoker across my chest, searing the flesh as it moved. "Once again I'm going to ask you, where are others of your kind?"

"How many times do I have to tell you to fuck off before you actually take a hint?"

Brother John smiled though I believe he was again on the verge of losing his temper and lashing out. "Don't you see how alone you are now? An abomination of God and yet forsaken by everything unholy—you have nothing else to gain with your silence. Just a little cooperation from you is all I am asking. Just tell us what we need to know, and your suffering will cease. Can't you see? I am offering you a way out of this. This is God's will."

"You are a real fucking joke!" I said to him.

"Explain!"

"You tie us up, beat us severely, promise to kill us, then talk about offering me a way out as though you are generous and doing me a favor! If God exists at all, he has nothing to do with what is going on here."

"You see? I try to be kind, and that kindness is met with blasphemy." John brought the end of the stoker under my chin and held it firmly there as it deeply burned through the soft flesh. "I am going to break you. I promise you, I will break you."

Brother John and the others in the room proceeded with my punishment for what seemed many hours. Truthfully, time seems to have little value when one is being tortured. I had no idea of how quickly or slowly time advanced. When the changeover begins, the pain I feel is immeasurable; there is no way I could put into words the suffering that I endure. If there is a silver lining, it is simply that it doesn't last long—I tend to black out within ninety seconds or so.

But while my suffering at the hands of the self-proclaimed Hammer of God could not compete with the pain of being ripped apart from the inside out, which I had become all-too familiar with, the duration of Brother John's inflictions seemed to push my very sanity beyond a recognizable threshold. It's true, torture someone long enough, cause them enough pain, and you will drive them to insanity.

I could feel the stoker, still red-hot from its frequent reintroduction to the fire, pierce my lower back and tear through my kidney where it was left. I finally cried out, as smoke and steam spilled from the wound and rose to my nostrils. There was no part of my body that remained uncut, unbruised, or unburned by my captives. Blood spilled from me, and yet the beating and torture continued carried out by fists, clubs, razors, even scissors, which seemed to open wounds wider then a traditional blade. The four men, including Brother John, took frequent turns, giving each other breaks when they needed them. Of course, I received no such breaks.

I tried to hear what was happening with Anne as she was no longer screaming. I had assumed that her punishments were much more cruel and unforgivable than what I endured. I wasn't sure what time it was, but suddenly I knew that it was "time" and within a few moments, several shouts alerted the men taking their turns with me that something horrible was up. They each grabbed their rifles that had been resting across the room on tables and proceeded toward the doorway. Before they even made it, however, screams and gunshots rang out. Brother John glared at me while two of the men proceeded down whatever hallway existed beyond the door. He approached me with the same slow approach he had used when cutting and burning me. "What's happening?" he demanded

"Maybe you should go find out," I answered as another horrible scream filled our ears.

He brought the barrel of the gun from his side and pointed it at my head. "It's time that you die!" he said with hate in his tone. Suddenly gunfire again rang out then more screaming; John quickly turned his attention away from me. "Stay here with him," he told the last member that remained in the room. Glancing at the nameless man who had demonstrated just as much cruelty as his "brothers," I observed he now had a deeply frightened look on his face.

Several more shots followed by a smashing sound… then silence. The man who remained with me put his rifle up to my temple. I couldn't actually see him or the rifle he held as that was the side my eyesight was compromised on, but I could feel the cold barrel pressed firmly against my bloodied skin. "These are silver bullets!" he said with a trembling voice. "Why aren't they working? Make this stop, or I will kill you!"

I turned my head and looked directly at this man and, for the first time, actually saw a man, and not a monster himself. He was hardly even a man really, more of a boy; I guessed him to be seventeen or eighteen. I noticed a large tattoo on his left shoulder—a large cross and an eagle. "Silver, you might as well use a squirt gun. It won't work. You've watched too many movies."

"I swear to God, I'll kill you!" he exclaimed frantically. "Make it stop!"

"I have no control over this. You're only hope is to run, run as fast as you can."

For a moment, he remained at my side with his rifle pointed at the side of my face. Then he frantically ran though an exit on the opposite side of the room. I was alone, strung up with blood trickling down my body and pooling beneath me as it ran off my toes and onto the floor.

For what seemed a long span of time, I hung there, slowly feeling my wounds healing in the miraculous way that they always do. Despite the fact that my torture session was over, my mind had far from recovered. I cannot even say if I was awake or asleep for the next hour or so, or was it only fifteen minutes? Again, time seemed to mean nothing to me at that moment.

Then I heard the breathing of something large; I knew it wasn't human. Slowly, Anne's monster entered through the door that had been left open. It approached me and seemed to study me, taking note of how I was strung up. Until then, I never really knew the extent of the intelligence of the wolf. In our discussions, Myra had speculated that the werewolf chooses who it kills and who it allows to live but never spoke about the extent of the creature's understanding of the world around it. While I will never know to what extent the wolf's intelligence is borrowed from the human being, it does make sense to me that if I can access the gifts of the monster when walking as a man—increased senses, strength, healing abilities—then why wouldn't the monster have access to the cognition and understanding of the man or woman that it is a part of? Maybe the dreams that we have are a common meeting ground. Maybe not.

This werewolf that had come to rescue me lacked the maliciousness that Myra's had years earlier. The creature walked on four legs and reminded me of a black bull with its broad and muscular back; I wondered if I looked like this. It rose up on its two hind legs and brought its nose to my face, gently touching me. I was amazed that a creature such as we were could demonstrate tenderness, but that is what she offered in that moment.

Without warning, the wolf, who stood nearly eight feet tall when upright, swung with deadly power and tore the cable that had suspended me. I dropped to the floor and must have lost consciousness. The next memory I have was waking and feeling a warm and dusty wind blowing into my face. After a struggle, I escaped the cable that had been wrapped cruelly around my wrists.

I exited the room, and as I walked down the hallway, I saw the worst carnage one could imagine. The wolf didn't just kill these men—she dismembered them. I stepped over hands that had been torn from wrists, ears that had been torn from heads, and torsos that had no limbs nor even a head remaining. The walls and floor were as if painted with blood and littered with shell casings. I remembered Anne's description of

Arthur's healing as he was shot presumably by these very individuals. She had stated that he seemed to heal almost immediately.

Judging from the number of shots fired, I can only imagine what the scene would have looked like the night before when the shit hit the fan. Desperate as they were with their silver bullets, they were unable to kill her. Good, they had it coming, this and so much more.

I exited the building and welcomed the sunlight that flooded the landscape. Even here, evidence of the violence that had occurred the night before with blood and body fragments scattered about. The building itself stood alone, selected so that no one would ever hear us screaming. Unfortunately for them, no one would ever hear their screams either.

I finally came across an intact body with a face I remembered well; Brother John had been struck in the abdomen and disemboweled in the process. He seemed much paler in the light of the sun, and as I stood over him, I wondered what his last thoughts were. I brought my shoeless foot to his face and, with inhuman power, crushed his head so that he was as unrecognizable as were his men who had been torn to pieces.

I rounded the corner of the building to meet what was left of the young man who had last retreated. His left arm had been torn from his body—the eagle tattoo ripped and torn in half, and his ribcage was opened and exposed to the flies that now buzzed excitedly around him. Anne allowed not a single survivor.

I listened with hearing that no human could possess and could hear the faint yet deep breathing of the one other living person to emerge from this tragedy. I found the front entranceway to the building and the vehicles that had been used to transport us here. Another body lying face down with what appeared an enormous hole dug through his back—evidently, he had attempted to make it to one of the trucks to escape.

Sitting on the ground and resting against the front tire of one of the trucks was Anne—blood covered and staring into nothingness. She knew I was there but did not acknowledge me. What does one say in a moment like that? Her eyes seemed fixated on some imaginary point extending beyond the earth between her feet. I wondered what those eyes witnessed; I wondered if there was anything I could say, anything I could do.

Not knowing what else to do, I sat on the ground next to her and didn't say a word. For the longest time, we just sat there, and although I wanted to comfort her, I didn't. As Myra would say, we're not human anymore—why should we act like it? Still, even with my humanity stripped from me, I could never be like that. I could never be so cold to someone who was hurt.

Eventually, Anne rested her head on my shoulder and I wrapped my arm around her. She cried and cried. I didn't ask, but I wondered if she cried because of what she had done or if she cried because of what had been done to her.

Several weeks later, Anne still wasn't the person that she had been when I first came upon her in Vegas; I wondered if she ever would be again. When we were alone and all was quiet, I asked her what happened on that night.

She turned to me and placed her hands on my face. With a soft and emotional tone, she answered, "Caleb, I love you with all my heart, but I never want to talk about that ever again."

"I understand," I said to her.

NINETEEN

THE FOLLOWING COUPLE of years seemed to pass by far too quickly. Charlie was quite disappointed when I informed him that my fighting days were over. But during our time together, we had each become millionaires several times over. I'm sure he was more then content with that.

As for Anne and I, we left Nevada and, after a few brief stops along the way, returned to the St. Louis area. Yes, we had our rough moments, but all in all, those days were the happiest I can ever recall—for whatever that's worth. I don't believe that Anne was ever a truly perfect match for me; despite being older than she had been when we first met, she still seemed needy and childish at times. Still, we were good company for each other.

I did the best I could to teach her to use and develop her potential without resorting to the brutal tactics used by Myra. For the most part, she proved to be a good student and quickly became adept at employing her strength, speed, and even her tracking skills. It seemed that she made a much better werewolf than I ever could have.

Always the optimist, she seemed to balance the often sour disposition I held. And although I would never actually give her the pleasure of knowing that I admitted to it, the truth is that she was right about everything she had predicted. As time went on, my role began to shift from being the protector and teacher to being her equal. The fondness I felt for her would in time grow into love, and she would become the person I would lean on for support.

Looking back, while I can say that I was pleased by the new direction my life had taken, I also have to confess it was probably the least productive period I had lived. It seemed that much of what we did, we did only to pass the time between one lunar cycle and the next. I guess there are only so many times that you can go to the zoo, only so many times you can visit the Arch, only so many Cardinal games you can watch, and only so many wineries and bed-and-breakfasts you can stay at before life becomes one long boring and monotonous stretch. I was never bored with Anne, of course. I was bored with life, bored with an area.

Anne did not have to work hard to convince me that we should again travel. Besides, money and time were certainly not restricting us. In fact, the only problem that we had was finding a safe and remote place for the becoming. After being on the road for as long as I had been though, I was actually pretty good at scouting for safe locations for us. I wanted to visit the northern New England area, maybe even head across into the Canadian side of the border, maybe hop over to Nova Scotia. Anne wanted to head west, however, and although I had been out that way quite a number of times, I thought it might be interesting to actually see sights like the Rockies with someone I cared about rather than on my own.

So after the end of that lunar cycle, I bought a new Chevy Blazer, and we hit the road. It was fun, with each day being a new adventure. I was right, seeing things with Anne made them special somehow. Although I had done my share of travel, I had never actually taken a vacation before.

Being much further along with my lycanthropic condition than was Anne, I really wasn't able to express my pleasure of this experience with the same enthusiasm as she did. Still, I enjoyed not only the trip but also my time with her. From time to time though, for some unexpected reason, thoughts of Trish would enter into my thinking. I wondered how she was doing; I wondered if she had found peace; I wondered if she ever thought of me. While these weren't necessarily unwelcome thoughts, I did my best to push it out of my head; a part of me felt guilty for even having them.

In the coming weeks, we were like aliens from another planet exploring earth, discovering new sights, and tapping into the beauty of everything around us that we had both taken for granted for most of our lives—sunrises and sunsets, mountains and valleys, flowers and trees. We traveled through Colorado, then north through Wyoming and into Montana. We spent some time in Washington then proceeded into Oregon, renting a cabin at the base of Mt. Hood.

It was during that time that Anne's mood suddenly changed. She became seemingly disturbed and jumpy. It was such a contrast from how she had behaved right up until then. At times, she even became emotional. I was uncertain of how to approach her with this; I asked her about it a couple of times, but her response was vague. Finally, she opened up.

"Caleb," she said to me, her tone more serious than usual, even for her "I would like you to take this and keep it safe." As she spoke, she withdrew from her backpack a black leather-bound journal.

"What's this?"

"Just some of my personal thoughts, my beliefs, maybe a forecast or two of things to come."

"Why are you giving this to me?"

"I'm not sure, but I think that something may happen to me soon, and if it does, it is important to me that this is kept safe." There was a strange look on her face that I knew myself at one time, a look that, if she were to live long enough, would no longer plague her—she was frightened.

"You believe that something is going to happen to you?"

"Something will happen to me, something ugly I'm afraid."

I looked into her face, examined her lovely smile that still possessed emotion. "Nonsense!" I said. "Even if there was something or someone capable of hurting you, which I don't believe there is, I wouldn't allow it to happen."

"Will you please keep this hidden and safe?" she asked, ignoring what I had said to her.

I took Anne's journal and the following day placed it in a safe-deposit box. I didn't really give it much thought beyond that, but many years later, I would eventually come back to retrieve it. As for Anne's statements, I wasn't sure what to make of them. I did consider the events that transpired in Nevada with the lunatic John and wondered how it had affected her. Had she been an older wolf, I do not believe there would have been any emotional scars—how could there be? She was so young to the condition, however, so much human left in her that I had no way of knowing how deeply she was hurt.

We are the most awesome and powerful creatures in creation. We are untouchable. Nothing can kill us. I took comfort in this mind-set though I realized it was flawed. Was I being foolish? Of course I was. Here is a word of caution—if a powerful psychic tells you that something bad is going to happen and you regard it as an emotional flaw that she has not yet overcome, then you are as fucking stupid as I was. My disregard for her warning was another of those mistakes that I have no excuse for.

It was the spring of 1989, and I had been a lycanthrope for well over a dozen years. In that time, I had hardly aged a day. Anne, who was in her late twenties at the time, looked about the same age as me, despite me being born decades before her. *Maybe this would work out with us,* I told myself.

Unfortunately, Anne was distant after arriving in Oregon. She would speak and smile like everything was okay, but she went about her day-to-day life in a much more reserved manner. It was as though she simply engaged with me for my sake. I became increasingly frustrated with her though I never really made my thoughts known.

We drove south into California, where we discovered a rather large park not far from the city of Gualala. It was a lush area with a number of trails and an impressive garden that Anne seemed delighted with. We spent an afternoon there, and for the first time in several weeks, Anne seemed genuinely pleased. The flowers, along with the distant smell of the ocean, and the beautiful weather seemed to create an almost paradise-like atmosphere there.

We should have probably stayed right there or headed home to St. Louis; after all, we had been on the road for some time. But I wanted to head to San Francisco first, maybe spend a little time taking in the interesting history the city held. I have no idea why I wanted to continue traveling when Anne had clearly had enough, but because of the decisions I made, I would feel responsible for the fate that was about to fall in our laps. Maybe it was this sense of responsibility or guilt that led me to do some of the incredible and unspeakable things that were in my near future. If I could go back to that day at the park and tell myself what was about to happen, tell myself what I was about to do, I wouldn't have believed it.

So to San Francisco we went, and given that we had plenty of time before the next becoming, I wanted to stay for week or two. We got a nice hotel room then set out to explore the city. The Golden Gate Bridge, Candlestick Park, and Lombard Street were among the initial sights. Fortunately, it seemed that while Anne was still in a bit of a funk, she seemed to enjoy herself again.

It was our fourth or fifth day there, and I headed to one of the butchers I had been visiting during our time in town. When I left, Anne was sleeping, and given that this was simply a food run, I felt no reason to awaken her. Maybe I should have.

I really gave no thought about my surroundings as I pulled into the parking lot of the butcher—I had been there twice already. My mind continued to dwell on Anne's mood and what that truly meant, if anything, for the future. As I took the key from the ignition, I immediately knew that I wasn't alone. In the air, I could smell them even though I could not see them—other lycanthropes. Exiting the Blazer, I scanned the area until finally my eyes met a man with broad shoulders and greasy shoulder-length hair who was approaching me. From around the corner of the building, I heard the footsteps of another approaching, and from within the building, another stepped out.

Trust me when I say that there is *nothing* comfortable about the situation I found myself in, but there was little I could do but to let them approach me. If there had been one, possibly two, I may have been able to at least defend myself, but with three of them, it would have been physically impossible for me to survive an aggressive encounter—if that was their intention. I stood my ground, hoping to negotiate but fully prepared to do whatever was required to walk away from this scenario.

They each took positions encircling me, but it seemed that none of them were eager to speak. So I began, "My name is Caleb. What can I do for you?"

"You are to come with us," the one facing me said.

"Who are you?"

"It doesn't really matter who I am," he stated. "The one who wants to see you is Wade—his is the only name you need to know."

"And what if I refuse?"

"We have our instructions. One way or another, we will carry them out." His tone, no surprise, was without emotion but stern enough to leave no doubt that he would carry out his directions with as much force as was necessary.

"In that case, I suppose we should go."

I walked with them to a blue van that had been parked just around the corner. From there, my captives drove me several miles away to the warehouse district. They neither spoke to me nor each other.

We arrived at an old warehouse, rusty and definitely not in the best condition. I was escorted inside where I was amazed to see many lycanthropes, each watching me as though they intended to descend upon me and tear me to shreds. I proceeded toward the far end of the structure and finally came face to face with the leader of this pack.

"My name is Wade," the man said as he advanced several steps toward me. His hair was short with more gray than brown left to it. He looked to be in his mid to late forties though his true age would be impossible to determine. His dress was casual to say the least; he wore jeans with the right leg torn from the ankle to above the knee and an old stained white t-shirt. Even with the overwhelming scents of seafood and various other meats, I could nonetheless tell that he hadn't bathed in at least several days.

"I trust that my lieutenants weren't too aggressive during your escort here?" he asked with the slightest hint of a grin, a false grin.

"Why am I here?"

"Right to the point," he said. "I like that. In fact, I respect that. So I will reciprocate that directness," he said as he began pacing. "You see, I don't know anything about you—your age, where you come from, whether or not you belong to a family, or even your true intentions in coming into this area. But here, there is an order to things, and what you must understand is," he said before pausing momentarily as though collecting his thoughts, "your being here puts me in a very awkward position."

He waited for me to offer a response, but when it became clear that my silence would continue, he proceeded. "This is a territory, and it belongs to me. I cannot simply allow just any wolf to come in here and profit from the society I've established while desecrating the very nature of the order that is in place."

"So what do you want from me?" I finally spoke.

"By rights, we would be justified in tearing you to pieces. However, it has been brought to my attention that you possess a number of traits that may prove beneficial to us. You are a very strong wolf, and I believe that you would fit in very well here."

"And what would my role here be?"

"One of my lieutenants of course. You would be a part of this family, take an ownership role of virtually the entire West Coast, from here to Baja. You would answer to me directly and carry out necessary tasks."

"Necessary tasks such as hunting down lycanthropes who wander into this territory?"

"Precisely," he answered, "in addition to other enforcement roles. You see, we have infiltrated law enforcement and government on every level. We influence the media and tug on the strings that affect every part of our society, a society that has been remarkably lucrative for everyone involved. There is no reason that you should not benefit from this as well."

"So this is about power? About securing yourself as the undisputed authority in your territory? You know, I've been in and out of your territory countless times over the last decade and have never, until now, run into any other lycanthropes."

Wade smiled, but the message behind it was a clear warning—Watch it! "Yes," he said calmly, "I was made aware of your presence on a number of occasions, mostly in the Los Angeles area but here in San Francisco as well. Fortunately for you, your trespasses were too brief to enforce or apprehend you—until now, that is.

"As for this establishment being about power, as wolves we already had that. I'm sure that you are as much aware of that as any of us. No, it's about an environment that allows us to be us. Not exactly consequence-free mind you. We do have rules after all. But an environment in which mistakes and mishaps can more easily be avoided or, if need be, rectified. You see, if a member of this family were to inadvertently kill one or more during the becoming, we have contingencies in place to deal with such an occurrence. Tell me," he asked, "you have found yourself under those circumstances, right?'

I remembered the Wyoming tragedy and the unforgivable role I played in it. I also thought of over a dozen close calls I had had over the years. Though I dared not confess anything about my mistakes, the truth of the matter was that it would have been nice had someone been there to cover up my sins or offer plausible explanation when I killed livestock, dogs, whatever.

"In addition, we are much better suited to deal with hunters when they pop up from time to time. Interesting story," he said with a slightly excited tone. "About a year and a half ago, a group of twelve or thirteen well-armed and well-experienced hunters were mutilated by a wolf in the Nevada badlands. Was that your doing?"

"I wouldn't know anything about that," I answered.

Wade stared at me for a long moment before offering again his artificial smile."Of course not." He then turned away from me and returned to the seat he had been in before I arrived. "So what do you say to my proposal?"

I knew that I needed to tread carefully here. Though I wanted to tell him to forcefully shove his offer up his ass, I was pretty sure that in doing so, I would be signing my own death warrant—effective immediately. As it was, there were six lycanthropes there, including Wade, a near impossible set of odds. "Can I give it some thought?"

"What the fuck is there to think about?" Wade asked firmly. "Either abandon whatever ties you have and join us or become our enemy."

"There is a matter I wish to negotiate."

"This isn't a negotiation!" he said spitefully.

"No!" I returned. This is the end of my fucking life as I knew it and the beginning of a new one! You will have my service should I choose to offer it or my death should I decline it. I think at the very least, you owe me one day to make my preparations, whatever they may be."

"Very well," Wade answered impatiently. "But make no mistake, this offer is a one-time deal only. Decline it or try to flee from this area, and our next meeting will be the one in which you are killed."

I turned to walk away, and I could tell that the five remaining lycanthropes were very reluctant to simply allow me to walk out the door, and yet they didn't dare go against the orders they had been given.

"You realize that even if you want to be the person you once were, you cannot. That person is gone, and probably for the better," he stated in a tone that I could easily hear.

"And what does that mean?"

"You think that you live life now in some 'Jekyll and Hyde' fashion, like a coin that's either heads or tails, but the sad truth is that you and the demon that resides within you share a much more symbiont relationship. Sure," he stated loudly as he took a step in my direction, "you walk around with all the unique benefits that someone in our position naturally enjoys, but do you think that that is all you borrow from the wolf? And don't you realize that the wolf borrows its intelligence from you? You can't honestly believe that your soul hasn't been corrupted by its influence?"

I hadn't yet even turned in his direction. To his questions, I said nothing.

"You better wake up," he stated. "Every day you lose ground to the demon you share a body with. The question isn't 'where do you stop and where does it begin,' but rather 'how could you have gone so long without realizing that you and it are one in the same.'" Wade laughed. "Something to ponder."

Fully aware that I was being watched from a distance, I casually made the long trek back to my car. Once behind the wheel, however, I drove with reckless haste back to the hotel. Nothing else mattered beyond grabbing Anne and moving as far east in the shortest time as possible. I considered the idea that Anne might object given how fond she was of the area—not that I cared. If I had to knock her ass out and toss her into the trunk, I would have done so. My plan was to be back on the road within fifteen minutes of arriving at the hotel. Even that window of time seemed unreasonably long considering that we would be running for our lives.

As I drove and reflected on the words that were shared between Wade and myself, my heart began racing in a way it hadn't in a very long time. The massive adrenaline rush brought with it a razor sharpness to my already inhuman reflexes and awareness. It was as though I was suddenly aware of every particle of dust on the dashboard that even mildly shifted as I drove. Of course, despite this aggressive alertness I was experiencing, there was no way of knowing what I was driving into.

As I exited the car, I already knew that something was horribly wrong. Ascending the steps in a blur, I arrived on the third floor seconds before making it to my room. I rushed inside only to be welcomed by a gruesome and appalling scene that my darkest nature could not have imagined.

Like something from an over-the-top horror movie, there was blood that seemed to cover the entire room—the walls, the carpet, the furniture, even the ceiling was as though it had been sprayed. My nose immediately alerted my brain to whose blood this was, but it didn't really register until my eyes, upon scanning the room, came to the remains of Anne. In shock, I dropped to my knees and attempted to reach out and touch her only to instantly pull my hand away. Her body had been dismembered, her arms, legs, and head torn from her torso, and then arranged at the foot of the bed.

I wanted to cry out. I tried even to scream. But I found myself without a voice by which to do so. Likewise, I wanted to cry for this woman whom I had only recently learned to love, this woman who spent her entire life in love with me. My tears were lost to me though just as my voice was. I lay on the bloody carpet several feet from Anne as pain washed over me in waves, attempting again and again to force the tears from within me. My mind was in a state of absolute shock, and as such, I think I must have simply shut down. I couldn't have even defended myself had I needed to.

I can't really be sure how long I lay there. During that time, my mind seemed strangely disconnected from my body. I remembered a very youthful Anne greeting me at the Vanderman Mansion—her glowing smile was almost irresistible. I remembered her hurt expression when I sent her away at the bus station, and I remembered the look of fear that she had brought with her to Vegas. These as well as countless other memories of her—most of them insignificant—erupted from the deepest recesses of my unconscious mind and flowed directly across my senses.

Without warning, the hurt that had temporarily crippled me seemed to evaporate, and in its place, a violent anger flooded into my heart and quickly purged every other thought or feeling that had peacefully resided there. Now understand, I'm a lycanthrope, and anger is a part of my day-to-day existence. But it is always an anger that is kept in check. It doesn't control me—I control it. But on this day, the hatred permeated through my very soul.

I rose slowly from the floor only to notice words scribbled on the wall with a black marker, "Your deal didn't apply to her," it read. I studied it for a long while, realizing that the plans running through my head would certainly lead to my death too. What I was going to do would amount to nothing short of suicide. I could have fled. There was no one to stop me after all, but the thought of running never even entered into my mind.

From the closet, I retrieved a trunk I had purchased and used during my fighting days. I removed all the clothing it held as well as the heavy mace that was given to me by Arthur. Pulling the already bloody sheets from the bed, I gently wrapped Anne's body and placed her into the trunk. After a moment of silence, I grabbed a few personal items and left the hotel with the trunk.

The events that happened the following day defy any explanation I could offer. I should have been killed that day; I shouldn't have been able to go on and do all the things I have done since, let alone pen these words. Still, there was something Myra had told me once, and while I hadn't really thought about it until the dust settled that day, I suppose that maybe it made sense.

"In certain circumstances, and under the most extreme conditions, you may find yourself in a situation where utilizing the rage you carry in check is necessary. I won't lie. It is unsettling like falling, but if you give into the anger, stop resisting and pull it forward into you. You will discover a destructive force that you were not aware that you possessed.

Self-control will be sacrificed, of course, but it will allow you impressive power."

In the early hours that morning, I drove up the coastline to revisit the beautiful garden path outside Gualala that Anne had enjoyed so much. I ventured up the same path we had taken nearly a month before, and throughout my walk, I felt almost as though Anne was there with me, walking by my side. After a lengthy period of reminiscing, I finally strolled off the path for a short distance and came upon a small clearing. Sitting beneath an old oak at the edge of the clearing, I took a moment to clear my mind and breathe. It was quiet and peaceful here—the perfect resting place for Anne.

Returning to the truck, I retrieved the trunk that housed her remains and brought her back to the clearing where I buried her. I remember thinking that I should say something. After all, isn't that what you're supposed to do? But I couldn't find words that were suitable, so I remained silent and let the sounds of the night speak for me. It was a beautiful night, serene and clear. This was the proverbial calm before the storm.

Before long, I knew that it was time for me to leave, but unlike my departure from Myra, Trish, Arthur, even Jessica, I made no attempt to fool myself into thinking that I would ever return here. I walked away from Anne's grave knowing I would never again step foot here.

My return to the San Francisco Bay area was surreal—like Wyatt Earp riding in to face off against the Clanton and Mclaury gang; this was my personal highway to hell.

As I approached the warehouse, there were two lycanthropes within sight—one positioned roughly one-half mile away on the rooftop of another building and one guarding the entranceway to the warehouse itself. I floored the Blazer and bore down on the sentry guarding the door; of course he was a fast runner, but not that fast. I struck him and knocked him to the ground before spinning around in the open parking lot and running over him again.

I exited the Blazer, and as I looked out at the not-too-distant rooftop where the other lycanthrope had been posted, I noted that he was no longer there—on his way to intercept me, no doubt. I pulled a gas can from the backseat along with the mace I had brought with me and approached the wounded but quickly recovering wolf-man I had run down. A quick and powerful kick to his face slowed that recovery down just a bit, long enough for me to douse him with gasoline and set him to flames. He screamed and kicked and flailed around on the ground, much longer than he would have had he been just a man.

In that instant, the second lycanthrope, which had been racing my direction, leapt toward me in a savage manner, not unlike his inner monster would have. Like Babe Ruth, I swung the wicked and heavy mace with preternatural strength and met the lycanthrope with its business end. The result was that I shattered the ribcage of the attacker and buried the mace into his chest cavity. As he then lay helplessly on his back, I placed my boot on his throat and tore the mace from within his chest. This time, using the weapon much like a golf club, I swung the instrument and removed his head in the process.

What happened next is kind of a blur. Things seemed to unwind so quickly that my memory actually failed to record the scene in the same detail it seems to record everything else. I know I went into the warehouse and met with several lycanthropes that were not pleased to see me.

I know that several of them began to subdue me as I already knew that they would. This would be my last day alive; they would kill me, and I would go to the great beyond bravely. I would meet up with Jessica on the other side maybe… Maybe Anne would be waiting to greet me also? This is what I wanted to think of at that moment; this would have been a fitting and proper final thought. But strangely, my mind wasn't conjuring any peaceful or loving thoughts.

Again, Anne's remains buried in the park came into my memory, thoughts of her mutilated body. This is where my thoughts lingered, but that was only the beginning of what was going through my mind in that instant where time seemed to slow down. I considered the torture we suffered at the hands of John. I thought about Arthur's murder and the loss of everything he had built. My mind raced from one tragedy to another, and once I started considering all the negative aspects of my life and how absolutely unfair that life had been, it seemed that I had initiated some kind of internal sequence that fed itself on the misery and pain that the world or fate or God had decided to inflict upon me.

Once this inner sequence reached a certain point, I seemed no longer in control—like a landslide, my temperament was suddenly a time bomb with seconds left on the clock.

I came there angry, of course, but with every passing second, I fell further and further into a rage that consumed not only my thoughts but also began to invade me physically. It was so strange, but I found myself going through something very similar to the becoming in the sense that I had no choice but to surrender my will to… something else. Whatever demon is within me, whatever dark half that lies dormant throughout most of the month, I completely succumbed to its power and hatred. I don't know what happened really. I remember only bits and pieces.

I know that I used the mace against the other lycanthropes, each with preternatural strength of their own. I used it the way Samson used the jawbone against the Philistines. When it was all over, I somehow accomplished the impossible by killing a dozen lycanthropes in addition to the two outside. But in my rage, I totally lost control, control of my body and control of my mind, and it took some time to reacquire that control.

Unfortunately, Wade was nowhere to be seen. I wanted to kill him more than anyone else; he had either gotten away, or more likely, he had never been there in the first place. But just because I had killed everyone here, I was far from finished feeding into my vengeance. After going through paperwork in the warehouse, I found several home address of various members of the pack, including Wade.

I took the addresses and then set fire to the warehouse before immediately heading to the first address on the list. It was a home belonging to the family of a lycanthrope I had killed named Otis Raikman. Everyone there was human and innocent of any wrongdoing against me, and yet I didn't care—Anne hadn't wronged anyone, and look what became of her. Their innocence would not save them either—I killed them all, men, women, children. No one associated with the pack was spared.

I spent the next several days going from one location to the next slaughtering anyone and everyone that I felt was worth something to any member of the pack—family, friends, coworkers, acquaintances, it didn't matter. I killed and killed and wasn't satisfied; it was a mass murder bloodbath. Law enforcement on both the local and state level launched a huge investigation—one of the largest in the state's history—trying to find what they thought were a group of people responsible for cult killings. To this day, I have absolutely no idea of how many people I killed.

Still, Wade and another lycanthrope named Garret managed to stay one step ahead of me throughout my spree. Then I had heard that they headed east and wanted to distance themselves from me, and so, I pursued them. Over the next six or seven months, I tracked them from location to location, often missing them by only a matter of hours. Sometimes I would lose them for weeks at a time only to pick up the trail again.

From one location to the next, they ran like fugitives, often leaving death in their wake. I was like a bounty hunter, except that my quest was deeply personal and all consuming. There were times when I wondered if it would ever end; I wondered if this was all my life truly amounted to—just the pointless futility of revenge when in the end Anne was gone forever and no amount of personal justice on my part would change that.

Finally, the day came when, seemingly by accident, I could faintly make out the scent of another wolf. I had tracked them all the way to Jacksonville, Florida. I had assumed that they had passed through town, that I was at least a week or so behind them. To my surprise, upon getting settled into town, I picked up the ever-so-faint trace of their scent in the distant wind.

I set out on foot, crossing several miles of neighborhoods, parks, and industrial areas, before finally making it downtown. I was so close; I could feel it. By now, I could even make out the two distinctive scents—they had been here for a while, walked on these streets long enough that tracking them was not terribly difficult. But there was something else too, something somehow familiar. Ordinarily, I would have investigated this other issue that made itself known, but I was not about to compromise this opportunity to finally kill both Wade and Garrett. As far as I was concerned, everything else was a distraction.

Then as though by providence, I suddenly saw Garrett—he was the long-haired, greasy lycanthrope who intercepted me at the butcher in San

Francisco. With the same preternatural ability to sense his surroundings that I possessed, he looked my direction and brought his eyes to meet mine. He bolted, and I followed. From street to street, over cars, through busy intersections, we ran faster than any human ever could, but I was about to over take him. He ran into a dark alleyway, which I thought was stupid, considering that even I knew that there was no easy way out of the other side.

Reaching the end of the alley, he slowed his pace, and a second later, I struck him with as much strength as I could possibly offer. My blow knocked him to the ground, and I immediately leapt on top of him. While I didn't have my mace with me, the large knife I carried would suffice to separate his brain from the rest of his body. He struggled, but my initial strike had dazed him enough that performing the task of killing him was a less-than-impossible feat. But I wasn't alone in the alley, and I don't really remember what happened next. I do know that I finished what I had started with Garret. I know that I rose to my feet looking to see who had joined me here, and then my awareness was immediately stopped—just like someone blowing a candle out.

TWENTY

I DREAMT. YES, I always dream, and I have repeatedly mentioned the horrific nature of these dreams as nearly every lycanthrope experiences them. Night after night, an unending torture visits me as I sleep. This is simply the way it is, the nature of the beast, if you will, the way it has been for me since I was first bitten.

There is a rather cruel irony in all this, wouldn't you think? The majority of my emotions ripped away from me as the years slowly roll by even as my body seems almost immune and virtually untouched by vast passages of time. And in all this, I find that it is when I sleep. It is when I dream that I am most human as it is then only that I seem to experience anything other than the inhuman anger that shadows me during my waking hours. Indeed, even now as I pen these words, I work to suppress that anger.

But it is the dreams in which I speak; it is in those moments that I can once again feel sorrow and fear. Who would want to experience these emotions? I suppose it is bittersweet, certainly more bitter than sweet, but in the dreams I have, as I have stated, I am terrorized, I am afraid, and I know a very human sense of grief and loss. When I wake, it is not Caleb the human. It is not Caleb the man who lies there, but rather, I am Caleb the monster. Instantly, whatever fear and grief I experienced while trapped in that dream state is completely gone and is suddenly an abstract notion that I find myself unable to relate to. It is so abstract, so bizarre and alien to what I am now, it would be like placing a Picasso painting beside a Sally Mann photograph and expecting to see a comparable likeness—there is none.

I awaken, and in that instant, I am an absolutely and entirely different being, and despite my greatest efforts, I am no longer able to relate, even on the most basic level, to who I am in my dreams—the frightened and trembling person I was an instant before I woke. Sorrow and fear, who would want to experience these emotions? I would. They are there in my dreams, yes, but I cannot relate to that. That isn't really who I am, not now. Oh fuck you! I don't expect you to understand any of this! Fear? Sorrow? What are those emotions to me? Nothing! Nothing!

Please forgive my temperament; I want to continue. I so desperately want to tell my story, this part in particular as it did serve as a strange and, in retrospect, a much-welcomed epiphany in my existence. It would mark a new beginning, a period in which I would reinvent myself. Please read on and I will explain. So where was I? Ah yes, I dreamt.

It seemed a familiar country road, a dirt road that I lazily strolled down. Each step I took was slow and deliberately leisurely. A part of me seemed to somehow expect something awful, though why I could not say as everything around me was so serene and peaceful. I could smell and even taste the dust that I stirred beneath my footsteps. The midday sun bore down, unobstructed by any cloud cover, and I found it quite warm. I removed my jacket, which was quite unseasonable for this time of year, and carelessly cast it to the side of the road. Why would I be wearing a winter coat in the summer? Strange, the thought remained in my mind only for a moment, then I dismissed it—it didn't really matter. Still, to discard of it in this fashion was quite uncharacteristic of me, but really, this didn't matter to me either.

The only important thing to me in that moment was the moment itself, and everything that accompanied it. I absolutely welcomed and loved the sunlight as it struck my face, neck, and exposed parts of my arms. It seemed to almost embrace me, wrapping itself around me lovingly as would a long-lost family member. I proceeded forward, abandoning the jacket forever.

There was a breeze and, with it, the most beautiful and fragrant scents. Flowers—daises in particular but many other flowers as well—the scent of grasses, trees, even the crisp fragrance of running water from a nearby creek. I inhaled these essences, and in taking them in, I imagined that they were somehow becoming a part of me. As such, I wasn't just an outsider strolling through this beautiful moment where space intersected with time, a moment that surely would not last, but I was becoming a part of it.

There was another scent in the air also, one just as lovely as the flowers—no, something even more wondrous, even more intoxicatingly beautiful. It was something from my past, a distant past maybe? I don't know. I couldn't remember though I fought to. I wanted to remember. This new scent, I loved it, and somehow I longed for it. What it was I could not say, but it suddenly evoked powerful feelings within me, and I wept in joy. I wept as I had never done before as though I had been rescued from something—saved.

How long had it been since tears of this kind had streamed from my eyes? I could remember no time when such immense peace and safety and joy touched me or elicited such a response. Yes, I cried out in happiness, and yes, such a feeling as happiness does indeed exist, only I had forgotten what it felt like. Why was I suddenly so happy? It was this scent, this enthralling scent from my past that had so moved me. And yet, I could not remember what it was. In fact, I could not remember anything before I was there, on that very dirt road. Where I had come from? How long had I been there? Why I was there? I could remember nothing, nor did I seem to care. Again, it didn't matter—the only thing that mattered was this moment.

I had no way of really tracking or following this beautiful scent as it was all around me in every direction. So I simply proceeded down the path as this seemed the natural thing for me to do. As I strolled, I deeply embraced every sensation—the dust, the daisies, the breeze, the sunlight. I even plucked a wild blackberry from its vine that grew along side of the road. Even Hemingway himself could not provide with words how the explosion of sweetness created in me a beautiful euphoria. And yet, this was really little more then icing on an already perfect cake.

I followed the road for some distance, lost in a most peculiar and trancelike state of mind, until I finally came upon a worn path leading into a wooded area. After only a moment of consideration, I left the dirt road and proceeded into the shade provided by a thick canopy of trees. But before I had gone even fifty yards on this shaded trail, I came across a sight that I could not have prepared myself for.

On the ground before me, a large white blanket had been spread out, and resting upon it—Anne. She was wearing a yellow sun dress, which seemed to make her dark complexion even more beautiful. She looked up and smiled at me, that same smile I had seen so many times. My mind wasn't working right—I knew this well enough. But while I knew something was wrong with the scene in front of me, I never really got the sense that this "wrong" or that this was a bad thing.

"Hey, stranger," she said to me. "Aren't you happy to see me?"

"Yes, of course I am," I answered though still in disbelief of what I was taking part in. "How are you here… I mean, how did you get here?"

"That's a silly question," she said still smiling at me. "I've been here waiting for you. I was beginning to think you weren't coming. Come lie next to me. I want to look into your face."

I did as she asked and slowly lowered myself next to her. For whatever reason, I could not figure out what was wrong here, what was wrong with me. "It seems so long since I have spoken with you."

She touched my face then leaned forward and kissed me. "Well, we're together now. Don't you want to be here with me?"

"I do… Yes, I very much want to be here with you. But aren't you gone?"

"Gone?"

"Aren't you dead?" I asked, the words spilling from me before I had time to acknowledge what I had even thought. She only smiled and kissed me again. I kissed her back. She spoke no further, but she continued to caress my face and hair, offering occasional kisses to my forehead as I stared into space, attempting to… struggling to make my mind function the way it should. I considered the scent that I had been so engrossed with, *this beautiful and impossible-to-ignore scent that I so loved. It wasn't Anne. Somehow Anne didn't belong here, did she? Did I care?*

Quickly, I threw myself on top of her and lustfully tore her dress open, revealing her breasts. Her brown eyes seemed only to invite more of my carnal instincts. I passionately kissed her lips, her neck, then her nipples. Ah, I wanted her, this person whom I had known when she was but an adolescent before she was a lycanthrope; she knew that we would be together some day. But even as I kissed her passionately and began to explore her, those strange thoughts returned to my mind. Wasn't she dead? Yes, I was sure of it. It seems that I had seen her remains, and yet, here she was—warm, healthy, alive.

It was real, it was magic, and I was so unbelievably happy. I continued kissing her until her body somehow became hard and cold. Then, in that exact instant, I was no longer capable of those emotions.

Was it a blessing or a curse? Either way, I was now awake, and I found myself in the most excruciating pain. My neck, my throat in particular, my chin, and even the area around my mouth felt as though the flesh had been torn from me. The rest of my body seemed without injury, but those injuries I did have were possibly the most severe I had endured since I had met with my condition after being attacked. Even the attempts of Brother John to "purify" me had left me in better condition than I was when I woke.

I was no longer bleeding, which I guess was a good thing, but when I swallowed, I not only felt the immense pain from the act but also felt the saliva trickle from my neck. Slowly and with exceeding difficulty, I rose to a seated position and swung my legs over the side of what seemed a large dusty dining room table.

I did not know where I was, but it appeared to be a somewhat rundown and no longer lived-in home. I faced what might have been a kitchen in decades past, but was now home only to the rats and vermin—I could smell them in the walls. Smoke and water stains decorated the walls, replacing the wallpaper that appeared in happier days. It appeared the carpet and tile had long since been removed, but nothing more had been done to improve the floors. A thick coat of dust and pollen covered what few items remained in this otherwise dead and gutted house.

Beneath the table, a large amount of blood that had spilled over its edges and onto the floor. Then suddenly, I realized that I detected a scent that I, for whatever reason, had ignored until then. Most likely—no, it was definitely the scent from my dream. I had been smelling it the whole time I had been unconscious on the table, which is why I had paid it so little mind upon waking. Unlike the limited ability my brain has when functioning during a dream, I was absolutely aware of whom that scent belonged. And just as if on cue, she entered the doorway on the opposite side of the kitchen.

"Welcome back to the world of the living," she said. Her voice, her face, her scent, her very essence, almost too difficult to believe. I wondered if I was again dreaming. She waited patiently for me to respond, but I could not. I only gazed in her direction, attempting to form a logical and rational explanation to which I could not do either. "It must come as quite a surprise to see me after all these years," Trish said with her trademark smile.

"Where are we? Do you live here?"

"No, it's just a house, just a place for you to heal up a bit."

"What happened?" I asked, my voice a strangely unfamiliar part of me due to injuries to my larynx.

"You were stupid. You were flanked by one individual while you killed another that he used like bait for you." Her tone was cold, not like I once remembered it. "He damn near took your entire head off with a single shot. Had he been just a little closer to you, I have no doubt that he would have succeeded in that."

Quickly, it all seemed to come back to me—the alley, killing Garret, then Wade stepping from the shadows. She was right; I was stupid to have been led into such a tactically obvious snare. Wade allowed the last member of his pack to be killed just so that he could end my life.

"What happened to him?" I demanded. It hurt terribly to speak at all, let alone with exclamation.

"Who?"

"The asshole with the shotgun!"

She smiled though her expression was an absolute mask that concealed a nothingness underneath. "You should consider yourself lucky that I was there to intercede. You wouldn't be breathing right now otherwise."

"Tell me what happened!" I said impatiently.

"I killed him—brutally. I figured that you would appreciate that."

I looked away from her and tried without success to again collect my thoughts. It seemed almost surreal—my dream of Anne, Trish here with me, Wade killed by Trish's own hand no less. I closed my eyes and recalled Wade and the offer he had made to me on that long-ago night. I remembered the torn apart remains of my beautiful Anne and the endless rage that had consumed me.

I should have been happy that he was dead; a part of me was. And yet, I could not help but feel that I had somehow been cheated. Oh. how I had lived for the notion of tearing his intestines out while was alive and watching. The things I would have done to him, the unspeakable things.

I breathed deeply and told myself that it was all over now, that I had no reason to continue with my rage. I told myself that I had to let that go. When I opened my eyes, I saw Trish still observing me, now with a mirror in her hands. Without a word, she handed it to me, and without the horror that would have rampaged through my mind during my more human years, I studied the damage. My throat looked like raw hamburger; I was surprised that I was even able to talk.

"Thank you for saving me," I said to her.

She again smiled. "So who is it that I killed, this asshole?"

I hesitated telling her much. I remained in a state of shock, a shock that would require more time for me to come to terms with then would my wounds to heal. Why was she here? That was what I wanted to know. What the hell? Still, I had time. We would discuss these things in due time. For now. her answer. "He was the leader of a pack I had encountered in California. He was the last of them. They're all gone now."

"I see. Well, he must have seriously pissed you off."

I wanted to be patient, but I could take no more of this. "He pissed me off about as much as you did!" It was my every intention to become confrontational at this point. I was still in anger mode, and in my opinion, I had more than enough reason to question her.

"Excuse me!" she said with a hostility equal to my own.

"I came back for you, and you were gone! You didn't even leave a message for me. You just up and left!"

In a tone much less aggressive than my own though still absolutely firm, she spoke. "Do you honestly believe that I owed you something? I begged you to stay with me. I begged, damn you! And you left anyway. What did you care about me? What did you care about the pain and hopelessness that I carried with me? No, you had to go off on your fool's errand! By the way," she asked sarcastically, "did you find any answers that you were looking for?"

I answered only with my silence. I immediately knew that this argument was over before it had begun. Despite what I felt, I was in the wrong. Everything that she was saying was right. I didn't hold any claims to her, she owed me nothing, and I had no right to expect anything that would restrict her wishes. This was a woman I loved once—no, this was a woman that I never stopped loving. This was Trish.

But even though I had been defeated in this our first and only quarrel, Trish was not quite ready to give up. "No, you learned nothing. You simply wasted your time in going there! As far as me, I did wait. I waited for days, then weeks, and yes, months passed without a call, without a letter, without so much as a fucking singing telegram! And now, after saving your life—*you're welcome by the way*—you scold me and speak as though I was a piece of property owned by you!"

I lunged toward her, and she must have thought I was attacking her as she tried pulling back to strike me, but I was too quick, and she was too wrapped up in her verbal counterassault. I put my powerful arms around her, and though she squirmed violently, I did not let go. I just held her. After a moment of struggle, she realized that I had surrendered to her. I did not wish to do battle with her. Never with her, ever again. Slowly, her struggle against my hold on her became an embrace, and just like that, our quarrel had ended.

"I am so sorry," I said to her. "Seeing you again, especially after everything that has happened… it's just… hard." I struggled with my words, but I had said enough—I could see that I had diffused whatever bomb that lay inside her.

"I've missed you," she said. "I thought I would never see you again."

"So what happened to you?" I asked, this time without the demanding and accusing tone I had used earlier.

She pulled away from me, and only then did I notice that in the strong embrace I had used, my wounds had once again began bleeding. Her white jacket was now very likely ruined as it was deeply stained with my blood. Even her hair, much longer than it had been when I saw her last, held traces of my blood, now dried and caked within it. Seeing my face when I noticed the damage I had done she spoke, "Don't worry, it's not really a big deal." It's always interesting, at least to me, that lycanthropes don't seem to worry about such issues.

"We have much to talk about, much to catch up on," she commented. "Are you hungry?"

"I am, but I don't know if I can eat yet—I can barely swallow."

"Well, do your best."

Moments later, Trish had brought in several bags of groceries, including eggs, milk, hamburger, pork, and fish. She advised me to stay inside so that no one would notice the strange man with the hideously injured neck that had bled all over his clothes. It was true. I was an absolute mess.

"How long did I sleep?"

"About a day and a half."

"Shit! And this is as much as I have healed?"

"You have no idea just how bad of shape you were in. You actually look pretty good right now—you have healed remarkably quickly even for one of us. You are *so* damn lucky to be alive." She handed me a gallon of whole milk and continued speaking while she opened the ten-pound packages of hamburger. "I dragged what was left of your body here and tossed you up on the table for what triage I could offer. I think I removed all the buckshot that was in you. I did the best I could anyway. It is possible that there might be something left. If so, you'll deal with it." Her tone was impersonal and cold. Just as I knew it would, she had lost so much of her humanity in the years since we knew had learned of each other.

"You don't sound very compassionate," I said jokingly as I took a large drink of the milk. Unfortunately, much of it seemed to spill and run from various holes in my throat.

"I'm afraid I haven't much compassion to offer these days." As she spoke, she turned to witness the scene of me drinking and spilling the milk. After a second, her face took on a most peculiar expression—her lips twisted somewhat, her nose wrinkled ever so slightly, her eyes seemed to enlarge, and some very fine lines formed on her cheeks. Clearly, she found the scene amusing. "That's interesting," she said as she turned away from me and tore open the pork steaks.

"What's interesting?" I asked. "That half of everything I swallowed just spilled into my lap?"

Even though her back was turned to me, I could tell that she was still smiling. "No, but your situation, that's fucking hilarious," she said chuckling lightly. "But that isn't what's interesting."

"So what is interesting?"

"It's nothing, but you should try to get more of that down if you can, you'll heal faster." This time she was the one joking.

"I'll do the best I can, but I want to know what you find interesting."

"You will not find it noteworthy or interesting, I'm sure."

"Try me. Besides, you can't just say something like that and not elaborate."

She paused for a moment, considering her words carefully as though she might be judged harshly for saying the wrong thing. "You know, I'm not really the same person I was when you knew me—so much of what I was I lost. But there was always something about you. It's like you revive some part of me—you bring some life into places within me where it seemed life could no longer exist." She was quite serious, and I was uncertain of what to think of her statement.

"I'm sorry," I said, "I don't understand."

She smiled. "I haven't laughed in over five years. What do you think of this? In all this time since I lived in Rockford, I have been in a state of emotional death and decline. And in these last years, I have been unable to even find humor in anything. It was something that was lost, gone from me and no longer existed. Then, after twenty minutes with you conscious, I find myself laughing at your sad state sadistically."

Her words struck me in the most unexpected way. I needed time to think about everything, including the dream from which I had only just woke a short while earlier. It seemed that I held too much information that I had not given proper thought to.

"Are you even listening to me?" Trish asked as she noticed my somewhat distracted state.

"I've heard every word you've said, and I have something that you might be interested in learning. But I need to organize my thoughts on that matter before I discuss it with you."

"All right."

"I promise, we will discuss the very topic of your feelings very soon. In the meantime, please tell me what happened after I left you in Rockford."

She looked at me in what I interpreted as a disappointment possibly because she thought I was dismissing her last statement or possibly the remark I had mentioned regarding leaving her in Rockford. Either way, her look was as much as she expressed as far as her inner thoughts were concerned.

"There is a lot to explain. Are you sure you really want to know?"

"Why, of course I want to know."

"In that case, I will tell you everything after we've eaten when we can sit down like civilized creatures, and not the animals that we all too often become." She expressed her sentiment coldly, but I couldn't have agreed with it more. I remembered the evenings that we had spent so many hours talking while in her kitchen or her living room. We each appreciated the propriety of conversation in an eloquent and almost formal fashion. We are demigods after all—wouldn't you think? Doesn't it make sense to discuss the deepest of thoughts in the most proper manner?

"You didn't by chance bring a bottle of wine with you?" I asked.

She smiled—genuinely, I believe. "I did, three bottles of the best Cabernet Sauvignon I could find. Maybe we should duct-tape your neck so that you can actually enjoy it once you swallow it." More humor, more for me to consider.

We spent the next couple of hours eating everything she had brought with her. We had even considered getting more food but decided that it could wait. As was the case when I was recovering from the severity of my injuries while with Myra in Alaska, the calories I took in greatly accelerated my ability to heal. By the time we had finished eating, I was quite visibly healed, and my voice, though fully functional when I awoke, was now much less scratchy and clearer and strong.

Our discussion during that time was light and pleasant, certainly a welcomed break from the near-constant silence I had endured since Anne's death. I loved listening to Trish speak, her voice so beautiful and feminine, yet her thoughts so articulate and logical. Nothing of an emotional chord was present when she spoke of her son—who, it seemed, was now working for the Chicago Fire Department, was married, and had two kids of his own.

"So you're a grandmother now!" I said, trying to elicit a smile. She did smile though it was absent of anything real. It was offered for my sake only. I have often wondered how two older lycanthropes would interact with one another. I think this was only a hint of what would eventually overtake us. Trish was older with the condition than was I, so naturally it had affected her to a greater degree. As for myself, I had thought my own humanity was gone by this point. But after seeing Trish, I knew that I still had feelings. Feelings for her, of course, but remnants of old emotions were still present. They were manifested not only in my love for her but also in the happiness that she was with me now, the anxiety of hearing the story she was to tell me, and the fear that she would leave me soon to resume whatever life she now had.

We continued to talk about trivial things; of course, I loved this too. She spoke of her frequent trips to Florida and her love of the beach. She expressed how she had seen the most beautiful and wondrous sights while diving in the warm waters of the Caribbean. She also told me about how she had experienced a profound increase in her strength and power as she had grown older—a knowledge that Myra had once passed on to me but was apparently withheld from Trish.

I had stories for her also though I did not reveal anything in detail, choosing instead to offer a much more detailed account at a more civil hour when we could talk as we once did. I remember telling her about my fights and how easily I earned tens of thousands of dollars and more in sparring sessions in which I simply could not lose. As I spoke, she seemed somehow lost in my words. Was she really though? Was it possibly that this beautiful woman could be interested in me? Funny, these were the same thoughts I had run through my mind over a decade earlier when we sat across from each other and provided each other the accounts of our lives up until that point. Just as we did once, we again spoke for hours on end.

The sun had set by now, and the last few rays were struggling to illuminate the sky. As Trish stepped out to her car to retrieve the wine, I took a moment to explore the decaying house. The structure really should have been condemned if it hadn't already been. It would have cost so much more to have made it livable than to have simply torn it down. Still, it had character, and yes, it had its "ghosts."

The only furniture in the house, other than the now bloodstained oak table that I had recovered on, was an old moldy and dusty sofa. I could smell the cigarette butts that were hidden deep within the cushions as well as the hair of a dog that had long ago rested on it. There were also several folding chairs stacked into a neat pile in one of the bedrooms. I considered what would be best for sitting and talking and found neither truly appealing.

Trish entered and gazed at the sofa with me, contemplating the same thought likely—the irony of a formal and sophisticated exchange on furniture that reeked of bodily fluids and rodent droppings. None of this would have bothered us, not really, but the surroundings were less than conducive to the intimate atmosphere that we had each imagined.

"Here," Trish said, tossing me a roll of bandaging. "It's dark out, so no one will likely notice us, but in the event that someone gets a decent look at you, at least they won't be alarmed at just how awful you look," she said smiling.

"Are we leaving?"

"I hope you haven't formed any attachment to this place," she was now mocking me clearly. It was good to see her attempting humor even if it was at my expense. "We can go somewhere much nicer than this. I have some place special to show you."

I carefully wrapped the cloth bandaging around my rapidly healing neck and used masking tape to secure it. I expected it to be totally healed by the following day; for the moment, however, Trish was right. I was a rather unpleasant sight.

"Throw this on also," she said as she held a large dark hooded sweater.

Even though it had been washed, it still retained a faint yet unmistakable scent of a man.

"You may keep that," I said firmly. "I don't want it." There was no real anger in my voice, but Trish's expression indicated to me that she knew full well why I declined the shirt, preferring the bloody rags instead. Her look seemed to convey how sorry that she was to even offer it to me.

How interesting, I was feeling something I hadn't know in some time—jealousy. I said nothing, of course, but I wanted to do great bodily harm to this individual, this very human individual. I had no doubt that Trish would name this person in due time.

What was I hoping for really? That somehow whatever had happened in Rockford all that time ago would be magically rekindled? That she would abandon whatever life she had developed for herself and come away with me at my beckon? What was inspiring this strange and foreign and unpleasant emotion that I was experiencing? I could find this weak human and tear his limbs from his body. No one could stop me. But would Trish defend him? So many strange feelings ran though me at that moment—all of which were quite unbecoming of the man I wanted Trish to see me as.

"Please forgive me," she said. "I didn't mean any disrespect, and I didn't mean to cause any hurt for you."

I stepped forward and without warning brought my lips to hers. She did not pull away, nor did she offer even the slightest hint of resistance. She seemed all too accepting of the physical intimacy that I offered. She tenderly touched my face as only she could. She then brought her kisses to the corners of my eyes.

"We should leave this place," she said. "I have much to talk to you about."

TWENTY-ONE

OUR RIDE WAS quiet, at least as far as conversation goes, with Trish offering only a few statements such as, "I think you are going to enjoy this place," and "I come here often." Her Jeep, on the other hand, was loud and seemed almost obnoxious with its engine roaring and the way it allowed to wind to whip at us. Our ride lasted nearly ninety minutes, during which time I simply gazed longingly into Trish's direction, a gaze that she occasionally returned with her lovely smile that seemed her trademark.

We arrived at a secluded beach at almost nine o'clock, the warm air blowing a strange yet sweet scent from some place far in the Atlantic. Trish was right; the surroundings were certainly peaceful, making this area an ideal retreat for someone seeking serenity. Without warning, Trish approached my left side and casually wrapped herself around my left arm, resting her beautiful locks on my shoulder.

"It's so crazy," she said, "these strange feelings that come over me when you are close to me."

I turned to face her. "Please tell me what you mean by this."

She sat down and kicked her shoes and socks off, digging her toes into the warm sand. "I'm not sure that you will really understand. I don't even understand it."

"Please," I repeated.

"Well, when you stayed with me in Rockford, I truly enjoyed your company, but there was something more to your visit. I felt it as soon as I came upon you in the old tool and dye building."

"Go on."

Trish shook her head slightly and offered a faint smile. "I just felt something. It was something I recognized but didn't really understand. The way we are, this lycanthropy, I had been like that for almost nine years. In that time, I did notice a loss of my ability to feel as I once did. I knew all too well that eventually I would end up just as Michael had, just as he warned me I would. I wasn't completely lost, not yet of course, but I was well on my way as I am sure you are now.

"But there was some spark inside of me. I couldn't explain it then, and I really can't explain it now, but I simply felt more emotion than I knew I was capable of. I was honestly, truly happy with your company. Was I selfish for not wanting you to leave? Of course I was, but I knew that I felt more human in those days than I had even before I had met Michael. Isn't that the stupidest fucking thing you have ever heard? That somehow being in your proximity seemed to magically instill and revitalize what I was losing?"

At first, I thought it was my imagination, but there were tears developing in her eyes. How was this possible? She was well beyond that emotion, and yet, I saw what I saw. "Even when I left you for a while, I seemed to carry some of that magic with me. You remember when I went to volunteer at the hospital? I didn't really have to put on so much of an act for the children. My smiles were real. And smile? I cannot remember ever smiling so much, wanting to laugh so much, feeling so happy inside then when you were there with me on those all-too-short hours. But as much as I pleaded with you, begged you, you left me. And as I watched you drive away, I held on to that magic as long as I could.

"It did go away, and in time all of my emotions, seemed to fade into an abyss, out of my reach forever. It was almost like an amputee wanting to use his removed limb. My ability to feel even something as simple as compassion for a sick child was lost to me. As the years went by, I accepted what I was—it was all I could really do. And like that amputee, I learned to survive without that now removed part of who I once was.

"And then you come into my life again, and again you bring your magic. And as I sit here, feeling things that I thought I would never feel again, I am uncertain of whether to love you or hate you."

Her moist eyes were now erupting tears. I considered putting my arms around her to offer comfort but wasn't sure if it was a welcomed gesture. As tears rolled down her cheeks, she did not attempt to wipe them away. Maybe there was a part of her that was enjoying this bittersweet experience, an experience that humans take for granted. Finally, I could take no more; I embraced her as my friend, my best friend, and felt her return the sentiment. She then wept for a great while. I did not speak. I only held her as she tucked her head into my chest and spilled out countless years of emotion.

I searched for the perfect words, and as it always seems when I need them most, they eluded me. I considered my response carefully then proceeded in the only way I could. "Trish," I began, "I need to offer to you my thoughts on this matter. While I cannot say why you are experiencing this, I too have acknowledged an uncanny feeling while in your proximity. This is something I have been meaning to talk to you about since before we left the house."

With difficulty, Trish pulled away from me and attempted to regain her composure. "I am sorry for my display. It would have been uncharacteristic of me even when I was human. Now, however, it is simply embarrassing, and I hope you do not think less of me for this." As she spoke, she finally wiped the now-retreating tears from her face and looked at me with swollen and red eyes.

I took her hand in mine and squeezed it firmly. Looking into her eyes—eyes that seemed deep and too human for someone such as Trish—I replied, "You never need to apologize for that. It is the most beautiful thing I have seen in you." At this, she smiled as she looked down at her toes in the sand. "Every night of my life since I first acquired this condition, I have been plagued by the most monstrous and horrific dreams. They are something that I have simply come to expect when I close my eyes for sleep. The only exception to this otherwise absolute rule are those nights I spent with you all that time ago and during my unconsciousness when you came upon me here.

"I went to see Arthur Denham, hoping to walk away with a greater insight into what I was. I thought that if he had a strategy for overcoming the worst part of our condition, that maybe he could share it, or maybe I could solve whatever mystery he may have failed to himself."

"And?" Trish asked, her voice still broken with emotion.

I frowned. "It seemed that his level of brilliance could only shadow my own. There was nothing to discover. He was an anomaly, nothing more, or so I thought." Trish listened as I carefully offered my account of the dialogue I shared with Arthur. I spoke to her of what remarkable and vast knowledge he seemed to possess. I told her of the advice he offered and how irrelevant it seemed to me at the time. "Trish, there is something about us being together. You must know this."

"You are special," she said smiling.

"No, it's not just me, but you too. Don't you see? You are not the only one of us who benefits from our time together."

"Benefits? Do you really think I believe this is somehow beneficial to me?"

"I don't understand. Isn't it?"

"I used to think so. I used to need and crave my emotions. As they slipped away, I died. The person you see here is not the person that you once knew."

"That is nonsense," I said trying to understand her reasoning "You would not have saved me if you were anyone else."

She smiled and touched my face gently; somehow, I know that she was about to offer something I did not wish to hear. "My dear Caleb, surely you must know that I am loyal to our friendship. I would have done anything to save you, killed anyone, and if need be, I would have died myself in the process. That is something you will always have in me. But what do you think is to come of us now? What are your designs upon me?"

I found myself confused by her questions and then realized that I had not really given the nature of our association or our future sufficient thought. I had been so caught up in the moment, so caught up in my own string of desperate emotions, that I had neglected consideration of her circumstances. Still, I answered as honestly as I could. "I want us to be together of course. I want to take you with me, and start a life together."

"But see," she said shaking her head, "this cannot happen, at least not now."

I'm sure that the look I offered to her more than made her aware of my immediate confusion. Her look, on the other hand, suggested a deep pain that was slowly rising from within her. "Whatever *human* you have in your life now," I began, "forget about him. Leave him and come away with me. Even if he is fully aware of what it is that you are, he could never possibly understand. Understanding is something he could never truly offer." My tone was direct and mean spirited. Yes, a true jealousy had taken hold of me—something I can honestly say that I had never felt before. I half expected another heated exchange of words as my statement was absolutely confrontational, but Trish offered only her sad eyes It seemed that I had been a bastard for so long that I didn't—or couldn't—understand the idea of not getting what I wanted.

Finally, Trish spoke, "If only it were that simple."

"It can be," I said, quickly cutting her off before she could continue with whatever she had planned to offer. "I've spent the last decade looking for you—hoping and praying that our paths would cross again. And here you are, the person of my dreams, the one individual that I could never drive from my mind, the one individual that I want and need more than anything. I have no doubt in my mind, especially now, that you and I were meant for each other."

Trish pulled her eyes away from mine before closing them altogether possibly in disappointment. Her head dropped slightly and shook in disagreement. But this was not a disagreement that I intended to lose; I would talk to her, scream at her if necessary, but in the end she would understand how important she was to me. "Trish, surely you must know that I fell in love with you when we met. You are simply something that I cannot walk away from. As of right now, there is nothing more important to me, nothing I need more than you."

"It's time that I tell you what has happened in my life since I last saw you." Her voice was broken with emotion as the tears that she had shed served to weaken the ability of her vocal chords. Interestingly, the significance of what she was to offer seemed only strengthened by those same emotions, those strange emotions that I was having such difficulty trying to understand and empathize with.

You must understand what emotion is like for us. Though I have tried, I feel certain that I have failed to truly convey how quickly and completely separate our lycanthropic nature is from what is considered a human response. While I was pleased with the knowledge that Trish was experiencing something that she believed lost forever, I myself felt no such emotion. Inside me, nothing moved—at least as far as I could tell. And yet, I was not old enough to be completely devoid of those feelings. Fear and anxiety had nearly left me entirely, joy was found only in the smallest doses, and sorrow was little more than a memory. Of course, I had an abundance of anger, and now this strange angerlike thing seemed to hang over me—jealousy. Despite all of this, I still did possess and acknowledge those emotions as weak as they had become in me.

But love, I cannot say that I entirely understand what love is. I suppose that I had always considered it an emotion as well, but maybe I had been wrong all along. I had long suspected that with time, I would lose my love for Jessica, and yet I hadn't. Now don't confuse love for something less elaborate such as grief or sorrow over the loss of a loved one, or happiness and excitement at the memories I carry. No, there is no further grief or sorrow for Jessica's loss. Neither is there happiness when I consider the time I did have with her. The inability to experience these feelings has made me almost machinelike as I feel absolutely nothing. But I still have love... I think I do anyway. But I don't know exactly what love is. I heard someone say once that love and hate were not emotions, but rather states of being. Again, an argument for the philosophers.

The point I wish to make here is that I absolutely meant everything I said to Trish. I was in love with her. I don't know, maybe there was some emotional pull that affected me in a very subtle way, something much less obvious than how she was affected. Maybe there is no real way that the reader of these accounts will understand what it is truly like to be robbed of one's emotional status yet retain their state of being. Of this matter, I will say no more.

"When you left me that morning, I felt utterly lost and defeated. Of course I didn't want to control you or hold you with me if it wasn't something you wanted yourself. And honestly, my intentions to keep you with me were nothing more than a selfish act on my part—an attempt to 'feel' again. But I would have been good to you. I would have been a good partner, a good lover, a good wife even if you would have wanted it."

I know I just finished saying that I had so little emotion left, and yet the preceding statement stabbed at the most sentimental part of my heart. *What had I done? How could I have been so foolish to have lost this beautiful woman?* As I listened to Trish begin her story, I realized that she again took on a strange gaze that I remembered her using when we had first met. I wanted to hold her hand just then but did not wish to interrupt as it seemed that she was somehow lost in her words.

With the sounds of the waves crashing on distant rocks, she continued, "But you said you would return, and that is all I had to go on. After a couple of months without so much as even a word from you, I made the trip to Madison myself." She then looked directly at me, offering a weak smile. "Oh, please forgive me. I would love to say that I had some concern about your well-being, but that wouldn't be the absolute truth. The fact is I thought perhaps that if I could see you, or rather if you could see me once more, then maybe, just maybe, you would want to come back with me. I was desperate. I was obsessed, and I was possibly at the lowest point in my life. I kept telling myself that I wasn't good enough, that you could never be content to stay with me. I told myself this, and yet I looked for you anyway.

"It was only a couple of days—how could someone come into my life and change everything in such a short time? But you did just that, and I would never again be the same.

"I found and spoke with a private investigator who told me that you had headed to New England, or so he believed anyway. With that information, I returned to Rockford a broken soul—you had abandoned me."

"Trish, please understand. I never abandoned you! I did come back for you, but you were already gone. I know that I was away for too long, and I know that I didn't offer you the courtesy that I should have, but I did come back, and I was heartbroken to find that you were no longer there! Please understand and believe me!" My words were filled with desperation—I absolutely needed her to understand that I offered the truth.

She smiled. "I know that. Or I should say, I know that now, but at the time, that is what I felt—alone and abandoned. I had lost everything that was once important to me—my family, my friends, even my son whom I loved more than life itself. My ability to truly feel much was gone, and so were you. You were my last and only hope, and without you, I no longer wished to live. I was going to kill myself, but do you know what stopped me?"

I nodded only.

"I thought at first that I couldn't because Josh would think less of me than what he did. But the person whose consideration I held in even higher esteem was you. I was afraid of what you would think of me if and when you were to learn that I ended my life. What horrible irony that because you left me, I had lost the one hope for humanity, and with that I had lost the one reason to continue breathing, and yet, because of my vanity, because of you, I was unable to do what was necessary to end my life.

"Eventually, the thoughts of ending my existence passed, but the need to reinvent myself took hold of me. I couldn't remain isolated any longer. I couldn't be Trish W—— any longer. I had to become someone, something else. So I sold the dance school, practically gave away the farm, and left for Chicago to be with my husband and son."

Her words hit me with the same destructive force as would a sledgehammer. It was her husband that she had been with; it was him that I smelled on the hooded sweater she offered me. Did I hate this man any less knowing that he was the husband she had mentioned in her story to me? No, just the opposite—I think I hated him more. Nothing about this seemed fair to me. She should have been with me; I felt as though she was created for me, the woman of my dreams, the woman beyond my dreams. Her heart was with me. I knew this and could see it in her eyes; and yet, this puny and pathetic human being had some kind of hold on her. Inside of me, I could feel my hatred welling up as I contemplated the gruesome and painful death I could—and possibly would—bring to him.

As though she were reading my thoughts she stated, "Yes, I am still with him now. And although I feel so strongly for you, I have an obligation to him."

"Why do you feel that you owe him something?" I demanded.

"It is as simple as this. He stayed with me even when I was badly injured. Even when I was a horrible and untrusting wife, he stayed with me. Now he is sick, very sick, and he has no one but me. I do feel that my obligation to him supersedes the feelings that I have for you. I hope you can understand. I feel that I have no choice in the matter."

"How sick is he?"

"He has pancreatic cancer. It's not his first battle with cancer, but this is much worse than what he has dealt with in the past. The only reason we are even in this part of the country is because he undergoes radiation here. Technically, if it weren't for him, I wouldn't have been in the area to have helped you when I did."

Her explanation softened my intense anger toward him but did nothing to derail the idea that we were meant to be together. "Do you love him?"

She smiled. "Even when we were first married, I never truly loved him. If I had, Michael would have never been a significant person in my life. He was always a good husband and father, but I never loved him." She paused for a moment as if carefully selecting her words. "I hope you know that I love you. I love you with all my heart. You are the only man I have ever said that to and truly meant it."

"So be with me!"

"I can't. I am so sorry, but I can't, and nothing you can say will make things any different than they are."

"That's unacceptable," I told her. "I would cherish you. I promise I would be good to you. You are my destiny, and I cannot let you go."

Ignoring my previous statement, Trish continued, "We will be leaving town tomorrow morning. There is so much I want to tell you, but I don't know where to begin, what to include, and what to leave out."

I looked at her, and clearly she could see the pain and frustration in my eyes. "Tell me what I can say to impress upon you the need I have for you."

"You've said everything you can say. It is what it is." She touched my face as she spoke.

I couldn't believe this was happening; it was as though my universe was falling apart all around me. "Trish, please don't do this, please! You're breaking my heart!"

"I know," she said. "I'm breaking my own heart in the process. I think you keep approaching the situation, expecting me to offer you a different answer. I'm sorry to say you are not going to find that answer tonight. I'm sorry."

In that instant I was defeated; I knew that I had lost her again, and I felt a giant hole open right through the center of me. This hole took the place of a piece of my soul; it carried with it an unendurable pain that I would have to burden. That hole would exist for many more years. There would be no amount of knowledge I could acquire, no accomplishment, nothing I could ever obtain that would be sufficient to fill it. Only Trish's presence in my life as my partner would fill it.

We sat quietly for the longest time, neither of us knowing what to say. Finally, Trish spoke, "As I said, I am leaving tomorrow, but I am here now. I'm right here this moment, and at this moment, I'm entirely yours."

I looked at her and she smiled. "What do you mean?"

"We should enjoy this time we have," she answered. Again, we were both momentarily quiet. It was just her and I and the sounds of the midnight waves washing up onto the warm sand. Finally, she pulled close to me and kissed me passionately. Within moments, we were both undressed and making love. It was so easy to get lost in her caring and tender embrace. When she touched me, when she kissed me, when she gazed deeply into my eyes, I could feel the depth of her feeling for me.

Several hours later, as we rested in the sand, our bodies side by side with our legs strangely wrapped around each other's, we spoke. We spoke as though we would always be together, as if this night would never end, as if we were going to remain on that beach in the weeks, months, and years to come. We both laughed almost like we were human; it seemed so natural. I was absolutely intoxicated by her presence.

Soon, Trish sat up then rose to her feet. "Come, run with me. Swim with me," she said as she extended her hand toward me. Once we were both standing, I followed her lead up the beach. What started as a brisk walk soon became a sprint through the sand by two unclothed super beings. We traveled with a speed no Olympic athlete could match even on his best day.

It soon became a game, one in which I was to chase her, try to catch her while she teased me laughing the whole time. I loved watching her run, watching her powerful and fully exposed muscular yet slender body propel her forward effortlessly. She was amazingly fast, certainly faster than I was, which surprised me greatly. Finally she allowed me to catch her some three or four miles down the beach. We were intimate again, and then she led me into the black nighttime waters to swim.

Afterward we made it back to the spot where our clothes were and, after dressing, decided to enjoy our wine—an eight-year-old Cabernet. Unfortunately, in our haste to leave the house earlier, neither of us had considered wine glasses, so we ultimately wound up sharing a small paper cup. I know, this probably sounds terribly uncosmopolitan, but it was the ending of the most romantic few hours of my life.

As we were finishing the bottle, the sad reality again began to make itself known. We both observed the moon and knew that at that exact time of night in exactly two weeks from that day, both of us would be nothing short of horrible and evil monsters. We both knew this as we watched the then-benign state of the lunar cycle, but neither of us mentioned it.

"I believe with all my heart that you and I were meant to be together," I told her.

She smiled and held my hand, and after taking the last sip of wine from the small cup, she replied, "I believe this too. You may not know this, but leaving you is absolutely tearing me apart. I love you like I have never loved anyone. I share closeness with you that I have never before felt."

I again wanted to argue with her to stay with me, but I did not. Still, the sorrow on my face seemed to make the argument for me. She then offered a strangely lycanthropic statement, "If it makes you feel any better, his odds of survival are quite slim." What an unusual thing for a woman who is choosing to stay with her husband to say. "You know," she began, "we have many more years ahead of us. We certainly have numerous decades, maybe lifetimes even. I don't know how much time John has. He has been battling cancer for a long while. Every time he thinks he has beaten it, it reappears. At this point, they say he has a less-than-five-percent chance of living beyond five years. They don't like giving numbers like that, but that is the cold, hard truth. I alone seem to hold the cure for his illness in my blood."

I looked at her sternly. "You wouldn't?"

"No, though he has asked if I would be willing to do that for him. I told him that he is still a man, and that is something to be proud of. If he were to become like me, I would be ashamed of him for needing it just as I am ashamed of myself. So with my refusal, I have practically revoked his last option and sentenced him to almost certain death."

"How do you feel about that?" I asked.

She offered me the most unusual look as she responded, "He is my husband, and he is the father of my son. He is also a good man that I have known for over three decades, and I don't want to see him die. As far as how I *feel* though, I am a lycanthrope, and I have no feelings for him. When he dies, and he will die, there will be no tears shed for him, and there will be no mourning.

"I know it's odd, considering my recent emotional outlet around you, but in your absence, I am a porcelain doll—devoid of expression. Whatever emotions I do have, they are created by and reserved exclusively for you.

"If you truly believe that we were meant to be together, then we will. You will just have to have faith. In the meantime, please always know that you are on my mind, and you are in my heart."

Her words stirred something deep within me, and I felt a mild hint of something that might evolve into tears, but despite how hard I tried, nothing happened.

"You are my best friend," she said.

"And you are mine."

Later, she drove us back into the city and kissed me one last time before leaving me at the motel. She told me she loved me one last time before she left. She also told me to take care of myself. Then she was gone.

So what more is there to say? Trish was gone. After spending so much time looking for her, I had all but given up. Then as if by providence, our paths had come together again. And yet, after what was certainly a touching reunion, she again slipped through my fingers as easily as smoke. Others might say that a relationship between us was simply not meant to be, but I could never accept this notion.

There was no one in this world that could ever be a substitute, no one who could hold a candle to her, no one who could ever make me feel as whole as she did.

The next evening I revisited the old condemned house that she had brought me to after saving me. The rats had carried off what remained of the food Trish had brought. Blood stains were now a part of the table and floor where I had been placed—almost like candle wax. And yes, I could still very easily smell Trish. Too easily, I thought. True, I had expected to encounter her scent, but this was quite strong. She wasn't there with me then, but she had been there relatively recently—though why I was unsure. There was really nothing here for her, no real reason for her to have come back to this awful and dismal building. But to be honest, there was no reason for me to have been there either. I guess I had hoped that by going back there, and by later traveling through the parts of town where she had walked, maybe I could just... connect with her somehow.

Is that a strange or unusual way to think? I would say to myself, "Trish was here," and by doing this—by retracing her footsteps, by sitting in those places that she had sat, by touching the objects that she had touched—I was closer to her. Well, crazy or not, that was my reason for being there.

I ventured into the next room, the one with the worn sofa. It was then and there that I noticed a black jacket that had been tossed over the back of one of the folding chairs, one of the chairs brought in from the bedroom. The jacket definitely belonged to Trish, and as I brought it to my face, I could smell her essence in it.

She had returned here... to leave her jacket? I didn't understand. I pulled the black suede object close to my chest, and closing my eyes, I held it as if it were a long-lost friend, as though it were Trish herself. What an odd thing for her to do. I wanted to ask her about this, but there was no way for me to contact her.

Later that same night, I returned to the alley where I had been shot. As I suspected, this was a crime scene now, and the alleyway had been roped off. It seemed that the area had been combed, the bodies and whatever evidence available had been taken away, and the long and dark corridor was now deserted. I looked up and observed the rooftop that Trish had followed me to and observed me from, the rooftop that she had descended from to save my life. It was a ten-floored building, and stood roughly 130 feet tall—I was quite simply amazed.

We are remarkably strong and able creatures, and yet only a few of us push ourselves to our full potential. It was almost disturbing really as I stood there contemplating a fall from that height. I had little understanding of my true limitations. Myra would have been disappointed in me were she to have known this. Even Trish, my most dear Trish, based on her tone, seemed to almost frown on how clumsily I carried myself and how I could so easily be lured into the situation I found myself in.

With this in mind, I decided that I must not remain ignorant of what I could do—I must test my limitations. Moments later, I stood on the same rooftop that I had observed from the ground—to me, it was Trish's rooftop. It was truly remarkable, the view she must have had from this vantage point. With my lycanthropic eyesight and hearing, I could easily spy upon people from impressive distances. Why had I not considered such as thing sooner? I was suddenly like an eagle looking down on to a field of mice.

At the far end of the street, perhaps a quarter of a mile away, I listened in to an intimate conversation between two lovers that had just finished a late evening meal. I also observed two men, who were some distance away from the couple, eye the young woman as she entered her romantic partner's car while he held the door for her. Even from that distance, I had no difficulty hearing with clarity the ugly and vulgar acts they claimed that they would do to her. By this, I was appalled. I wanted to kill them both.

I turned my attention to the opposite end of the street. Here, a man on a payphone was making arrangements for a cocaine purchase. As I listened with the fullest extent of my preternatural ability, I could even hear the man with whom he was speaking—a man named Durbin. It's funny that after all these years, I can still remember that name even as insignificant as it was.

I then approached and stood at the very edge, looking down into the dark and uninviting alley. Just then, a mild trepidation passed over me. If I were human, the likelihood of surviving such a fall would be slim; to walk away unscathed would have been nothing short of miraculous. I remember staring down at that moment and wondering if I would have been willing to take such a leap if Trish had chosen to remain with me. I wondered if I was doing this simply because she had left. I looked at the distant spot where I would fall, and a reluctance to act began to creep into my mind. I hesitated—only for a moment—then, before I had any further opportunity to talk myself out of it, I boldly stepped off the ledge.

As one would imagine, the fall itself took several seconds. A lot can go though your mind in only a few seconds, however. There are people who take their lives by jumping from tall structures certainly taller than this one. Although no one will ever know for sure, it would seem to me that in those seconds—those seconds where time seems to move so slowly—the jumper would regret their decision. It would be almost like watching a guillotine blade slowly falling toward one's neck.

The same could not be said for me, however. Although I was uneasy about falling from such a height, I knew that this would be far from sufficient to kill me. There was, of course, the idea of breaking every bone in my body, but even this I would miraculously heal from. Besides, Trish had accomplished such a feat and did not even consider it remarkable.

In the instant I hit the ground, a violent jolt was sent through my entire body. Every bone, every joint, every muscle felt the impact, followed by a brief instant of disorientation in my mind and by a numbness that, for only an instant, swept through my being. I found myself, still in one piece, on my hands and knees. It seemed that my lower extremities had taken the brunt of the impact, then I fell forward, catching myself. For a second or two, I didn't move; I then slowly rose to my feet. There was a considerable stiffness in my ankles, knees, hips, and all along my spine—a stiffness that would pass within an hour or two, but beyond that, I was unharmed.

I am sure that Trish performed this same task with much more grace than I had, but I had done it. I had taken a leap unlike any other, and in the process, I learned a little more about myself and about my abilities. I left the scene just as it was and went to find something to eat.

A few hours later, I returned to the same rooftop—"Trish's rooftop." Trish had stated that she had spanned these building of approximate height from one rooftop to the next with a single leap. This seemed almost as fantastic as jumping to the ground, almost. The distance between Trish's rooftop and that of the neighboring building was maybe twenty-three to thirty feet. Knowing now that at least my body could take such a fall, I backed up so that I could run toward the edge. With more confidence in myself than I had earlier in the evening, I sprinted toward the ledge, and with all the power my hips and legs could muster, I leapt from the top of one building to the roof of the next. The task proved easy enough; in fact, I had used more power than was even necessary.

By the end of the night, I felt that I had become an accomplished acrobat and could glide from building top to building top almost effortlessly. I could observe and track any human being—or lycanthrope—in the downtown area and could plummet to the earth from terrible heights without so much as a scratch.

After hours of trial and error, I had temporarily satisfied my need to discover my physical limitations. While I was pleased with what I had learned and by what I could now do, the truth was that I remained in an awful depressed state. Why could she not be with me? Did she not know how much I needed her, how much I loved her? The sorrow I felt in light of her absence overshadowed any sense of achievement.

It was thoughts such as these that ran though my mind when I suddenly came upon—him. It was the vulgar man that I had spied upon hours earlier. By now, it was almost four-thirty in the morning. I first observed him as I stood atop a five-story building owned by an insurance company. I quickly closed the distance between us by moving from one rooftop to the next, just as I had practiced throughout the night. As I neared him, I gracefully fell to the ground then advanced toward him without his awareness. At this point, I was finally able to use my olfactory senses to their fullest potential.

Although I've never been a good judge of age, I would expect that he was in his early twenties. He stood about six foot two—taller than me—and I estimated that he weighed about 220 pounds, an impressive-sized man to be sure. He was an unclean individual who had not bathed in at least several days. He did attempt to mask his somewhat crusty body odor with an overly generous amount of cheap cologne. He had consumed several beers throughout the night, and Jack Daniel's more recently. I could smell the alcohol on his breath and seeping through the pores of his unbathed skin.

What else would you like me to tell you about him? There was nothing he could hide. He was a heavy smoker, he did not use deodorant, and he had eaten french fries hours earlier. I can also tell you that he had been with a woman earlier in the night—a whore, no doubt. I could smell her fluids in his pants, on his face, on his fingers. Yes, he had left her only recently.

He wore jeans and a black Metallica t-shirt. His hair was dark and greasy but not long, and he was clean-shaven. Strange really that someone would be interested in removing facial hair but absolutely neglect overall cleanliness and hygiene Even his teeth smelled as though they were rotting in his mouth.

So why did I take such an interest in this individual? Well, that's easy really because like I said earlier, I wanted to kill him. Although I had killed a number of people, I had never stalked anyone before. So here I was, like a cat stalking whatever poor and miserable creature it had set its sights on.

The streets were absolutely empty, dead, but it wouldn't remain that way for long. Soon, traffic would pick up, and those early birds would be out getting their worms. I quietly walked up behind him as he pulled a cigarette from its pack and placed it between his lips. I grabbed him by the back of his neck and forced him off the main street and on to a darkly lit side street.

"What the fuck's your problem?" he shouted out with more fear than anger. His voice suddenly reminded me of those things he had said about the young blonde woman he and his friend had watched earlier. Oh, how loathsome and detestable I found him.

He withdrew a large folding knife from his pocket. "I'm going to fuck you up, motherfucker!" he shouted. His shouting would attract attention, I knew this, but I also knew that this wouldn't last too long. I think he expected me to flee upon hearing his threat as he merely stood speechless at my lack of a fearful response.

"Do your best," I told him.

After several seconds of him simply standing there, I stepped toward him. He quickly stabbed at me with the point of his blade. But he was as slow as a human could be and less than competent with a bladed object. With ease, I grabbed his right hand, which held the weapon, and with an intense grip that no human could possess, I broke every bone in his hand. Before he could scream out, I struck him very hard in the sternum, breaking every one of his ribs as easily as if they were crackers.

This blow was no doubt sufficient to cause his ribs to puncture and therefore collapse both of his lungs while sending his heart into a state of shock. But he was still alive and making direct eye contact with me for the first time. Blood pooled in his mouth then began to spill over his lips. He then lost control of his bladder and pissed all over himself as he stood there.

"Don't feel too bad," I said to him coldly. "You never had a chance." With those words, I grabbed his throat and forcefully removed his thyroid cartilage from his body, tearing his anterior neck wide open. I let him drop to the ground where he squirmed and kicked and bled until life passed out of him.

I tossed the crushed handful of flesh onto his corpse and walked away. Within twenty minutes, police would be on the scene; they would probably connect this murder to the ones that occurred just down the street several nights before. They would double their efforts, interview everyone in a three-block radius. It is likely that they would speak with the whore whom he shared a bed with and his vulgar friend who was lucky enough to not cross my path on this night. All this, to catch a killer in their midst. But no one would ever know it was me, just someone passing through town.

So am I an evil person? I certainly wouldn't argue with anyone who believes that I am. Still, I can say that I don't want to be evil. Was it Trish's rejection that ultimately led me to kill this man? Oh, don't feel sorry for him—he was far from a saint. But I could not help but think that perhaps I took out my frustration that I felt about Trish on him. Maybe on any other night, I would have been revolted by this individual but would have left him in peace—after all, he didn't do anything to me. He didn't even know I existed until the moment before I killed him. Of course, there is one other thought, a notion that I did not really consider until just now in fact.

I had just mentioned that he did nothing to me, which is true, but I found myself hating him for those things that he said about the blonde woman. I didn't really mention this before, but the woman we had both noticed reminded me of Heather Locklear who coincidentally bore a close resemblance to Trish. I remember thinking at the time, just how fortunate the young man who was with her was to have her. Of course, I am attributing Trish's traits and personality to this woman who only resembled her; she may have been, for all I know, a total bitch. Still, it occurs to me that I may have been less angered by what he said and more outraged by the fact that his statements were about a woman who reminded me of Trish. Maybe he just picked the wrong woman to comment on at the wrong time. Perhaps, there was a part of my subconscious that was trying to protect Trish. Either way, I feel no remorse for that bastard; I am glad he is dead, and the world is certainly a better place without him.

Later that morning, I left town, and for once again, I began to consider thoughts of ending it all. Everything had always been a game, at least in some fashion or another, but now it was a game that I no longer wanted to play.

Twenty-Two

I DROVE NORTH AND then west with no real destination in mind. What was there left for me really? I had done all that I had set out to do, and after seeing Trish, I had no desire to return to the life I knew before Anne had entered it. It wasn't really much of a life anyway, more of a preoccupation while the years passed.

I passed through the Carolinas and into Virginia before heading into Kentucky. I stopped here and there in no hurry to make it anywhere specific. One of these stops occurred as I was traveling into Louisville. It had been several days since I saw Trish, and she occupied my mind without mercy. I was sitting at a diner and ordered an unreasonable amount of food as was my style.

"You must be one of the hungriest customers we've had," the waitress commented with a smile. I smiled back, but what I really wanted to do was to tell her to go fuck herself. I would have been willing to tip her more if she would have simply brought my order without talking to me; I wasn't really in the mood to be patronized.

So as I sat there, regretting my life and hating my waitress, I stared out the window at an ugly building positioned across the street; in one of the windows, a small For Sale sign. *What a miserable-looking building,* I thought to myself.

Finally, my waitress brought the first portions of my order, and I continued gazing through the window, not only at the building but at the neighborhood in general as well. As I ate, the wheels in my mind began unexpectedly turning. The more I studied the structure, the more character it seemed to have. Eventually, my mind began to run a number of what-if scenarios. These were the first positive thoughts I had had since watching Trish's taillights disappear.

I exited the diner and proceeded across the intersection to view the building—my building—more closely. A little work and this could be a respectable site for any number of businesses, but I had something very specific in mind. On one side of the structure, a modest parking area, bordered by a chain-link fence that separated this property from an open grassy area. If I was going to realize my plan, I would need to acquire this area as well.

I turned my attention again to the building itself. Although the doors were locked, I had little problem entering through a broken window on the third floor. Twenty seconds later, I stood in a large and open room that reminded me of the old tool and dye business in Rockford where I had first met Trish. Ah, yes, I knew that I was going to have to work especially hard to push her image out of my mind. I knew that I wanted to do something healthy and constructive this time though—I had no further desire to drown my memory of her with alcohol, fighting, and a virtually endless supply of meaningless casual encounters. No, I wanted—needed—to do something positive with my energies, and while I could never be as altruistic as Arthur, I could be respectable. I could even learn to respect myself.

I toured the building and found it to be in relatively good condition. Before I left, I had a mental image of how everything would look in six to eight months. It would be a lot of work and would likely cost me half of my fortune, but it would belong to me; in all my life before then, I can honestly say that I never had anything that belonged exclusively to me.

Of course, I would have to relocate to Louisville where I knew not a soul. But as I considered it, I realized that it would not be any different from St. Louis, where I felt that I knew the city herself but none of her residents.

Later that day, I rented a small furnished apartment that would serve as my temporary home. I then made all the necessary calls and agreed to meet the realtor the following day. Amazingly, everything seemed to fall right into place, and by that week's end, I was the owner of both the building and the neighboring lot.

Unfortunately, the full of the moon was fast approaching, and before I could dive into renovation, I was required to tend to the becoming. I drove east to the Daniel Boone National Forest and eventually settled in an area park officials called the Clifty Wilderness. While I found this spot less than perfectly suited for what I needed, it sufficed.

It was such a strange feeling as I sat there in the middle of nowhere, waiting for my body to painfully twist and contort until I lost consciousness and allowed the monster to take control. It was strange because everything I had been dealing with during the preceding full moon seemed so far and distant now. A month earlier, a peculiar hatred flowed through me, and like a strong and pungent odor, I was seemingly unable to wash it from me. In addition, while I pursued Wade across the country, I in turn was pursued by a sense of ultimate hopelessness and loss once I was to achieve my objective and remove Wade from all existence. From time to time, I wondered what I would do when it was all over and my objective complete. My rage prevented me from dwelling on this idea, but it would cross my mind, and when it did, I had no answer. I only knew that the life I lived before Anne entered into it was not one I could ever go back to. In fact, when I thought about who I was just eighteen months earlier, I would become filled with disgust with myself.

But suddenly, just within that last week, everything turned around, and I felt a sense of purpose, purpose that didn't involve ripping anyone's throat out. All I can say is that in one instant, I had found myself sinking into the darkest abyss of an emotionless depression, and in the next instant, I was rescued by yet another beautiful epiphany. As for the origins of that epiphany, maybe all the factors in my life—the news of Arthur's death, Anne's unexpected emergence into my life and the tragedy of her loss, my quest for revenge, Trish's temporary reemergence—maybe those factors cumulated into the proverbial perfect storm as I sat in my booth at the small diner and stared out the window.

I stayed at the park until well into the next day. I was lucky that month, with the beast rearing its head only once. Clearly, I needed to adopt a method of dealing with this monthly occurrence in a better way than what I had been.

I arrived back in Louisville on a Tuesday, and after examining the building I had purchased, I realized that I needed to secure a second location, a very private and secure structure. Initially, I had considered running a business in the location I had purchased and possibly living in the upstairs floor. My plan was fine, except during the full of the moon. I wanted to employ a strategy similar to the one used by Trish and Arthur—imprison myself during the becoming. Unfortunately, this was not a practical consideration at this site.

Before I could get too much started with my newest business endeavor, I would have to take care of my problems with my inner monster. Specifically, I needed a place somewhat removed from my place of business or where I lived, some place where I could safely lock myself up during that part of the lunar cycle.

I searched for several days and considered several options before I found the perfect site—an old rundown and long-forgotten church. Built in the thirties, it was once called the Asbury Nondenominational Church of Christ. As far as I could tell, it had been many years since a congregation met to worship here. It was dusty, dilapidated, condemned by the city. As I walked down the main aisle toward what was once the pulpit, I could tell that this had become a semifrequent hangout for teenagers as the floor was littered with condoms and beer bottles—this, I would definitely need to bring to an immediate halt.

The only part of the building that I would have any use for was the basement, and upon my examination of it, I found it to be ideal. After purchasing this piece of real estate (the previous owner was more than happy to part with it), I spent the rest of that week securing the church—new doors, new locks, bars on the windows. I also put a large chain-link fence around the property's perimeter; and to further deter anyone who might be inclined to climb over it, I installed motion sensors that would light up the outside of the church as light as day should anyone step within thirty yards of the structure.

I had already ordered the materials I needed to construct an indestructible cage. Upon its completion, I had everything I needed for the next full moon. Essentially, the prison was roughly a twenty-foot-by–twenty-foot square. Once inside, I would toss the key onto the floor several feet beyond the reach of the bars. I would then disrobe, if I hadn't done so already, and wait for my dark nature to take its course. The following morning, I would awaken, amazed that the cage had managed to confine the immense strength and power of the demon. I would retrieve a simple wire hanger that I had kept taped to the top of the prison, and with it, I could reach the key that would allow me exit this cage.

From time to time, I would wonder what would ever happen if, for whatever reason, I was unable to retrieve the key that would always serve as my lifeline once I was Caleb again. I cannot imagine what I could possibly do as no one would ever know where I was, and as such, no one would ever come to my rescue. Fortunately, in all the years that I have utilized my self-imprisonment as a method of containing the monster, I have never faced the problem of being unable to get out.

I was more than a little nervous the first few times that I used the cage, and I specifically remember thinking to myself on that first night that I had made a terrible mistake in doing this. I know that it worked well for Trish as well as Arthur, but this was a first for me. Eventually though, I would become accustomed to it and wonder how I ever managed without it. Obviously, this way of maintaining the demon would have been impractical during my time traveling, but with the life I was ready to begin, this would become more than just a practicality. It would be a necessity.

With that particular personal problem now tackled, I was free to devote my time and energy to my business plans. Within four months of my spotting the building from my diner seat, a health club appropriately named the Beast opened its doors to the public. Yes, I had opened a gym, and while it might not have been something most would have done in my position, it was something that worked especially well for me. Now this certainly wasn't my ultimate goal—to own a gym and live upstairs—but it was a step in a direction for me. More importantly, it served to anchor me to the community and provided a home base from which I could build a name and reputation.

The main floor, or ground floor, housed the free weights and machines, everything a bodybuilder, power lifter, athlete, or weekend warrior could ever want—benches in every style, squat racks, pulley machines, dumbbells ranging from 5 to 160 pounds, Nautilus lines, and more. The second floor was divided into two parts—a cardio area, complete with treadmills, stationary bikes, ellipticals, the works, while the other side was utilized as an open area for floor exercises and classes such as Pilates and yoga as well martial arts classes. As I mentioned, the third floor was my personal living space—nothing too special, except the four large freezers that I kept stocked with various foods.

Business was slow at first, with only a handful of individuals interested in the new gym in town. I was actually perfectly content with this; after all, I certainly wasn't depending on business for the sake of survival. You could say that I considered this to be more of a pastime or hobby than an actual business. However, each month new members joined, and shortly the Beast began to take on the look of a real health club.

There was no pool, no basketball or racquetball courts, and no daycare. Because of this, there were critics who insisted that the Beast wasn't really a family-friendly gym, and I usually agreed with them. As far as I was concerned, if you were looking for somewhere to take your kids so that they could be looked after, try a daycare or babysitter; if you were looking to splash around and swim, there were a number of pools available in Louisville. If, however, you were looking for a real fucking workout without all the pansy-ass frills, a place where people were serious about their goals and knew what the hell they wanted from a gym, then you were definitely at the right place. And while it was—and still is—true that I didn't have basketball or racquetball courts, I also didn't have a football field, soccer field, tennis courts, roller skating ring, or horse track, I still ran one of the best hardcore gyms ever.

To this day, my doors are still open. While I certainly don't intend to use this writing as a forum for promoting a business that I own, I would encourage anyone interested in a real workout to check it out.

I had always considered myself an introvert, and anyone who knew me would agree to this fact. Unfortunately, my position at this new enterprise was one which required me to work with the public, usually in a very informal way. I did have people working for me—front desk personnel, housekeepers, and a couple of trainers, but I was still expected to make my presence known, especially during those first years of business. Despite my often shy and withdrawn personality, however, I actually enjoyed walking through the gym, talking with members, often even working out with them. *How interesting,* I often thought, *that these guys in the weight room are being spotted as they attempt to max out by the owner who just happens to be a werewolf.*

And so had begun the newest and greatest phase of my unnaturally long life. Without question, this time would prove to be more valuable than anything else I had ever done before or since. It was a period of growth and self-discovery. I realize how fucking cheesy that must sound, but cheesy or not, it was true.

I'll explain. I am what I am—a lycanthrope, a werewolf, wolfman, skinwalker. You can use whatever description you like. It doesn't change the truth—I am what I am. This was a cold hard fact that for the longest time, I could not accept about myself, at least not on every level. This was also something that I had admired in others who knew and accepted about themselves—Myra, Arthur, and yes, especially my beloved Trish. Hell, even Anne seemed more in touch with who she was despite her initial ignorance.

But me? No. From my first moments as a new creature, I was at odds with myself. This wasn't denial; far from it. I knew exactly *what* I was, but for whatever reason, I had difficulty accepting me for me. One could argue that I existed in this way long before my Alaskan hunting trip, and maybe that is true also. Maybe I was the inescapable result of those long-ago tragedies that I would wear like a badge for decades.

Until my time in Louisville, I had lived like a man in mourning. Because I couldn't accept fate at face value during my early life, I chose to run from my problems, and even as a demigod, a newly invented being, I still ran. It was my own fault that I lost Trish, my own fault that it took so many years to accept the simple lessons that Arthur tried to make available to me.

But here I was—Caleb V——, proud resident of Kentucky, owner of the Beast Fitness Center, and frequent workout partner of countless gym rats that would often show up in the hopes watching me press quarter of a ton or more off my chest with relative ease.

With the establishment of the church, which I began to refer to as the sanctum to myself, as a getaway during the becoming and the gym up and practically running itself, I had time to devote to anything I wanted, so I went back to college. In the coming years, I would earn degrees in criminal justice, art history, and biology. It didn't take long before I remembered just how humbling it was to be a student, but I enjoyed it nonetheless.

I will admit, there were times when the arrogance of various professors angered me, especially considering that, in fairness, I often had a deep understanding of subjects that they simply could not appreciate. My mind operated far beyond the limits of my classmates and instructors. I was bright enough to carry two full-time schedules easier than I did one when I first attended college in St. Louis (I was pretty stressed out when I was young and married to the devil incarnate).

Several years passed during this time, and when I wasn't in class, I began traveling. I toured Europe on several occasions, and in doing so, deepened my appreciation of my lot in life. No, my life wasn't perfect, very far from it really, but it did allow me to engage and experience the world as no one could. There are a number of endeavors that I engaged in during that time that I would welcome the opportunity to share. Another time perhaps. As interesting as those accounts are, they will do nothing but distract me from telling my story here.

There was one minor tragedy that I should probably talk about, however. Now after reading this, you may think that I am the absolute stupidest creature to have ever been born. Trust me when I say this—I have never hated myself as much as I did on account of this particular oversight.

By this time, several years had passed since coming to Louisville, and though I am sure you grow tired of reading about my continued feelings for Trish, they always have and continue to make me who I am. In fact, I firmly believe that they somehow anchor within me the remaining humanity I have left. Although I had done the best I could to busy my mind in the generous amount of time since I had last seen Trish, from time to time I still found myself staring into space and allowing my memory to recreate her image, her voice, even her very scent in my mind.

For no particular reason, while in one of my reminiscing moments, I found myself remembering how wonderful it was to hold her, remembering how at peace I was and how safe I felt in her company. I began wishing I had a photograph of her, something I could stare into and channel my sorrow toward. One thought led to another when suddenly it occurred to me that I was still in possession of the jacket Trish had left in the dusty old house in Florida.

Like a drug addict desperately looking for another high, I quickly ran upstairs into my private apartment, opened one of my closets, and removed the black leather jacket. I actually placed it far in the back of the closet in the hopes that if I didn't see it, I would possibly not think of her. Obviously, it was an object that I could never destroy or throw out, but at the same time, it was one that I tried never to look at. But on that particular day, I remember pulling it from the closet as though I had done so a thousand times when, in fact, this was the first time I had even looked at the jacket since "hiding" it there.

Ah yes, even after the passing of several years, Trish's beautiful scent was still right there. Then I did something I should have done many years earlier, something I should have done the very night that I recovered the jacket. Why I hadn't inspected the pockets beforehand, I will never know, nor can I forgive myself for not having done so. So as you can probably imagine, my heart seemed to stop and bleed painfully as I removed from the jacket's pocket a letter that I was intended to read the day following my last encounter with Trish. It read,

> Dear Caleb,
>
> What can I say, except that I love you? Please forgive me if it seems that I am indecisive. I feel pulled in many directions. On the one hand, I feel bound by my obligations for the sake of my son who is still very much a part of our lives, for my family, and for the human being that I once was. I know that it would have been easy to walk out on me

after my accident, but John stayed by my side even when he learned of the affair. I guess I felt that doing the same for him was something that I just had to do. At the same time, I am betraying my heart and soul by walking away from you.

As I write this letter to you now, I cannot help but feel that I have made the wrong decision. I knew it when I was driving away from you. I know that you were right with everything you said, and I feel the same way—we should be together. As it is, I cannot bear the thought of being away from you any longer than what is absolutely necessary. What I am trying to say is that I want to be with you now, and I want you to take me with you.

I will remain at the G——Hotel for another two days. I will be waiting for you. If for whatever reason you are unable to meet up with me, please call me at (815) 332-XXXX. I hope and pray that my earlier statements have not dissuaded you. I desperately need you in my life.

Yours Forever,

Trish

With Trish's letter in my hand, I slowly sat back on to my bed and allowed the message that she had penned to slowly sink in. What had I done? What must she have thought of me? What must she think of me now? I wanted to scream out... cry... curl up into a ball, but I was emotionally beyond all that. But I wasn't beyond love. I was never beyond love. I knew it was a long shot, considering the time that had passed, but I did try calling the number that she had provided. Not surprising, however, that particular number was no longer in service.

I'm sure Trish probably assumed that I had a change of heart regarding my offer to her; maybe she thought I was angry with her. Surely her husband had died by this point. Did that matter? What was I to do now?

I tried telling myself that my life was better off without her, that the heartache I had experienced for so long would only be rehashed if

I were to pursue her again. It's true, not a day ever went by that I didn't wonder about her, but clearly the universe had different plans. After all, we tried... and we tried... and we tried; it didn't really seem that it was meant to be.

I don't know that there was much logic in my arguments, but I was trying to convince myself of something I could never truly believe. The one thing I did know was that I needed to think my way through the decision of whether to contact her. Unfortunately, there were issues that would again prevent me from immediately searching for Trish, let alone pursuing a renewal of my association with her.

I was deep in the woods and uncertain of where I was, and yet, everything seemed somehow familiar. There was fresh snow on the ground, three or four inches maybe, and I could see tracks made by various animals within the last hour of so—fox and rabbit among them.

I closed my eyes to allow my hearing and olfactory senses to work undistracted. Within an instant, I was aware of the chipmunks that were hibernating deep within a nearby tree and various winter birds that, while I could smell them, remained eerily silent. In the far distance, I could hear the heavy footsteps of a deer as it made its way though the snow.

I opened my eyes and quickly traversed through two hundred or so yards of dense woodland to the east, positioning myself downwind of the animal, thereby ensuring that while I could smell the deer, it would be unaware of my presence. It was an adult doe, half a mile to the southwest. She was strong and healthy, the picture of natural vitality. But there was something more, something I couldn't get a handle on—like the woods that surrounded me, this doe's scent was somehow familiar. It was as though it wasn't just a deer, but something I knew once before, a long time ago.

With the speed and grace that only a lycanthrope could, I quickly and quietly advanced toward the doe. Her scent grew stronger as I approached until at one hundred yards I caught sight of her. Using the trees as cover, I crept closer and closer, much as a cat would. While there would be no way I could outrun a deer, if I got close enough, I wouldn't have to.

I was drew close, very close. I could hear her breathing, could practically hear her heart beating, and then she saw me. She did not bolt and run; in fact, she didn't even seem afraid of me. Her sad eyes looked at me as though I were her friend, a friend that would never harm her. I slowly moved from behind the tree and cautiously approached the doe. Still, she did not run, but instead took steps to meet me. Amazed at what was actually happening, I reached out touched her gentle face then stroked her soft neck as though she were a newborn colt.

This would have been impossibly strange had I been human— a wild animal acting in such a calm manner when in the presence of a person, let alone the physical contact. As for lycanthropes, every animal I have ever come across, domestic or wild, seems to recognize me as the ultimate predator. The only exception to that rule was during my time with Trish. Obviously, there was something about her that was special among us. Outside of her goats and kittens, no animal had allowed me to pet it since becoming what I am; that was over thirty-five years ago.

And yet here I was, with a wild doe no less. My original thought while stalking it was to kill it if for no other reason than sport alone, but there was no way I could do that now. I continued stroking her soft coat until I noticed something bizarre—there was blood trickling from the animal's ears. As I took notice of that, the doe began bleeding from its nose and eyes as well.

Quite suddenly and without warning, she fell to the ground and began convulsing. I backed away in horror as the animal painted the freshly fallen snow with its blood as it threw its head to and fro. Then just as quickly as it had begun, it was over. The animal ceased to move, ceased to breath, ceased to live. For several long moments, I stood in disbelief, wondering how this could have happened. But it seemed that the worst wasn't over for this poor deer as something began to squirm in its abdomen, like fingers wiggling under a sheet.

The scene, already horrific, became increasingly macabre as the mouth of the doe opened slowly, followed by a very humanlike scream and accompanied by blood with a syrup consistency that flowed from its tongue. I averted my eyes when maggots as large as my thumbs began to tear through the animal's coat and erupt from the carcass.

Although I was no longer watching the decimation of what was a beautiful animal, I could hear its flesh being pulled apart. A loud gunshot in the distance then rang out, diverting my attention from the sounds coming from the deer. The gunshot, which echoed off the surrounding hills, *carried with it a strange sense emergency as though instinctively I knew something terrible had happened.*

I immediately ran as quickly as my legs could take me, traversing a mile and a half of this rough terrain in minutes. As I ran, the sunlight faded from the sky in a most unnatural way, replaced by a starless pseudo-nighttime cover, a black void that spanned from horizon to horizon. This is how the world ends, I told myself as I ended my fanatic run, shocked to find myself staring at Myra's cabin.

I turned and viewed the dark forest that I had emerged from. The trees seemed engulfed in a strange black fog that served to hide something ugly and menacing that had been following me. I backed away from the tree line and toward the relative safety of the cabin as malevolent eyes seemed to watch my every move. A part of me was ready to fight if need be, but fight what? Somehow, I already knew—it was the deer... kind of. More accurately, it was death. But I knew that it wasn't coming for me. I was nothing but an unwilling bystander here. It only took an instant to realize who it was coming for.

"Myra!" I screamed as I pulled myself out of my nightmare. For the longest while, I sat at the edge of my bed telling myself over and over again that it was only a dream, just another fucked-up dream. But there was something different about this dream though I wasn't sure why.

In the days that followed, I couldn't stop thinking about Myra; even Trish and the letter I had discovered seemed ineffective to remove my thoughts from the woman who made me who I was. In all the years since I left her, I had never felt such an irresistible need to reach out to her. It was as though I knew that she was in danger. Was it possible that my dream was an omen, a warning?

After another Myra-inspired dream equally as disturbing as the first, I felt that I had no choice but to go to her. Maybe she needed me, maybe she was in danger, or maybe they were just dreams. I wasn't sure, but I was obsessed, and I needed to go to her if only to put my mind at ease. Several days later, I booked a flight to Alaska; my chief concern was how Myra would feel about me after all these years.

TWENTY-THREE

AS I APPROACHED the cabin, I remember a sense of dread overcoming me, like those few moments one might experience at the gallows just before execution is carried out. Yes, over the years I had contemplated what it would be like if and when I was to ever return there. I often wondered what it would be like to speak with Myra again, to be on terms with her as an equal rather than the student role I had played before.

Indeed, when I first left Myra all those years earlier, I had planned on returning within a short time—maybe after a year or two. Of course, I was still overwhelmed by her on one hand and needing her for comfort on the other. Upon leaving Myra, I was alone in the world and felt much as a child might upon leaving home for the first time—and permanently. But while Myra always held a very special and intimate place in my heart, there was little more she could truly offer me. From that point forward, the world would become my classroom.

So here I was back where it all started. I exited the car, uncertain of what to expect—surely, Myra was well aware that I was here, but would she welcome me with open arms or loath me for this uninvited trespass? The cabin was identical to what it was decades earlier—picturesque and beautiful but somehow creepy, like something from an *Evil Dead* movie.

"Myra!" I shouted, loud enough for her to have heard within a two-mile radius with her preternatural hearing. When I heard no response, a sick feeling began to well in my stomach. In that instant, the foreboding feeling that I had been experiencing in the weeks before quickly came to a head—I knew that Myra was dead.

I remembered Myra telling me how it was common for lycanthropes to share a deep-seated psychic link with those who they had created. I knew then that this is why Myra had been in my thoughts over and over again.

I entered the cabin and proceeded slowly but directly through it; from the family room through the kitchen, everything seemed just as it should have been, untouched. It wasn't until I peered through kitchen window facing the posterior of the cabin that I saw her remains. I exited the cabin and approached the body, half expecting to wake from another of my horrible dreams—this was no dream.

I could still see her face, but the back of her head was gone; in her hands, a 12-gauge shotgun. In life Myra was so beautiful, perfect in every way. I remembered every delicate line, every delicate curve; she could have been a goddess. In death however, she was ugly, as ugly as everyone gets when they die, maybe even more so in her case. I suspected that she committed the act on herself on or about the time I had my initial dream of her—about two weeks earlier. Her body, though decomposed, was just as it had been when it landed on the ground as there were no predatory animals in the area—thanks to the wolf.

I wrapped her in one of the white comforters that still bore my bloodstains from three and a half decades ago. I carried her body deep into the woods and buried her under the tree where she had first spied upon me the morning after I was attacked. Despite my lack of emotion, everything seemed remarkably surreal; I couldn't believe that this was happening.

As the sun began to set, I slowly ventured back to the cabin like a soldier having just lost a battle. At the cabin I lit a candle and retraced my steps through the kitchen where I saw a letter that Myra had intended for me to find resting on the table. It read,

My Dear Caleb,

If you find this letter as I suspect you will, then you, no doubt, are well aware of my demise. I'm sure that you are disappointed in my decision, and for that, I am deeply apologetic.

I know you have many questions. Why would I do this? What could have led me to such a low point in my life? Why did I not search you out before this? While I do have the answers to these questions, they will do little to further your understanding of my contingencies.

I have lived a long and lonesome life, the vast majority of it a monster, and during my time here, I've accomplished little—and of that, nothing positive. Someone once told me that guilt was the greatest folly of humankind, a burden that limits the capabilities of those who experience it. Well, I have committed a great number of evil acts, and yet I would give my very soul—if I possess it still it—to feel even a moment of remorse for what I've done.

I lied to you when I said that we get used to existing without feeling. I was hoping to spare you the harsh reality of what you would inevitably face. The unfortunate truth of the matter is that I want to feel something, anything, yet I cannot. I am sorry, Caleb, but I will not continue to live like this; I would rather terminate my existence than to live and breathe without desire or want for anything.

I owe you a greater apology than I could ever offer to paper. I hope and pray that you will find the peace that you search for, the peace that I was unable to find. Good luck, Caleb. You are one of the best of us.

With deepest sincerity
Myra

I spent the next several days reflecting on the events in my life that had led me to this point. I thought about my time spent with Myra, brief as it was. I thought about Trish, Arthur, Anne, all the other individuals that had come into my life and had left just as quickly. It seemed that I was destined to have people enter into my life only so that they could be taken from me. Now while this thought hardly applied to Myra, considering the lengthy span of time since I had last seen her, I nonetheless felt a profound sense of loss—not just of her but of everyone I had known as well.

Again, for the first time in many years, I was revisited by an old idea that I had almost forgotten about. Before coming to Alaska for the first time all those years earlier, I was so desperate for the world to stop, desperate for a stillness of heart that I had thought again and again of taking measures just as Myra had done. I wanted to be numb, numb to the pain that ate through my soul like acid. Though it took decades, it seemed that I was finally getting what I wanted—a numbness. Ironically, I had long ago learned that feeling nothing would be a worse fate than feeling everything even if it was unbearable.

As I remained in the cabin, surrounded by Myra's scent, by her very presence, I wished that she hadn't done what she did—my spirit was broken. But while I do not know her specific reasoning, I shared her desire to end everything. While I had invested several years prior to this attempting to reinvent myself in the style of Arthur, I realized then and there that someday I would do just as Myra had done.

I spent three days in her cabin, half expecting to see her walk though the door or offer some lesson to me that she had forgotten to in the years before. I sat in her chair that she would so lazily relax in while she read. On the small table next to the chair was a half-burned candle and a copy of Dostoyevsky's *The Idiot*. I remembered her offering me her opinion of Russians and wondered what she thought about this author. I wondered if perhaps she had just finished reading this particular book before writing my letter and terminating her own life.

From time to time, I would find myself gazing in the corner where my pallet once rested. Now it was just an empty corner, but memories came rushing back, memories of her lying next to me and wrapping her strong arms around me.

I also took that time to do what I wouldn't have dared to do during my earlier stint at the cabin—I reentered Myra's bedroom and sorted through her most private possessions. There were clothes, of course, even a few items belonging to a man (I remembered her offering me clothes after my attack). In her closet, I found a box of pictures, all black and white. I also found several journals, very old journals; as I flipped through them, the entries were dated as far back as 1916. I considered offering to these pages what I had read, chronicling her story, but I won't do that; her story will remain just as she wanted it—private.

I can say that as tragic as my story has been, it could not hold a candle to the pain that Myra experienced in her life. I learned of the personal atrocities that she had faced and dealt with, unspeakable horrors that occurred long before I was even born. I learned so much about who this amazing woman was, things I wish she could have spoken to me about. She never let me into her innermost thoughts during our time together, and she never had a chance to after I left. But then again, sometimes there are things best left unspoken.

My initial plan was to head back to Louisville and resume life as it had been, but for reasons I cannot say, I booked myself a flight back to Louisiana, back to my childhood home. Maybe it was the nostalgia I had been feeling during my return to Alaska that led me to pursue more, drove me to reopen those buried skeletons that I had turned my back on. Three days later, I was back in the Pelican State.

It had been almost thirty years since I had last seen the bayou, and yet the minute I smelled it, I knew that I was home. I walked in the footsteps that I had when I was a child. The house that I grew up in had been replaced by a newer home, a nicer home and other homes had been built around it. And although much had changed both in Lafayette and on the shady dirt road where I grew up, the swamp was exactly as it had been since before the first settlers had arrived.

While it was interesting to see the area and to taste the flavors in the gumbo I remembered from my childhood, I did have a reason for my return. I rented a boat from one of the local sugar cane farmers and made my way into the heart of the bayou, back to the place of my childhood fears.

As if driven with some kind of mentally programmed map, I navigated directly to the large piece of land that was home to a monster. Within moments of my arrival, the monster and I were aware of each other's presence. I was in no rush, casually walking in the direction of the camp where half a century ago, two of my friends and I foolishly ventured. I was there soon enough.

Much like Myra's cabin, Pruitt's camp had not changed despite all the years that had passed. Animal bones hung from trees, and a fire blazed over a very large cast-iron pot, simmering whatever Pruitt had pulled from the swamp. And there he was, sitting patiently by the fire, waiting for me. He rose to his feet as I approached, and a smile swept across his face.

"Seems that you and I may have crossed blades once before, yes?" he asked as he studied me. "Are you still looking for your monster?" It seemed that his intention was to taunt me.

"How many years have you been out here?"

Pruitt smiled, widening the youthfully deceptive lines on his face—he was a man who looked to be in his midfifties. "This has been my land since before your grandfather was born. I have watched as generation after generation has come and gone." Suddenly, Pruitt's demeanor changed; as the smile melted from his face, a scowl became apparent, and his jaws tightened. "And all the while, I've kept to myself, trying to keep my distance from those fuckers that feel the need to trespass here."

There was a strange mixture of feelings that began to run through me. On the one hand, I hated him for what I had long-since known—he had killed Aaron all those years ago. And yet, hadn't he done everything he could to ensure that the tragedy that happened would be avoided? My mind revisited the exchange that occurred between Pruitt, Aaron, Holly, and me. He was ugly, crude, and frightening, and perhaps intended to protect us through fear. Maybe he had hoped that his behavior would keep us away.

Was he guilty of anything that I myself hadn't committed? No. I knew it when I was young, and I knew it now—Aaron's death was of his own doing, his own foolishness. Pruitt was a vile and hateful man, but as I looked into his wild and savage eyes, I knew that he wasn't the evil being that I had suspected him of being for all those years.

"But you couldn't stay away, could you?" he asked in seething disgust.

It wasn't difficult to see that Pruitt's temperament was escalating—my very presence here was prompting his rage. My first instinct was to attempt to diffuse the situation, to explain my innocence and Aaron's youthful audacity, but just as suddenly, I realized that I owed nothing to this individual.

"I didn't come here to apologize," I said to him. As I spoke, he slowly took several steps in my direction. His movements seemed almost catlike—slow and deliberate as though his intention was to pounce—and in the next instant, he did just that.

As he lunged toward me, I stepped forward, grabbed him by the throat with my right hand, and slammed him into the ground. He was older, and therefore, I expected him to be stronger than I was, but this wasn't the case. "I am not the boy that I once was," I said to him. Within ten minutes, I had killed him.

There was a time when I would have felt guilt for taking his life—I had already logically concluded that he didn't intentionally kill anyone unlike Wade and his family. However, the time for feeling guilt for any reason had long since passed.

I spent that night in Lafayette, and during that time, I thought about Myra's letter, thought about how badly she wanted to feel something even if it was an unpleasant emotion. There was one more thing I needed to do before heading back to Louisville.

A couple of days later, I found myself walking thought the streets of St. Louis, revisiting some of my old haunts, essentially, avoiding what I had come here to do. Unfortunately, I only had about five days before the lunar cycle forced me to lock myself up. With that in mind, I revisited the cemetery where Jessica had been buried—a place I had been unable to bring myself to since her funeral.

Expecting the worst, I approached her headstone and waited for what would not come—grief.

EPILOGUE

SO THERE YOU have it—my story. What else is there to say? I'm alive, just like the rest of humanity. But whatever it is that I have become, whatever it is to be a lycanthrope, it has brought me to a place where I have nothing left in common with humanity. I live day by day; I remain ever vigilant of the lunar cycle, and barring anything unforeseen, it is likely that I will be around for another seven or eight decades.

I exist as a preternatural creature—a shape-shifter, a metamorphic monster. If you've read my story, then you know that I'm not alone as a lycanthrope. There are others. But what of other supernatural entities? Are there other different types of monster? Of this, I am sorry to say that I know nothing.

In the time I have lived as a lycanthrope, I have never seen a vampire, zombie, or extraterrestrial. I have seen good and evil. In a strange way, I've become the very face of evil at various times. However, as for as I can tell, good and evil are, by and large, human characteristics. I have acquired no knowledge, despite my searching, to definitively prove that either God or Satan exists or of the existence of angels or demons. Yes, I've heard stories of demonic possessions, and at the opposite end of the spectrum, I have heard stories of miracles, but I have never witnessed anything of this nature.

You could say that in recent decades, I've lost much of my faith, along with my humanity. I will tell you that I find no comfort in the notion of a godless, atheistic world. The absence of God seems to make life a seemingly empty and pointless journey.

So are lycanthropes the lone preternatural creature on the planet? No, I don't think so. While I've never seen a vampire—at least to the best of my knowledge—there are other nonlycanthrope things that I have witnessed. Ghosts, spirits, I have had countless encounters with them. In fact, they seem to exist almost everywhere. Most humans lack the ability to sense the subtleties of their surroundings; most—including myself when I was human—are totally ignorant of the spirits or entities that we share our homes with.

I will give you a quick lesson on hauntings, and bear in mind, this information comes not from any afterlife experience, psychic ability, or spirit guide, but rather from the observations of preternaturally sensitive being. As far as I can tell, there are four different types of hauntings. Most are residual hauntings, meaning that there is no spirit or ghost involved. For whatever reason, residual hauntings play out over and over again like a skipping record. These phenomenon, while remarkable at first, interest me little now as there are so many of them, each mundane and insignificant and each occurring just beyond the perceptions of most human abilities, but not mine. Even animals such as dogs and cats, though fully aware of their existence, seem to pay little mind to them.

Poltergeists, or at least what I call poltergeists, are quite interesting to observe although there isn't any kind of spirit involved with these either. My understanding is that these poltergeist episodes are a telekinetic phenomenon caused by a human who, in most cases, remains unaware that they are responsible for the often violent manipulation of their environment. I have witnessed two such poltergeist episodes, both involving adolescent girls of about thirteen or fourteen years of age who, I believe, were responsible for the occurrences but lacked an understanding or awareness that they were causing the episode. In both cases, the girls had recently experienced what would no doubt be traumatic. The first girl who lived in Brooklyn had been brutally sexually assaulted by a street gang while the other girl who lived in rural Ohio was the sole survivor of an automobile accident that killed both of her parents.

Each had come from drastically different backgrounds and were set almost ten years apart. And yet, what these two girls were capable of—the things that happened in their presence—were identical. Objects would be wildly thrown from shelves, windows would shatter, carpet would tear from the floor, and anyone in the immediate vicinity of the girl would be thrown away from the child usually into a wall and often pinned there until the episode subsided.

As fascinating as these poltergeist events were, these were not true hauntings. True spirit entities or spirit hauntings are the only actual ghosts, and while less common than the nonspirit residual hauntings I mentioned, they seem abundant enough for me.

As I mentioned, it would seem that most animals with heightened senses—such as dogs and cats—would be aware of these spirit entities, especially as they do tend to interact with the physical world on different levels. Often, residual hauntings manifest much as a movie would—you can if you are sensitive enough actually see what appears to be a man or woman standing at a window or ascending/descending a staircase each morning at a certain time, but that is it. There is no interaction, no awareness of any kind. There is simply nothing there but an image that plays out over and over.

A true spirit, on the other hand, while seemingly possessing a conscience, doesn't have any kind of recognizable body—at least as far as I can tell. If they are visible at all, it is ordinarily in the form of smoke or mist or possibly a glowing orb that appears to float in midair. If I had to guess, I would say that these spirits behave as though they don't realize they are dead. They are often like Alzheimer's patients, wandering from room to room, confused and uncertain of where they are or even what year it is.

Certain spirits seem to have more energy than others, and in some cases, they are quite capable of manipulating objects in their surroundings. They can lock or unlock doors, turn faucets or light switches on or off, open cabinets or doors, even take items and relocate them for whatever bizarre reason—again, they often behave in a confused and illogical manner. In many cases, keys, pictures, or other objects will disappear from a table or countertop only to reappear weeks later under the kitchen sink or in the back of a closet.

Of course, while the idea of a mystery in which I have specialized tools at my disposal did seem to captivate my interest, what attracted me most to the spirits of the dead is the notion of life after death. Clearly, there is something there. Maybe if there is an afterlife, perhaps there is a God?

Unfortunately, I have had little success in ever approaching or getting near a spirit. While they are often oblivious to the living—humans that are usually operating in their midst. They seem to recognize and acknowledge me and stay as far from me as they can. They act quite frightened in my presence—though as to why, I cannot say. It would not seem that I could conceivably bring any harm to them.

There is another type of haunting, and unfortunately I have little to offer regarding what exactly it is. These are entities of some sort though I do not believe they are human in origin; I don't believe they were ever alive. Unlike other entities or apparitions that I can easily observe, this other type of entity is much more difficult to locate. I am assuming that they are aware of the presence of the living as well as my presence. They seem relatively benign, moving from here to there in the shadows as though hiding from people, who clearly cannot see them. Unlike spirits that remain active around the clock, these other entities appear to be nocturnal in nature. Clearly, a closer investigation is necessary for a better understanding. No, I have not ruled out the idea of angels or demons when considering the nature of these entities, but again, while they are aware of human beings, they seem to have little or nothing to do with them, disregarding them in most cases—disregarding me as well.

I should note, if you haven't already guessed, that in recent years I have sought out the peculiar and unusual, stories and rumors of "otherworldly" individuals, bizarre and unexplained phenomena, and of course monsters such as myself. It is unfortunate, however, that the majority of these searches were absolutely fruitless—just stories, frequent spirit entities, and exaggerations of accounts by individuals, intoxicated more often than not, whose stories were rationally explained.

In addition to the spirit world, I have encountered humans with exceptional abilities. There is little more that I offer to elaborate further on the psychics that live among us. Mind you, I don't mean the generic astrology psychics that offer information about your zodiac sign, but rather, those who share Anne's talents. While a mystery to me, she possessed the ability to see events often years before they happened with remarkable detail. But there are other types of gifted people.

As a child in Louisiana, voodoo was a mystical and often feared religion, especially for the colored families in the area. I remember that it often frightened Aaron though he rarely admitted to this. To me, it had always seemed too bizarre to be taken seriously, and those who practiced it were a bit obsessed with ideas that I could not understand.

For all their attempts, the bayou priestesses were unable to cause one person to fall in love with another, offer vengeance for a wronged individual, or generate wealth for a family who desperately needed financial relief. In addition to this, although there were stories of fantastic "miracles" performed by these witchdoctors, I know of no one who had even the slightest relief of pain by visiting a voodoo spell-caster.

Despite my hesitancy to believe in individuals who held supernatural abilities to cast spells, I have come to learn that they do in fact exist. Maybe they utilize a type of energy that the poltergeist girls unknowingly possess; but this is purely a speculation on my part. When asking about the source of their abilities, I've received various answers about faith, Christ, and non-Christian deities. Ultimately, these are individuals with incredible abilities who seem only slightly more educated about what they can do than the poltergeist girls. Whereas the girls who experience poltergeist phenomena tend to look at spirit or demon causes, the witches—although many do not call themselves witches—tend to believe that their religion is credit for their abilities.

In 1999, I met a young woman named Patricia S—— in Albuquerque, New Mexico. She was beautiful, intelligent, deeply religious, and most of all, quite deadly. She was well aware of what she could do, though would refrain as she felt that it was a misuse of a gift that God had granted her Because of her hesitancy to practice or strengthen her abilities, her true potential would likely never be discovered. She was nineteen when I first met her, but I felt as though her soul was much older than her years.

During our meeting in New Mexico, I watched her push an aggressive ex-boyfriend into cardiac arrest using the power of her mind. He lived because she allowed him to live. Of course, I was fascinated.

If Patricia were to become angered, her energies could be channeled into a destructive weapon. On the opposite end of the spectrum, she worked as a healer and offered her services to those who could not, or would not, seek conventional medical intervention. Amazingly, although shunned or ignored by health care professionals, Patricia's ability to work with those who were ill or injured and show improvements in or alleviate their conditions seemed to, in many cases, exceed those of the medical profession.

Now, Patricia was an accomplished herbalist and homeopathic philosopher. She was a strong believer in the concept of natural healing or allowing the body to heal itself. While noteworthy, none of this truly interested me. What set Patricia apart wasn't the fact that she understood herbs or knew how energy channels moved through the body, but rather the power of her mind—specifically, how she could use it to heal those who were ill or dying.

I actually spent a considerable time with Patricia, and while I was there, a man came to her for help. Apparently, he had been diagnosed with an inoperable brain tumor and told that he had only six to eight months to live. His headaches, which plagued him daily, were treated with a strong narcotic pain medicine. He was instructed to make arrangements for the inevitable. Modern medicine had little more to offer this man, so out of desperation, he sought out Patricia. I met this man on two separate occasions—when he first came to Patricia and a year later when he was fully recovered and living his life as though nothing had ever been wrong with him. Of course, when Patricia treated him, it was in a private manner, and I was not permitted to observe. But I could smell the disease in him, and the physicians were correct—he would die soon. I honestly do not know what Patricia offered or performed for this individual, but within six months, the tumor was gone, baffling the doctors who had offered his bleak diagnosis.

Does this not sound too supernatural to you? Well, consider this then. Patricia's mind and the power it could generate seemed determined entirely on her emotions. It was only when she became afraid that her ex-boyfriend's heart stopped beating. On another occasion, when she became deeply angry, she psychokinetically tore tires from a truck.

There is one other preternatural subject that I have witnessed that I should address here. Regretfully, this too I have little to offer but what I have seen with my own eyes It was winter of 1986, and I was fighting in Miami, Florida, when I noticed a strange individual in the crowd paying particularly close attention to me. He was a Caucasian man, about thirty years of age, and dressed all in black. There was something quite different about this individual, and my first thought was—lycanthrope. I realized, almost immediately, however, that while he certainly was not human, he was not anything like me either.

After the fight, I made my way to speak with him, and seeing me approach, he made a hasty departure Quickly, I was in pursuit of him and learned that he was much faster than I, and apparently much stronger as well as he leapt up and scaled a building like something out of a comic book. I did my best to track him, but he was simply gone. This would have been unusual enough, but I did see this same individual about two years ago in southern Illinois—still watching me. He had two other individuals in his company, each dressed identical to him, and each very well groomed and attractive as he was—another man, this one with dark hair, and a blonde woman.

As I had done twenty years earlier, I went in pursuit of these individuals only to lose track of them. From what I could tell, the man that I had witnessed years earlier had remained absolutely unchanged. Although I do not know what they were, nor do I have any clues as to their origins, I have come to regard them as the Immortals. No special reason why I call them this, except that I get the feeling that while they do appear young, they are in fact much, much older, older than any lycanthrope. Again, I don't know this for certain. It is only a feeling.

But enough of this, I have droned on long enough with my thoughts here. There was a reason that I offered my story to paper, and on more than one occasion during my writing, I have forgotten my intentions.

I'll be honest with you. When I began this writing, my intention was to end my existence upon its completion. I know you've read over and over again about losing one's humanity, but I'm sure that to most, this concept is too abstract to wrap one's mind around. I don't know, I've never considered myself a strong person, certainly nothing like Myra. Bearing that in mind, how could I be expected to proceed forward in life when even Myra, as strong as she was, could find no reason to live?

But maybe that's the real issue—the fact that I can find no reason to proceed through life. I've lost nearly everyone who was ever important to me—most of them violently. What's worse, I've long since lost the ability to grieve for those who have died. Do you believe that fact makes it easier for me? Like I have said before, it's as though I need to breath. I must breath, and yet there is no oxygen. No, I don't suppose you would understand.

It's true though, I was planning on this writing being my final act in this life. Go back and reread the introduction; perhaps you will look at my story in a different light. This was to be "my confession," my personal request for forgiveness—forgiveness for being what I am. Though truthfully, I don't know who I'm asking to forgive me—a supreme being, the Architect of Creation, the Almighty God? If such a creator exists, does he recognize me? Does he loathe me? Or are my attempts futile as God does not exist? No, if he does exist, I can't imagine that he pays any mind to me whatsoever.

Either way, I have to consider the notion that forgiveness and contrition have their limitations, and certainly I have overstepped those acceptable limits.

As I'm sure you've aware, I have invested my energies in recent years in the pursuit of knowledge and understanding of the metaphysical world. It seems, however, that I have come as far as I can within this world. Even what I have been taught exists without evidence—again, a requirement of faith. And I'm not interested in faith; instead, I want confirmation, proof. Proof of divinity, proof of... something, a reason to exist.

As ironic as this may sound, I have found that reason during the construction of these pages. I believe in love. It exists, it is out there, everywhere; I have felt it myself. I no longer feel things the way a man or woman feels things, but I know love, and I know loss. Every day, I think of those whom I have loved, those whom I have lost—Myra, Anne, Sharon, Kelsey, and let us never forget my dear and beloved Jessica. Yes, my list extends beyond those names I have offered in these pages. There are a lot of names, but I have lived a long time.

Somehow, the pieces finally seem to fit—I am a monster, a monster that never wanted to be a monster who never asked for such a curse or blessing. I wanted nothing but love and peace. Instead, I was given everything... except what I wanted. I shouldn't complain though. Love is for poets, and a poet I am not. Either way, you need not worry about me taking my life now as I have no intention of proceeding with that course of action.

So what am I to do now? I think I will go north and west, and see where the road leads me. Would you like to know where I have resided for the last year where I have penned these words you now read? No place too spectacular, I have been living in Rockford, Illinois, with my last living friend—my absolute best friend. Come try to find me if you wish. By the time these papers find their way into your hands, I will have long since departed.

So what final piece of advice can I offer? Strange how it feels as though I should have something deeply insightful to say here, but I don't, and I honestly don't care. Still, maybe there is something to be gained from my experiences If so, do with this what you must. Good luck to you, whoever you are.

Caleb V.
July 2, 2012

CONFESSIONS OF A LYCANTHROPE

CHRONICLE 2

FIREWALK

(EXCERPT)

G. L. EDWARDS

I DON'T BELIEVE I could have possibly picked a creepier night to do this. As soon as Jennifer returned home from her classes that she had been attending, she told me that she had been having bad feelings. This was before I told her about the Grizzles or what we were doing that night.

Never before had I seen her act so nervous. Keep in mind, Jenn is not a typical young woman. She does, after all, talk to the deceased. The minute we pulled into the driveway of the house, she gasped, "This isn't right."

Tony was waiting for us in his car, but he seemed a different man than the one in my office earlier. This man had terror in his eyes. Simply sitting in his driveway horrified him. As Jennifer and I walked to his car, he rolled down the window and handed me the key to the door. "I'm not going in, and I'm not staying here!" As he spoke, his voice seemed to break slightly as he worked hard to maintain his composure. "I just saw someone in the upstairs window. It was an old woman, and she was looking directly at me and smiling! This house is fucking evil!"

I watched as Tony's hands were shaking on the steering wheel. This August was one of the hottest on record, yet this night seemed cool, almost chilly to Jennifer. Despite the odd temperature of the evening, a bead of sweat ran from Tony's temple to the side of his neck. "Man, don't go in there. There is something bad in there!"

"He's right," Jennifer said as she faced the house. "There is something bad in there." Jennifer, a 115-pound young woman, spoke with the courage that Tony, a rather large and strapping man, lacked.

With the key in my hand, I said, "I'll call you tomorrow." Turning toward the house, I felt a strong breeze blow into my face. Tony's engine started and his little blue Escort disappeared into the night.

Far in the distance, I could see the porch light of the nearest neighbor, roughly a mile and a half to the west. The house itself was a nice structure to look at—it seemed benevolent enough. It was an impressively large plantation home, built some time in the first half of the nineteenth century—maybe around 1840 or so. The idea of having a building that had survived the Civil War, the Lincoln assassination, the first flight by the Wright brothers, the *Titanic* disaster, and man's walk on the moon was quite appealing to me.

Clearly, this house had had its share of facelifts over the years, maybe even a few renovations but seemed to retain a vintage feel that would attract anyone with an affinity for history. The large and impressive deck spanned the entire length of the front of the house, and hedge bushes lined both sides.

As we ascended the front steps, I noticed the hair on Jenn's neck and arms were standing up. She never once told me that she didn't want to do this or that she was ever frightened. She bravely and obediently followed me up the steps to the front door.

The door was already unlocked, and I opened it. We stepped through the threshold and noticed a considerable drop in the temperature. Once inside, we walked to the center of the living room, and as we stood there, I asked Jennifer how she felt.

With a savage intensity in her eyes that I had never seen before, she answered, "This house and everything around it is dark. It doesn't want us here. It absolutely doesn't want *you* here. I have never felt anything so dark in my life." Looking around the room, she added, "There are no spirits here. No parted soul inhabit this dwelling. The entities in this house are not afraid of you."

"So what exactly is in this house?" I asked.

She offered a bewildered look as though uncertain of how to answer the question. "There is not one but many of them," she said as her heart rate began to rise. "Whatever it is that is here with us, it wants to split us up—it is going to try to separate us. Oh my god, there is nothing human about the apparitions in this house. They never were human. These are actual demonic entities. These are demons!" Jennifer was visibly frightened and retreated into the corner of the room.

"Tell me what you see."

"There was a family here after the war, after the Civil War—they were tortured to death! There were twin daughters that lived here at the turn of the century. They had blonde hair and were twelve years old—they were both cut to pieces!"

Jennifer was describing to me what she was seeing. She stared into the room as though watching events unfold on a film or video. Suddenly her face expressed something even more horrific than what she had already described. "Oh my god! No!" she screamed with tears running down her face. "It was only a baby!" she cried out.

Although I could not see or hear the things that she was observing, I did feel the temperature continue to drop sharply, probably fifteen or twenty degrees in a matter of seconds. There was also a foul and nauseating odor that filled the room—like rotten cabbage and raw sewage.

Suddenly, something unseen shoved me into the wall forcefully. I could feel as this "force" attempted to bind me in the way that Tony described that it had done with him. Whatever it was, it was quite impressively strong and would have no difficulty pinning even someone such as Tony. I, however, was much stronger than Tony and seemingly stronger than the entity that tried to hold me.

Breaking free of its hold on me, I grabbed Jennifer and proceeded toward the front entranceway that we had walked through only moments earlier. As though the house understood our intentions, the door slammed shut; the locks immediately engaged. I then pulled Jennifer into the next room—the kitchen—which apparently enraged the demon, for we both heard a chilling and angry howl like that of a wild dog coming from the living room.

As I turned my attention to Jennifer, she appeared disorientated, mumbling about the atrocities this house had seen. Suddenly, everything went quiet in the living room—the growling and howling noises that had originated from that room after our departure simply stopped, and everything was amazingly quite.

I listened with all the preternatural ability I had; there was nothing but Jennifer's erratic heart rate that seemed to make any noise within the entire house. The awful stench still continued to hang in the air. It was almost as though the house was attempting to hide something that I would otherwise have detected by masking everything with this most foul and offensive odor.

Just then, I heard something quickly slide off the counter across the kitchen and immediately placed myself between it and Jennifer, who continued to babble, seemingly unaware of what was happening in the present moment. No sooner had I placed myself in harm's way than three large kitchen knives plunged deep into my abdomen, shoulder, and neck.

If I had been anyone else, the knives would have killed me. With a brief and intense jolt of pain, I removed each blade from within me and broke it from its handle.

I would heal from this, of course, but I would need a few hours before doing too much more. In addition, I realized that while Jennifer was an asset when it came to understanding what was happening, she was also of little use in her tranced state. It seemed that it was time for us to leave as it was unlikely that I would be able to keep her safe within this house for much longer. This was not going at all as I had hoped or planned.

I suddenly realized then that we were not alone in the kitchen. A shirtless man appeared from nowhere and was now standing in the center of the room only a few feet from us. His skin was an ashy gray, except the areas around his eyes, which were yellow as though with jaundice. He smelled diseased, like a mixture of moldy bread and urine. Unlike his skin, his eyes were all white, and he didn't seem to have pupils. He gazed at me in a strange manner; it would seem that he was studying the wounds that I had received—no doubt, wondering why I was still alive at all, let alone still standing.

"You will not leave here," he said in a raspy voice. As he spoke, his mouth seemed filled with pus pockets, his breath was like old sour milk. He quickly advanced and reached for me, and I drew back and struck him hard. I felt the bones in his face breaking as they made contact with my fist, but then suddenly he was gone.

I turned to see Jennifer still in a strange trancelike state as though she were somehow living in the past as well as the present. I became annoyed and shook her, "Jennifer!" I shouted but received no response.

I was uncertain of what to do next. A part of me considered standing my ground, and had Jennifer not been with me, there would have been no reason not to. Although I clearly did not understand exactly what I was dealing with, it seemed unlikely that whatever it was could kill me. There was also a feeling that something was happening within the house and that the longer we stayed within it, the worse it would become.

I picked Jennifer up and slung her over my shoulder. Of course, I was bleeding on her, but she would have to forgive me for that. There was a flight of steps that led out of the kitchen and into the great unknown of this house. I ascended the stairwell quickly, three steps at a time, when suddenly a roaring sound enveloped the kitchen behind me. It sounded like a locomotive screaming as it raced by on tracks. The deafening sound seemed to pursue me as I advanced quickly up the steps. I dared not stop for Jennifer's sake and charged ahead into an upstairs hallway and through a large window at the end of that hallway. Using my body to shield Jennifer, I leapt through the glass window, half expecting it to not break as I did. As I dropped from the second floor window, I swung Jennifer from my shoulder to my arms.

Returning to the car that was still peacefully parked in the driveway, I rested a semiconscious Jennifer in the passenger seat then proceeded to remove the shards of glass from my face, shoulder, and arms. These wounds too would heal—likely within an hour.

Upon examining Jennifer, I found her eyes glassy and frozen with fear even now that she was safely out of the house. Whatever it was that she had witnessed, it somehow traumatized her. I looked back at the house, which utterly amazed me. We hadn't been inside five minutes before the violent occurrences began. While I was hardly finished with the house, Jennifer was little more than a liability to me at this point, and it would be pointless to have her reenter the dwelling.

The hour-long drive back into S——, seemed adequate enough to bring Jennifer out of her trance and back to her annoying self. Unfortunately, the details that she remembered—vague as they were—seemed of little help as far as how to deal with the house. She was able, however, to provide some useful information on the nature of the home.

Apparently, there are places, here and there, that for whatever reason serve as entranceways for a host of dark entities. These demonic things seem to come through these places and often commit atrocities when they do. Jennifer informed me that the Grizzle home was built over just such a passageway. This was a very dangerous and unpredictable type of haunting that nothing good could come from.

"There are worse things than you in this world," she said. "This house is one of them. Please don't go back. This is a fight you cannot win."

As I stated, she was unable to offer any methods for dealing with anything like this. As far as she knew, there was no way to stop the entities from coming into this world. She told me that it was an anomaly, something that has existed long before there were ever people.

I dropped a seemingly healthy Jennifer off at the office, and despite her insistent and constant pleading for me not to, I returned to the house. Upon my return, the wounds I had incurred during my first visit had vanished, and I pulled into the driveway fresh and ready to deal with whatever I should come across.

As I got out of my car and looked closely at the house, I could feel something strange emanating from it. Though I am hardly a psychic, I am capable of experiencing perceptions beyond human limits. Was it simply my imagination, or did the house seem to almost smile at me? Unlike the Grizzles, unlike Jennifer, and unlike anyone else that may have come to examine this house, I was incapable of fear, incapable of worry or concern. In fact, the only emotion that I was capable of experiencing seemed to grow within me—anger.

It seemed fascinating though I wouldn't have thought it possible to have harmed or injured any kind of ghost, spirit, or demon. However, it did seem that whatever was in the house was susceptible to pain. I realized this when I struck the demon in the kitchen. For just an instant before it vanished, I was aware of its pain that resulted from my strike. Logic indicated that if I could injure it, I could kill it—and I had every intention on killing as I gazed at the house.

I opened my trunk, and from it, I retrieved a heavy flanged mace. A bit Gothic looking, yes, but it certainly did the job. That is, whatever it struck, it demolished. I acquired this unusual weapon some years ago as a gift from another lycanthrope named Arthur Denham. I have offered an account of my exchange with Mr. Denham in my preceding chronicle, and although I hold the greatest respect for this individual, I will not go into our meeting here.

From what I was told, the mace was the favored weapon of an enormous Germanic soldier who died on the battlefield in a war against Serbia. Although uncertain of how old this weapon is, it is in near perfect condition—indestructible and impervious to anything short of being melted down. I would imagine that with its weight, even the above-average man in strength would find difficulty yielding this weapon. I would also imagine that the warrior whom this weapon belonged to took great pride in himself for being able to use it effectively. As for myself, I swung it with ease.

I again climbed the six steps leading up to the deck, and again the front door was unlocked. I cautiously entered the living room and scanned the environment from left to right, expecting macabre and bizarre minions to leap toward me; I sensed nothing out of the ordinary, however. To my right, I could see the entrance to the kitchen, on my left—the family room. I wanted to further examine the kitchen as I didn't have a chance to closely go through it when Jenn and I were last here, and because this was the room where the gray man had shown himself.

Again, I found nothing unusual in the kitchen; it was as I had left it earlier. Ugly yellow tiles on the floor, oak wall and base cabinets, a green refrigerator and stove, a small table against one wall. The three broken blades were on the floor where I had left them, next to a small pool of dried blood that I had spilled when retracting them from my body.

I considered retracing the path I had taken earlier and going up the steps to the second floor but wanted to explore the downstairs first before going upstairs. I left the kitchen and proceeded through the living room and into the family room. In it, there were various pictures on the walls—the Grizzles and their friends and family. There was a sofa against one wall, two recliners at forty-five-degree angles that faced the sofa, and a coffee table between them—nothing unusual.

Beyond the family room, a long hallway with a door leading outside and another doorway at the halls end. Opening this doorway, I found steps leading into the basement. Being as alert and on edge as I was, I could not be certain if I was hearing something come from downstairs or if I was imagining it. Even my mind loves to play tricks on me from time to time.

This was not my imagination though. I was certain of it. As I listened, the sounds of a baby crying filled my sensitive ears. Even with my extraordinary senses, I could only barely detect the sounds coming from beyond the doorway where I stood. As I listened, I could make out the sounds of an infant crying. I remembered what Jennifer had said, that there were no spirits in this house, only demons. Apparently, the crying that I was listening to was also demonic.

I descended the steps, uncertain of what to expect but certain that something ugly was about to happen. The basement air filled my nostrils with a damp and musty odor. Peering into the gloomy "dungeon," I could see a very faint light at the bottom of the steps. I crept slowly down, allowing all my senses to detect every possible sight, sound, and scent. The hazy illumination originated from a twenty-five-watt bulb that hung from the basement's farthest corner. While quite dim, I had little difficulty seeing everything around me.

On the side of the basement with the most light, numerous boxes lined the walls and were stacked on top of one another. If my nose served me, these boxes were, at least in part, filled with old moth-eaten, moldy clothing and dusty papers or books. Next to the boxes were several metal filing cabinets—it would seem that they were quite old as I could smell the rust all the way through them. There was also a desk, and it too was old and mold filled.

The desk was used, it seemed, as a place to manage business and finances. Various papers were scattered across it, including electric bills dating to 1961, love letters to and from a woman named Samantha, and even an elementary school report card from that same year. Half a century of dust had collected on the desk, making it impossible to read any of the paperwork until it had been shaken off.

I then decided to explore the less dimly lit half of the basement, which seemed blanketed with darkness. As I gazed into this darkness, it appeared as something more than a simple absence of light. It seemed, rather, to take on almost physical characteristics as though one could reach out with his hand and grab it. Stepping into the dark shadows, I felt engulfed by the blackness. There was an eerie quality possessed within this basement, something that seemed to swallow any energy that entered it.

I felt as if I was being watched by someone, but upon scanning the area around me, I could see nothing to indicate that I wasn't alone. However, I would have been stupid to believe that I was alone. You know that sinister feeling that children as well as grown adults get, that feeling that creeps over you when you know that you are alone but cannot convince some small irrational part of your mind of this fact. The feeling that something evil is lurking, watching, and just waiting for us to take one more step, that feeling that something has quietly walked up behind you and at any second will grab you from behind.

This darker side of the basement also seemed much more damp

than the other. The mildew I could smell thrived on the concrete walls, ceiling, and floor. As I looked around, there was little that captivated my interest. An old table, a dresser, and an armoire, each would have been splendid antiques had they been cared for. As it was, they had nearly disintegrated and were falling apart. Passing this furniture, I observed still more boxes.

In the farthest corner of the basement, opposite the side of the hanging light, where the blackest part of this living darkness stood, there was a large tarp that covered the wall. As I tore the tarp from the wall, I found that it concealed a door. While I stood there, studying the doorway, I could again feel the temperature quickly dropping.

I found the door tightly secured and reinforced from the other side. The thick wood of the door felt quite solid and seemed several inches thick. It was as though whoever had put the door in wanted the concrete walls to fall apart and deteriorate long before this door would. With a considerably sizable kick, the door shattered almost like glass, sending wood fragments in all directions. It did so partially due to its age but more so because of the sheer power I had put behind the kick. When this door was pit in, it was done with the intention of keeping most anyone out, but they hadn't intended for someone such as myself to be searching here either.

Past the entrance, a hallway that seemed swallowed by the blackness beyond, a blackness that exceeded anything the basement could offer so far. As remarkable as my night vision is, even I was having some difficulty seeing much in this total absence of light. I slowly proceeded forward and could feel the darkness engulf me as the temperatures continued to drop. I followed the hall for about fifty feet, then it opened up to a single chamber. This chamber measured approximately 100 feet by 120 feet. The walls were filled with lined with various pictograms of which I could not make out in the absence of light and two unlit torches that hung from either side of the chamber.

As best as I could tell, this was a shrine of some sort—a holy or sacred place that was dedicated to something evil. I was, no doubt, the first person to set foot into this area in well over a century. The air was stale, dusty, and moldy. The walls were quite moist, like the walls of the basement, and the moisture was beginning to freeze as the mercury dropped.

Against the far wall, a most unusual piece of furniture for this setting—a child's crib. I slowly approached the crib, trying to estimate its age. Suddenly, there was a movement from within the crib. An infant's sounds, those that I had heard upstairs, accompanied the movement I saw. Without fear of what I might find, I proceeded to the front of the crib and peered into its lace-lined contents. There, a baby of about six months stared back at me. It was far too dark in this room for any human to be able to see anything, let alone an infant, and yet, clearly this impossible child looked right at me.

For the longest moment, this baby and I exchanged looks without blinking. I could not smell anything human here, nor could I detect even the tiniest heartbeat that I would have expected. There was no body heat emanating from the crib. Despite this, the baby was moving and making tiny sounds that babies make. After several seconds, though, what at first appeared a tiny baby began to change. Its eyes seemed to take on a reptilian shape, its fingers becoming claws. A row of daggerlike teeth revealed itself as it opened its mouth, allowing a forked tongue to taste the air. With this, a mucuslike substance formed within its mouth and ran from its lips, and it used its claw hands to pull itself out of the crib.

Curiously, I watched all this take place, refusing to take my eyes off the creature while knowing fully well that another being had entered this chamber. After a brief instant the "baby" suddenly sprang toward me from its crib with its seemingly deadly teeth bared. In its eyes, an evil that I've seen before, an evil that I've glimpsed in even my own reflection in years past.

As would an experienced predator, its attack targeted my throat as it leapt toward me. With a swiftness equal to its own, I thrust my body backward and heaved the mace with a deadly power and accuracy. The result ended in an explosion of body parts. For an instant, the air showered me with this creature's blood as it did the wall nearest me. At my foot lay a tiny arm/claw, still twitching. The creature's head and upper torso lay lifeless and unmoving against the chamber's opposite wall.

With this done, I turned to see who or what had entered this secret room and was here with me now. I figured the odds were better on seeing a "what" rather than a "who." In just that instant, both torches ignited and this room was flooded with bright light. This bothered me considerably for a couple of reasons. For one, there is a comfort I have in the darkness since my eyesight allows me to see with detail what others cannot (you can imagine the advantage this gives me). More than this, though, I realized that the forces I was dealing with here were capable of pyrokinetics. I was sure that if capable of lighting a torch at will, there would be little difficulty of employing this ability as a weapon against me.

I was able to see the symbols on the walls now—inverted pentagrams between a strange cross. I glanced at them only for an instant before looking directly into a semifamiliar set of eyes. The being who stood facing me was the same one that I had encountered in the kitchen with Jennifer. He stood nearly six feet tall and was rather lanky. His shorts, the only clothing he wore, were filthy and seemed so old that they may tear and disintegrate at any time. His hair was dark and oily, his black veins were visible through his gray skin, and yes, he brought with him his disgusting diseased odor. The left side of his face was badly disfigured from the blow that I had delivered to him earlier. Despite this, he offered no visible sign of pain or discomfort.

He stood there, gazing at me as I did him. He appeared a man, but he was not what he appeared, any more than the baby was what it first appeared. His strange eyes that had no pupils or irises made knowing specifically what he was looking at impossible; I know only that he was intently studying me, searching my body, part by part. It didn't appear that he was going to step forward or reach out for me as he had done upstairs, but I prepared myself for just such an action nonetheless.

For a moment it was difficult to say who was examining who more closely. As we stood, a droplet of blood trickled down the side of my cheek. This was tickling me, and I wanted to wipe clean all the little creature's blood from my face. I resisted this urge though and focused on my curious adversary who was still engrossed with his study of me.

Finally, he spoke. His voice was raspy and disturbing to listen to. "You're not human." As he said this, his face held the queerest look.

"There's a news flash,"

"What *are* you?"

"Does it matter?"

"I don't know," he said. "What is it that you want here?"

Ignoring his question, I began examining the room in greater detail now that it was illuminated. My eyes returned again to the odd cross painted on the wall with what was likely blood. It was like a cross but with an inverted question mark.

"Are you interested in that?"

"What is it?"

"Ah, that is the Satanic cross. It questions the deity of God. It is the representation of the three crown princes—Satan, Belial, and Leviathan—and symbolizes complete power under Lucifer."

"I see."

"Are you a believer then?"

"No."

"Does it frighten you then?"

"Fear is a human emotion that I am incapable of, and I honestly couldn't care less for your shit hole of a shrine here."

Obviously insulted, the gray man stepped backward. He paused for a moment, contemplating what to say next. "Again, what do you want here?"

Upstairs, I heard a man screaming in pain. My eyes momentarily darted away then returned to the demon in my presence. It quickly occurred to me the he wanted to keep me here even if only for a few moments. He didn't want me to help whoever was upstairs; he didn't want a repeat performance of Jennifer's rescue from the house.

He quickly moved himself so that he was blocking the exit. "Make no doubt, I will burn you to ashes if I must!" he said threateningly. "Now I will ask only once more. Why are you here?"

"Why am I here?" I repeated casually as I stepped toward him. "I'm here to kill you, of course." Immediately upon saying this, I spun clockwise with my mace targeting his head. At the last second, he raised his hands in defense, but it did him no good. The mace struck with such force that it removed his head from his neck.

His headless body wobbled for several seconds then collapsed. The demon's head had come to rest on the floor several feet away and appeared dead. I approached the head and stood over it. The ceiling in this room was high, allowing me the room to draw back the mace and swing it downward as though I were splitting wood or driving a heavy spike. Just as would a watermelon, the mace sent tiny fragments of his head in every direction.

I proceeded out of the room but caught sight of the infant creature's remains, still lifeless on the floor. Using my boot to stomp down on it, I achieved the same result that the mace did with the gray man. Again, I heard the loud screams upstairs. I hastily dashed away from the chamber as the torches continued to burn behind me.

Once I reached the main part of the basement, three other beings stood waiting for me. Underestimating the strength I possessed, two of them grabbed me, one on each arm, and each with a supernatural strength of their own. These three were much like the one I had just killed a moment ago—grotesque looking, sickly pale, and smelling of disease.

I let go of the mace, and with both hands free, I seized the two demons by their throats and lifted them off their feet. The third demon stood in amazement as I did this. Then with a precise and deadly swiftness, I jerked downward as hard as I could while retaining my grip at their necks. This motion was sufficient enough to tear both of their throats out. These demons, while certainly stronger than any person, were not immortal or at least not in this realm.

The two dead bodies dropped on both sides of me while I clung to the grayish bloody flesh in my hands. Tossing aside what were throats just seconds before, I retrieved the mace and buried it into the chest of the third demon who only watched as I had killed the others.

Climbing the steps toward the first floor, entities that remained both invisible and intangible pushed at me and struck at me with inhuman power and strength. It seemed that their only goal was to prevent me from helping whoever was upstairs. I fought against the countless demons that attempted to slow or stop me.

Upon finally reaching the second floor, I listened for the screams that had ceased several moments earlier while I fought through the barrage of beatings I had endured to get there. My first thought was that it was all a ploy to lure me upstairs, but then I suddenly smelled what was very much human blood—unlike the horrid diseased blood of the demons.

The scent was coming from a bedroom at the far end of the hallway, the same hallway that Jennifer and I had exited through earlier in the evening.

With a force many times what was needed, I smashed through the door of this bedroom. The sight before me was unbelievable. As best I could tell, Tony Grizzle had returned to the house and, for whatever reason, reentered it. His arms and legs had been slowly torn from his torso, and his face looked as though acid had been poured on it. His death was an excruciating one.

I was at a loss for even what to do at this point. In that moment, I felt something enter the room. I remained motionless, waiting for something to happen. And then something extremely powerful—much more powerful than anything else I had come across in my life—seized me.

Made in United States
Orlando, FL
18 May 2024